The Laws of Attraction

A Novel in the *Triorion* universe

By LJ Hachmeister

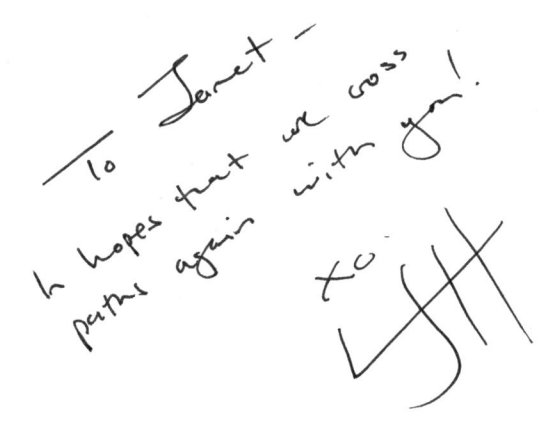

Copyright © 2017 by Source 7 Productions, LLC

www.triorion.com

First Edition

This is a work of fiction. All names, characters, events and situations portrayed in this book are products of the author's imagination. Any resemblance to actual persons or events is purely coincidental.

All rights reserved. No part of this book may be used or reproduced in any manner whatsoever without written permission, except in the case of brief quotations embodied in critical articles or reviews. Please do not participate in or encourage the piracy of copyrighted materials in violation of the author's rights. Purchase only authorized editions.

Cover art and design by L. J. Hachmeister and Nicole Peschel

Source 7 Productions, LLC

Lakewood, CO

Novels by L. J. Hachmeister

Triorion: The Series

Triorion: Awakening (Book One)

Triorion: Abomination (Book Two)

Triorion: Reborn, part I (Book Three)

Triorion: Reborn, part II (Book Four)

Triorion Universe

The Laws of Attraction

Forthcoming

Shadowless -- Outlier (Volume One)

Triorion: Nemesis (Book Five)

Short Stories

"The Gift," from *Triorion: The Series*

"Heart of the Dragon" from *Dragon Writers*

This book is dedicated to the real Niks and Syra, my loves, my heart, the best parts of being here.

And, of course, to Rex. You are loved.

The Laws of Attraction

Chapter 1

Four years ago, even a glimpse of Lt. James Gryggs would have turned her stomach into butterflies. Now, as he stepped out of the shower and back into his living quarters, water dripping down his chiseled, muscular body, Niks felt only her conditioned response: A reminder to herself that she had nabbed the hottest rising officer in the Dominion Core, and a vague sense of routine and muted thrill as he toweled himself off in front of the portal window to the stars.

"Doesn't your shift start in twenty minutes, nurse?" he said, regarding her with his signature half-smile. Propping his foot up on the end of the bed, he twisted just right, highlighting the long muscles of his back and popping out his abs.

Niks glanced at the holographic clock on the nightstand. 0440. An ungodly hour to even conceive of waking, even in the timeless, star-speckled cold of deep space.

"Just five more minutes," she said, pulling up the bedsheets to her chin and wishing back the comforts of sleep.

"I have a better idea," he said, crawling up onto the bed. His held himself up with his strong arms, just above her, his blue eyes glinting with mischief.

"You're still wet, James."

Ignoring her annoyance, he kissed soft spot behind her ear. "And you will be, too."

She smiled as he bit her earlobe and pulled down the sheets, exposing her in her white t-shirt and underwear.

"Gods, I've missed you," he whispered.

As much as she wanted to be irritable with him, she couldn't help but relax to his touch as his fingers glided down her contours, stopping only at her hips to reposition himself directly above her.

"You're beautiful, Nikkia," he said, grazing his lips against hers, then bending down for a real kiss. Before she could admonish him for calling her by her full name, he slipped his tongue inside her mouth.

In the back of her mind she complimented herself for the gentle skill of his kiss, the way his tongue danced around hers.

I'm a good teacher, she mused.

Four years ago, when they first met on a starbase closer to the Homeworlds, she thought someone as good-looking as James would have had plenty of experience kissing women, but the young officer never saw himself like everyone else did, and his ambition to climb the ranks in the Dominion Core pulled his sights away from all other distractions, including women.

But I got him. The thought still excited her. Even aboard the *Mercy*, a d-class starship on a three-year medical relief mission with just over two hundred crew members, she still felt the envious eye of those who found the blue-eyed Lieutenant Commander attractive.

Still…

His hands, calloused from years of rigorous training, grazed up her abdomen, and underneath her shirt. Holding on to the bedframe with one hand, he cupped the underside of her breast, then squeezed.

Then to the other…

As anticipated, his hand moved to the other breast, giving the same attention. His fingers played with the tops of her nipples, waiting for her to react before pinching them as he bit into her neck.

She pushed up against him, feeling his muscles press back, the massiveness of his body against hers, the giant that could crush her in a second.

Except, he wouldn't. After four years, she had the routine down pat.

Five, four, three, two…

Having spent the allotted time in foreplay, he propped up one of her legs on his shoulder, and pushed aside the crotch of her underwear with his fingers, and set his length against the junction of her thighs. Closing her eyes, she relaxed her body, not ready for him, but not wanting him to stop either.

James loves me, and I love him. This is what's supposed to happen.

He entered her, pushing himself up to her limit. The roughness of it, the pain and pleasure, made her gasp. Arching her back, she reached out and grabbed the tangled bedsheets as his hips pressed against hers.

"Oh God…God…" she moaned.

He thrust harder, deeper than she thought she could stand, but she didn't want him to stop. Not this close, when he would finish, be satisfied, affirming their perfect relationship.

With a grunt, he gave one final thrust, holding himself inside her until spent. Exhaling, he came down next to her, holding her close in his sculpted arms.

At least I'll have a good excuse to go straight to bed tonight.

She hated the thought, but didn't disagree with the sentiment either. Sleep was a premium aboard a medical mission starship, and sometimes sex got in the way.

"That was great," he said a little too loudly in her ear.

Rolling over, she faced him, taking his hands off her hips and holding them just away from her chest.

"You're going to have to take another shower," she joked.

"Worth it," he said, kissing her on the forehead and squeezing her hands. Blue eyes, filled with nothing but adoration, stared back at her as he whispered her favorite words: "Love you."

She smiled. "Love you, too."

As he rolled out of bed and made his way back to the shower, Niks yawned and stretched, and prepared herself for the long shift ahead.

"*Chak*," she muttered, seeing the time. Not a second later, a blue-text message flashed on her wristband.

Early morning nookie again? Get your skanky ass into admitting already.

She didn't have to see the sender to know who sent the message. *Sy.*

Syra Gaoshin, her best friend, worst influence, and the cause and solution to most heartbreak aboard the *Mercy*. More polar opposites couldn't be found in the entire Starways galaxy, but Niks didn't know how to get by a day without Sy anymore. Not after surviving nursing school together, and all the action and misadventures of a deep space medical missions.

Hold off Meow for me, okay? Niks texted back. So far the grumpy charge nurse, Maio Kull, who joined them at the last resupply two weeks ago, didn't seem to despise her as much as she did Syra. Still, she didn't want to chance upsetting the waspish Dominion Core officer, and risk punishment. Not that Syra made it any easier for her to avoid trouble by nicknaming her "Meow" on day one, forever ruining her ability to properly pronounce her name.

Throwing on her scrubs, Niks tried to do something with her mess of dark hair before settling on her usual ponytail. She afforded herself only a quick glance in the mirror, light green eyes flashing back at her, deciding once again to skip any kind of cover-up.

"Later, honey," she shouted as she hopped out of the automatic door still wrestling one of her boots on.

"Haha, you just got laid."

Niks yelped, not expecting Syra to be standing right outside her door, arms crossed, with a devilish grin plastered to her face.

"Jeez, Sy—"

"Come on, they just unfroze your dreamy Lieutenant Commander. I figured you'd be late these next few shifts."

"You're not funny," Niks said, turning her back to Syra and signaling for a lift with a wave of her hand.

Snorting, Syra slapped her on the back as the automatic flatbed transport system whistled down the hall toward them. "Did he at least do something other than—"

Niks whirled around. "And stop right there."

With a sigh, Syra muttered just loud enough for her to hear as they both stepped aboard the lift: "Mr. Predictable strikes again."

Ignoring Syra, Niks pulled up the surgical assignments on her wristband interface. "Forty-five patients in holding today from a transport ship attack on the booster highway; twenty-two of which are slated for immediate surgery. Another fourteen-hour shift."

"Ugh," Syra said, gazing out to the stars as the lift whisked them down the windowed corridor toward the medical bays. The soft light of the constellations brought out the blue tones in her Nagoorian friend's skin. "This quadrant is killing me. So many sick people, too much war. I've never looked forward to cryosleep as much as I have this last month."

Picking up on the fatigue in her friend's voice, Niks touched the back of Syra's hand. "You okay?"

Syra pulled at one of the ringlets of auburn hair falling around her shoulders, avoiding Niks' gaze. "Yeah. Just need a break."

"Sounds like you miss Azzi."

The mention of Syra's ex-boyfriend elicited more than the frown Niks expected. Syra's tight fist connected with her shoulder.

"Ow," she said, rubbing her sore shoulder.

"That *assino* can stay asleep for another two months—make that two hundred years—as far as I'm concerned."

Niks held tight to the safety railing as the lift banked around the corner, but Syra crossed her arms leaned up against the lift interface.

"You guys are the worst couple ever," Niks remarked. "Thank the Gods they put you two on different sleep cycles."

Syra's entire demeanor changed. A secret pinched down the corners of her eyes, and tightened her lips. Still, a few words escaped. "Not quite the worst."

"Huh?"

Before Niks could question her further, the lift stopped at the double-doors of admitting.

"Aren't you getting off?" Niks asked as Syra stayed on the lift.

Syra regarded her right hand. "Well, definitely later tonight, but—"

"Seriously…"

"You are no fun today."

Niks crossed her arms, not playing into Syra's jabs.

"They floated me. I'm playing circulator for the day. I'll see you around, k?"

"Alright. Well, let's try and break together then?"

Syra leaned over and socked her friend again, this time with a smile. "You smell like sex. Good luck getting that past Meow."

Blushing, Niks sniffed at her scrubs, then her armpits. "Jeez, oh no, I—"

"Ha!" Syra said, chuckling as the lift took off further down the corridor to drop her off at the surgical suites.

Sighing, Niks waived her wristband in front of the admitting doors, triggering the green-filter scanner. A buzz and click later, the admitting doors opened, and the smell of disinfectant and gangrene hit her like a starclass freighter at light speed.

"Help me—"

"Nurse, please—"

"I can't—this pain—please someone—"

It's going to be a rough shift, she thought, hearing the cries and moans of all the patients.

As soon as her boots hit the white-tiled admissions floor, charge nurse Maio rounded the med station in the center of the bay and scowled at her. The grey, bristled hair on the back of her neck stood on end, and the beak-tip of her nose jutted out as if to peck Niks on the forehead. Niks still wasn't sure of Maio's species, but Syra had been kind enough to make it even more awkward the last time she got drunk and loud at the bars: *"Just 'cause she's humanoid enough to stand on two legs don't mean she's not a giant chicken-cat assino!"*

"You're three minutes late," Maio said, pointing at her own wristband.

"Sorry," Niks muttered, keeping her gaze down and heading to her locker behind the circular med station desk to pick up her equipment.

She caught Meow twitching her whiskers as she walked past, but applied cleanser to her hand from one of the sanitizing dispensers and rubbed it on her pants and scrub top before the charge nurse could manage a second sniff.

Damn you, Sy!

After grabbing her equipment and clicking on her accessory belt, Niks downloaded her assignment to her wristband.

I've only been assigned one patient?

She tapped the wristband, but it didn't phase the yellow holographic projection dancing just centimenters above her wrist.

Weird, she thought. That would leave forty-four other patients to only two other admitting and triage nurses. *Maio must have screwed up the schedule.*

Instead of questioning the charge, Niks headed straight for her first and only patient waiting in bay 5, "John Doe." When she tried to pull up the detailed patient information, only blank fields came up.

What the hell? Am I supposed to triage him or prep him for surgery?

Maio intercepted her before she could pull back the curtain.

"Hand me your bioscanner," the charge nurse said, holding out her four-fingered hand.

"W-what?"

Maio stood firm, yellow eyes zeroing in on Niks as she removed the bioscanner from her belt with trembling hands and gave it up.

After shoving the palm-sized scanner in her white jacket pocket and giving Niks another once-over, Maio continued. "You've been selected to be trained on our new patient guidance system, the Med Oculus."

Niks didn't know what to say. In the short span of Maio's tenure, the formidable charge nurse hadn't done much more than take notes on her dataclip, bark orders, and write up anyone who deviated from their scripted duty. She hated military-trained nurses. When she signed up for duty with Syra, the representatives of the Sentient Outreach and Humanities Organization, or SOHO, promised her that the medical missions would operate free of the military influence, but that didn't last long. Not with the war going on between the Dominion Core and the United Starways Coalition, and so many quadrants and systems in a state of unrest. Now, every starship needed some kind of escort, lest the crew risk raids, assault, capture—or worse.

What is this? Niks thought as Maio offered her a thick green visor with a wrap-around stabilizing head attachment. Three lights flashed in white near a small keypad that would situate over the right ear. Maio then handed her a silver glove for her left hand that covered only her thumb and first two fingers. When she turned over the glove, Niks spied the tiny metal discs at the fingertips.

"This device will allow you the same patient information as a regular bioscanner—and more. Partial immersion."

"Immersion?"

"Yes. The high-density transceivers imbedded in the glove and visor will grant you a certain level of sensory insight into the patient. Your interpretations, plus the data from the internal scan, will help upload more accurate information for diagnosis and treatment."

Niks' heart thumped against her chest. The visor felt too heavy in her hands; she wanted to throw it back at Maio and run straight to James.

"T-this is..." She couldn't complete the sentence. *Like a Prodgy's ability.*

Prodgy Healers, the most legendary telepaths of all the Starways galaxy. With a simple touch, they could diagnose and heal the most grievous wounds. But their ability to Fall—to become dark agents of death and disease, destroying living tissue with a mere thought— made them the most dangerous species of all. *They're the reason the wars between the Dominion Core and the USC started—*

She still remembered the chilling message in the Core training videos:

"Dissemblers are a hidden enemy—know who you are dealing with. Register all telepaths; bring them in to your local Core embassy for screening. Protect your children. Protect your home. Protect your life."

All telepaths—all leeches—are dangerous, she thought.

"Your hesitancy is unfounded," Maio said, reading the terror in her face. "This technology is the beginning of true patient care without the Dissembler threat. Will you or won't you participate?"

Fears swirling in her head, Niks managed to squeak out a question: "Why me?"

Maio grunted, as if she didn't want to answer. "The designer is human, so he made the primary interface compatible with human neurons. That leaves you and nurse Idall as the only candidates. Between the two, you've correctly identified thirty telepaths in the last six months of the *Mercy's* missions. I have my reservations, but the board feels that your skill as a nurse, and your loyalty to telepath registration makes you the ideal candidate for this trial program."

Trial program. She looked again at the visor in her hand. *Why would the Dominion want to run medical trials on new equipment out in deep space?*

The answer came in a silent scream from the back of her mind. *Because this is technically a SOHO starship, unaffiliated with any military—so no one is watching.*

"I—"

Before she could answer, a familiar hand weighed down on her shoulder.

"Nurse Kull—I'll take it from here."

Wheeling around, Niks couldn't believe her eyes. *James?* "L-lieutenant Commander—"

Maio glared at the two of them, then disappeared behind the blue curtain separating the general pre-op and treatment area from the individual bays.

"What's going on?" she whispered, still holding onto the visor and glove as if they would bite her. "You knew about this and didn't tell me?"

James tightened his jaw. "This tech has been highly classified. I just got the go-ahead from my commanding officer to start the trials right after you left this morning."

"This is too weird, James. I can't do this."

"You're a good nurse, Niks. That's why you were selected."

"No, because I'm one of the two humans with medical training aboard this ship."

"Stop it. You know you're the best."

"But I—I don't want to be…" The words fell off her lips, dying in the space between them.

James looked around the room. Other medical staff, ducking in and out of their assigned bays as patients continued to call out, paid no attention to their interaction. From the way he straightened his spine and clasped his hands behind his back, Niks could tell he wanted to hug her, but couldn't. Not now. Not on duty.

"Trust me about this. I think it will help."

"Help?!" Niks fumed. "You had a hand in this?"

James lowered his voice and steeled his gaze to hers. "I recommended you to Maio, to the Dominion board, and to the reps from SOHO. This is yours if you want it, Niks. I think you can take patient care to the next level."

Niks shoved the equipment into his chest. "You don't get to decide what's best for me."

Ripping back the curtain to the patient bay, Niks prepared to tell off Maio and dig out her bioscanner from the charge nurse's jacket. But Maio, standing over a yellow-skinned patient with her dataclip, looked at her with an expectant frown, stopping her in place. "I told the board you wouldn't do it. You lack the proper constitution."

All of the breath left her lungs. Niks looked back and forth between Maio and the patient, not knowing what to say or do. In the back of her mind, she recognized the holographic readouts of the patient's status just above the interface headboard: *comatose; reason unknown*. But the patient's contorted facial expressions and rigid body positioning didn't corroborate the scanners' diagnosis.

"What's wrong with him?" Niks asked.

Maio maintained her cold tone. "Whoever attacked the transport ship used a combination nerve gas and hemotoxin to disable all of the occupants. It's affected each species in a different way. However, both the handhelds and bed scanners are having a hard time reading this man's biodata. I would suspect he has an internal bleed, but without any type of confirmation, the only option left is for exploratory surgery."

Forgetting herself for a moment, Niks did a quick visual assessment. The man lay naked on a warming exam table, each muscle in his body tensed. IV fluid lines, draped from the ceiling, attached to his arms and neck. *Hardened yellow skin, humanoid appearance in height, serrated nose...must be an outerworlder, possibly a Cerran.*

"Exploratory surgery is a huge risk if he's been exposed to hemotoxins..." Niks mumbled, still caught up in her assessment.

"Now you see why we wanted to introduce the Med Oculus on John Doe," James said, coming up behind her again. "Through your senses, nurse Rison, we could get a read on him, upload the necessary information for the med teams. You can save his life."

Niks took a step away from the lieutenant commander, standing across from Maio and leaving James at the foot of the bed. Balling her hands into fists, she thought of all the reasons she should, and shouldn't.

Is this wrong?
I won't betray my parents—
Can I do something like this?
This is a patient's life—
—but I don't want to be like them*—*

Her mother and father's faces jerked across her mind; the phantom smell of burning buildings and fresh blood touched her nose, filling her with terrible memories she fought to keep at bay.

"Find someone else," she blurted out.

Tears brimming her lids, she ran back to her locker and plopped down on the bench.

How could he do this to me? she thought, holding her breath to keep from sobbing. James knew her past; he knew more than most people did about her parents, even Syra. *I thought he cared—*

Red warning lights flashed on her wristband as an announcement came over the intercom.

"All hands prepare for incoming. All hands—"

The ship quaked, and even in a windowless medical theater, Niks imagined something massive narrowly missing the *Mercy*.

Another battle. More patients.

No time for tears.

Niks fished through her locker, finding her backup bioscanner, and attached it to her belt. With a deep breath, she collected herself, and prepared for the worst.

***

Dominion soldiers brought in new patients by the dozens, filling the treatment bays beyond capacity. The freshly wounded lay everywhere, in the aisles and jamming up the pathways in and out of the preop and treatment area. As much as she tried, Niks couldn't get past the horrid smell of burnt flesh permeating the air.

"Rison—you've got four admits coming in—get going!" Maio shouted over the commotion as medical staff flew all around trying to manage what they could.

Frustrated and already running low patience and supplies, Niks crouched down next to a battered, delirious woman on the floor, trying to keep her covered with an old curtain improvised as a blanket as she scanned her wounds. The woman appeared to be from Arkana by the thickness of her forehead and prominence of her jaw. Readings confirmed her suspicion when she identified a four-lobed pancreas. However, something didn't feel right as Niks scanned the rest of her body, looking beyond the superficial burns and abrasions.

From what little information they got before patients got dumped into their department, attackers hit another transport on the booster highway. The starship, carrying about four hundred people, suffered total engine failure and broke from faster-than-light speed, barely missing collision with the *Mercy*.

Her blood is too thin—she's going to bleed out, she thought, waving the scanner over her chest. Reaching into her accessory belt, she pulled up a coagulation booster and pressed the hypoinjector into the woman's neck, but stopped herself when she scanned her brain. *Readings are off the charts...*

Gut kicking in, she recalled her first patient of the day, and what Maio relayed about the mysterious condition of John Doe: *"Whoever attacked the transport ship used a combination nerve gas and hemotoxin to disable all of the occupants. It's affected each species in a different way."*

Amidst the screams and cries, Niks made the connection.

Same attackers. But why?

The question butted up against her thoughts as Niks worked to stabilize the woman's vital signs, hooking up fluids and applying cooling bandages to the burns. As she finished her initial assessment and first response, she held the bioscanner over the woman's chest to upload the patient information to the ship's shared database so she could obtain treatment orders from one of the doctors circulating amongst the wounded. Before she hit send, the woman's hand shot up and grabbed her wrist.

"Please don't..." she said through swollen lips. Her dark eyes pleaded with Niks. "They'll...take me..."

Niks looked again at the bioscanner. *She's definitely Arkanan, but...*

"Why?" Niks asked, leaning closer to the woman.

With a trembling finger, the woman tapped on Niks' bioscanner, zooming in on the snapshots of her brain, and the areas highlighted by the neuro gas's effects.

"I'm not a monster," the woman whispered, tears sliding down her cheeks.

Before Niks could make the connection, the woman went into a seizure.

"Need assistance in bay five!" Niks shouted, trying to keep the rest of the patients safe as the woman bucked off the floor.

Maio and two other nurses rushed in, helping her administer a sedative to relieve the woman's seizure. After settling the woman, Maio looked at the bioscan Niks obtained on her.

"I think she was exposed to the same combination nerve gas/hemotoxin that we saw with the other transport," Niks said, unsure why Maio scrutinized her patient so heavily.

I performed all of the correct first response. What the hell is she going to write me up for?

"That is a correct assessment," Maio said, but she didn't give back the bioscanner. "Anything else?"

Niks bit her lip, blocking out the screams and the cries of the wounded. She remembered her patient's plea: *"Please don't...they'll take me..."*

"She didn't want me to upload her bioscan. She sounded worried that someone would take her."

And her last words: *"I'm not a monster."*

Mind racing, Niks grabbed the bioscanner out of Maio's hands. "What if the nerve gas/hemotoxin highlights the extrasensory pathways of a telepath?"

Maio's forehead creased, but only for a second. "Upload your data immediately. I'll call for a containment crew. Good call, nurse Rison."

As Maio typed in command codes on her wristband to summon Dominion soldiers, Niks told herself to feel proud. This catch—this kind of way to positively identify so many leeches—would certainly serve a great purpose.

But as she turned back to begin treatment on the next patient, she couldn't help but feel the Arkanan woman's dark eyes, open but unseeing as she lay in her post-seizure state, staring into her, even as the soldiers carted her away.

***

"Daaang, girl—you got *seventy-five* leeches tagged?" Syra slapped Niks on the shoulder. "That's a haul. Never heard of such a thing."

Niks cradled her untouched drink in her hand, unable to feel the same level of exuberance her best friend felt over her incredible discovery earlier that day. Sitting on a stool, she scooted up to a broken exam table and laid down her head on the cool metal.

What's wrong with me? she thought, looking at the digital clock on her wristband. *2350. I should be in bed.*

In the worst times, and some of the best, they came here, to storage room E, deep in the bowels of the *Mercy*. No one ever came by, unless they needed to stash away some junked-out piece of equipment. Otherwise, it proved to be the only place on the entire cramped ship to get away from it all.

"You haven't finished your drink," Syra pointed out as she poured herself another round of her homemade concoction from an old canteen into a specimen cup they stole from pre-op.

"That's because this tastes like engine runoff and something you scraped off your boots," Niks said, holding up her specimen cup full of turbid brown fluid. Light from the stars, streaming in from the horizontal widow, reflected off the floating particulates. "Are you trying to poison me?"

"I'm trying to get you drunk, and lord knows that wouldn't happen in our watered-down cantina," Syra said, pulling up a broken stool and setting it next to Niks. With only three of the four legs intact, it took Syra a moment to find her balance by tipping forward. "It's not like you're going to tell me what's bothering you unless you're sauced."

Niks had to give her that. Talking about feelings wasn't exactly her strong point, especially about James to Syra. For whatever reason, it made her uncomfortable.

"It's Mr. Predictable, isn't it?" Syra asked, taking a slug from her cup.

Sighing, Niks relented a little. "Maybe. I guess. And that's just the thing—he did something awful today; something I'd never think he'd do."

"What?" Syra said, setting down her cup and looking at her intently. "Did that *chakker* hurt you? Am I going to have to kick his buff little *assino*?"

Niks snorted. "Maybe."

Leaning over, Syra brought Niks' cup to her mouth and pinched her nose. "Drink, friend. Then talk."

"Get off," Niks said, pushing her away and taking a drink herself. The harsh liquid set her throat aflame, but she stifled a gag and cough, not wanting to bear her friend's harassments.

"That's better. So…?"

Once the burning subsided, Niks continued, her throat a little tighter than before. "So, he 'recommended' me for some military medical equipment trial—something called 'Med Oculus.' Meow tried to get me to use it this morning on a comatose patient when the scanners couldn't read him. I wouldn't care, but it's military, and it's…"

The words caught in her throat.

Syra nodded at her drink. Niks took a mouthful, nearly puking it all up, but forced herself to keep it down with a hard swallow.

Gotta tell Sy. Gotta tell someone.

"The Med Oculus just sounds like leech tricks," she said, rushing the words. Taking a deep breath, she steadied herself: "I don't want to be in someone else's head, feel their pain—just sounds like Dissembler evil."

Syra frowned. "Weird."

"I know."

"No, I mean you're weird. That's not a leech trick. Just sounds like modified neuro tech."

"Huh?"

"Ohmygawd, how can you be so well-traveled, and so oblivious?" Syra chuckled as she pulled up some holographics on her wristband. "Skins and tails—virtual reality prostitution—any of this sound familiar?"

Niks shrugged her shoulders, not recognizing any of the high-tech gear rotating on the holographic axis.

"Jeez, Niks," Syra chortled and shut off the images. "It's all neuro tech—the hottest illegal nerveware on the streets. Cleanest way to climax. Operator jacks you in, gets you off by various nerve stimulation, then you're done. No awkward goodbyes, limited cleanup—no trips to the STD clinic at 0400 for a mysterious rash..."

"You speaking from experience?"

The familiar, devilish grin cut across her best friend's face. "Don't you be judging me, Ms. Predictable, just because I'm not afraid to live once in a while."

"Just 'once in a while?'"

Syra pushed Niks' drink closer to her face. "You need to loosen up. Neuro tech is pretty rad. And besides, you love being a nurse, helping people—this might be the next step."

Niks went rigid. "You sound just like James."

"Uckk, don't say that. I could never be that boring," Syra said, making a disgusted face.

Silence fell between them, with only the ticking sound of the ventilation system filling the elongating space.

As a tingling warmth of alcohol spread throughout her body, Niks verbalized some of the thoughts circulating in her head: "I don't want him thinking he knows what's best for me."

Syra scooted closer, enough to wrap her arm around Niks and hold her at the waist. "I can't believe I'm saying this, but I really do think he's trying to help. For being a stiff military chump, he's putty in your hands, Niks. That guy would do anything for you."

Unable to find the words, Niks rested her head on Syra's shoulder as old hurts pricked her sinuses and formed an aching lump in her throat. She wanted to tell Syra everything—the truth about the death of her parents, her deepest fears, about James and all the feelings she couldn't face alone—but she could never find her voice.

Syra turned her head so that her lips grazed Niks' ear and whispered. "You're my bestie, ya know. You can tell me anything."

Tears slid down her cheeks, but Niks held back the sob bursting from her chest.

Syra kissed the side of her face. "I'm here."

Niks took another large draft. Vision wobbling, she slurred out what she could. "My parents... it all happened so fast..."

With Syra's brew unhinging her self-control, the memory of the terrible event unfolded before her eyes. Nine years old again, Niks found herself clinging to her parents' hands as her mom and dad shouted at the top of their lungs. Out of nowhere, protesters for telepath rights marched down the main street, surprising the residents of New Earth city on the evening of an otherwise sleepy Fall day.

"We need to get out Nikkia of here," her dad yelled over to her mom as the townspeople and rioters exchanged heated words.

"We're not monsters," one of the telepaths said, waving his white flag with the symbol of extrasensory perceptions stamped in the middle. "We will not be forced to register!"

It didn't take long for things to turn violent, not with the residents fearing the psychic manipulation the Dominion Core warned of on daily interspace broadcasts. Nikkia watched their grocer, a sweet, grey-haired man who always gave her a piece of candy at checkout, pick up a glass bottle from the recycling cans outside his store and cock it back, ready to throw. "Get out of here, leeches!"

Others joined in: "You're not welcome here!"

"We're not going to let you hurt our children!"

Someone hurled a brick, hitting one of the protestors in the chest. The telepath holding the flag waved off the townspeople, trying to keep them back. "We're not monsters—"

Her dad, trying to push his way through the thick mob of people now shouting and brandishing weapons, shouted to her mother: "Police blocked the exits. I don't know how we're going to—"

Screams and explosions erupted in the town square. Clouds of smoke blotted out the setting sun as hot debris rained down from above.

Mom, Dad—

Chaos surrounded her, a confusion of people running every which way. Smoke filled her lungs as the taste of copper spread in her mouth—

MOM—DAD—

The smoke cleared, enough for her to see her parents, trampled and bloodied, lying in the middle of the sidewalk—and the man who had held the flag chanting over their unmoving bodies.

Mom…Dad…?

"Don't hurt them!" *she screamed, running toward the telepath at full speed.*

Strong arms gathered her up, pulled her away.

"No," *she cried, beating her fists against her rescuer's arms.* "Mom, Dad—go back—GO BACK!"

"Hey," Syra said, jarring her back to reality as Niks fought against her friend's grip. "It's over. Whatever happened, it's done now. You're here, with me, in good ol' storage room E, our little sanctuary."

Niks opened her eyes. No smoke, no taste of blood in her mouth. Only the slate-gray walls, broken machinery, and the stars of an unnamed nebula twinkling light years away.

And Syra.

Pressed against her chest, Niks could hear her friend's heartbeat, smell her sweet perfume just above the medicinal scent of antiseptics soaked into their scrubs. Her touch felt good, safe, reliable, as it had for the last ten years.

"Thanks, Sy," she whispered, pulling back to sit up. Still, she didn't let go, partially because she feared spilling out of her chair. However, she braved releasing one hand to grab at Sy's full specimen cup. "*Chak*—whaddidya put in these things?"

"You really don't want to know," Syra said, swiping the empty cup to fill it as Niks downed the rest of what was out.

"It's getting late," her friend said, checking her wristband before handing Niks her refill. "Last call, k?"

"No." Niks pawed at her friend's canteen, but Syra held it out of reach. "Let's finish it."

"I'd like not to drown my liver."

"Don't wuss out now—"

"Jeez," Syra said, wrestling her onto the broken exam table. The entire metal slab wobbled, but stayed upright as Syra mounted her. "What the hell got into you? I've never seen you this worked up."

Niks fought against her friend's hands pinning her down, but stopped when she realized Syra staring back at her, chestnut eyes intense and full of concern.

Gods, she's beautiful. The thought floated through her head as another part of her realized why all of the men, women, and everyone else, pined for the blue-skinned Nagoorian.

We've been friends for so long...

Breath caught in her chest, Niks gazed back, expecting—waiting for something—for—

"Why are you looking at me like that?" Syra said. But there was no sarcasm in her voice, no accusation; only curiosity. Chestnut eyes narrowed, taking in more than Niks' inebriated demeanor.

Surprised, and feeling exposed, Niks put up another battle to be released, but less so than before. "I should get back—James will be waiting."

"Mr. Predictable can wait."

"No, I—"

"Here's how it's going to go: No matter what time you get back to his quarters, he's going to sit you down and talk to you about your 'feelings' and your plain vanilla relationship while feeding you rations and water to help lessen what is going to be a massive hangover tomorrow. Within twenty nauseating minutes, he'll manipulate you back into thinking everything is just fine again. Then you're going to have the same sex you've been having for years, on your back, barely wet, with no orgasm for you—not unless you imagine someone else banging your sweet little flower."

"*Chak* you, Syra."

"No, *chak* you—for the love of God, Niks. You need it," Syra said, putting her face within centimeters of Niks'. "You need to live outside yourself for a moment, expand your horizons—challenge yourself. Stop being the scared little girl playing it safe. That isn't what life is about."

Niks fought back against the pressure building in her chest. "We're ten zillion miles away from home—doesn't that count as pushing boundaries?"

Syra released one of her arms, bringing her hand to Niks' face. Cupping her cheek, Syra looked into Nik's eyes in a beckoning challenge, daring her farther than she could ever go. "Kiss me."

"W-what?"

Lowering herself, Syra's breasts pressed into Niks' chest, her mouth grazing Niks' lips.

So soft...

Niks tasted her, taking in the hot alcohol in her breath punctured by the sweetness of her purple lipstick.

"Kiss me."

Niks froze, unable to handle the confusion of feelings tearing her at the seams.

We're just friends, I could never—
(Syra; so beautiful, I've always—)
I couldn't
It's just the alcohol
(Maybe this one time)
James wouldn't find out—

Fearing what she could not understand, she allowed herself the easiest escape.

No, this isn't me!

Niks bucked her hips up, launching Syra forward. Wiggling free, Niks fell off the table, too drunk to catch herself on the shelves.

"You okay?" Syra said, peering over the table with a giggle.

Heaving for breath, Niks swallowed the dry contents of her mouth and rolled over, her back flat against the cold tiles. "You're an *assino*."

"You should have kissed me. I might have believed you then, ya big square."

Syra hopped off the table and gathered the evidence of their drunken night, tucking the canteen between her plump breasts and tossing the specimen containers into her purse. "Come on, I'll ride the lift with you back to his quarters."

"Can't I just stay at your place?" Niks asked as Syra lifted her up by the armpits.

Syra looked at her with bemusement, but filtered any discomfort from her response. "No, not tonight. Don't want Mr. Predictable banging on my door and interrupting my fun."

Stumbling over her own feet, Niks found herself strangely disappointed, and unable to keep the frustration out of her voice. "You're gonna hook up—tonight?!"

"Hey, this girl's got needs," Syra said, opening up the storage door and assisting Niks back out into the empty corridor. She typed in command codes on her wristband, summoning a lift. "And so do you. Don't forget that."

"I'm perfectly satisfied," Niks said, closing her eyes to keep the room from spinning away. "I've got the hottest boyfriend in the Starways who loves me."

Syra chuckled, keeping her arm around her friend as she wobbled back and forth. "And the biggest blue clit in all the universe."

"What?!"

"Nothing!" Syra said, waving her right hand in truce as the automated lift came whizzing around the corner.

Niks' legs felt like water as Syra hauled her up onto the lift. Upset, but not sure why, Niks nudged her friend in the ribs with her elbow. "Wish you weren't an *assino*."

As they sped down the hallway, Niks leaned heavily on Syra, dreading the long talk with James, and the inevitable outcome. Once they came within sight of his quarters, Syra kissed her cheek and whispered back: "I wish you weren't so afraid to be you."

Niks closed her eyes, inner voice rising in the wake of her inhibition.

Me too.

Chapter 2

Just wanna sleep, Niks thought, trying to keep from toppling over as James guided her to the single couch in his living quarters.

"We need to talk, Nikkia," he said as he plopped her down on one of the cushions.

Damn you, Sy!

"Stop," she said, batting his hands away as he tried to offer her water and electroyle-infused rations from the food dispenser.

"I'm glad you came home; I thought you'd end up at Syra's." Brushing off his uniform pants, James sat next to her and took her hands. With wide, big blue eyes, he said in his most serious tone, "I'm worried about you."

Chak *you, Sy.* Not that her best friend would be thinking at all about her at the moment. Niks imagined her already at the cantina, hitting on one of the newbie soldiers recently transferred to their ship—maybe even two—and sealing the deal with the glint in her eye, hips swaying side-to-side as she called for a lift back to her quarters.

But I have Mr. Predict—
James. I have James.

"I know you're upset about the Med Oculus," he said, firming his grip. His massive hands dwarfed hers, but he didn't apply too much pressure. "But I really believe this is a fantastic opportunity for you, Nikkia."

"Stop calling me that," she said, trying to scoot away from him, but she'd already reached the end of the couch. Wrenching her hands free, she crossed her arms and faced away from him, looking out the circular window to the stars. "And I don't want to hear any of your military *gorsh-shit.* I'm your girlfriend, not your test subject."

"You're right. This is your choice. I just thought after you signed a contract with SOHO you understood the risks and rewards of operating in deep space."

Even drunk, Niks caught the inflection in his voice. "What?"

James leaned forward on his knees and formed a steeple with his hands. "Didn't you read the fine print in your contract with SOHO? The non-disclosure contract with the Dominion?"

A wave of nausea rippled through her gut. Bracing her abdomen, she tried keep the liquid contents of her stomach down.

James, however, took her silence as an admission of negligence.

"You never read the fine print," he chuckled. "For the *Mercy's* protection, SOHO has allowed the Dominion to trial new medical treatments."

"I didn't volunteer to help the military," she said, unamused by his patronizing tone.

"You help identify telepaths."

She blushed, unsure of why she felt embarrassed and angry at the same time. "That's different."

Assuming a less dominant stature, James rest his arm on the top of the couch, his fingertips brushing the end of her ponytail. "Helping others is what you do best, Niks. I'm just trying to give you what you've always wanted."

The words perched on the edge of her throat, wanting to be screamed: *You don't know what I want.*

But she held back, frozen as his fingers glided over her shoulder and touched her chin. He moved closer, encroaching on her space, as he directed her face to his. "You're still upset. Talk to me."

Staring into his blue eyes, she thought of a million different responses, all of which demanded to be heard, and none of which she felt comfortable enough to say. Instead, he did what he always did when she couldn't come up with anything.

"We can't have a good relationship if we don't have trust," he said in his smoothest voice. "You're confused and angry right now, some of it at me; you think I stepped out of line."

She dropped her gaze, but he picked up her chin again. "I know your parents were killed in telepath riots—"

"My parents were killed by leeches," she said, jerking her face out of his hand. She wanted to add, *you inconsiderate, overbearing jerk*, but she bit down on her lip before the words could escape.

James cupped her cheek. "I know. It's all in your employee file."

For the second time that night, Niks blushed. *He had no right—*

"Shhhhhh," he said, wrapping his other arm around her shoulder and pulling her to his chest. Face smashed against his hard pectoral muscles, she couldn't manage more than a muffled grunt in reply. "I'm here; I'll protect you. You don't need to worry about anything."

As much as she wanted to protest, his arms felt good around her. Thick and strong, they promised the kind of protection stolen away from her long ago.

She pulled back a little, enough to look up at him, seeing the familiar cropped, dirty-blonde hair and blue eyes, and clean-shaven face. None of the other men she'd dated ever compared to him, and she couldn't imagine a better partner. *Career-minded, intelligent, good-looking, built, loving...*

Rattling through her usual list, she couldn't hold on to her anger—especially when he slid one of his hands up her thigh, his blue eyes still gazing at her with unwavering attention.

Unfulfilled needs quieted her stomach, and all other considerations. Turning to him, she allowed his hand to travel under her scrubs, skimming the undersides of her breasts.

"Here," he said, shoving the glass of water between them as she went in for a kiss. "Drink this first."

Irked, but pawning it off as something she should have expected from him, she swished the water around her mouth to get rid of some of the aftertaste of booze, and then swallowed.

"And this," he said, offering her the food ration again.

Syra's face popped up in her mind. *"...he's going to sit you down and talk to you about your 'feelings' and your plain vanilla relationship while feeding you rations and water..."*

No, she thought, fighting against Syra's words. *It's not like that. We're not that—that—*

James pushed her down on the couch, and kissed the soft spot behind her ear, nibbling down her neckline. As he used one of his hands to hold himself up, he undid the ties on her scrub pants.

"Then you're going to have the same sex you've been having for years..."

"*Chak,*" she whispered.

"Huh?" he said, not pausing as he folded her scrub pants and put them on the coffee table.

"Nothing," she said, pulling him back in.

He kissed her, massaging her breasts in the same circular motion as his tongue.

I guess that's sorta different...?

Sitting up, he unbuttoned his uniform top and then pulled it over his head. His hardened abdominal muscles, and the light hair descending his chest and belly button, made her smile.

All man, all mine…

As he unzipped his pants and moved himself on top of her, she closed her eyes and allowed him to pin her arms over her head. Moving aside the crotch of her underwear, he pressed against her warmth, but did not enter.

Surprised, she opened her eyes, but the excitement dulled when she found him looking down on her, eyes glinting in the starlight. "I love you, Nikkia Rison."

He pushed himself inside her and she cried out, unready for all of him at once. Still, she didn't tell him to stop, not even as he gripped her waist and pumped harder, his hips grinding into hers.

"…no orgasm for you—not unless you imagine someone else banging your sweet little flower…"

Damn you, Sy.

As James thrust in again and again, sweat beading across his brow, Niks closed her eyes. *Just finish already so I can get on with this hangover.*

Curving her back, she drew him in deeper. Despite the pain, she moaned for him, making him quicken his pace.

"Nikkia… Nikkia…"

Gods, I hate when he does that.

One final thrust. He held on her hips too tight, making her wince. But after a few seconds he caught his breath, rolled her to her side, and moved in behind her for the obligatory cuddle.

"Glad we talked," he said, giving her a squeeze.

That was a discussion?

Nausea came back, with vengeance. This time, as she fought to untangle herself from his grip, she couldn't hold herself back. She threw up all over the coffee table, knocking over the water glass and spoiling the food rations.

"Nikkia!" he said, jumping up and sweeping her up in his arms. Carrying her to the bathroom, he gently set her down and held her hair as she emptied the rest of her stomach into the commode.

"Sorry," she muttered, wiping her mouth with the back of her hand.

James didn't say anything, handing her a towel to clean her face as he flushed away the translucent brown remnants of her binge.

He's always there for me. As she stared at the water swirling down the commode, she thought of Syra, of the kiss that didn't happen, and of all the reasons she wanted to get drunk with her friend in storage room E that night.

I'm not happy.

The thought stunned her at first, but left her numb as James assisted her back up and carried her to bed. He helped her change her scrub top and into a clean t-shirt and fresh underwear, and before tucking her in, tried to get her to eat and drink again.

"I'm fine," she said, pulling the sheets up to her nose and assuming the fetal position.

James kissed her forehead, "Love you, babe."

Babe. That's even worse than Nikkia.

Not that he knew that, or how much she hated cuddling after sex. As soon as he switched off the lights, he wiggled over to her and draped one of his huge arms around her body and pulled her in close.

Stifled by his body heat, but too exhausted and nauseated to do anything about it, she laid there in the dark, staring out to the cosmos framed by the portal window. Shimmering in the cold of space, the stars offered her no solace, no guidance, as her mind and heart warred over the truth of her greatest need and yearning.

But as she drifted off, promising herself that she'd find contentment in the morning, she imagined Syra on top of her again, only a breath of space between their lips, and the kiss that should never, and would never, happen.

***

Sirens blasted Niks awake only four hours later. James shot out of bed, and within the span it took her to reorient herself to her surroundings, the Dominion Core lieutenant had already changed into his battle uniform.

"*Chak*," Niks muttered, stumbling over to the dresser and sifting through the small collection of her clothes he allowed her to keep in the middle drawer. Very little made sense in the blue and green sea of scrub tops as the expected headache, and wailing sirens, racked her skull.

Only granny-panties? she thought, unable to find anything else. "I swear his drawer eats my thongs."

Assuming his authority, James called up the bridge on his wristband, holding the device in front of his face. "Report."

Niks scooted out of range, not wanting the entire command crew to see her changing. *Did you forget I'm here?*

A young-looking soldier, one of the new transfers, appeared in the projection. "We received a distress signal from La Raja, capital city of planet Neeis. Their president reported anti-telepath terrorist attacks on city hall, government buildings, and hotels. Casualty reports are in the thousands."

Niks' stomach knotted. *We've exceeded max capacity before.*

But not like this. The *Mercy* could hold up to five-hundred patients, not thousands. Even if they rapidly unfroze the crews resting in cryosleep and sent mobile units to the ground, they still didn't have the resources to treat that many injured.

"What other starships can assist?" James asked.

"None within jump range. The *Callieo* and the *Ventoris* estimate they can reach orbit within forty-eight hours."

Forty-eight hours, Niks thought. Hands shaking, she turned them into fists. *That's too late.*

"What's our ETA?"

"Commander Hickson is pushing this next jump. We'll be in transport range in fifteen minutes."

Grabbing whatever she could find, Niks threw on mismatched scrubs and headed for the door.

"Niks—" James said, breaking his conversation as she stepped outside. "Hold on, I'll ride the lift with—"

She didn't wait, signaling for a lift and climbing aboard the transporter jam-packed with medical staff heading to their stations.

Jin Idall, nurse and only other human hired by SOHO, offered her part of the railing as the lift sped off again.

"Did you hear?" she said as she collected her long black hair and shoved it into a surgical cap. Sweet but reserved, Jin kept a straight face as they neared the admitting unit.

Niks tapped her wristband, but nothing came up. *Damn—no assignments yet. That's a bad sign.* "More terrorist attacks and we're the closest starship."

Some of the other medical staff listening in on their conversation muttered under their breath, but kept any overt anxieties to themselves. As the crew of the *Mercy,* they'd all faced back-to-back shifts, missions in the heart of warzones, and other high-stress situations.

Then why does this feel different? she wondered.

"Are you okay?" Jin said, giving Niks the side-eye.

Catching a glimpse of her reflection in the shiny finish of the lift railing, Niks winced. The puffiness of her eyes and pallor would certainly cause alarm—and get Maio's attention. Not to mention the probable stink of Syra's devil-begotten concoction seeping from her pores.

"I-I'm fine. Just couldn't sleep last night."

"Sure," Jin chortled. Crossing her arms, she nodded at the other lift racing down the hall carrying another wave of medical staff, including Syra. "She owes you at least a fluid resuscitation. Better tank up before this gets hot."

"Thanks," Niks muttered, annoyed and embarrassed.

Syra caught up with her as the lift dropped them off at admitting. How she looked well-rested, her makeup fresh and her hair perfectly curled, Niks didn't know.

"I don't need to ask, do I?" Syra said, looking Niks up and down, half-smiling, half-cringing.

Already self-conscious of her ragged appearance and mismatched scrubs, Niks grabbed her friend by the arm and pulled her in close. "You owe me some fluid resuscitation—and probably a dose of vetynol for this headache."

Syra giggled, and followed her through to admitting. "Fair enough."

Pulling Syra along, Niks lead her friend through the crowd of medical staff milling around the nurse's station waiting to be briefed, back to one of the storage rooms. Niks grabbed the fluid kit off the shelf, and a few other meds, and set them down a cart before taking a seat on top of a mobile biosystems analyzer.

"Give me your arm," Syra said, unwrapping the kit and priming the fluid line.

Niks offered her left arm, and with the other, covered up her eyes, too embarrassed and frustrated to look her friend in the face.

"It's not that bad, is it?" Syra asked as she attached the fluid to Nik's forearm and hooked the bag to one of the shelves. "I've seen you way worse."

"No," Niks muttered, watching the yellow-tinged fluid flow into her veins.

After injecting a cocktail of drugs into one of the IV ports to ease her hangover symptoms, Syra crouched down and rested her hands on Niks' knees. "What's up, girlie? Talk to me."

Those eyes, Niks thought, taking in only a glimpse of the warm brown of Syra's gaze. Her friend's hands felt good on her legs, the touch full of care and interest, and willingness to hear her through.

But she didn't want to admit the frustration and anxiety she didn't understand, or even attempt to verbalize the emotions roiling through her. Instead, she looked up at the rapid-infusion bag, watching the last few drops shoot down the IV line.

In three minutes I'll feel better.

And yet, she still slipped: "So, last night, did you even get his name?"

The question came out with a hint of jealousy she hadn't intended, but Niks covered it up with a nervous chuckle.

"You know the answer to that." Licking her lips, she moved her hands up Niks' thighs. "But I must say—those fresh recruits sure work harder than the veterans!"

Niks laughed as Syra raised and lowered her eyebrows and stood up to shimmy her breasts in her face. Be it the rapid infusion, or her friend's ridiculousness, she felt better, the uncomfortable truths of the night before fading back from her immediate concern.

"Alright," Syra said, pulling out the IV and bundling up the kit to throw in the trash. "Better?"

"Yes, much." Niks stood up and gave her friend a hug, not letting go even when Syra tried to pull away a second time. Turning her head, she whispered into her friend's ear: "Thank you."

Syra kissed her on the cheek, and gave her one last squeeze. "Come on—we'd better get going before Meow sniffs us out and assigns us to the lame-o transport team or something."

Sneaking out of the storage room, the two made their way back to the nurse's station where the medical staff talked nervously amongst themselves, whispering rumors and worries about the mission ahead.

"Attention," Maio said, standing behind the nurse's station with two Dominion physicians and James. "Due to the critical situation on Neeis, we are reviving all medical staff in cryosleep. I have divided our current crew into five teams: ground rescue, stabilization and transport will be working off-ship. After reviving the crewmembers in cryosleep, the remaining two onboard teams will work surgeries and transitioning our sickest patients into cryostasis for transport back to Dominion. Check your wristbands for your assignments, and report immediately to your designated areas for further briefing."

"Is it safe?" one of the med techs asked.

Maio shot him a glare before responding. "All teams have been assigned to a compliment of Dominion soldiers. Dismissed."

Everyone, including Niks, immediately checked their wristband.

"*Chak*," she muttered as she read the blue text scrolling across the face of her wristband. *Transport team? I'm one of the strongest nurses—I shouldn't be babysitting!*

Syra rested her chin on Niks' shoulder and pointed at the signature at the end of the assignment. "Looks like someone's boyfriend is getting a little protective."

Fuming, Niks shouldered her way through the crowd to James. The lieutenant, deep in conversation with Maio, did not notice her until she came up beside him.

"May I speak to you in private, *sir*?"

"Nurse Rison, you are due on the transport ship," Maio snapped.

"One moment, nurse Kull," the Lieutenant said, pulling Niks into the center of the nurse's station.

"We're launching in twenty, Nikkia; this better be urgent."

Turning her wrist to face him, she pointed at the blue text. "Why did you assign me to the transport team?"

James' face remained cool and calm. "Nurse Kull and I felt—"

"No, you felt," she said. "Meow would have put me in triage, or at least ground rescue."

"Meow?"

Shaking her head, she corrected her pronunciation. "*Maio*. Look, you don't have to protect me."

"It's not like that."

Niks detected the hesitation, saw the way he averted his eyes. *He's lying.*

"We based the decision off the Med Oculus," James tried to explain. "Jin Idall volunteered to try it, and so we assigned her to oversee triage."

"Then put me on ground rescue."

James clenched his jaw and assumed an authoritative tone. "This is not your decision, nurse Rison."

Furious, but without immediate recourse, she glared at him and muttered. "Yes, sir."

As she walked away, heading toward the docking back to meet the rest of the transport team, Syra intercepted her at the lifts.

"Hey—chin up. There'll be plenty of opportunity to help."

"Easy for you to say," Niks said, noticing the scrolling text on Syra's wristband. Assigned to the triage team under Jin, Syra would see most of the action, and not be stuck on the same transport vessel going to and from the surface.

"Keep your head on straight and don't do anything I would do," Syra said as Niks boarded a lift.

"That doesn't leave much," Niks said with a heavy sigh.

Syra grinned. "That's my girl."

***

All of her anger and frustration vanished the second Niks stepped off the ramp of transport-1 and onto the blistered streets of La Raja. Dying light flared the bombed-out government buildings to the east, while the fires still raging near the infamous pleasure hotels gave off green and purple light from whatever toxic grit fueled their flames. Bodies, broken and bloodied, lay strewn about in the hundreds.

My Gods... she thought, heart pounding in her chest. She'd expected more of the nerve gas/hemotoxin, but not the bombings that took out at least two-thirds of the city, and hid the morning sun beneath a smear of brown clouds.

"Rison—double-check the stretchers and freezer cases," said Lieutenant Daniels, commanding officer for the transport team, as he pointed her back inside the ship.

Niks didn't move, at least not right away. *I should be with them,* she thought, watching the second transport vessel drop off Jin's crew closer to the heart of the city. *Would they have let me go if I had said yes to using the Med Oculus?*

The question made her uncomfortable, so she buried it away. Adjusting the connectors from her hazard suit to her oxygen mask and tightening the straps to her medical backpack, Niks reluctantly went back inside, safe and protected just as James ordered.

Niks surveyed the transport vessel. Arranged to hold up to twenty litter patients and ten freezer cases to transport the most critical patients back to the *Mercy,* she expected their crew to make continuous runs from surface to the starship and back at least every two hours.

This is unfair, she thought, punching in the diagnostic commands into the freezer cases. *He can't take nursing away from me. It's the one thing...*

She stopped herself before she could finish the thought, but the sentiment remained. *(...that's mine).*

Within ten minutes of checking the stretchers and freezers, patients started arriving by the dozens. Dominion soldiers and SOHO med techs dropped off the most severely wounded, coordinating with Lieutenant Daniels as to whom to transport first.

This is horrible, Niks thought, holding the hand of a man missing most of his face and right arm from a blast. "You're safe now. We're taking you aboard a medical vessel. Everything will be all right."

Working as fast as she could, she prepped him for a freezer case to buy him some time as he garbled and moaned through the jagged hole in his face.

"New priority, nurse Rison," Daniels said, walking up to her as she infused cryoprep into the patient's IV line.

By the hard set look on his face, Niks expected the worst—cutting corners, sparing supplies for only the ones who had a chance to make it, even sacrificing their own quarters aboard the *Mercy*—but not what he asked.

"Freezer cases are only to be used for patients with positive extrasensory brain scans."

Niks' breath caught in her chest as she looked back down at her patient. With what little sense he had left, the injured man clung to her hazard suit, knuckles turning white as he fought to stay conscious. Blood pooled around his head despite the hemepatches, and it would be only a matter of minutes before he went into heart failure.

He won't make it if we don't freeze him—

Daniels looked over her shoulder as she waved the bioscanner above the patient's head. "Turf him," the Dominion officer said, snapping his fingers at two soldiers and then walking away.

Niks stood in shock, not knowing what to do. *I can't just let him die—*

But the decision had already been made. The Dominion soldiers lifted the injured man off the stretcher and carried him off the transport ship, dumping him off near a broken slab of cement with the rest of the dead or dying citizens.

Before she could absorb the horror of the first patient, several more patients came through. Niks worked in a daze, trying to save whom she could, but ultimately losing to the military's surprising rule over patient priority.

This isn't right, she thought, watching other SOHO medical staff abandon patients on the surface. *Why does the military only want us saving leeches?*

After the second departure and return to surface, she couldn't ignore her conscience any longer.

Not the kids, she thought, heart aching as Dominion soldiers pulled a badly burned little girl from her stretcher when she didn't test positive.

"Mommy—Mommy—" the little girl sobbed, her arms reaching out to Niks as the soldiers carried her off.

"You can't do this," she said, flinging off her bloodied gloves and storming over to Lieutenant Daniels. "I don't want to lose patients like this."

"You have no authority on the matter, nurse. Now, get back to work or—"

An explosion rocketed the entire transport vessel, hurling Niks against the wall. Racking her head against a monitor, she fell to the floor, dazed and ears ringing as a flurry of activity played out before her.

"Another attack—take cover!" someone shouted.

Smoke filled her lungs; she tasted copper in her mouth.

(Mom, Dad—)

Panicked, but unable to find her footing, she scrambled across the grated floor, trying to find purchase as the ship groaned and quaked.

"Daniels to helmsman—take off!" she heard the lieutenant shout above the fray.

No, Niks thought, fighting her way past the soldiers and medical staff rushing on board. *I can't leave them*—Syra, Jin, and all of her friends stranded in the heart of the city—not to mention the injured citizens.

As the engines rumbled to life, one of the other nurses grabbed Niks's arms as the soldiers raised the ramp. "What are you doing?"

"I won't abandon them!" she shouted, wrenching free and flinging herself out of the closing space between the ramp and the door seal.

She hit the ground hard, sending shooting pains up her shoulder and neck. With no time to spare, she collected herself and stumbled as far away as she could as the blue anti-grav pods lit up and lifted the transport vessel off the ground.

"Rison!"

Strong hands grabbed her by the armpits and dragged her behind the fragments of a wall as the transport vessel fired its engines and blasted away to the orbiting starship above.

"Vyers?" she said, thankful to see her fellow med tech taking shelter behind the wall with her. At over two meters tall and weighing over 115 kilograms, the hulking Trigonian looked as if he had taken a beating in the recent wave of attacks. Bits of glass and debris peppered his face, and burn marks scored his hazard suit, but he didn't look at all concerned with his own injuries.

"There's a group of people trapped in one of the hotels, but Jin and several other members of the triage team are down."

"Where's Syra?"

"She's okay—went back out into the field to help the injured."

That sounded about right. No matter what, Syra never stopped, even in the worst conditions.

"We'll just do what we can until the Dominion secures the situation," Niks said, checking her backpack for supplies. A few hyposyringes looked damaged, and her bioscanner.

Dammit, she thought, tapping the bioscanner. The screen remained black.

But it didn't matter. As long as she could still stand, she would do something, even if it meant tearing apart her hazard suit to fashion tourniquets.

"Can I patch you up?"

Vyers shook his head. "Nah; it's just scratches. The ground team needs you. I'll stay here, see if anyone else pops up."

"Alright—be careful, Alex."

The med tech gave a two-finger salute. "You too, Niks."

Picking their way through the smoke and rubble, Niks found Jin Idall and the other members of the triage team in the broken-down tent. Supplies and stretchers fragments smoldered in the aftermath of whatever bomb struck their location.

"Niks…" Jin Idall, badly wounded, lifted a lacerated arm to flag her down as the others medical staff tended to the most severely injured.

"I'm here," Niks said, kneeling beside her on the ground and feeling for a pulse on her neck.

Weak, but stable, she thought as she surveyed the rest of her body. *But she might have internal injuries I can't see.*

"I'm fine," Jin said between ragged breaths. "Get back into the field. Hotels…people trapped…"

Niks slapped several dermpatches and a painkiller to Jin's arm. "I won't leave you like this."

Shaking her head, Jin looked her in the eyes, a weak smile upon her face. "Trust your intuition."

But that was just it. Niks didn't like Jin's pallor, or the way her skin temperature registered below 34 degrees Celsius on the sensor tips of her gloves and the readout on her visor. Her gut screamed at her about the seriousness of her hidden wounds, but she couldn't take a risk of injecting her with the wrong stabilization medication.

Then she saw it. Besides Jin, covered in soot. *The Med Oculus. I can't—*

But Jin. I can't leave Jin to die.

With trembling fingers, she dusted off the visor and glove for the Med Oculus.

"You don't have to," Jin said, voice fading.

Niks' cheeks burned red. *She must know about my freak-out.*

Explosions boomed in the distance. Screams peaked, then faded.

(Mom, Dad…)

Niks held onto tight to the Oculus, torn by conflicting emotions. But even as old fears played out across her mind, her own words surfaced amongst the tumult as she stared at Jin: *"Nursing is the only thing that's mine."*

Taking a deep breath, she slid off her own glove and replaced it with the Oculus glove. "Can you coach me through it?"

Jin offered a weak smile. "Not going to lie; it's a little jarring."

"I'll be fine," Niks said, trying to sound more confident than she felt.

"It kinda feels like falling. Maybe like how Alice felt when she fell down the rabbit hole."

Niks laughed; she hadn't heard a reference to something from Old Earth in ages. "And then I wake up in Wonderland?"

"Not quite." Jin's voice turned serious. "You're so close—closer than you've ever been to someone."

Bringing up her hands, Jin folded them above her heart and squeezed her eyes shut. "It's terrible and wonderful all at the same time."

Niks braced herself as the ground quaked, and people shouted outside the tent.

"You can do this, Niks," Jin said, resting her hand on her arm. "Get me back so we can help more people."

"You're right." Niks jammed the visor down over her eyes, and adjusted the head attachment. In the far right of the visor, vital signs graphs and stat analysis appeared, but no numbers populated the field. She could still see Jin clearly, though cast in shades of green. "Okay, what's next?"

Jin pulled open the tears in her biohazard suit, exposing her black and blue skin. Color paling, she whispered: "The glove…your eyes now…"

Terrified for her friend, Niks placed her gloved hand on Jin's stomach. She expected the visor to show stats, maybe even zero in on the internal injuries, but even with Jin's warning, she didn't expect the fall.

Oh God—

Vision wobbling, her brain and body disconnected, like a sailor flung from their ship into a swallowing black ocean. Niks wanted to tear off the visor, but her body, a sluggish thing in the distance, could not be reached.

Panicked, she wanted to feel something—suffocation, even pain—not the deadened drift of being pulled apart from herself.

Then, awareness. Niks' eyes stung as a light flashed all around her, slowly spinning away into blinking stars. Blood vessels and viscera appeared before her as she skimmed across the reddish-brown hues of Jin's liver.

That wasn't at all like falling.

But her thoughts didn't linger for very long on the dysphoric experience as she felt the connection back to her body reestablish, and she became aware of not only her internal view, but of her hand atop Jin's abdomen.

"You okay?"

Niks heard Jin's words, but at a distance and muffled, as if spoken through a wall.

"Yeah…this is incredible," she said as she moved her hand over Jin's abdomen. Vital signs and stats scrolled across far to her right, but she didn't pay them much attention. The rush of blood, the rolling waves of peristalsis deeper in Jin's digestive track, the hard surface of bone and the sponginess of marrow—she could touch and sense everything.

"What?" Jin said as Niks stopped over her spleen.

Blood pooled around the ruptured organ. Niks eyed the vital signs, and the blood chemistries as she hovered over the injury. *She needs a transfusion, direct dose of CellStat, and a ImmunBoost.*

"Okay, I know what to do. What's next?"

"Use your right hand… hit the center button on the keypad near your ear… disengage connection."

"Why?" Niks asked, fumbling to find the correct button.

"Maio…really strict about it."

Niks found the center button and hit it. A tidal wave of warmth filled her as she returned in full to her own body. "Isn't she always?"

Jin's chortle turned into a wince. "Good point. Still… you wouldn't want to get stuck in my guts, would you?"

Still a bit shaken, Niks dug around the medical kits and bags until she found what she needed to treat her friend. "As pretty as yours are," she said, injecting the gelatinous CellStat directly into her spleen, "I don't think I'd want to be stuck inside anyone's guts."

After setting up the transfusion and covering Jin up with supply bag to serve as a blanket, she kneeled back beside her. "Better?"

"Already," Jin said, touching her arm again. "Thanks."

"Alright, I'm going back out there."

"Wait." Jin grabbed on to her hand. "Don't use it alone."

"What—why?" Niks said, looking at the Med Oculus glove through the green visor.

"It's still experimental—take someone with you—just in case."

Niks looked around. Other nurses, doctors, and techs were already dealing with massive traumas, and with low supplies—and no extra bioscanners—what else could she do? "I'll be careful."

Worry creased Jin's forehead. "Niks—"

Niks squeezed Jin's hand. "I'll catch up with Syra, okay?"

"Be careful," she stressed, still not letting go over her hand. The words trembling on her lips brought tears to her eyes. "I still feel…"

Huh? Niks didn't understand Jin's fear, or the sudden emotion calving the normally reserved and collected young nurse.

"Rest," she said, freeing her hand. "I'll be back soon."

As she took off into the bombed-out city, searching for her best friend and the survivors of the latest attack, Med Oculus strapped to her belt, she couldn't help but feel like she left something behind in the tent. She paused about a hundred meters away and looked back. Medical staff dipped in and out of the battered tent, carrying supplies and bloodied instruments.

Jin will be alright, she told herself, adjusting the filter mask over her face.

Still, something lingered. A sentiment, a longing she could not claim.

Turning away, she focused on the dark skyline ahead, to the wild fires streaking up to the sky, and a world torn apart by fear and pain.

Chapter 3

The sun took on a reddish glow, peering at Niks through the cracked-out windows and broken structural beams as she made her way toward the worst-hit parts of La Raja.

Maybe it's not such a bad thing, Niks thought as she passed by the bombed-out remains of one of the pleasure hotels in the infamous District. Broken displays and tawdry ornamental finishings lay strewn about in the rubble, a few neon signs sputtering in the ash. The blend of old-fashion hotel rooms with traditional furnishings, high-tech arcades and virtual reality boutiques certainly fulfilled every fantasy imaginable.

How could anyone do any of this? she thought, kicking a paper advertisement for *"two naughty girls at the same time!"* out of her way. Jacking into arcades, getting off on simulations—or, even more appalling—sex with prostitutes—

Not everyone is as lucky as I am, I guess, she thought, imagining James' strong embrace, and the safety of his kiss. Blanketing herself in the best times with him, she worked past her discomfort at the sight of all the sex and pleasure, and moved forward.

"Syra—are you there?" she said, tapping her wristband to try again for a location on her best friend, or any of the other missing members of the triage team.

Nothing, she thought, staring at the flashing question mark projecting from the wrist display. The bombs must have done something to scrabble the personnel signals, too.

"Help!"

Niks whipped her head in the direction of the cry.

"Over here!" someone else shouted. The voice sounded familiar.

Niks ran toward the cries, picking her way through overturned stimulation beds and broken lightning fixtures until she popped out into a break between buildings and some kind of alley. Several people lay trapped beneath iron beams, most unconscious or dead.

"Niks!"

Relief swept over her as Niks spotted Syra, rescue bag slung over her shoulder, and a few other members of the triage team hustling over toward the alley.

"Thank God you're okay," Niks said, stopping Syra with a hug.

Syra cocked her head. "Come on—it's me."

Not wasting any time, Syra moved past Niks and assisted the other team members unearthing the injured from the beams. Working in tandem, as they had done for years, Niks and Syra brought out the patients, and set up a plan.

"I'm down to bare minimum supplies," Syra said, opening-up her rescue bag and rifling through the last few remnants of bandages, hypos, and intravenous fluids.

"Transports took off after the last bomb. I don't know when they're returning," Niks said, looking up to the smoke-filled sky. High in orbit, she imagined James and Commander Hickson devising a counterattack to the last terrorist bombings, or at the very least, a strategy to safely return and extract the teams still left on the planet.

"Best we can do then," Syra said, feeling for the closest patient's pulse as she waved a bioscanner over his chest. The man, dressed in black leather and brandishing more weapons and tattoos on his body than Niks could count, seemed more like a hitman than a patron of La Raja's offerings. Blood and ash covered his face and body, but the suspicious looking bite marks on his arms didn't look like they could have been caused by the bombings.

Niks tilted Syra's bioscanner toward her as her friend reached his head. "Careful."

"What?"

Niks looked over Syra's shoulder. Only one Dominion soldier left in their lot, his attention focused on helping extract the other trapped citizens. "Daniels ordered us to save only the telepaths for transport."

Brows pinched together, Syra looked down at her bioscanner, the unconscious patient, and then back to Niks. "*Godich* military," she cursed under her breath, adjusting the mask situated over her nose and mouth. It took her friend less than a heartbeat to make her decision. "*Chak* 'em."

"No leech is worth it," Niks muttered.

Syra quirked an eyebrow at her. "Everyone deserves a chance, Niks."

Anger and resentment spiked her chest, flushed her cheeks, but Niks didn't contend her friend. Her nursing vow—to provide equal, quality healthcare for all—meant the world to her, and she took the credo to heart. But in the same space occupied something less ideal, toxic in its rage, kept locked away from the image she held of herself.

Shaking off the weight of her unwanted feelings, Niks did her rounds on the others as Syra worked to stabilize her patient. Ali Deckers, or "Decks," the only other nurse amongst the crew, waved Niks over.

"Don't all these guys look like they're from the same gang?" she said, pointing to the other men and alien hybrids pulled from the debris.

She's right. All of them dressed in similar black clothing and bore different kinds of weapons—from clubs, to brass knuckles, knives, and chains. Niks squatted next to Decks' patient and saw the fatal bite mark on his neck, and wild scratch marks scoring his face. "Looks like he got in a fight with a feral cat."

Decks sighed as she shifted the straps to the backpack on her shoulders. "I don't want to use the last of my supplies on gang members."

Niks didn't try to argue with her. Eventually, everyone from SOHO suffered some level of despondency by the pain and suffering, poverty, or inhumane conditions they encountered on the missions. And she got it. Not everyone was as forgiving and non-judgmental as Syra, and sometimes decisions—the harshest kind—had to be made in crisis situations.

"Sy," Decks called out, "what if we head to Red House? We can treat the children with what we have left."

Red House. Sounded familiar. Thinking back, Niks remembered hearing something about an orphanage for all the illegitimate children born in the heated passions of the hotels.

"I've got four more dead, one circling the drain," one of the med techs called out as he assessed the other suspected gang members pulled from the wreckage.

Sitting back on her heels, Syra read the body language of the rest of the triage team. Niks inferred the expression hardening her eyes as she laid a hand on her patient's still chest. "Is there anyone else?"

The Dominion soldier poked his head back between the fallen beams, fanning the dusty air and looking through the intricate webwork of collapsed steel, bricks, and girders. "Think we got everybody."

"Okay," Syra said, her voice even. Niks knew better, especially when she saw her best friend grab her rescue bag without making eye contact with the rest of the crew. "…let's keep going."

As the other eight team members picked up their supplies and headed back north, Niks paused. Movement in the alley caught her eye. Walking over to the criss-crossing beams, she spotted a hand covered in faded, interweaving gray tattoos rise up from the ash, and from the shadows came a weak cough.

Someone's still there. She stopped herself before she said anything aloud. *What if it's another gang member?*

Syra came up behind her and touched the back of her hand. "Everything okay?"

"I don't care… I can't leave them," Niks whispered, nodding her head toward the hand.

Even without knowing the full truth about her past, Syra still got her. With a gentle smile, Syra whispered: "Go on. I'll circle back after I get everyone to Red House safely. Here," she said, digging out a resuscitation pack and handing it to Niks. "This is the last one."

"Thanks," Niks said, ducking under the first beam.

"Be careful—and don't do anything I would do!" Syra called as she headed back with the rest of the crew.

Niks stayed focused on the person trapped underneath the debris as she carefully made her way over, under, and through the wreckage. Broken wires snagged at her hazard suit, and dust dirtied her mask. Frustrated and unable to see, she pulled off the mask and slung it on her belt. Through the fetid miasma of smoke and toxins polluting the air, she detected something else—something impossible and wonderful just beneath the stink. It reminded her of Syra, or perhaps her mother's perfume; feminine, calming.

"You're going to be okay," she said, touching the patient's hand. Long fingers curled into a fist, followed by a groan.

Pushing off bricks and dusting off the patient, Niks didn't uncover the gang member she expected crumpled up against the building. Dark orange eyes with yellow accents, like a twilight sky shattered by lightning, popped open as Niks felt for a pulse along the patient's neck.

"You're going to be okay," Niks repeated, but this time with less confidence as her attention kept returning to the woman's face. Despite the abrasions on her forehead and cheeks, or the swelling around her left socket, Niks couldn't ignore the woman's strange allure. Dark blue and green hair, shaved close to her head on one side, long on the other, accented the angles of her high cheekbones. And the multiple tattoos, all symbolic or geometric, looping around her entire right side, or at least what she could see in the gaps between her torn clothing and ash-covered skin, gave her a wild, outerworld look, despite the rest of her human features.

My God...

She couldn't help herself. Lustrous and vibrant, the woman's eyes, an amber-fire that lured her gaze, made her dig deep into the years of nursing experience to refocus and concentrate on the assessment.

"My name is Niks. I'm a nurse with the Sentient Outreach and Humanities Organization. I'm going to stabilize you and then get you to safety, okay?"

The woman groaned, lifting her head, but then letting it fall back to the wall. Niks felt along the woman's body, trying to detect any gross abnormalities, wounds, or breaks.

"No...stop..." the woman said, her voice throaty, strained.

Niks palpated the woman's abdomen, concerned about the hardness in the right upper quadrant, and the way she guarded her ribs. Through the rips in the patient's clothing, Niks spied blunt trauma sites, but from the pattern, it looked it wasn't made from bricks or fallen beams, more like—

A bat, or a club.

Niks thought about the gang members they pulled from the same alley. *Was this woman getting beaten?*

It explained the bite wounds on the gang members, and some of the claw marks. Niks checked the woman's fingers and found bloodied, balled-up skin underneath black-painted nails.

"Get...away..." the woman said, blood sputtering from her mouth.

She's afraid, she told herself, holding the woman's arm down as, even weakened and severely injured, she tried to push Niks away. *I can't leave her like this.*

Niks opened the resuscitation kit, but stopped herself. *What if she's not human?*

Some humanoids or hybrids wouldn't be able to tolerate some of the meds in the kit, and the reaction could be fatal.

Only one choice.

Grabbing the Med Oculus off her belt, Niks popped on the visor. She paused as she slid on the glove, Jin's warning resurfacing: *"Don't use it alone…"*

Her stomach twisted with old fears, but anger and shame made her grit her teeth as she remembered the look of disappointment upon James' face when she wouldn't use it, and the smug satisfaction on Maio's. Even Syra and their recent drunken escapade crossed her mind, as did the feeling of embarrassment and cowardice at her best friend's words: *"Stop being the scared little girl playing it safe."*

No, she decided, *I'm not leaving her.*

Besides, she had saved Jin's life. *I can do this.*

Pressing her gloved fingertips to the patient's stomach, she closed her eyes and prepared for the fall.

But it didn't come. Niks opened her eyes, the world cast in green hues.

Why isn't it working? she thought, tapping the visor. The stats and the graphs appeared in the far upper-right of her visual field, and the readouts showed a link to the glove.

"Don't…" the woman said, blood continuing to trickle from her mouth. "Don't…want your…"

The rest of the sentence fell off in a garble as the woman's head lolled to the right.

She's unconscious. Niks felt for the patient's femoral pulse with her right hand, but couldn't palpate anything. *Dammit. Work!*

Once again, she pressed her gloved hand to the patient's abdomen. As soon as the metallic discs touched the woman's skin, Niks' vision jerked down, then crashed against an invisible surface. Disoriented, she tried to gain some sort of bearing as a whirlwind of images, sounds, and sensations roiled all around her.

"You were always the best—"

Blue eyes, full of longing and hidden grief—
—"What do you know about love?"
Lips parting wetly, legs opening, inviting. Warm, pink center; salty, sweet.
A man's chest against herself, covered in hair, muscular. Teeth biting into skin, his hands rough against her hips.
(Nobody sees me.)
An image jerked in front of Nik's, more formed than the rest:
Someone pushed her out into a dark alley. Stumbling over her sprained ankle, she fell to her knees. Her face felt both aching and numb after so many punches, but still, she held her head high and stood back up. Men in black leather surrounded her, all of them sporting weapons. One stepped forward, cigarette in hand, a smile denting his hideous face. "Last time I ask, darling. Your tech—give it up."
Fatigue, terror—and defiance. "Shove it."
"Then die, ratchakker."
Niks fought to right herself as wave after wave of foreign memories crashed over her, pain ghosting through her with every punch, kick, and blow that landed on the patient's body.
What's happening to me? she thought. *This didn't happen with Jin—*
Then it all stopped at once, like a hurricane dispersing at the height of the storm.
Breathing hard, Niks found herself on top of the patient's still heart, chaotic electrical activity bouncing around the surrounding tissue.
No!
The stats and graphs on his visor flashed red-warning signs of the patient's cardiac arrest. Still, she stopped herself. *I can't leave until I know the cause.*
Every second that passed squeezed down on her nerves, ramping up her anxiety, but she carefully scanned up and down the patient. Broken ribs, a collapsed lung, and a liver laceration all concerned her, but not as much as what she found pooling near the patient's left kidney.
What is that?
Touching the fluid discoloring and inflaming the surrounding tissues, she sensed something acerbic, highly toxic.

This is poison, she thought, tracing the puncture wound that introduced the fluid. *This is what caused the arrest.*

Something beeped. In the upper right-hand corner of her visor, the analysis field gave a readout of the fluid.

Diatox, she realized as she read the chemical list. A popular sensory enhancer used on the streets, Diatox would be a staple drug on Neeis. However, injected in this much quantity, it would cause severe pain—and potentially arrest.

Keeping her left hand on the patient's abdomen, she ripped open the resuscitation kit with her right. Despite the perceived distance from her body, she knew the kit by heart, feeling for the short hypo at the bottom of the carrier. After identifying the smooth, cylindrical surface, she popped off the bottom with her thumb and depressed it against the woman's belly.

In another situation she might have appreciated the direct view of the antitoxin taking action and neutralizing the poison, or how when she shot the patient again in the chest, the adrenaline kicking the heart into gear. Except in that moment, something happened; a light sparked in the shadow, unseen gears clicked into place. That, and the patient's right elbow smacked her across the face, sending the visor flying off her head.

"*Chak!*"

Niks fell hard, knocking her head against one of the broken slabs and cutting her arm on a splintered beam. Head swimming and stomach revolting against the maelstrom of stimuli, she could do nothing but lay on her side as the patient crawled out from underneath the wreckage and staggered away.

The world seesawed and teetered, and when Niks tried to call out for help, the contents of her stomach throttled up through her mouth. After emptying her belly, and heaving for another ten minutes, she finally felt relief as the world righted itself again.

"Niks!"

Syra—

"Oh *sycha,* are you okay?"

Niks allowed Syra to drag her out of the wrecked alley, not caring about the scrapes and bumps against her body, or the hard feel of the asphalt against her back as Syra laid her down in the middle of the street.

"Talk to me," Syra said, already going to work assessing Niks' injuries.

"I'm okay... just..."

"Just nothing. Jeez. What happened?"

"Did you see her?" Niks said, grabbing Syra's arm as she applied a pressure bandage to the cut on her arm.

"Who?"

"Woman...blue-green hair, tall, tattoos..."

Syra shook her head. "No, sorry. And she'd better stay far away if she did this to you."

Still nauseated, Niks tried to sit up, but ended up laying back down and pointing to the alley. "Med Oculus... I tried to help..."

"Yeah, and this is how she thanks you," Syra said, touching the growing red and purple mass under Niks' right eye.

"Please—find her—she's still hurt—"

"Shhh," Syra said, holding her down by the shoulder. "Let me get you back on your feet, then we can figure that out."

Too exhausted to fight with Syra, she closed her eyes and allowed her friend to tend to her injuries and symptoms. Emotions she didn't expect—relief, worry, fear and curiosity—flowed through her as Syra injected her with antiemetics, pain killers, and a bolus of fluid expanders.

Who was that? she thought, both angry and concerned at the same time.

The woman's eyes, lit by dark fires of a world Niks could never conceive in her wildest dreams, appeared behind her closed lids. She tried to imagine someone else—anything else—

James. God, he's probably so worried.

(Deep orange, like the raging center of the sun)

Or Jin—is she okay?

And all the other patients she needed to tend to.

(Fractured, lightning struck)

Stop it; get focused.

But she couldn't shake the eerie feeling. Even when Syra finished her treatment, refitted her mask, and helped her back over to the alley to collect the broken visor of the Med Oculus, she still felt something else; a presence far in the distance, too far out to reach, or to understand.

"Didn't I tell you not to do anything stupid?" Syra said, taking remains of the Med Oculus visor from her.

"You said not to do anything you would do."

"Exactly."

Niks laughed, and despite the ache it brought to the bruise near her eye, she appreciated her friend's humor, now more than ever.

"Come on," Syra said, taking her by the hand and leading her away from the alley, "we finally got a radio signal in from the *Mercy*. Transports are coming back in thirty with fighter escorts."

Niks nodded, not knowing what else to say. An unnamable fear unfurled within her chest, sending chills down her spine. At first she attributed it to the bombings, or the mission itself—or even James, and how she couldn't decide if she was still mad at him, or needed him now more than ever.

"You really okay?" Syra said as Niks looked back at the alley. Syra's hand moved from Nik's hand to her shoulder, squaring her to the Nagoorian. "Did I miscalculate your head trauma?"

Something isn't right.

But she couldn't let on. She didn't want to get pulled from the mission, not with so many more patients that needed her help. What happened with the tattooed woman was just a fluke—and with the Med Oculus broken, she wouldn't have to worry about putting herself out like that again.

"You wish. Then you'd rationalize hoarding all the booze for yourself tonight."

Syra grinned. "That's my girl."

As they walked off together into swirling dust and debris, ash still raining down from the congested sky, Niks fought the temptation to look back, to whatever—or whomever—called out from the shadows, whispering secret desires and forbidden thrills she could barely comprehend.

Don't, she told herself, shuttering out the titillating sensations with a deep breath and a squeeze of her fists. She decided the patient must have been a bad person—a deviant, prone to salacious activities—and that these sensations must be the aftereffects of the abrupt severance. *This will pass. I can't let her get in my head.*

The wind answered with indifference, howling through the cracks and holes in a world broken open and splayed out under the watchful eye of the sun.

Chapter 4

"I think I could sleep for a week," Syra said, resting her head on Niks' shoulder. Turbulence from the transport's choppy ride through Neeis' upper atmosphere made Syra's head come down a little too hard on Niks' shoulder, and she winced and sat back up straight in her seat. Niks didn't say a word, even as her back protested the upright posture of the seats anchored to the fuselage or the tightness of the harness keeping her in place between Syra and one of the patient litters.

"I hope this is the last run," Syra added, craning her neck to look out of the oval window as the stars blinked into view, as did their orbiting starship, the *Mercy*.

Exhausted herself, Niks didn't respond, drawn inward by the intensity of recent events and sluice of emotions. Her thoughts bounced around from the horror of the terrorist attacks and all of the victims, to the shock of the Dominion military prioritizing telepaths for transport.

And, *her*. The woman with the dark orange eyes and tattoos winding and interweaving all around the right side of her body.

Stop.

Niks forced herself to look to her left, down the treatment cabin of the transport ship. The patients crammed in litters cried and moaned, most delirious on pain medications, while the extrasensory positive ones trapped in the freezer cases drifted in limbo, unaware of the fate determined for them by the Dominion. Still, as much as she wanted to acknowledge the pain and the suffering of the patients, or her outrage at the military—and James—she couldn't shake the vague, unsettling feeling that she left something behind.

It's the children at Red House, she convinced herself, thinking of all the orphans they treated but didn't transport, as the military dictated only telepaths and persons of interest to be brought back to the *Mercy*.

But even that didn't sit quite right.

"Hey—where are you?" Syra said, nudging her in the ribs.

"Here. Just wiped."

"Okay," Syra said, looking her up and down. "Maybe no drinks tonight then. You look like you need real sleep."

Niks whipped her head around to Syra. "No—I could definitely use a stiff drink."

The concerned look etched across Syra's brow eased up. "Alright, but I'm out of the good stuff. Cantina it is."

"Ugh," Niks lamented, "it's so watered-down."

"It's all we got, sista."

Niks shook her head. "Fine. I don't care how long it takes—we're getting sauced."

"Alright then," Syra said, looking both surprised and amused.

Niks took one last look down the cabin as the tractor beam locked on to the transport to guide them into the *Mercy*. The cries and moans escalated as pain medications waned, and the ship engines rumbled down. *Just finish this shift, get tanked with Syra—it'll be okay.*

Or so she wanted to believe.

***

After her sixth shot, Niks finally felt something other than the exhaustion and unease. The cheap cantina alcohol warmed her muscles and slowed down her mind so that the anxieties and body aches became a distant problem.

"God, I still can't get away from that stink," Syra said over the bar chatter and rock music, sniffing the sleeves of her green scrub top. Niks silently agreed. Even though they both changed into fresh scrubs, the pungent residue from the bombs, smoke, and the effluvia of blood and decay still floated above the usual bar smells.

"A few more shots should do it," Niks said, signaling the overwhelmed bartender for another round.

"I can't decide if I'm a good friend for letting you blow off steam, or a bad nurse for letting you drink post-head injury."

Frustrated that the bartender had yet to look their way, Niks tried again, waving both her hands this time and leaning over the bar.

"Hey, what's the rush?" Syra said, still nursing number five.

Niks tapped her empty shot glass on the bar, aggravated by the wait. Since the all of the *Mercy's* personnel had been taken out of cryosleep to aid with the crisis on Neeis, the tiny cantina, usually only patronized by the newbie soldiers and medical staff who had yet to figure out how to concoct their own brew, stood jam-packed with people all trying to get drunk off the terrible SOHO-grade alcohol.

Syra hit her in the shoulder. "I said—what's the rush?"

"Sorry," Niks mumbled, eyeing Syra's unattended sixth shot. With a roll of her eyes and a shrug of her shoulders, her friend let her snag it. Niks downed the harsh liquid in one gulp, hoping that the synthesized vodka would do something more than give her a headache in the morning. Wiping her mouth with the back of her hand, Niks added: "Just not eager to get back."

Syra held up her shot before knocking it back. "You're not—but I am."

"Huh?" Niks said as Syra got up and fixed her top, making sure her rounded breasts peeked out just right in the V-neck of her scrubs.

"Don't give me that look," Syra said, scanning the room for a suitable mate—or mates, depending on her mood. "If you weren't pissed at him, you'd go home right now to Mr. Predictable."

Niks scoffed. "So?"

"So, why are you complaining? At least you have someone to go back to. I have to go on the hunt each night."

"Like that really bothers you."

Syra touched her own nose. "Mmmm. Beats routine."

With a little kick step, Syra merged into the crowd, zeroing in on her prey.

Seriously—those guys? Niks thought as Syra thrust herself between a pair of Dominion deckhands. Between the two of them, they didn't have enough upper lip hair to count for half a mustache. *She always likes the young ones.*

Normally, Niks would take a seat on one of the barstools and watch the charade from afar, both judging and secretly uncomfortable by her friend's more adventurous lifestyle. This time, she didn't want to sit down, not even when the bartender finally made his way over to her and asked her order.

"Give me the strongest thing you've got," Niks said, unable to keep her eyes of Syra as her friend rubbed her hand up and down the two young men's arms. The bartender slid her a single shot of something pink and bubbling, but she didn't pay it a second thought as she guzzled it down, even as raked her throat and sizzled inside her stomach.

Syra...

Tension built in her chest with every stroke, every coquettish laugh Syra employed. Before she could stop herself, Niks pushed her way through to the crowd, popping out at her friend's side.

"Niks? What are you doing?" Syra whispered out of the corner of her mouth.

Niks didn't know what to say, confused herself.

"Boys, this is my friend Niks," Syra said, trying to salvage the situation as best she could. "Niks, this is…"

Of course she doesn't know their names, Niks thought, half-heartedly smiling as each of the young men offered an eager salute. Still, she saw the attraction. The one with darker skin and red-flecked eyes possessed both humanoid and alien features, while the other looked Trigonian, with a strong jaw and prominent muscles that she imagined wrapping around her body and—

What am I doing?

"You heading back, Niks?" Syra said, giving her both the arched eyebrows and nod to the door as a strong hint to stop interrupting her fun.

The smart thing—the way she'd always go—would be to stumble out, get a lift back to James', and just deal with the consequences. But as she looked into her friend's eyes, seeing the expectation, the known response, she couldn't stand the idea.

"So—what's your name?" she said, turning to the Trigonian. Mirroring Syra, she put her hands on her hips to spread her chest.

The Trigonian smiled, big white teeth gleaming in the low-light of the bar. He said something back, but Niks couldn't hear it over the thrashing guitar solo.

As Niks cozied in, pressing herself against the deckhand, and motioning for him to tilt his head so she could talk into his ear, Syra yanked her away.

"What are you doing?" Niks shouted as Syra dragged her into the corner, away from the thudding speakers and bar noise.

"What are *you* doing?" Syra said, crossing her arms and looking her up and down.

Feeling more than tipsy, Niks steadied herself on the wall, trying to keep her balance. "Can't I have a little fun, too?"

"Mr. Predictable isn't going to like this."

"Mr. Predictable isn't here," Niks semi-slurred, twirling her finger around.

Syra cocked her head to the side, confused, but unable to stifle the laugh. "Right. So, what—which one you want—the dreamboat Trigonian or 'dark and mysterious?'"

Hiccupping, Niks replied: "both."

"Uh-huh."

To prove her point, Niks rammed her way back through the crowd, to the two young deckhands still hanging out right where they left them. But when they turned to her, both lowering their drinks, desire in their eyes, she froze.

What am I doing?

Something inside her, beyond her rational thought, answered with a stumble-step forward into the Trigonian's arms.

"Whoa, you okay?" he answered.

With a sly smile, the other added: "Should we take you home, nurse?"

"It's alright, boys." Syra pried her from the Trigonian's arms and held her close. "Another time, k?"

As Syra guided her out of the bar and signaled for a lift, the effects of the last shot hit her full force, setting her head spinning.

"I grossly underestimated how hard you hit your noggin," Syra commented, still holding Niks around the waist as she helped her on to the lift.

"No, don't," Niks mumbled, pushing away Syra's hand before her friend could input the number to James' quarters. Unexpected tears pricked her eyes, and she buried her head into her friend's shoulder. "Let me stay with you."

"Huh?"

"Please," Niks said, keeping close even as her friend tried to lift her head up to look at her face. "Not tonight."

The lift beeped in a request for coordinates, but Syra didn't move and neither did Niks. When the lift beeped a second time, a sob hit her, making her breath hitch and a gasp escape her lips. Grip softening, Syra kissed the top of Niks' head and whispered: "Okay."

Though the lift ride jostled the liquid contents of her stomach, Niks kept it together, holding on to Syra, understanding the nausea, but not the butterflies dancing in her chest.

It's just Syra's, she thought as the lift dropped them off in front of her quarters.

They'd done sleepovers like this hundreds of times over the course of their friendship.

And yet, as her best friend assisted her to bed and unlaced her boots, Niks felt both guilt and excitement as Syra moved to take off her scrub bottoms.

"Cute! Where'ja get those?" Syra said, pointing to the black lace Niks had accidentally put on in the rush to get ready that morning.

Blushing, Niks giggled and tried to take her own scrub top off, but got caught up in the tight V-neck.

"Oooh, yeah," Syra laughed as she helped Niks the rest of the way with her top.

"I was hurrying," Niks said, crossing her arms over her chest to hide the raggedy old black sports bra.

"You're adorable." Still chuckling, Syra stripped down, not showing any concern about walking around stark naked as she looked for suitable pajamas in the mess of scrubs and lingerie strewn about her tiny quarters.

Syra...

Long legs, perfect hour-glass figure, flawless blue skin and a strut that would seduce any person regardless of their sexual orientation. Even after a hellacious shift and enduring terrible conditions, Syra's auburn hair looked freshly styled, falling over her shoulders and down her back with perfect curls.

...so beautiful...

Niks found herself reaching out, wanting to catch Syra's arm as she passed by scrounging through another pile of clothes, but pulled back as her friend turned around, old t-shirt in hand.

"Are you sure you're okay?" Syra said, looking at Niks with the same concern and curiosity she had shown in storage room E.

Ashamed and unsure of herself, the tears started back up, streaking down her face. "Y-yes. I guess. I don't know."

Syra pulled the t-shirt over her head and then sat down next to Niks on the bed.

"This is the second time I've said it—I've never seen you like this, hon. I'm really worried about you. And what was up with hitting on those deckhands in cantina? That's not your style."

Niks turned away, not wanting Syra to see any more of her tears.

"Look," Syra said, pulling her down at the waist to lay on her side. Her friend cuddled up behind her and pulled the sheets up over them. "We can talk about this tomorrow morning when we're both a little less 'drink.' Just know that I'll always be here—and you don't have to be anything but you around me, k?"

"K," Niks whispered back.

Still, as she drifted off, Syra pressed up behind her, warm Nagoorian body heating her between the cool sheets, Niks couldn't help but feel something more—a distant sense of hunger and need lapping up against the shores of her mind, unsettling the perfect construct of the world she had created.

**

Strong arms grabbed her by the hips and threw her down on the bed.

Where am I?

Two men, both young and unfamiliar, looked down on her with hungry eyes. One, wiry and naked, the other, red-headed, freckled, and still wearing checkered boxer-briefs.

Niks could make out a dirty lamp without a shade, a tangle of bedsheets, and the bland decorations of a cheap motel.

"Turn around," the naked one said.

"No, you," she replied in a deep, seductive voice.

Is that me?

No. Not her. Someone else.

But how?

When she looked down at her body, she saw definition and tone in her usual soft places, and tattoos adorning her right side. Scrapes, cuts, and bruises in various stages of healing, marred otherwise flawless skin. Her breasts appeared bigger, pierced, and as she rolled to her side to pull down one of the men, she felt something tug around her pelvis.

What is—OH MY GOD—

A blue, erect phallus, attached to the harness strapped to her hips, got caught up in the sheets.

Never—no—not me—can't be—

But the reality of sensation, too real to be a dream, couldn't be ignored as she slapped the naked man into submission until he lay down flat on his stomach. Though slender, the man's back rippled with muscle, his light hair mussed from foreplay as he buried his head into the pillow, awaiting his punishment.

"You said you liked it rough," she heard herself say as she stretched over and grabbed a bottle of lube, already down to the last drops, off the nightstand.

"You, there," she said, pointing the red-head to take a position behind her. "And wear this."

As she straddled the first man, she handed the red-head a bandana off her arm. With a timid smile, the red-head took it, turning it into a blindfold as he came up behind her.

"Hope you're warmed up enough," she said, applying a few drops to the blue phallus and rubbing it over the head.

The red-head behind her got closer, pressing himself against her back. She felt every taut muscle, every rough hair as he kneaded the muscles of her shoulders, sliding down the curve of her hips, and working his way down to her buttocks.

Bending over and leaning on her elbow, she grabbed the phallus with one hand and pulled on the naked man's hair to tip back his head. "You're mine."

The man laying face down splayed out his fingers as she thrust inside, then bunched up the sheets in his fists. He moaned with every pump of her hips as she moved back and forth, slowly building up speed.

A satisfied smile crossed her face, even though Niks wanted only to run away and detach herself from such vulgarity. But she couldn't, not even when the man behind her spread her cheeks, fumbling to find her wet opening. She paused for just a split second, allowing the man behind her to enter her warmth, feeling him slide inside her all the way up to his pelvis.

Still wearing his boxer briefs, *she chuckled, sensing the brush of fabric against her buttocks.* What a newb.

But the observation didn't come from Niks, nor did her reaction as the man behind her pulled back and slid back inside again, this time with more force.

"Neither one of you come until I say," she said as they interlocked in pleasure.

Niks tried to find something, anything, to latch on to apart from the groans, the incredible synchronicity of three beings moving *together in unison, the feel of rough hands on her hips, her breasts bouncing up and down—*

"Oh God, Rex, please—" the man on bottom said, scrunching up the bedsheets until they ripped off the mattress.

"Don't come until I say," she said, yanking his head farther back and biting his ear.

The red head bent down with her and ground his fists into the mattress, the curvature of his manhood hitting the spot inside her that turned her own wetness and need in the undulations of pleasure.

"Rex, please—"

Niks could no longer differentiate her own self in the heat of passion, caught in the wake of the rising orgasm as their sweat-slicked bodies slid back and forth. Legs quaking, she thrust herself inside the prone man up to his limits at the same time the man behind her pushed himself up against hers, stretching her forward. Lust-crazed, she wanted more, plunging back inside with force, and the man behind her responded with equal vigor. As blood rushed to her clit, nerve endings exploding, she cried out: "now."

Niks woke with a gasp, throwing the sweat-soaked sheets from her body.

Oh God—what just—

Frenzied, she looked around, expecting a heap of bodies and a mess of bodily fluid, but found nothing.

Almost nothing, at least.

Heat rushed to her cheeks when she moved her legs and felt the squishy moisture in her underpants.

Oh no, Syra—

Whipping her head to the right, she found her best friend sleeping with her arms over her head, snoring up a storm, oblivious to her experience.

Thank God, Niks thought, touching the crotch of her underpants. Thoroughly soaked through, she couldn't believe she came in her sleep. *This has never happened before...*

It thrilled and frightened her.

Was that real?

She laughed at the thought, but couldn't put it aside, either. The sensations felt all too visceral, accessible, unlike the remoteness of a dream. And that body—

Niks gasped, bringing a hand over her mouth.

I know that body.

The tattoos, the familiar geometric and symbolic designs interweaving around the right-half of the woman's body.

My patient—

Rex. Or at least that's the name the men cried out.

Rex?

The thought echoed across her mind in a way she didn't expect, as if reverberating down a long tunnel. For a moment, she expected a response, but got only a semi-snort, then elongated snore from her sleeping bed companion.

Niks got up, mindful not to wake Syra, and tip-toed to the bathroom. After shutting the sliding door, she stood in cramped bathroom and splashed some water on her face. When she came back up, she caught a glimpse of herself in the mirror. The light of the stars and the planet below shining through the oval window brought a soft glow to her face.

Don't be foolish, she told herself, touching her cheeks, her black and blue right eye, then her lips, trying to ground herself in the tactile sensation. *It was just a dream.*

"You were just a dream," she whispered, reaching out and touching the mirror. Sliding her finger down the cold surface, she tried to put aside the strange phenomenon, or the nerve endings still tingling between legs. After all, she had gotten worked up in the cantina, and the combination of work-stress and whatever hideous rotgut she had knocked back in the last shot could have easily created the crazy dream. That, and she hadn't climaxed in ages.

My body just overreacted.

Yes, that's it.

And yet, as she turned to go back to bed, chastising herself for the entire night and promising herself to straighten things out between her and James in the morning, she couldn't put aside the image of the tattooed woman, the freedom of her body, or the satisfaction she felt aggressing her playmates.

Everything will be better in the morning, she thought, promising herself to focus on patient care, and her duties as a girlfriend and nurse as she slipped back into Syra's bed.

Pulling sheets back up to her neck and staring up at the bare gray ceiling beams, Niks forced herself to think of James, of all the things she could be thankful for in their relationship, as a sigh rose from up deep within at another satisfying conquest.

Chapter 5

Blue eyes, the same rich color as an afternoon summer sky, appeared overhead.

"Don't look at me like that," she said, voice full of gravel, batting away the man's hands as he tried to help her up.

But once again, not her voice. Niks tried to get some bearing, but like before, could do very little as if the silent audience in someone else's dream.

This can't be happening, she thought, distressed but unable to find any way to free herself from the voyeuristic experience.

Niks saw through a different set of eyes as she reoriented to her surroundings. Lying in a half-opened tube with exposed wires and side panel scanning apparatus, her body moved sluggishly to any commands, as if her neurons just switched back on.

Is this a revitalization coffin? she wondered. She thought she saw a logo etched into one of the interface panels, but her eyes panned away before she could discern anything more.

"I needed to blow off some steam," she said, irked by the man's silence as he watched her climb out of the tube.

When her bare feet touched the cold laminate floor, Niks shivered. Still fuzzy, as if waking up from a dream within a dream, Niks rubbed her eyes and looked over her naked body as the other man watched on from just a few feet away.

The tattoos—

The same geometric designs and symbols adorned her right side, as she had seen in the dream before. However, the cuts and bruises present earlier had vanished. She tested her ribs, and put pressure on her abdomen. A faint ache radiated from both sites, but nothing concerning.

After completing her assessment and clearing her throat, she turned her attention back to the man. "You going to just stand there?" she said in a voice luxurious and rich as she held out her arm.

The man frowned at her, but threw her the set of clothes draped over a rickety old wooden chair. As she sorted through the pieces of the ribbed black and grey jumpsuit, tactical scarf, and a hooded wrap, an errant thought echoed through her mind: Can't stay here much longer.

Apprehension sunk into her bones, and an itch to move out as soon as possible, but Niks sensed the man across from her, arms crossed in front of him with a steadfast gaze, wouldn't be receptive.

As silence passed between them while she dressed, Niks tried to get an idea of her surroundings and of the man in the room with her. In her periphery, she made out peeling beige wallpaper, another bare lamp on the nightstand, and a mattress pulled from the bed frame and set against the windows to block out the light, very similar to the first room she found herself in. A desk, covered with tools, wires, and computer components, caught her attention, in addition to the second view of the cylindrical tube crammed up against the far wall. As much as it looked like a military-grade revitalization tube, it had missing components, in addition to modifications she didn't recognize.

The man intrigued her the most. Catching only glimpses of his face as she continued to dress, she couldn't help but notice his handsome features. Tousled brown hair, a strong nose and jaw, a perfect, symmetrical face—and startling blue eyes that purported to hold back unconscionable secrets. But his striking face juxtaposed to the rest of her body made her gasp.

What happened to him?

Even though clothed in a stained white t-shirt and military fatigue pants, she could see the disfigurations mangling the lower half of his body as he took a seat in the old, squeaky chair and rolled up a pant leg. Grabbing some tools from the desk, he fiddled with the exposed gears and wires of his prosthetic leg. Both of his arms appeared badly burned. Skin grafts had been attempted, though with mismatching skin tones and the crisscrossing appearance of overlapping derma-mesh.

"I can't stay here," she said, looking around for something on the floor covered in red dust and silver filings from whatever projects they ran out of their room. When she found a pair of beat-up hypercolor high-tops, she slid them on one at a time, hopping around on the opposite foot. "And neither can you."

The man looked up, stolid expression unaffected by her declaration.

"Look, I overheard those SOHO medics—the Dominion is transporting out telepaths."

"Don't overreact," the man said in a flat tone, going back to fiddling with the mechanical parts of his leg.

"So what—stay here and wait to get caught? La Raja is a sanctuary city for telepaths—you don't think the Dominion is going to use this last wave of terrorist attacks to justify setting up shop?"

The man didn't respond. Niks sensed that this was typical, and frustration, not her own, heated her cheeks and turned her hands into fists.

"Remy, you godich ratchakker, *I am not in the mood for any of your* gorsh-shit."

Remy, *Niks thought, letting the man's name sink into her. Feelings poured over her in a wave of sensory information:* She felt his hands, calloused and strong, one around her neck, the other bracing her back. Leaning in, he kissed her softly, his warm tongue melting into hers. But slamming up against the sensual memories came more heated emotions: aggravation, upset words, and flashes of him upending a room after a terrible fight.

"Where you going to go, Rex?" he said, still not looking up as he fiddled with his prosthetic leg. "Once you leave orbit, you're going to have every tech thief on your *assino.*"

Rex—

Niks' stomach flip-flopped, excited and nervous at hearing her name again.

"Yeah, and I've got the Takuzi on my tail if I stay here." She kicked the mattress flopped against the windows. "Oh—and the godich *Dominion Core.*"

"The boss's top henchmen died in that blast."

"Don't be ignorant. At best it will buy me some time until Akanno gets another team together and figures out I didn't die in that alley, too."

Remy looked up, this time with a perturbed expression. "Half the city got bombed, Rex. Who says Akanno survived?"

"It wasn't your *assino* that got jacked with Diatox, beaten, and then crushed," she said, giving him the middle finger.

With a heavy sigh, Remy set down his tools on the desk and rested an elbow on his fake knee. "For once in your life, Rex, be chakking *patient, see how things shake out.*"

"No," she said, moving in front of the cracked half-mirror hanging off the door. *"It's too dangerous."*

Impossible—

But the reflection in the mirror confirmed the truth as Rex did her hair, running her hands through the green and blue locks to get the perfect flip over the right side of her face. Of all her familiar features, Niks recognized the woman's eyes, as dark orange as the sunset on New Earth, splintered with yellow accents as she pulled off a stray eyelash from her cheek.

My patient—but how is this possible?

Rex squinted, leaning forward to the mirror as if she saw something she didn't like. Alarmed, Niks tried to pull away, but could do nothing as the woman reached out to the mirror, dark orange eyes alight and inquisitive.

"What the—?"

As soon as Rex's fingers touched the mirror, Niks peeled back, falling away and in, as if sucked down an emptying drain.

No—no—

"No!"

Niks shot up straight in bed, kicking off the sheets, her right arm elbowing Syra in the head.

"Ow!" Syra said. "Whad'ja do that for?"

"S-sorry." Niks tried to provide some comfort as Syra rubbed her left temple and sat up in bed. "Just had a crazy dream."

"What—fighting assassins?"

Niks caught hold of Syra long enough to examine the swelling lump on her head. "No. Weird stuff with a patient. And…"

Cheeks blooming red, Niks swallowed away the rest of her explanation, hoping Syra wouldn't pick up on her embarrassment. But Syra being Syra, her eyes narrowed and she grabbed on to Niks' hand.

"I know that look. What you holding back, girl?"

"N-nothing."

"Nothing my *assino*. Did that bartender give you a splash of the ol' pink bubbly?"

Niks frowned, but then recalled the horrible last shot she took right before she made a fool of herself in front of Syra and the deckhands. "Yeah…"

"Oh, that'll mess ya up." Syra let her go, slid out of bed, and headed to the bathroom. "Last time I took a shot of that poison piss," she said, shouting from the toilet as she did her business, "it was with our former OR supervisor—and then she and I ended up in the docking bay control station with not a single shred of clothing between us."

As Syra continued on with the sordid details of her encounter, relief washed over Niks.

That's got to be the reason for those crazy-vivid dreams.

At least it sat better than any other explanation she wanted to consider.

"…dear *God* was she a good kisser."

On any other day, Niks would roll her eyes at Syra, unable to imagine such a thing as kissing another female. But in light of the licentious nature of her recent dream, she couldn't quite bring herself to the same judgement.

I should get going, she thought, glancing over at the nightstand clock. *0430.* Chak. *That means that any second—*

The door chimed not once, but twice.

Syra popped her head out of the bathroom and lifted an eyebrow. "Ah, Mr. Predictable, right on time."

Niks rummaged through the sea of clothes next to the bed, finding the only pair of scrubs not saturating in perfume, mystery stains, or smelling like the floor of the cantina. "Can I?"

"Yeah," Syra said, pulling on a pair of scrub bottoms draped across her dresser and slipping back into the bathroom. "See you in a few."

"Thanks."

Dreading the impending lecture, Niks took a deep breath and opened the door lock.

"Nikkia." Standing with his arms clasped behind his back in full battle uniform, James looked down at her with steely blue eyes and a tight jaw. Behind him, an automated lift hovered in place, awaiting a destination. "I will escort you to the medical wing."

Niks resisted the urge to look back to Syra, and stepped forward onto the lift with the lieutenant commander. After an uncomfortable thirty seconds of silence as they whizzed down the hall, she finally caved. "Sorry I didn't come home last night. Sy and I—"

"We will discuss that later," James said, keeping his gaze pinned forward. "Right now, there are more exigent matters."

Niks didn't like the inflection in his words, or the serious tone of his voice. *Something's wrong.*

Long shifts, more wounded refugees, supply rationing—even the threat of a warzone didn't bother her—but something in the way he wouldn't look at her, the way he kept his stiff posture and militant expression told her that her concerns paled to what he held back.

"Tell me," she whispered, focusing all of her attention on him.

James eyes flitted to the left and right, to the corners where mounted cameras spied on every interaction in the public and authorized personnel zones. "There have been some staff reassignments within the Dominion. Commander Hickson has a new advisor. His name is Commandant Rogman, Chief of Military Acquisitions."

Rogman. She didn't like the way it sounded, or the way James' forehead knotted when he said the man's name.

"I understand that you used the Med Oculus to save Jin Idall," James said, finally looking at her.

She barely eked out a response: "yes."

"Did you use it on anyone else?"

The fervor in his voice frightened her, and she looked away with quick a shake of her head. *Wait—what? I should tell him—*

Something in her gut clamped down, insides screaming: *(No, don't.)*

"Thank God," he said, pinching the bridge of his nose.

"Why—what's happening?"

James gripped the edge of the rail as the lift turned the corner and slowed in front of the admitting doors.

"I'm meeting with Commander Hickson and Chief Rogman. I'll find you as soon as I'm done," he said, offering her a hand down. Niks accepted, only because she wanted his touch, the affirmation of his strength right then. She'd never seen James act like this, paranoid and clandestine.

"I don't like this," she dared to say out loud, holding on even as he tried to pull away.

"Neither do I," he whispered, squeezing her hand before taking it back. "Stay focused, stay sharp—and keep off of Maio's radar, alright?"

"Alright," she said, frustrated and scared at the same time as she watched the lift take off again, and James disappear down the corridor.

Why am I afraid? she chastised herself. *Who is Rogman, and what could he possibly do to me?*

It's not like she'd done anything wrong—well, maybe lie to James about using the Med Oculus, but it couldn't have been that big a deal. Besides, it was broken, lying in medical engineering beyond the repair of their techs, so it couldn't be used anytime soon.

Then why this terrible feeling? she thought as she waved her wristband in front of the double doors.

But as soon as Niks stepped foot inside admitting, the chaos of it all—patients lying on makeshift beds, along the hallways on the floor, body fluid spills, supplies strewn about, nurses and doctors running about and shouting above the cries of the wounded—reeled her in, and she focused herself on what mattered most.

Chapter 6

"Need some help?"

Niks didn't look up as Syra came up beside her in one of the triage bays, slipping on some protective gloves and helping her hold down her thrashing patient by the chest.

"Thought you were in surgical," Niks said as she calculated the safe amount of a hemodynamic booster she could give the young male patient missing half of his left leg and screaming in a Rajash, the native language of Neeis. His black blood painted the walls and her yellow gown scrub cover, but she didn't pause, trying to get his vitals stabilized.

"Got tagged out by second shift, thought I'd see if you were having all the fun," Syra said, plugging in an IV to his neck and helping Niks secure a secondary line in one of his arms.

"*Chak*," Niks said, looking through the empty medicine vials on the shelf. She pulled open a few of the bay drawers, but found nothing useful leftover in the decimated medical kits and triage packages. "I don't have enough dermapatches or promorph."

The male patient, his screams turning to breathless whimpers as his vitals dipped, turned his head to her. In broken Common, he whispered: "Please... help me..."

"I'll get a doc," Syra said, ducking out of the bay as the patient lost consciousness.

Niks looked at the scanner readouts over the patient bed, noting the vitals and chemistries, but couldn't correlate all the findings.

He shouldn't be losing his pressure—not with all the vasopress I gave him. She looked again at the injured leg severed just below the knee; the temporary hemelocks, pressed over the wound site in glowing yellow octagonal patches, appeared as if they had stopped the bleeding.

Biting her lip, she did a manual exam, palpating his abdomen and rechecking intact sites for anything the scanners may have missed. Then, as her gloved hands circled back around to his chest, she felt a tiny opening just under his armpits.

What is this? she thought, examining the bilateral slits, edged with red, and wet, like the gills of a fish. *He's not Neeisin.*

At least not fully. He had the characteristic double pupils, six fingers, and protruding spine plates at the cervical level, but the anatomical oddity underneath his armpits indicated another ancestral line.

Niks rescanned the patient again, but the species identification module reported Neeisin a second time.

What the hell?

Out of nowhere, fractured images of the bombed-out city flashed through her mind. Surprised, but not fighting her intuition, she remembered back, summoning her memories of the crumbling buildings she passed by until her mind hitched on a curved symbol etched underneath the broken neon sign for a windowless clinic.

Iyo Kono.

Of course. Why wouldn't Neeis, the planet of pleasure, be closely affiliated with the infamous Iyo Kono, an orbiting black market of restoration clinics and body modification boutiques? Iyo Kono operated light years away, but as her thoughts came together, she remembered spying several other "health consultation clinics" occupying both the main streets and the back alleys.

What if this is a body mod? Niks felt along the slits, pulling open the right side to reveal a row of fine teeth.

"What's the patient status?" Dr. Vo asked as he and Syra came around to the other side of the patient. Niks ran him through the scans and vitals, and the medication administration list.

"Then why is he losing pressure?"

"I think he's a body modder," she said, revealing the slits under the patient's armpits. "He's probably on high-dose remicoroids to suppress his immune system and maybe some other street drugs that are interfering with the vasopress."

The name of a drug came out of nowhere, spilling off her lips before she had time to think about it: "like methoc—he's probably on methoc! That would explain the opposite effects of the vasopress."

"Very impressive, nurse Rison." Vo scribbled something on his tablet, not making eye-contact with her.

"I could run a specified blood series to confirm," Niks suggested. But by the concern on Syra's face, the way her friend stood back, no longer engaging in patient care, Niks feared the worst.

"That won't be necessary. There's a new patient arrival in bay 12. Please go and assist nurse Idall."

"But he needs treatment or he'll die—"

Gentle hands pulled her back, but Niks resisted, even as Syra whispered for her to come along.

It hit her like a star-class freighter as she watched Dr. Vo clear the monitors and signal for a med tech to clear the bay.

"You can't deny him treatment because he's not a leech!" Niks shouted, wrenching her hand free from Syra.

The heads of the other nurses, doctors, and med techs turned her way, and for a split second, the commotion around them came to a standstill.

"Nurse Rison, report to nurse Maio," Dr. Vo said, closing the curtain behind him and looking everywhere but at her as if to tell the rest of the staff to get busy.

Tears in her eyes, Niks stormed off to the nurse's station, Syra running behind her.

"Wait—wait—" Syra caught hold of her arm and pulled her into the stock room. "Think about what you're doing."

"Saving patients," Niks said, butting up against an empty row of shelves in attempts to break free.

Syra wouldn't let her go completely, touching her shoulder as she looked at Niks with her widened brown eyes. "When was the last time you took a break?"

At first she didn't care, but then, with a frown, Niks looked at the time on her wristband. 1837. She'd been on the clock since 0500, and even though the second shift had arrived hours ago, she didn't give up her post. Not now, not with the entire admitting bay still full of patients, and so many people in pain and needing medical care.

"You're exhausted; you've been working yourself raw for days now," Syra said, pushing an errant strand of Niks' hair behind her ear. "Just stop and breathe a minute, k?"

"Okay."

Taking a stilted breath, Niks resisted wiping the tears from her eyes, not with Syra staring at her, as her friend's hand moving from her shoulder to on top of her crossed arms.

Syra smiled and rubbed the tops of her hands. "Better, right?"

"That's not going to fix—"

"Shh," Syra said, pressing closer to Niks as a med tech ducked in the stock room looking for something, finding only empty shelves, and running back out. "I know you're upset. Let's just do what we can right now."

"I can't let people die," Niks said, tears reforming anew. "Not for a *chakking* leech."

Syra wiped the ones that escaped down her cheek on her own sleeve before holding her in a tight hug. "I know, it's messed up, but I promise we'll figure this out, okay?"

Resting her head on Syra's shoulder, Niks took another breath, this one reaching the bottoms of her lungs. As she held it in, she thought of James, and how upset he'd been as he'd dropped her off before her shift. *He knows something.* Her whole body tensed. *Why didn't he tell me about any of this from the start?*

"You're amping up again," Syra said, still holding on but leaning back to look her in the face.

"Sorry," she said, exhaling sharply as she untangled herself from Syra. "Look, I'd better go see Maio."

"Ugh, Meow." Syra rolled her eyes and made a scratching motion with her left hand. "She'd better have nothing but nice things to say to you."

"Ha."

"Seriously—I saw you making some great calls today, Niks. How'd you figure that out about the methoc?"

Niks furrowed her brow, uncertain of her own luck on that one. "Don't know."

Tapping her between the eyes with her index finger, Syra undid the knot in Niks' forehead. "It's like there's a bioscanner in this big head of yours."

"Not like it did any good for the last patient," she mumbled, turning away.

"Hey—I'll help out Jin while you deal with Meow. Come find after me, alright?" Syra said, snagging her back for a quick hug and kiss on the cheek before exiting the stock room and heading to bay 12.

Dreading the certain lecture, Niks trudged over to the nurse's station. The med techs monitoring the patient traffic did not look up from their flashing screens as she rounded the desk, blue and red hues of data reflecting off their impassive faces.

"Where's Maio?" she asked to the half dozen techs. None of them answered, though one pointed to the secured med room in the center of the station.

Niks flashed her wristband on the scanner. As soon as the door slid open, Maio's harsh voice hit her like a hammer to the skull.

"I've told you twice now to keep the cryofreeze locked up for the transfers," the charge nurse screamed at the cowering pharmacy technician clutching bags of the liquid blue medication.

"B-but Dr. Nara ordered these bags for the staff members with post-cryo thaw syndrome," he sputtered.

"And Dr. Vo overrode her orders this afternoon," Maio said, ripping the bags from his hands and returning them to the shelves.

So, Dr. Vo is on Maio's side. Niks stored the information away for later as the pharmacy tech scampered out of the med room, prehensile tail tucked between his legs.

"Rison," Maio said, her voice turning cold. "Why am I getting behavioral reports on you from Dr. Vo?"

Niks ground her teeth together, trying to mind her words, but finding herself slipping in the pull of exhaustion and frustration. "I joined SOHO to save patients—not selectively treat those with telepathic powers."

"I thought you, above all the others, would appreciate the efforts of the Eeclian Dominion," Maio said, walking past Niks and closing the door to the med room.

Standing so close to Maio, Niks detected a musty animal scent beneath the cloying floral perfume that made her wrinkle her nose.

"You've had no problem turning in telepaths to Dominion registration," Maio said, yellow eyes narrowing.

Niks shifted her weight between her feet, but kept her gaze. "It never interfered with patient care."

"We're in the middle of a war right now," Maio said, advancing so that Niks had to take a step back into the shelves just to keep a comfortable distance from the charge's beak-tipped nose. "Sacrifices must be made to secure the victory of the righteous."

A retort perched on her tongue, but she swallowed it back as Maio took another step forward. The charge nurse's smell permeated her nose, infiltrating her lungs, seizing the breath in her chest. Niks' attention divided, her mind unable to resolve the conflict of smells: sickly sweet and pungent—like a predator trying to mask its stench.

"You will do as instructed, nurse Rison, or I will relieve you of duty."

Before Niks could muster up a response, Maio's wristband chirped. Maio glared at her once more before checking the flashing light. The charge nurse's eyes widened, and she accepted the incoming call.

"Commandant," Maio said, breathless and reverent. "I didn't expect you to—"

A mustached man with an austere face and a chest full of military decorations appeared in a holographic projection a few centimeters above Maio's wristband. "Nurse Maio—secure Jin Idall, priority one, and await my orders."

"Yes, Commandant. I will have her available to you immediately."

The image on the wristband went out with a blip.

Who was that? Niks drew in a quick breath, but held her tongue as Maio blew past her, legs brushing together as she headed to bay 12. *Wait—what do they want with Jin?*

The most recent conversation with James entered her mind: *"There have been some staff reassignments within the Dominion..."*

Was that Rogman?

And his questions about the Med Oculus—and using it on Jin.

Oh no—

Exiting the med room, she tried not to run as she made her way to bay 12. By the time she got there, Maio had already summoned a security team to escort Jin Idall out of triage.

"Wait—what is this about?" Jin said, confused as the Dominion soldiers held on to her arms. As Jin passed by her, panicked and looking for help, she locked eyes with Nik. Her expectant look tugged at Niks heart. After all, Niks should do something—stop the soldiers, demand an explanation—at least get her purse out of her locker. *Something.*

But Niks did nothing, frozen in fear as she watched her friend dragged away.

"What was that all about?" Syra whispered, popping her head out of bay 12 as Maio returned to the nurse's station, and the rest of the teams got back to work.

Stomach in knots, Niks could do nothing more than shrug her shoulders and avoid Syra's eyes.

Her friend looked her up and down. "Tell me later. Right now, help me with this patient."

Niks followed her inside the curtain, reflexively surveying the patient as Syra broke down the situation. Still, as she dove into action, helping Syra with the bleeders and pumping the unconscious woman full of volume expanders, her mind couldn't let go of her inaction.

Why didn't I do anything?

—and more importantly, why the Dominion would be interested enough in Jin to pull her from duty during a crisis.

As Syra attended to the blast wounds on the woman's legs, Niks cleaned the lacerations on her forehead.

"Do you have any more gauze?" Syra asked, pressing an absorbent dressing with one hand on the patient's leg as she dug around the bay drawers with another.

"This is the last one," Niks replied, holding up the blood-soaked square.

"Okay, I'll go see if I can find more."

As Syra ran out, Niks debated rinsing the bloodied gauze in case no more could be found. Instead of deciding, she found herself staring at the patient. Just a week ago, treating the woman, Neeisin in appearance just like her last patient, wouldn't have made her think twice. Now, knowing what she was a—

(leech)

—and knowing that she had sacrificed care on her previous patient to help this one—

(monster).

No. Stop it. She scrunched up the bloodied gauze in her fist. *She's your patient.*

Niks remembered Syra's words—*"Everyone deserves a chance"*— but she couldn't let up, not even as the blood spilled over her gloved knuckles, dripping onto the woman's forehead.

(Mom, Dad—)

Smoke in her lungs, the taste of copper—

(Where are you?)

Her parents, trampled and bloodied, lying in the middle of the sidewalk—

(Mom...Dad?)

—*and the leech chanting over their unmoving bodies.*

("Don't hurt them!")

"Got some!" Syra said, bursting back in with an armful of gauze. "Thank the Gods for Decks and her hoarding."

Seeing Niks poised over the patient with a clenched fist, Syra paused. "What'd I miss?"

"Nothing," Niks whispered, turning quickly and dropping the gauze into the trash. Forcing herself forward, she grabbed a dermawand off the tray and returned back to the patient to close some of the smaller cuts.

Syra made a few adjustments to the monitors, checked the IV lines, then made her way over to Niks' side. Standing shoulder-to-shoulder as she assisted with the laceration closing, Syra said firmly: "Talk. Now."

"Am I...?" Niks looked again at their patient, dermawand shaking in her hand, trying to understand the blur of tears forming in her eyes. James, her last patient, Jin, and nurse Maio all flashed through her mind. *...a coward?*

Before Syra could prod the rest out of her, the bay curtain parted, and a dark, hulking figure stepped inside clutching his head.

"Azzi?" Niks said, wiping her eyes with her forearm sleeve. She hadn't seen the SOHO pilot in months, not since they put him on opposite cryo rotation. Despite his tank-like, athletic build, he looked weak, especially hunched over and shielding his eyes from the light.

"Oh no!" Syra slapped the edge of the exam table. "What the hell do you want?"

"Damn, baby—is that any way to great me after all this time?" Azzi dared a quick look from underneath his hand. Jet black eyes contrasted the bright white smile he half managed before he winced and took cover again.

"They should have kept you a popsicle," Syra said, her movements more aggressive and aggravated as she tossed dirty bandages to the floor between her and her ex-boyfriend. "Low-life, two-timing, sonofa—"

Niks interjected. "What do you need, Azzi?"

"Headache. Bad," he said, baritone voice rumbling through the bay. "Can't find anyone to help me."

With a scoff, Syra pointed a bloody glove toward the exit. "Try the ejection hatch in the docking bay."

Azzi grinned. "Still a sweetheart, aren't ya, Sy?"

Niks de-gloved and touched Syra on the shoulder. "I'll take care of it."

"Good. 'Cause all he'd get from me is a kick in the—"

"Come on," Niks said, taking Azzi by the hand and leading him to the stock room before it got any uglier.

"Thanks, Niks," he said as she seated him on one of the extra stools and turned down the lights.

"When did you get thawed?" Niks said, checking his pupils with her penlight off of her accessory belt.

"This morning. Hey—what happened to your eye?"

Niks had almost forgotten about the black-and-blue bruise around her right eye. "Patient care drama."

"Looks badass."

Niks chortled, but then something else occurred to her: *James didn't say anything about it this morning…did he even notice?*

"Anyway, I think I overhead one of the techs say something about a rapid unfreeze."

"You could be right," Niks said as she checked his radial pulse. "They're pulling all staff out of cryo because of the crisis on Neeis. At least that's what the Dominion told us grunts."

"*Goddich* military," he said, rubbing his forehead. "This is the worst headache I've ever had. I puked twice trying to get here, and then the line to get in…"

"I know," Niks said, imagining the scores of patients that hadn't even made it inside the triage unit yet, gumming up the outer corridors and waiting areas. After checking his nailbeds and finding the tell-tale bluish discolorations, and the redness of his sclera, she sighed and gave him a pat on his muscular shoulder. "Sorry, Azz."

"I had to slip in as two guards were carting off Idall. What's up with that? Everything okay?"

Niks stiffened. "I don't know… But I do know that you've got post-cryo thaw syndrome," she said, redirecting the conversation. "The only cure is a low dose of cryofreeze…or time."

The Tanzian pilot looked up, black eyes searching her face. "I don't like the way you said 'time.'"

Niks bit her lip as she contemplated the options. "The charge nurse, Maio, has got all the cryofreeze locked up in the med room."

"What?" Azzi said, half-chuckling. "How is that in short supply?"

"When you're freezing every last leech for transfer to a Dominion vessel."

The faint smile drained from Azzi's face. "Those *ratchakkers*...So that's why I woke up early. It also explains why I'm sharing my quarters now with three other people."

She nodded. "After this never-ending shift, I've got to go clean out my place. I gave up my room and listed myself with Sy just so she wouldn't get stuck with a roommate. Not that I'll be there very much."

"The girl does like her own space," Azzi said, shaking his head. "So that means you're still with James—I didn't miss anything good, did I?"

Niks let him inspect her hands for a moment before taking them back, cheeks blushing. "No—nothing yet."

"Soon. That boy loves you like crazy."

Leaning against the shelf, Niks stared at the floor, the words slipping away before she could stop them: "A little too much."

"What?" Azzi said, pressing his palm against his forehead.

"Nothing."

"You have nothing to worry about; you two are going to make it. Me and Sy—there are still strong feelings there, and if we don't kill each other first, maybe something will come out of it."

Niks bristled, not at the thought of Azzi and Syra fighting, or their on again/off again relationship—that she had gotten used to over the last few years. But the thought of her and James, married, forever bound to each other, inescapable—

Suffocating—

Covering her mouth with one hand, she stopped herself, and tried to correct her course of thinking: *The perfect guy, marriage, family; it's what I've always wanted.*

A voice from within, far off and unfamiliar, laughed, crumbling the illusion right before her eyes.

Azzi got up with a grunt, still clutching his head. "Look, I'm just going to ride this out in my quarters."

Snapping to, Niks pushed him back down. "No. *Chak* Meow."

"Meow?"

"It's a Sy thing."

"Ah," Azzi said, looking up at her with his sweet, doe-eyed expression. "You gonna nab some cryofreeze?"

Niks gnawed on the inside of her cheek. Stealing and going against orders was something she needed Syra for; not something she would ever dare do alone. Still...

I can't leave him like this. Frustrated with herself, she bit down on her cheek a little too hard, drawing blood. *Do something.*

The instinct hit her before she could stop herself. Her hands reached up to his temples, and with two fingers, she massaged in opposing circles. Head falling back, she imagined his pain, a heavy block of ice, melting away until it completely dissolved.

"Wow..."

Niks gasped and retracted her hands. *What did I—?*

"That took the edge off. Jeez, Niks," Azzi said, his familiar big-bear smile returning. He stood up, dwarfing her as he stood tall, and stretched out. "I feel great. Where'd you learn that?"

"I—I..."

Azzi swept her up in a huge, his gigantic arms lifting her off the ground. Squeezing her tight, he whispered in his low baritone voice: "You're a great nurse, Niks."

After setting her down, he said something to her about needing to get back, and about her taking a break, but she barely heard him.

What did I just do?

I acted on instinct, she told herself. *...But not my own.*

The thought sent chills down her spine, but she couldn't rationalize the feeling, her response, or any of what just transpired.

"You look a little pale, Niks."

She waved Azzi off. "I'm fine. I'll just go make sure Sy is okay, then head to James'."

"Alright, little missy. You take care."

With another hug—this one a bit gentler—he exited the stock room.

Absent-mindedly, Niks searched the ravaged shelves for anything useful scraps to take back to Syra, trying to ignore the tension building beneath her breastbone.

I'm okay. Everything will be okay.

She looped the thought over and over again in her mind as she gathered a few random materials in her arms until she felt the pressure dissipate.

It was just a fluke.

The same dismissive laughter returned.

She caught of glimpse of her reflection in the door as she shouldered her way out of the stock room, not recognizing the stranger staring back in the mirror-finish.

***

"No talking," Niks said, pushing James aside as she stepped inside his quarters.

"Nikkia, we have to—"

"No," she said, flopping down face-first on his bed. Everything hurt, every muscle aching for rest. "Just sleep."

She heard the quiet *swish* of the front door closing, and then his padded footsteps as he crossed the carpeted floor and stood at the end of the bed. Only a few seconds passed before he sat down beside her and rested one of his hands on her back.

"We need to talk."

Not again, she thought. She didn't want to hear about not coming home last night, Rogman, the Med Oculus, Jin, the crisis on Neeis—any of it. And she especially did not want to dredge up any of the uncomfortable feelings still nipping at the back of her mind over the strange course of events over the last forty-eight hours. *Just silence. And sleep.*

His hand moved underneath her shirt. The warmth of his palm, and the light touch of his fingers made her relax a little.

"I'm worried about you, Nikkia."

She tensed right back up. *No lectures. No talking.*

Something inside her stirred, especially as his hand moved to the small of her back. Turning on her side, she looked up and into the striking blue of his eyes, blood dancing in her fatigued muscles.

The thought came with a rush of carnal heat: *I'll get you to shut up.*

"What are you do—"

Grabbing him by the neck, she pulled herself up and into him, kissing him with unfettered aggression. As he brought up his hands to her face, she wrapped her legs around his waist, drawing him in closer.

"Nikkia—"

She brought him back in, pressing her tongue against his. For a moment he allowed her kiss, taking as much of him in as possible, sucking and licking until he pushed away again.

"Stop this," he said, turning his face to the side.

She slipped her left hand down his pants, to the hardness forming between his legs. As he struggled to find the words, his eyes rolling up in their sockets, she found his shaft, stroking it upwards as she pumped her hips back and forth.

As she backed away, teasing with her tongue down his neck and lifting up his undershirt to lick his chest, she kept her left hand working.

"Oh God..." he moaned as she unzipped his pants and popped him loose.

She hadn't taken him in so long; long enough that for a moment she hesitated, fearful of the lack of practice.

But as she opened her mouth, ready to pleasure him into climax, he blocked her with his hands. "Stop. This isn't you."

"What?" she exclaimed. "Yes, it is."

"No," he said, standing up and hiking up his pants. "This is weird."

Niks didn't understand. *Why won't he let me do what I want?*

After removing his clothes, James set them down on the dresser and returned to her, covering his manhood with his right hand. He stood at the head of the bed, and tapped the pillow with his left, an expectant look upon his face.

Confused, she crawled up and laid down, watching him undo the tie to her scrubs and then remove her pants.

For chak's *sake...*

He crawled on top of her, kissing her neck and fondling her breasts underneath her scrub shirt before making his signature move.

At least let me remove my—

No chance. Before she could get her hands down, he had already moved the crotch to her underwear aside and pressed himself inside her, all the way up to his hips.

Niks stifled a gasp, not ready as usual, but not willing to let him hear her reaction. She kept silent, even as he pumped harder, his neck, shoulder and chest muscles straining.

Staring up at the gray ceiling beams, she counted the seconds tick by with every groan and grunt he made. Ninety-five dry and agonizing seconds later, he finished with an elongated moan, and rolled off to the side.

"There," he said between breaths. "That was great."

Niks said nothing, still staring at the ceiling, arms at her side.

"We'll talk tomorrow, okay?"

She rolled over, away from him, facing the observation window to the stars.

"Babe?"

"Yeah," she said, her voice flat. "Tomorrow."

After patting her on hip, he walked over the bathroom and got in the shower.

Thinking her only audience was the stars twinkling in the distance, she whispered ever so softly: "I want more."

Chapter 7

Lying on her back, Niks woke to a strong hand sliding up the top of her right leg. At first she thought it was James, but in the dim light of the stars shining through the observation window, she made out his shape in the bed to the left, turned away from her.

Then who—?

Down below, emerging from the shadowy jumble of bedsheets came a partially shaved head, and long, muscular arms, the right side covered in tattoos. Niks wanted to cry out, but orange eyes, mesmerizing in their intensity, ripped the breath from her lungs.

That woman...

Impossible. Not here, aboard the Mercy, *as James slumbered beside her in his bed.*

A dream—not real—she can't—

But her touch didn't carry the distant, detached sensation of a dream as her hand slid higher up her thigh, and when her face came into view, Niks' heart thumped against her chest.

A strong jaw, a feminine nose, high cheekbones; beautiful, full lips.

Rex.

The name resounded across the room, as if she had screamed it. Orange eyes narrowed, like a predator zeroing in on its prey.

Niks wanted to cry out, to wake James, but another part of her, in need of something she could not name, held her tongue.

"You called for me," Rex said, voice low and husky as she put one knee on the bed, besides Niks' hip, the other off to the side, her hand on her upper thigh. Niks caught a glance of her in the blue light, naked body stunning, before she leaned in. The woman came within inches of her face, lips parting in a fiendish smile. "What do you want?"

Rex's hand moved higher. The feel of the woman's black-painted nails as they grazed the skin of her outer thigh, descending toward her center, awakened every nerve in her body. She shuddered, unable to control her body's reactions as her fingers slipped underneath her underwear.

"You've been neglected."

Knowledgeable fingers parted her, finding the sensitive bundle of nerves, and moved in a circular motion.

"I'll take care of you."

Niks breathed in sharply, taking in her scent, as Rex kissed the side of her cheek. The pleasure of her touch, the intoxicating smell of her—natural, no hint of perfume—filled her with desires untold. As she continued to massage her below, Rex grabbed her hair and pulled her back, exposing the meat of her neck. Niks gasped as Rex bit down, not too hard, but enough to send a skittering of goosebumps down her side.

"No..." Niks uttered as Rex removed her hand from her underwear.

Rex brought her lips to her ear, teasing her tongue along the rim. "Patience."

Straddling Niks, the orange-eyed woman came into full view in the light of the stars. Niks couldn't believe the sight of her; lean and muscular, yet feminine, her breasts high and round, pierced nipples erect.

The woman rocked her hips back and forth, her shaved mound rubbing up against her belly. Niks felt the woman's warm wetness against her skin, and her own between her legs broadening with every gyration. The tattoos decorating her right half came alive in her movements, weaving around in an intricate dance as her muscles rippled, changing from indigo blue to electric purple.

Leaning forward again, the woman cupped Niks' cheek and rubbed her thumb across her lips. Without thought, Niks opened her mouth, inviting the woman in, wanting to feel the softness of her lips, taste the honey-sweetness of her mouth.

"So eager," Rex whispered, staying just out of reach.

Unable to take her teasing anymore, Niks lunged forward. Rex caught her by the neck with one hand and eased her back down, her breasts pressing up against her scrub top.

"We have a few things to get out of the way."

On some remote level Niks heard James' rhythmic snoring, but she didn't care if he was laying right beside her, or if he rolled over and saw everything. The scope of her world narrowed into just the two of them, on half of a bed, the light of the cosmos illuminating impossibilities she would never even dream of.

Niks obeyed the woman's command as she pulled her up with two fingers in the v-neck of her scrub top until she sat pressed against the front of Rex's warm body. Sliding her warm hands up her side, Rex got underneath her top and slid it over her head. Orange eyes fell to her bra, the raggedy old one she had yet to change after two long shifts, but disgust never registered as it would have with James. Instead, a prurient smile spread across the woman's face as she undid the latches of Niks' bra with one hand, and brought the other one just underneath her chin.

"*You're beautiful.*"

Her words sang across Niks' mind, both weakening her muscles and filling her with warmth. And when Rex pushed her back down, her perfect breasts bouncing, tattoos glowing, Niks couldn't help but think the same.

No—I can't—this is—

Any chance for her to sabotage the moment ended as soon as Rex kissed her, opening her mouth with her tongue. The tattooed woman pulled herself down tight against her skin, breasts rubbing against Niks' bare chest as she positioned herself between her legs and continued to move her hips into her in a slow, thrusting motion.

The bombardment of sensation sent electricity thrumming throughout Niks' body—the feel of the woman's tongue massaging hers, the thrill of her fingers running through her hair, her other hand finding her breast and squeezing with just the right amount of pressure. Niks tried to pull away when Rex found her hardened nipple and tugged it between her thumb and forefinger, eliciting a cry.

"*What do you want?*" *she whispered, releasing her for one agonizing moment before coming back for another kiss. This time, she sucked on her lower lip, then descended down her neck, her hands never stopping, finding her most sensitive areas.*

Need throbbed between her legs, and with every one of Rex's thrusts, Niks lost herself in the haze of passion. When Rex's mouth found one of her nipples, she could no longer contain herself, rising up with her hips and chest to push herself closer and closer. Rex responded in fiercer thrusts, and cupping the roundness of her bottom with one hand while still teasing her nipples with her tongue and fingers.

"*More... I want... more...*" *Niks said between breaths.*

Rex sat back, her tattoos now a heated red, her hair flipped in front of her fiery orange eyes. With the same devilish smile, she spread Niks apart and scooted back so that she lay on her stomach, head between her legs.

I've never—wait no—

Rex claimed her with her mouth, silencing her fears with the very first swirl of her tongue. A moan escaped from her lips as Rex sucked and stroked, tongue stoking the flames of her desire.

Niks grabbed the bedsheets in both hands and yanked up, but lost her strength as Rex slid one finger, then two inside her. Arching her back, she relished the feel as Rex's tongue, coupled with her curved fingers, drove her higher and higher with every thrust.

"Oh God—"

Raw need drove her every moan, every cry out to God. And when Rex slipped in a third finger, she threw her head back and cried out.

"Please... Please... I need... please..."

Keeping her fingers inside Niks, Rex pulled herself back on top of her, and held her close, touching her forehead against hers. Niks couldn't look away, not even as her fire-born eyes stared down at her, and through her, watching her every strain and cry as Rex increased the force of her pumps. She held her close with her arm around her shoulders, not letting her go, delighting in her pleasure.

"Oh God—oh God—OH GOD!"

Niks' body convulsed, waves of passion washing over her in an explosive release. She wrapped her arms around Rex, not wanting to let her go as the free fall of fire and pleasure cascaded through her.

Is this real?

Niks didn't move. Neither did Rex. Only the noise of their breathing, still hot and heavy, sounded between them as the feeling slowly returned to her legs.

"Who are you?" she whispered.

Rex pulled away a bit, orange eyes filled with satisfaction. "Your desire."

Niks reached out, wanting to touch her face, to bring her in closer, to understand, when—

"Babe?"

Niks peeled back her eyes with a gasp as a hand rocked her at the hip bone.

"You okay?"

It took a moment before the images wobbling above her head solidified into a familiar face.

James.

No tattooed woman on top of her, no feel of her body weight, their breasts rubbing against each other, heat and sweat exchanging between them. And yet, still on her back, sheets down by her knees, she felt damp all over, her scrub top dotted with sweat, and her underwear soaked with—

Oh my God.

"Y-yeah," she said, pushing up on her hands to sit up. As soon as she felt the squishiness between her legs, she crossed them and pulled the sheets up to her collarbone.

"You were moaning in your sleep," James said, still hovering above her. He gave her a wink. "Dreamin' about me again?"

Niks nodded just to get him to go away.

"That's what I thought."

He kissed her on the cheek and scooted closer, enveloping her entire left side with his body.

"I'm too hot, James," she said, trying to unlock his arms from around her chest. When he wouldn't let go, she shoved herself out, spilling out of the bed and stumbling to her feet.

"What's wrong?" he said as she locked herself in the bathroom.

Niks sat on the toilet, confused and upset, wanting to run away and curl up into a ball at the same time.

"Lights off," she whispered to the operating system. If she could, she would have blotted out the starlight streaming through the oval window, too.

"Babe?" James knocked on the bathroom door twice. "Are you feeling okay?"

Don't give him any reason to worry, she told herself, clearing her throat. "Just give me a minute."

Moving to the sink, she regarded herself in the mirror. Her hair, a tangled brown mess, looked so mundane, her plain face and unmarked skin just as uninteresting. Even her eyes, green like the first buds of spring—her favorite feature—paled in the light of the stars.

I want...

She stopped herself, not wanting to complete the thought, even as fiery orange eyes danced through her mind. Hugging her arms across her chest, she closed her eyes, remembering the feel of smooth skin against hers; the feel of soft kisses—and gentle bites—down her neck and—

"Babe—I've got to get ready."

Niks snapped to, dropping her arms to her side.

Come on, she reprimanded herself, *none of that was real. Get your head together.*

After splashing some water on her face and taking a deep breath, she opened up the bathroom door again. James stood just outside, one arm leaning against the doorframe, left eyebrow canted.

"You sure you're okay?" he said, looking her over. "Hey—what happened to your eye?"

Now he notices? She didn't offer him anything other than a quick smile and a confident, "yes, I'm fine. Just a rowdy patient."

After he showered, and she did the same, she got ready as quickly as possible, even though her next shift didn't start for another hour.

I should go, she thought, wringing her hands together as she dispensed a nutrition bar from the food generator. Despite her gurgling stomach, she didn't think she had the nerves to eat anything just yet, but she took the bar and stuffed it in her scrub top pocket.

"Nikkia," James said, grabbing her by the wrist as she walked to the front door. "We need to talk. Please."

Just get it over with, she thought, following him to the couch.

"I know you're upset about Jin," he said, turning to her.

Jin. Her stomach folded over itself. *How could I think of anything else?*

And the Med Oculus—Rogman—the crisis on Neeis, and the Dominion's prioritization of the leeches—

"I can't disclose much," he said, trying to take her hand. She allowed him to, but as he leaned in, she stayed stiff and upright, facing forward. "But I can say that Jin used the Med Oculus on several patients down on Neeis before screening them. And La Raja, being a sanctuary city for telepaths…"

Jin used the Med Oculus on telepaths… Her heart pounded in her chest, but she kept her composure.

"So?" she said, still avoiding his gaze.

"Jin reported some unusual symptoms after use on certain patients, and those side-effects caught the attention of Dominion Intelligence."

Niks finally looked at him. "Rogman?"

James nodded. "Not someone you want interested in your activity."

"Why?" she asked, terrified by the hard look in James' eyes.

Shaking his head, he said evenly: "I serve the Dominion for justice and honor. He's the kind that joins the military because he finds war and unrest appealing."

James has never spoken against anyone in the Dominion, she realized. It must be bad. *And Maio worships him...*

The thought made her shudder.

"So, that's why you asked if I used it on anyone else?"

"Yes..." he said, shifting his gaze away from her. "I feel awful. I had no idea that something like this was possible. I was so eager to have you headline the program, help you advance your career and conquer some of your personal obstacles; I didn't consider all the variables."

Having rarely seen him so upset, she reflexively changed gears and suppressed her own feelings, putting her hand on his shoulder to comfort him. "You just wanted to help me. You couldn't have anticipated this kind of outcome."

"I'm supposed to protect you," he said. With increasing fierceness in his voice, he gripped the edge of the couch, knuckles turning white. "I couldn't live with myself if I caused you harm."

"James," she said, touching his face and playing with the close-cropped hair on the back of his neck. "I'm okay. I'm here."

"Thank God," he said, placing a hand on her thigh. "I know you; you would have used that Med Oculus to save everyone and anyone—and then you'd be where Jin is."

Niks held her breath, but it didn't stop the thought from forming. *Rex...*

No. It couldn't be. She was probably just some ordinary Neeisin citizen with body mods, or a thrill-seeking tourist from the Homeworlds. Telepathy was such a rare trait in the Starways; less than one percent of the population possessed any of the four known variations of the condition.

But La Raja is a sanctuary city...

Statistically, the crew of the *Mercy* had transported and frozen over a hundred telepaths in the last day off of Neeis.

...meaning that over 10% of our patient population has had some kind of telepathic ability.

A one in ten chance.

What if...?

Summoning up her most confident tone, she asked: "What kind of symptoms did Jin report?"

James formed a steeple with his hands and placed them under his chin. "I'm sorry, Nikkia—that's all classified now."

"Don't do this, James," she said, unable to keep the frustration out of her voice. "She's my friend."

"I know. I'm sorry."

"Not sorry enough," she said, rising.

"Do you know why I love you?" James said as she stormed off toward the front door.

Despite herself, she paused.

"You're *smart, resourceful*, and you always do the right thing. That means something, Nikkia, especially in these times."

The way he said it; the emphasis on "smart" and "resourceful." *Is he trying to tell me something?*

"I'm a nurse," she said, exiting his quarters and flagging for a lift. As she stepped aboard, she turned to him, not surprised to see him standing in the doorway, tight-jawed, lips pressed together. She hated the stone-walled expression on his face; it always showed her where his love for her ended, and how deep his commitment to the Dominion ran. "I will always fight for those who can't."

***

"You got ground crew?" Syra said, peeking over her shoulder as Niks scrolled through the assignments on her wristband. Niks checked for Jin's name, but she didn't pop up in any of the areas. In fact, she couldn't even find her on the staff roster.

"Yeah, I requested it." Niks closed the projection and tried to sound nonchalant. "I feel like I need to get off the ship for a while."

She wanted to say more—to confess everything to Syra—but between the other women milling around the lockers, getting ready for their shift, and her own uncertainties undermining her confidence, Niks kept her anxieties to herself.

Syra clicked on her accessory belt and stood up, leaving Niks sitting on the bench by herself. After rifling through her locker, she came back with a small bag of heart-shaped Swarts, Syra's favorite candy, and one of the precious few non-synthesized food items on the *Mercy*.

"Here."

"What?" Niks said, taking her offering but still holding out her hand. "No—I can't take your last bag, Sy."

"Come on. Let me be a good friend," Syra said, closing Niks' hand over the bag.

Niks laid her other hand on top of Syra's. Somehow, even if she didn't say anything, Syra always knew. "You always are."

"You can buy me a drink after our shift. Make it two."

"Deal," she said, stuffing the sweet and tart candy in one of her accessory belt pouches.

As Syra turned to head toward the door, Niks asked: "Hey, would it be okay if I crashed at your place tonight?"

Syra returned to her side on the locker room bench. Just above a whisper she asked: "Everything okay with Mr. Predictable?"

Niks shrugged. "Yes. No. I don't know."

Without missing a beat, Syra put her arm around Niks' shoulders. "You do technically share half my place now, Nikalicious."

"You don't mind?"

"Only if you elbow me in the head again."

Niks blushed. "Thanks."

"See ya, k?" Syra said, pecking her on the cheek before taking off toward the surgical suites.

With a sigh, Niks picked herself up and exited the locker room, falling into the flow of the other medical staff heading down the corridor and toward the lifts to the docking bays.

"Hold up, Niks."

Decks and Vyers caught up with her, both of them toting gigantic medical bags on each shoulder.

"Where'd you get those?" Niks asked as the two squeezed onto a lift with her and several other Dominion staff members she didn't recognize.

"Resupply," Decks said, showing off the bag stuffed with high tech synth bandages and sim-skins.

"That's not SOHO." Niks flipped open the lid to Vyers' bag, spotting the black and blue logo. *Dominion Core.*

"The *Callieo* and *Ventoris* arrived a few hours ago," Decks explained. "Things are already better."

"Yeah," Vyers chimed in. "Having two warships in orbit makes you feel a lot safer."

Niks said nothing, closing the lid to Vyers' bag and attempting not to eye the Dominion staff trying too hard to appear as if they weren't listening to the SOHO staff's interaction.

"You won't believe the mobile units they have set up," Decks said, eyes wide with enthusiasm. "We'll be able to treat so many people."

"You'll love it, Niks," Vyers said, patting her on the shoulder. "Oh—and no more haz suits. The *Callieo* treated the air. Last shift says it still stinks, but at least it won't burn your lungs out."

As they de-boarded the lift and headed for the transports, Decks pulled her aside.

"Hey—have you heard anything about Jin?"

Niks tried not to be obvious as she looked left and right, waiting for the Dominion personnel to be out of earshot.

"Not really."

"I saw her get escorted out of triage yesterday by Dominion soldiers, and now she's off assignments. She's not the type to get in trouble."

Niks took one last look around and covered her mouth up. "I think it has something to do with the Med Oculus."

"What?" Decks exclaimed, then caught herself when a few Dominion soldiers milling around the control console looked their way.

"Don't say anything," Niks muttered under her breath as they proceeded to their ship.

"We're SOHO, Niks," she said, taking her seat next to Niks and clicking on her safety harness. Leaning over, she whispered in her ear: "We help people. Anything else isn't what I signed up for."

Eyeing the score of Dominion soldiers strapping in to the transport's seats, she whispered back: "I know."

***

Niks didn't believe her eyes as stepped off the transport and onto Neeisin soil. Dominion scout ships circled above the city in three ship patrols, while crawlers, tank-like all-terrain vehicles, and soldiers perused the broken streets. Large white tents with mobile generators and com dishes had been set up on the SOHO team's sites both on the perimeter, and from what Niks could tell by the drones hovering in the distance, in the heart of the city.

This isn't a SOHO operation anymore, she thought, tipping back her head and smelling the air. Only a tinge of smoke, no burn. And the skies, just yesterday congested with angry brown clouds of toxic chemicals and grit, had been scrubbed blue. If she didn't see it with her own eyes she wouldn't have believed any of it, especially the sight of the unobstructed sun shining out to the northeast just over the mountainous horizon. *Recoveries and reconstructions never happen this fast.*

Niks stepped out of the way as a group of soldiers marched past her towing a line of anti-grav freezer cases behind her.

The sound of their boots crunching over the broken glass and burnt rubble, and the sight of their blue and black uniforms triggered the memory of Rex's worry: *"...you don't think the Dominion is going to use this last wave of terrorist attacks to justify setting up shop?"*

A shudder ran through her body, and she grabbed the loose parts of her jacket, pulling it closer to her body. For a moment she felt exposed, vulnerable; like a rabbit surrounded by wolves.

Think of James, she told herself, trying to push away the feeling with the idea of her boyfriend. *There are good men and women in the Dominion. They're here to help.*

But the line of freezer cases on the return trip to one of the transports compelled her to justify their actions.

They're just telepaths, she reasoned, clinging to old sentiments. *It's for the war.*

Besides, with the Dominion resources, they could treat everyone now—it's not like she had to sacrifice care for a non-telepath to save a leech. If the Dominion needed to cart of telepaths in the name of securing the Starways, then that was military business, not hers.

As Niks made her way over to perimeter camp, her wristband buzzed.

"*Chak,*" she muttered, seeing the incoming transmission from Maio. With a sigh, she accepted the call, the stern-faced Maio popping up on hologram.

"Rison," Maio said in her most authoritative voice, "report to Dr. Naum."

But I'm supposed to be on the triage team, Niks thought as the transmission ended and the route to station thirteen flashed on her wristband. Curious, she checked her assignment status.

What's this all about? Her name was in gray, status inactive on the triage team. *Something's wrong.*

Biting her lip, she resisted the urge to call up James. Instead, she typed a private message out on her wristband, one vague enough that it would pass through regular watch filters, but hopefully alert her overprotective boyfriend. *Going to be a late night.*

She waited as long as she could to hear back from him, slowing her walk toward station thirteen until Dominion soldiers standing outside the tent flagged her down.

"What's this about?" she asked as she ducked under the tent flap.

When the man in the white surgical suit and gray apron across the tent turned to her, she wanted to reach out, stuff her words back in her mouth, and shrink into herself.

"I'm Dr. Charl Naum," he said, voice cool as rain as he set down a silver instrument back on a tray. Although she couldn't recall ever meeting him, or hearing his name before, the sight of him took all the moisture out of her mouth, sent her heart pounding in his chest. Something about his dark hair and flinty eyes—or perhaps his aquiline nose and lips devoid of bracketing laugh lines—made her itch to turn around and run out.

Standing at around 1.8 meters, the long and lean doctor possessed an aura about him that chilled the air, silenced all else as he crossed over to Niks. Even the three other Dominion nurses waited in the corners of the tent, still as statues, awaiting command.

The doctor removed his heavy-duty black exam gloves and offered her a cold, veiny hand. She took it reluctantly, avoiding his eyes.

"Nurse Rison, thank you for coming. This won't take but a moment."

Niks tried to take back her hand, but he led her to the middle of the tent where a single exam table sat under the scrutiny of four round exam lights. The rest of the tent, lined with medical equipment and trays full of instruments she didn't recognize, offered no clues to what Dr. Naum intended to do.

"I—I'm SOHO," she squeaked out as two of the other masked nurses animated and pulled her back onto the table.

"Yes," he said, his face disclosing no answers as he replaced his black glove. "The Dominion appreciates the cooperation of your organization, and your continued loyalty to the preservation of peace and order in the Starways."

"What is this?" she said as one of the nurses tried to roll up the sleeve of her jacket. Niks blocked her hand and sat straight up. When the other nurses moved in to restrain her, Naum waved his hand.

"No need to worry, nurse Rison." He smiled, revealing a massive row of teeth. Even though he appeared human, in some remote corner of her mind, she thought of a Great White Shark. "We are only here to evaluate your health."

"My health?"

"Yes," the doctor said, turning his back to her as he plucked an instrument off one of the trays. He returned back holding a hypoinjector and an even broader smile. "You have used the Med Oculus. There have been concerning reports about the side effects of that device. We are doing this to ensure your safety."

Niks stiffened. *Jin—*

"I feel fine," she said, eyeing the crimson medication swirling around in the hypoinjector chamber. "I don't consent to any treatment or evaluation."

"Your consent was obtained the moment you used Dominion property," he said, inputting the dose into the hypoinjector. "It's in your SOHO contract."

Niks eyed the exit, mind spinning, the edge of panic gnawing at her nerves. *Where are you, James?*

"If you do not let me help you," he said, voice frigid, "I will take you back to the *Ventoris* for a more in-depth analysis."

Feeling like a trapped animal, Niks tensed to leap off the table and bolt when a sense of calm pervaded her like a warm blanket wrapping around her body. *(Everything is going to be alright.)*

What?! She couldn't fathom how as one of the nurses got behind her and held out her arm for Dr. Naum. *They'll know I used it on someone else—what if she was a telepath? Jin, oh God—I don't want to be taken away, too—*

The sentiment broadened. She felt safe, hidden, as if layered in protective armor. Invisible fingers grazed the back of her neck, and the idea returned, this time spoken in Rex's voice: *Everything will be alright.*

"You don't have to do that," Niks said, removing the nurse's hand and offering her arm to Dr. Naum. Scrunching her brow to appear perturbed, Niks looked the doctor in the eye. "Let's do this already. I've got patients to treat."

The doctor paused, as did the other nurses, surprised by her sudden attitude shift. The confidence, the firm tone didn't at all sound like her—and she liked it.

Naum depressed the hypoinjector against her brachial artery. At first Niks felt nothing, then a hot rush of molten lava coursed up her arm and spread across her chest.

"God—"

Breath stripped from her, she pawed at her throat, unable to pass any air through her collapsed trachea.

"Relax. The feeling will pass," Dr. Naum said in a most bored-sounding tone as he returned the hypoinjector on a tray.

Nausea threatened to upend her belly, but with no way to breathe, she didn't know how anything would pass.

Oh God—help me—

"Lie back," Naum said, pushing her down on the table as the other nurses ran various kinds of bioscanners up and down her body.

Just as she thought her chest might burst, her throat relaxed, and she gulped in air. As her breathing normalized, she realized that everything sounded more and more distant, as if she was floating away from herself. If she had wanted to fight or resist, she felt too far away from herself to do anything about it.

Out of the corner of her eye, she watched as Dr. Naum downloaded the scans to his tablet and read the report. "Is this right?" he asked, sounding disappointed.

"Yes, sir," one of the nurses replied. "Recent concussion, no markers."

"How fortunate," he said, sounding anything but sincere. He leaned over her, in her face, close enough that she could detect the sourness of his breath. "Good news, nurse; you're clear for return to duty. However, it has come to my attention that you were the last person to use the Med Oculus. How did it get damaged?"

Niks felt something cold pressed against her forearm. With concerted effort, she turned her head to the left and saw Dr. Naum holding another hypoinjector to a vein in her arm. The black fluid in the chamber made her panic, but struggling did nothing, her efforts coming out as weak movements that the other nurses didn't even both to hold down.

"Well?" Naum said, depressing some of the fluid into her arm.

Niks never felt such an acute tide of sickness, even when she came down with Tycen's Fever as a child. Whatever Naum injected into her sent spasms up and down her body, followed by deep chills and a sense of impending doom.

Why is he doing this?

"A p-patient," she sputtered, unable to control herself but doing everything she could to get him to stop.

"Not nurse Idall?"

Niks tried again, speaking through fuzzy lips and a thick tongue. "I w-wanted to help... trapped patient... she fought me... it got knocked off... broke."

Naum switched out hypoinjectors and depressed a third drug into her system. Like a cleansing ocean wave, all of the discomforting symptoms washed away within seconds, and her body relaxed.

"I apologize about that, nurse Rison," Dr. Naum said, helping her sit up. "The evaluation is quite uncomfortable, but it is for your safety. We've found that the use of the Med Oculus on the wrong kind of patient can have disastrous effects, and we didn't want you to needlessly suffer."

I don't believe you, she thought, balling up her trembling hands. But she couldn't say anything. Not now, not with Dr. Naum still in control, and no one to come to her rescue.

"When the Med Oculus was damaged," Dr. Naum said as he ran another bioscanner up and down her body, "not all of the components were recovered. We need you to take us to that exact location."

Her first compulsion was to lie, but Dr. Naum must have picked up on her hesitancy. Leaning in again, he came within centimeters of her face. "At this very moment my guards are escorting your friend, nurse Gaoshin, to the city perimeter."

Syra. Her stomach twisted in two. *Don't you bastards hurt her—*

"We understand she revived you when you were injured. She is going to help us back to that spot, as you will." He lifted her chin up with his gloved hand, meeting her with vicious gaze that could cut through steel. "If either one of you leads us to the incorrect location, there will be trouble."

Niks said nothing as he let her go, allowing herself to be lifted up at the armpits by the soldiers and dragged outside.

Syra, she thought, closing her eyes as the soldiers boarded her onto a hovercart, still holding her at the arms. As the transport lurched forward, she opened her eyes, seeing the wasted city before her. *You know what we have to do.*

Chapter 8

As the Dominion transport whizzed down La Raja's rough terrain of broken masonry, her stomach still queasy and her muscles weak, Niks clung to her only hope in that moment. *Syra...*

Years flew by in her mind. She remembered their first class together in nursing school with the notorious Professor Sherk, and all the wonderfully painful moments when Syra would pass notes or whisper commentary during lecture, and she had to hold all her laughter in. The campus parties that Niks would have otherwise avoided, but Syra dragged her to and somehow, despite her uptight nature, would get her to have a good time. The first time Syra nursed her hangover; the slew of her adventurous friend's lovers coming in and out of their dorm room at odd hours, but Syra dropping everything if Niks so much as looked down. Consoling Syra until late into the night when her parents wouldn't come to visit her, or attend her graduation. Going with Syra to the People's Clinic when she had a scare and making sure that Yarri, the boy who hurt her, paid in the most unconventional—yet apropos—way. Convincing Syra to sign-up for SOHO; traveling across the stars with her best friend on the greatest adventure of their lives. Inseparable from day one, best friends for life.

And now they faced a situation she didn't quite understand, an enemy that posed as their ally, and a threat that went farther than just jeopardizing her own safety. This was beyond rage parties gone wrong, alcohol poisoning, or triple-shifts during a medical crisis. She sensed something deeper, like a sickness that went down into her bones.

Niks let her right hand fall to her accessory belt, feeling the pouch bulge where she had stored Syra's candy. *Come on, Sy; feel me on this.*

"Where to next, nurse Rison?" Dr. Naum asked, squeezing her upper arm with his black-gloved hand as the transport slowed down near the arcade district.

Niks looked around, the familiar broken-down signs, canted cement, and fallen archways that she'd traveled through on foot not just fifty-six hours ago. If she went left, she'd lead them to the collapsed alleyway, to the scene of their encounter.

No, I can't, she thought, every cell in her body screaming to run in the opposite direction. Not just for her safety, but...

Wait...why?

She didn't understand her compulsion then; the desperate need that arose from within and wrapped around her chest like a clinging hug, like something—or someone—she needed to protect.

Shaking her head, she tried to think more rationally. *Where would you go, Sy?*

"Nurse Rison?"

The black-gloved hand squeezed even harder, eliciting a wince from Niks.

"Okay—stop," she said, hunching over the railing to the hovercart. She pointed over to the dilapidated, four-story building farther north where a SOHO airlift circled and volunteer workers could be seen on the rooftop and scaling the walls. No Dominion presence, only *Mercy* crew and La Raja citizens. "It's there."

"Location?" Naum asked the hovercart operator.

"Red House, sir; an orphanage for children," the operator replied after highlighting the holographic street readout on his console.

Naum snapped at the operator. "Then get us there, post-haste."

Bracing her stomach with one hand, Niks counted her breaths as the Dominion transport whipped down the streets and wound through collapsed buildings. As soon as Niks saw a second Dominion transport pulling up to Red House, she stifled a smile.

Sy...

And right on cue, Niks could hear her best friend's snark through the construction noise telling the Dominion soldiers to get their hands off of her as she jumped of the transport.

"You're not through," Naum whispered into Niks' ear before the soldiers helped her down off the transport.

Legs still wobbly, Niks allowed the soldiers to hold her up on either side as bulldozers and cranes passed in front of them. At least four dozen salvage and restoration volunteers buzzed around Red House while the orphans, covered head to toe in dust and dirt, played in the safety area down the block surrounded by yellow tape.

"There," Niks said, pointing to the ground occupied by a mammoth excavator.

"There?" Dr. Naum hissed at her, "you can't be serious."

Seconds later, Syra walked up with her escorts and pointed at the same spot on the ground. "Under that beast. Can I get back to work now?"

Naum gave her one last glare before yelling at the soldiers to find the foreman to move the excavator.

Niks waited, head bowed, avoiding looking at Syra as the Neeisin workers moved the excavator, and the Dominion squad scanned the area. When they came up empty-handed, Dr. Naum returned to her, cold eyes burning.

"We'll be watching you, Rison."

Thinking of Syra and drawing from whatever compelled her to protect their secret, she lifted her head and looked Dr. Naum in the eye, donning her best innocent smile. "I'm right in plain sight."

***

Still feeling dizzy and nauseated from whatever toxic concoction Dr. Naum shot her up with, Niks reported in sick and returned back to the *Mercy*. In her desperation, she stopped by James' place, but he wasn't there.

Where are you? She tapped her wristband, pulling up the numerous sent messages to her boyfriend. No response; nothing since she last saw him that morning, and when she checked his status, it came up "unavailable."

Frustrated, Niks pulled down the bedsheets of his perfectly made bed and slid in, not caring she still had her boots or scrubs on. James would throw a fit, and for some reason, she wanted that reaction from him.

Her wristband beeped.

Nikalicious—you'd better be resting your pretty little thang. Get over to my place, now, or I'll be forced to kidnap you at the end of my shift. XO – Sy.

Despite herself, she giggled and threw off the covers. Even talking in their special code so as not to alert the military watchdogs, Syra somehow got her to laugh.

She typed back: *On my way. Miss you already.*

As she crawled out of bed, she noticed she left a mud stain on his bottom sheet. *Serves him right.*

Realizing how angry she was, she decided it wouldn't be the best thing to see James right now, and Syra would certainly take care of her better than he would.

At least she knows when to back off, she thought, remembering her last night with him. That, and she needed to talk to Syra about what happened at Red House without the scrutiny of message filters, cameras, or voice recorders. *Or the enemy,* she thought, thinking once again of James. *How could he let any of this happen? He wasn't there for me.*

As soon as the lift dropped her off at Syra's place, she kicked off her boots, ripped off her scrubs, and dove into the unmade bed. Any other day she might have noticed the smell of perfume and mingling body odors, but right then, all she cared about was escape from the horrible events of the day, and the reprieve of sleep.

Or, at least, that's what she would have felt before the incident with the Med Oculus.

The realization hit her hard: *I haven't had a single dream without...*

Oh, God...

She squeezed her eyes shut, tried not to think about *her*.

But her subconscious whispered back: *(Rex...)*

Maybe it's a transient effect of the Med Oculus.

But she couldn't convince all of herself, especially not the butterflies fluttering in her stomach.

Curling up into a ball, Niks pulled the sheets over her head, and whispered underneath their gray protection: "You're not real..."

***

"You're unreal," she said through a voice pitched half an octave lower.

Not again, Niks thought, *awakening behind the familiar mask of the woman she did not know. A chill ran through her, and as she came to her senses, she found herself on some kind of rooftop in the outskirts of the city, the nighttime stars shining down from above. The metropolis flickered and glowed, full of sleek skyscrapers and traditional multi-tiered buildings. Below, the relentless roar of traffic and whine of the hovercraft battled the chattering rooftop fans.*

La Raja?

Perhaps, but she couldn't be certain as her sight was directed to the humanoid woman in the sparkling blue dress shivering at the edge of the rooftop. Although Niks had never seen the woman before, the sight of her pulled at her chest, filling her with a wide range of sentiments, from lust to resentment, to a strange tinge of heartache. Her dark complexion and plaited black hair with purple-tips stood out against the lighted backdrop, but her expression struck her just as much as her beauty. Light eyes, angled down to the stream of traffic below but drawn inward, carried with them unspoken pains, ones that Niks couldn't help but feel a part of.

"You haven't returned any of my calls for months, and now you followed me here," the woman said as Rex came up behind her and slid her hands around her waist. Despite her serious tone, the woman's voice carried a honeyed melody that only professional songbirds possessed. "What are you doing, Rex?"

Rex loosened the tactical scarf around her neck so that she could see the half-cocked smile on her face. "Enjoying the sights."

Stiff at first, the woman allowed herself to be taken by her warmth, pressing back as Rex hugged her from behind. Standing several centimeters taller than the woman, Rex rested her cheek against the top of her head and whispered: "Come away with me."

"Now who's unreal?" she scoffed, pushing out of her arms and heading back to the rooftop door.

Rex caught up to her, grabbing her hand and pulling her back. "Thea—"

Thea.

The woman's name hit her hard, bringing with it a barrage of disjointed memories and emotions. A crowded lounge, red velvet walls; smoke swirling inside the spotlights shining on a stunning smile. The dulcet sound of her voice rising above her mediocre instrumental backup. Niks felt as if her lungs filled with too much air as she remembered their delicious first kiss, and passionate sex that lasted until morning. Then came the purposely missed calls, telling herself that she didn't care; not consoling Thea when she cried herself to sleep just next to her on a bare mattress, naked and covered in only a soiled blanket.

"—stay here with me tonight," Rex said, running her fingers down the side of her face. She made sure to look in her eyes, giving her the reassurance she needed right then.

"No, Rex, I—"

She bent down and kissed her, just barely, on the lips. When Thea sucked in her breath, she kissed her again, this time parting her blue-painted lips with her tongue.

Shuddering, Niks couldn't help herself as her perspective split. From one angle, she felt herself as Rex, hoisting Thea up on to an elevated cement structure and standing between her spread legs. In another, physical reactions took hold as she remembered the feel of Rex's hands on her, the intoxicating smell, the way she teased and tormented—and wickedly pleasured.

"You're the devil, Rex," Thea whispered as Rex pushed her against the warm exterior of the exhaust vent with a hollow thud.

"Is that a no?"

Thea closed her eyes, her voice catching as Rex slipped one hand under the bottom of her dress and between her thighs. "No."

Delighting in her submission, Rex worked her hand in deeper, until she felt stubbly hair on the edge of her fingertips.

"Why Thea," Rex said, her other hand traveling up the curve of her hip and grasping her side. "You always surprise me."

Thea grabbed the back of Rex's head, intertwining her fingers into her hair and wrapping her legs around her waist. "Keep going."

With a smile, Rex freed herself from Thea's hands and undid the scarf wrapped around her neck. "Make a single noise, and I'll stop," she said, tying Thea's arms behind her back.

Thea tipped her head back as Rex hiked her dress up to her hips and licked her first finger. Still holding her at the waist with one hand, Rex teased the outside of her sex with a light touch, giving attention to each fold, each crevice, until all of Thea's muscles tensed.

Slowly, enough to draw in Thea's breath, Rex inserted her finger. She relished the warmth, the slippery feel, the rippled flesh. She explored her as she had done many times before, taking her time to find the spot that elicited Thea's convulsive arches.

"Not a sound," Rex reminded her as she crooked her finger. Now, as she moved her finger in and out, timing it with the thrust of her hips, she rubbed against her spot, careful not to increase the pressure too fast.

No, she wanted this to last, for Thea to break, to cry out her name, for all the bustling city to quiet in the wake of her pleasure.

Legs quaking, Thea tried to lean forward, but Rex pushed her back.

"Eyes closed. I have a surprise for you."

Once Thea complied, Rex dug into the side pocket of her jumpsuit with her free hand and produced what looked like a silver bullet.

What's that? Niks wondered, remembering herself. She wanted to pull back, uncomfortable at the sight of the object, but not knowing why, and not able to look away. *No, wait—what is she—?*

Niks trembled, torn by thrill and revulsion as Rex twisted the base of the bullet between her teeth, and it came to life, vibrating like a buzzing bee. With a lick, she wetted the tip, preparing it for—

Oh, God—she isn't going to—

As her right hand continued to slowly pump, Rex pressed the vibrating silver bullet against the woman's other entrance. Muscles puckered, Thea didn't let her in, not until Rex moved the tip around in a circle, moistening her entrance before easing inside.

NOT THERE—

Thea twisted her head back and forth, her legs quivering, as Rex pushed the vibrating bullet in deeper and deeper. Her breaths came in short, quick gasps, her neck muscles taut as she bit back her cries.

Rex slid her finger out enough just so that she could add two more. When she thrust back inside, Thea made a grunting sound and tightened her legs around Rex's waist.

This can't be right—

"That's right," she whispered, plunging deeper and more forcefully each time. The wetness between her fingers slicked all the way back to her hand, dripping down her wrist. When she felt her tighten, nearing her peak, Rex let go of her waist with her free hand and circled the round, erect tissue with her thumb. "Come into me..."

Thea screamed, belting out a high tone that could have shattered glass. Niks felt herself holding on just as tight as Rex, not wanting to let go of that fleeting moment of perfection. Still, once

Thea's legs relaxed, Niks shrugged off any sense of satisfaction, wanting only to run away.

This is wrong—

(Is it?)

But she could not. And she bore the same witness as Thea wormed her way out of Rex's ties and looked at her with fresh need.

Rex stayed between her legs, gazing back until Thea brought her hand up to her face and touched her lips.

"Kiss me again."

Rex did not, staying back. When Thea leaned in to try again, reaching for her breast, Rex stepped back and held her away.

"Why won't you ever give me you?" she asked. Furious, she thrust Rex's scarf back into her hands. "Why do I even try? It's always going to be this way, isn't it?"

"Thea..."

Thea slid off the cement structure, pushing her dress down and rearranging herself in a haphazard fashion. "You chak how you want, on your terms, always—but do you ever let anyone in?"

"Well, that's not true—"

"You know what I mean," Thea said, fixing one of her heels.

Rex took a step forward, but nothing more. Lips trembling, eyes glistening, Thea stabbed a finger at her. "You're not chakking real, Rex. You're here, but it's just a scene. You're a godich operator all the chakking time."

An operator—like a sim-stim operator?

It would explain why she found her on Neeis.

"I'm leaving, Rex, and I'm never coming back. I've wasted too many good years on you."

Wait—why aren't you saying anything? Niks wondered as Thea flung open the rooftop door and stormed down the stairs. She expected regret, a feeling of longing—something from Rex. And yet she only grafted a sense of numbness, of a disconnect from everything that just happened, and from the emotions of—

My girlfriend?

The understanding splashed over her like a dive into a cold pool. Niks couldn't believe the wash of emotions flooding through her, or how Rex could still say nothing in light of her true—though complex—feelings.

Follow her—why won't you follow her?!

Instead, Rex walked to the edge of the rooftop and gazed down the thirty-story drop. She took a step up onto the lip of the building, the toe of her hypercolor high-tops hanging off the edge.

Please, Rex—

Down below, movement near the front door awning caught her eye. Rex spotted her emerging from under the flashing sign for Suba House, a sparkling blue speck on the sidewalk. After hailing for a taxi, she paused and looked up. Rex didn't look away, nor step back as the northern breeze cut through the buildings, leaving her teetering on the edge.

"Goodbye, Thea."

Chapter 9

Niks lurched forward in the non-space, wanting to reach out with arms she didn't have to pull Rex back. DON'T JUMP—

"No!" she screamed, tearing at the gray skies up above.

"Hey, it's just me!"

Firm hands held her by the shoulders until she got her bearings. No gray skies, just gray sheets, all in a jumble around her, and Syra, twisted sideways, sitting next to her on the edge of the bed.

"S-sorry, Sy," she said, sitting up and pressing her palm against her forehead.

That dream—so real again—

No, none of that could have been...

"It's okay," Syra said, moving her hand aside so she could feel her forehead. Niks didn't like the concerned look on Syra's face. "I came back as soon as I could. Decks was sweet enough to cover for me so I could catch the early transport back."

How long was I asleep? Niks thought, looking at her wristband. 1450. Only a couple hours had passed, and yet she felt spent, emotionally and physically, as if she'd been up all night.

"What happened down there?" Syra said, scooting closer and taking Niks' left hand in her lap. "Did those Dominion psychos hurt you?"

Niks inhaled sharply as her own memories returned to her, as did the awareness of the awful aftereffects of the injection. Clutching her stomach with one hand, she pressed her face into Syra's chest. "It was awful," she said, tears forming in her eyes. "Maio sent me to a 'Dr. Naum' in one of the Dominion mobile units."

Syra stroked her hair, patient for her to continue. When Niks couldn't find the words, she helped her along. "What did he want?"

Tears slid down her cheeks, and she buried her head even harder into Syra's shoulder. "He forced me to get some kind of injection and then asked me all these questions about the Med Oculus. It made me sick; it was the worst feeling in the whole world. I would have done anything to get him to stop."

Syra gently pushed her up and pointed to the medical tote she propped against the bed. "I brought some supplies and a refurbished bioscanner. It hasn't been reintegrated into the system yet, so we can scan you without it uploading to the net, and erase all the data. You all right if I take care of you?"

Niks nodded and lay back down, wiping her face with the back of her hand.

"I never liked that SOHO buddied up with the Dominion," Syra said in a low voice as she ran the bioscanner up and down Niks' body. "I didn't like it five years ago, and I certainly like it even less now. It's a *godich* conflict of interest to have the military involved in our medical missions."

"I know," Niks whispered. "None of this feels right. And Jin…"

Syra paused and slid her hand into Niks'. "We're all worried about her."

The words came rushing out before she could censor herself: "What if they're freezing her and shipping her off with the other leeches?"

Syra squeezed her hand. "Has James said anything about any of this mess?"

Eyes hot and tongue loosened, she ground out the words through a clenched jaw. "He hasn't exactly been there for me lately."

Picking up on her signals, Syra went back to scanning her, but keeping an eye on her reddening face. "Does Mr. Predictable know what you did to my ex?"

"Which one?"

Syra snorted. "Yarri."

"Ha—no," Niks said, shaking her head. "I don't tell that story to anyone I want to date."

"Maybe you should. Might scare them in line. Lord knows that boy probably still can't sleep with the lights off."

Niks sighed. "I've never had to worry about anything like that with James before."

"Well, he's going to need to do some explaining to you," Syra said, flipping over the bioscanner so Niks could see the results. "Like why that *ratchakker* gave you a dose of that neuro toxin—he think you're a leech? There's no way we signed up for this kind of treatment."

Niks couldn't believe her eyes. An emetic, a neuro toxin—and a slew of other drugs she barely recognized—still circulated in her system. The shock of it all didn't mask the feeling of violation creeping into her bones. In that moment she didn't recognize herself, wanted to run out of her own skin and hide.

"Don't you start worrying," Syra said, rummaging through the medical tote. "You and me will figure this out, sista, k? Just like old times."

Her friend's reassurance lessened the tension building between her shoulder blades. Still, when Syra produced a hypoinjector, she shot up and grabbed at Syra's hand.

"It's just an anti-nausea and something to help with muscle recovery," she said calmly, showing her the yellow fluid sloshing around in the chamber.

Niks relaxed back down on the bed and offered Syra her arm. "Sorry."

"Don't you even," Syra said, pressing the hypoinjector into her arm. "This is some messed up *sycha*. But you know we're going to get through it."

"Thanks, Sy," Niks said, feeling immediate relief from Syra's cocktail. "You're the best."

"I know." Leaning over, Syra found Niks' accessory belt on the floor and plucked out the bag of candy from one of the pouches. With a smile, she set it on the nightstand next to her bed. "For when you're feeling better."

"Thank you," Niks said as Syra fiddled with the bioscanner, deleting the files before returning it into the medical tote.

"You need to sleep some more—it'll speed up your recovery." Syra pulled open the nightstand drawer and rifled through the mishmash of condoms and vibrating toys until she found a yellow packet with a triple z stamped on the top. "Take this."

"Where are you going?" Niks asked as she took the packet from Syra.

"Gonna pull some strings, see what's really going on with our good friends in the Dominion Core," Syra said, standing up, shouldering the medical tote and puffing out her chest.

"No, Sy," Niks said, grabbing the end of her scrub top and pulling her back.

"You have nothing to worry about, darling." Syra crouched low and made knife hands, eyes darting side to side. "I'm like a super spy assassin all in one."

"Right," Niks snorted.

"Get some sleep," Syra said, kissing her on the cheek. "And call me if you need anything."

"Wait, Sy..."

Why can't I say it? she thought, not understanding her own hesitancy. She had to tell someone about her weird dreams, work out what the hell was going on—but then it hit her. *If it is anything, and I tell Syra, she'll get in trouble too.*

Nobody can know.

Niks forced a smiled. "Love you."

"Love you more," Syra said, giving her the two-finger salute as she exited her quarters.

Niks checked her wristband again. No new calls or messages.

"*Chak* it all," she muttered, sliding off her wristband and throwing it across the room.

With a sigh, she broke open the yellow packet, and popped the octagonal pill in her mouth. As it dissolved, the sweet taste made her stomach turn over, but she kept it down, swallowing the gritty material with a scrunched-up face.

Niks curled up again, bringing the sheets up to her chin. As she waited for the sedative to take hold, she cleared her mind, focusing only on her breathing.

"Everything is going to be okay," she whispered, staring out at the floor covered in Syra's clothes and discarded takeout boxes from weeks ago. She didn't believe it, not one bit, but she kept repeating it, over and over again, until her eyes drifted shut.

***

"Everything is chakked.*"*

No... Niks lamented, waking behind Rex's eyes once more. Why is this happening?

"Calm down," Remy said, looking up from the heap of circuits and mechanical parts on the desk as she paced back and forth in the room. Niks noticed the slight drawl to his words this time, reminding her of the characters on the Old Westerns her grandfather used to make her watch, or perhaps the New Earth Cajuns. "Walk me through what happened."

"Nothing," Rex said walking over to the covered window. Poking her fingers between the window and the mattress, she pulled

back the lumpy foam and glimpsed outside. Dominion patrols, in groups of crawlers and troops units, marched down the street in tight formation, shining their search lights every which way. "Those military bastards are on every chakking corner. There's no safe route to the District."

With a grunt, Remy got up from his chair and joined her side. "Cool your heels awhile. Wait 'til it all blows over. The United Starways Coalition won't let the Dominion Core occupy a sanctuary city."

"Great—that just brings more military. Told you we should have left," she said, shoving him out of the way and walking over to the desk. The mess of computer innards and dissected holographic projectors didn't make sense to Niks, but as Rex studied the parts, an idea formed in her mind.

Their latest project…

Niks tried to look elsewhere, catching only glimpses of homemade headsets and visors stacked over to the right of the desk. *Thea called her an operator—and this looks like neuro tech…*

Something else, a revelation she could not quite grasp, floated just in front of her.

So, if Rex is a sim-stim operator, she thought, trying to understand what her gut pulled her toward, *Remy must build her tech.*

"Do you have another unit ready?" Rex asked, sifting through the pile of electronic parts. "Soldiers get lonely, right?"

Remy stretched, his abdominal muscles visible in the gap between his white t-shirt and fatigues. "I need a 122-red and four ionized resons."

"What? I just got you those—"

"And you broke my last headset in your little adventure with the Takuzi in that alley. Told you not to operate in the District; you're too hot right now."

Rex slammed her hand against the desk, rattling the gear. "Then what am I supposed to do?"

A strong feeling charged through her, filling her with a sense of challenged pride and dignity. (Don't take this away from me.)

It's all I have, Niks thought, relating to the sentiment.

Remy leaned against the wall, parting the mattress to look out the window. By the way his eyes changed focus on the activity down below, his posture tensing, Niks sensed through Rex's frustration that the conversation was over.

He must be ex-military, Niks thought, noticing the way his hands twitched, as if firing or grasping at a weapon. She'd seen in before in the veterans she treated long ago in nursing school. But when she tried to glean something more from the situation, Rex turned away, already on the move before she could get too disappointed in him.

Grabbing her scarf and hooded warp off the hook near the door, she muttered, "I'm going out."

As Rex hunched her shoulders and walked down the dingy corridor, Niks couldn't differentiate where Rex's anxieties ended and hers began. Even with her face covered she felt exposed, and each footstep on the stained shag carpet made her want to return back to the room.

This place isn't in the District, Niks thought, spying an empty vending machine and a dead courtesy com as Rex hurried to the stairs. Roaches, alerted to her presence, skittered back to their hiding places. The hideous wallpaper, a faded and peeling floral print with tawdry golden accents, reminded her of the cheap motels she'd heard about on the east side of the La Raja.

She paused at the top of the spiral iron steps, leaning over and listening for several seconds. In the distance, she heard street noise through a broken window, and an argument brewing on the bottom of the stairwell between two shadowy figures. Farther away, a boombox shrieked some kind of metalcore. Still, Rex didn't seem fazed, listening for something else. Or someone else.

Relaxing her grip on the railing and closing her eyes, Rex took in a deep breath.

What's happening? Niks thought, panicking as her mind stretched forward, into a space she shouldn't be able to occupy. In the bloodlit darkness behind Rex's eyes, images appeared all around her, immaterial like ghosts, and the faint outline of furniture and other inanimate objects. An array of smells—cigarette smoke, incense, stale booze, sweat and spent passions—filled her nose and fragments of conversations gummed up her ears.

Niks didn't believe her own senses, how the ghosts produced an array of colors, some warm and inviting, others frigid and repulsive.

At yet, captivated by the accessibility of their auras, she wanted more, to reach out, press closer—

Rex opened her eyes again, returning them to the stairwell. Something lingered from the event, the sense of someone in her mind punctuated by sweet lilacs, drawing her forward. Without a sound, Rex descended the stairwell to the next floor, her hypercolor hightops remaining a cool purple. A few drunks and junkies huddled against the wall, sputtering nonsense or asking for change, but Rex paid them no mind. Neither did Niks. She had to find them—the one that smelled like lilacs—of the presence on the fringe of her awareness.

Rex made it down the hallway, under the sputtering hallway lights, to number 435. With smooth, quick movements, Rex removed two of her dangling earrings, worked them inside the keyhole, and popped the lock. After returning her accessories, Rex pressed her hands against the plastic door, opening it just a crack and letting her senses bleed out ahead. Groans emanated from inside, but nothing that alerted Rex.

Tip-toeing inside, she ran her right hand along the bubbled surface of the bare wall to keep herself balanced inside the dimly lit room. Only a cluster of lit candle nubs melted atop a graffitied desk gave her any visual aid. But she didn't need it to know who made the grunts and groans. Niks perceived her surroundings just as Rex did, through a heightened sense that told her the semi-conscious people sprawled across the cushion-less couch and bare bed posed no threat.

Niks caught glimpses of tourniquets, empty syringes, wire bundles, and broken circuits on the floor as Rex moved toward the covered window. Green and red lights flashed in the dark. As her eyes adjusted, she could make out the outlines of four bodies, and the oblong headgear they wore. An idea formed in the back of her mind: They're jacked in.

Niks didn't understand the meaning at first, but as one of them groaned and writhed on the bed, she put part of the missing pieces together. This is neuro tech…

But somehow she perceived it all to be tainted, foul, cheap; a terrible imitation. The drugs, paraphernalia, and the low-grade gear disgusted her. She didn't understand the impression, but Niks didn't have a chance to dwell on it as Rex released the blinds. The flood light from the alleyway pierced the dark room, but Rex never looked back to see whose room she crashed. Instead, she cracked open the window and stuck her head outside.

Less than a meter away sat the next building, another sagging yellow brick motel with most of its windows boarded up or blown out. To her right, Niks could make out the edge of a glowing neon sign, and some of the letters—XEN. Below her, a significant four-story drop would surely kill her, even if she was lucky enough to land in overstuffed dumpster buzzing with flies. The garbage smell wafted up to her, and even though the sour smells bothered Niks, Rex didn't seem to care. Her gaze fixed on the two Dominion soldiers standing with their backs to them at the end of the alley.

Stay that way, *assinos*. Another thought echoed in her head as Rex gripped the window frame: You'd better be there.

By the time Niks pieced together Rex's intent, she had already wedged herself out of the window, and crouched on the sill, hypercolor hightops swirling with bright pinks and orange. Using only one hand to hold the underside of the head, she tried to gauge the distance of the opposing window. Though the glass had long been shattered, bits remained in the frame, like clear, jagged teeth.

Oh, no—don't—!

Niks would have squeezed her eyes shut if she could. Instead she screamed as Rex did a 180 spin and leapt over to the other window. The brief elation she felt as she stuck the landing wiped out as sharp pain bit into her right hand.

Niks wanted to cry out just as much as Rex, but the tattooed woman bit her tongue and tumbled inside. She didn't care that she struck some hard piece of furniture, or that she banged her head against the bare floor.

Clutching her wrist, she brought her right hand to her face. Tiny glass shards stuck out from the palm, blood streaking down her arm.

"What the—?"

Rex whipped her head toward the speaker. A slim, humanoid woman in her late 20s, sporting an antiquated bowl-cut and a threadbare bathrobe sprung up from her desk. Above the garbage stink drifting in from the broken window, the smell of lilacs touched her nose, making her heart beat a little faster.

"Who are you—what do you want?"

"Relax, it's just me," Rex said, she removed her hoodie and lowered her scarf to reveal her nonchalant smile.

"Rex, for saint's sake."

"Sorry, darling."

"Oh, your hand—"

"It's nothing," Rex said, still holding her wrist as she stood up. "But can I use your bathroom?"

"Y-yeah."

Rex took a quick survey, even as she gave the woman another smile. The room arrangements didn't look that much different than wherever she'd come from, though this woman's bed had a frame and mismatched and weathered—but clean—sheets. A simple desk and a shoddy chair opposed the bed, and a dresser topped with real books, a near-empty bottle of lilac lotion, and a camera case squeezed up against the wall next to the window. Rex found the bathroom behind the mini refrigerator. Though the wash stall didn't have a regular shower head, and the faucet opening had all but crusted over with lime scale deposits, Niks felt a sense of jealousy trickle through.

A working toilet…

Rex jangled the silver handle to the toilet, marveling at the prize.

The woman popped her head in, hazel eyes going back and forth between Rex's face and her bloody hand. "Can I help?"

"No."

Niks sensed the tension in the air just as she did with Thea. The woman's concern vanished from her face, and she crossed her arms with a frown. "So, you just commando roll into my room for fun? It's only been three weeks, Rex. You usually disappear for a lot longer."

Rex didn't look up as she plucked out the glass shards with her black nails. "I've been busy, Sam."

Sam.

Again, just the mention of a name shook loose memories and sensations Niks couldn't take in all at once. She heard stifled laughter, a line of poetry she couldn't place. Tablets and leaves of real paper scattered about, ink spills on a marble surface; the dusty smell of a library, or traditional bookshop. She gazed into hazel eyes, felt full, kissable lips upon her cheeks. Gentle hands reached out to her, wanting to trace every curve and contour, but she held them away with the same aching lump in her throat she'd felt before. Words sped through her mind, chosen in haste, misunderstood, overshadowed by heartache.

Sam's another ex… But that label didn't feel right. Rex wasn't the type to have girlfriends, or at least that's what Niks sensed.

"Busy? Yeah, I've heard," Sam said, sounding both irritated and tired. "My sources say Boss Akanno has a note on your head that would buy most of the sim-stim junkies a lifetime in the clouds."

Without a hint of sarcasm, her inflection unemotional, Rex replied: "Your sources are usually right."

"Ah, okay," Sam said, tightening her arms across her chest. "So, what is it then? Why are you here?"

Rex took her time, rinsing the blood and grime from her hand and then looking at the side of the medicine cabinet mirror. A tiny control panel blinked on the side.

"It's locked," Sam said.

Rex looked back at her, eyebrow lifted.

With a sigh, Sam said, "0814. And you can only have a dermapatch. Stay away from my pain meds."

Rex complied, opening the cabinet and regarding the rows of meds. As she plucked out a dermapatch from a box, she noted the bottles of anti-depressants, anti-anxieties, muscle relaxers, and synthopioids.

"I thought you just took something for your back," Rex commented.

Sam reached over and slammed the cabinet door shut. "Your information is a little outdated, as usual."

Ignoring the insult, Rex focused on Sam's close proximity, leveling her eyes and offering her a sly half-smile. Cheeks reddening, Sam pulled away and retreated into the bedroom.

"I came to see you, Sam. I was worried about you after the attacks," she said as she applied the dermapatch. Niks felt Rex's annoyance at the ticklish feel as the synthetic skin meshed and integrated into the damaged tissue, closing the wound. "I'm sorry I couldn't get here sooner."

Sitting at the edge of the bed, Sam turned her head, but only enough to give Rex the side of her eye. "It's not like I live on the other side of town."

"Yeah, but most nets are down—and have you looked out your window?" As soon as she said it, Rex wanted to rephrase, especially since the only window in Sam's room faced the other motel. Still, if she stuck her head out and looked to her right, she'd see the Dominion guards at the end of the alley. "It's not like I could come through your front door."

Sam's arms loosened, and she shook her head. "I know how bad it is. Jones got killed in one of the bombings; I had to cover his report."

Cognizance seeped into Niks' mind: Sam is a journalist for the Trigonian news. Jones was her net anchor.

Niks thought Rex would naturally comfort her, or say something, anything appropriate to acknowledge her partner's death. Instead, she approached her, letting her hips sway from side to side. When she got within arm's reach, she extended her hand, fingers grazing the side of Sam's face.

"You think I'm that easy?" Sam jerked her head away and looked up at her, hazel eyes misty, lips pressed together in a tight line.

No way—Sam won't go for this, Niks thought, sensing Rex's intention. Not with how rigid she appeared, or the vexation in her voice.

But something shifted inside Rex, a hidden light flicked on in the dark. As she concentrated on her gaze, heat built in her chest and spread through her limbs, projecting into Sam's face. "I think you've missed me."

Sam's shoulders slackened, her lips parted. Sensing her opening, Rex took Sam's hand and brought it up to her hip, then slid it back, on the round of her backside. Rex flexed her buttock, and closed her hand on Sam's, letting her feel the tightness of her muscles. Without prompting, Sam lifted her other hand up, and Rex positioned it on the opposite side in the same place.

"You're incorrigible," she said as Rex stepped in closer, putting herself between Sam's legs.

"Do you want me to go?" Rex cupped Sam's cheek, gazing into her eyes with intent.

What is she doing? But Niks couldn't hold on to her fear, or her curiosity for long. She'd only ever been on the receiving end of such aggression, and to see Sam's reaction, the way her pupils dilated, and her tongue licked her bottom lip in anticipation charged her senses.

"Don't go," Sam said, flexing her hands and pulling Rex forward, into her.

Wait—how did she?—

Rex ran her hand down her neck, using her nails to elicit a chill that made Sam shiver and draw closer.

"Who attacked La Raja?" she asked, running her other hand through Sam's mousy brown hair.

"Don't know," she said, eyelids drooping as Rex massaged her head. "Dominion won't release any information."

"What about Akanno—did he live through the bombings?"

Sam's eyes shut as Rex slid her fingers down the front of her bathrobe, feeling the soft tops of her breasts.

"Yes," she whispered.

Niks tried to pull away, wanting to understand Sam's complete mood shift. *How is she seducing her like this?*

"Where is he?" Rex asked as she loosened the sash tying together Sam's bathrobe. Purring softly in her ear, Rex pulled her bathrobe down, revealing her small breasts, and a dragonfly tattoo descending her left side.

The journalist pressed closer, her words breathless, as Rex's fingers reached lower, beneath her navel, playing along the split between her legs. "The SnakePit..."

Idiot, Niks heard her think. *With as much illegal neuro tech as he pushed, Akanno should have fled, at the very least, to the next city the second the Dominion touched down—not stay put in his own bar in the heart of the District.*

"How are you doing this?" Sam said, eyes swimming in their sockets as Niks continued to work her fingers deeper into her folds, stroking and massaging. "I'm really pissed at you."

Gotta go—

Niks didn't understand the thoughts running through Rex's head, especially the compulsion to bail on Sam and, after teasing her, leave her unfulfilled. *Why now, when you have her right where you want her?*

Rex's logic made no sense to her, or her heightened anxiety. *Gotta settle with Akanno.*

(I don't want to hurt her.)

But you will if you leave her! Niks *thought, even though Rex didn't seem to hear her.*

"You're not leaving," Sam said, catching Rex's hand as she started to withdraw.

Niks *felt the shift inside Rex, the disconnect as she looked into Sam's eyes. Whatever intimate connection they had, Sam bridged the gap between them, not Rex, even though she initiated everything.*

Why are you afraid of her? Niks *thought.*

Though Rex had withdrawn within herself, she did not stop, pushing Sam back onto her bed and flipping her onto her side. She couldn't stand Sam looking at her, not with those brilliant hazel eyes, the gaze that carried their shared history, and projected Sam's deep, and complicated, feelings for her.

You shouldn't care, Rex thought, *summoning anger for Sam, though her words rang hollow to Niks.*

Shocked and confused, Niks sat back as Rex laid down behind her and brought Sam's right leg up, robe still halfway around her waist. Sliding her left hand over her shoulder and grasping her breast, Rex pulled Sam in close, laying her head on hers. As she tugged on her nipple, rolling the pebbled tip between her thumb and forefinger, she walked her other hand down again, over her hips, around the buttocks, and settling between the slit between her legs. Taller than Sam, she had the reach to press one finger inside her warmth, but not too far, circling around, then moving in and out, in a steady rhythm.

"I want you, Rex," Sam said, her breath ragged. "All of you."

Niks sensed the dichotomy in Rex, the need to run, and the ego-driven desire to finish what she started. And something, stronger than both, pushing her to take a risk she normally wouldn't dare.

Sam is safe, Rex told herself, *justifying the dangerous gamble.*

What are you going to…? Niks *lost her words, breath caught in her chest as Rex's intent came to mind.* But that's not possible—

"I'm going to do something a little different. Keep your eyes closed." Rex pulled off the sash to Sam's bathrobe and tied it over her eyes. "And this, just in case you want to peek."

Rolling Sam onto her stomach, Rex kneeled over the backs of her legs. Sam grabbed the pillows in tight fists, already anticipating the surprise.

"Do you trust me, Sam?"

Sam hesitated, then whispered: *"yes."*

Wetting her fingers of her right hand with her tongue, Rex leaned forward, over Sam, and slid two fingers in her opening. When she felt Sam relax, she pulled back a little and pressed her another finger against the tight sphincter just above.

"Breathe, Sam."

A small breath, not even a gasp. But Rex slid the third finger in gently, waiting again until Sam released the pillows from her tight grip.

Niks reacted to Sam's moaning as Rex moved her arm back and forth, penetrating with more and more depth each time, aligning with her need. Even in the confusion of Rex's emotions, the tension of her strange relationship with Sam, or her own hang-ups, Niks caught herself wishing herself in Sam's place.

Her touch…

Guided, personal, expert. Nothing she'd ever experienced before with James, and even as her fears tried to conjure up reasons why it was wrong, nothing she would ever want—she couldn't stop herself from reacting.

I want you, Rex.

And then Rex made the move to push all of their boundaries.

Tilting her head back, she reached into herself, drawing forth from a place deep within. Niks never conceived of such an inner dimension, a place that could contain wavelengths of light and sound. Visceral warmth touched Niks' mind, pulling her away from her fears and immersing her in the purity of the shared sensations.

How is this possible?

She not only sensed Rex—she also felt Sam, as if Rex dissolved the space between them. Without barriers, Rex adjusted the angle and depth of her fingers until she hit all of Sam's most sensitive areas. Heat stacked upon heat as she augmented each thrust with pulsations of light, pushing Sam closer to climax.

When the journalist's body went taut, Rex drove in deep and held her close. Concentrating on the rising waves inside of Sam, Rex allowed the kaleidoscope of colors to flow through her, bursting out of her fingertips in a trumpet blast. All else fell away—the rough feel of over-starched sheets, the faint garbage smell against lilacs and sweat, the creaking and grinding of the rusted bed springs.

Oh God—

Submerged in the multiple perspectives, Niks would have screamed just as loudly as Sam as the journalist's entire body convulsed to Rex's extrasensory touch. She flung the two pillows in opposite directions off the bed, writhing beneath her in pleasure.

Who are you, Rex—how could you do this? Niks thought, stunned and reveling.

Rex dismounted, already redirecting her concentration as Sam struggled to regain her breath, still blindfolded and splayed across the bed.

"That... that was amazing."

With quiet steps, Rex moved over to the dresser and unzipped the camera case. Inside, she found backup batteries, an accessory interface module, and a signal booster.

She's done this before, Niks gathered as Rex swiped what she needed and closed the case back up.

"You might as well take a book, too." Sam removed the blindfold and turned onto her side, but didn't look at Rex, her eyes distant, unfocused. "I think you still have two or three of mine."

Guilt nibbled at her stomach, but Rex shoved it aside. Under normal circumstances, she'd just leave without saying a thing, but something hot and heavy pressing against her sternum forced out her words. "You shouldn't have gotten attached."

No... Niks thought, sensing the feelings Rex ignored, *that's not what you mean.*

"Don't come back," Sam whispered as Rex walked over to the window.

Rex placed one foot on the windowsill, her hightop solid black. Other words perched on her lips, but she could never speak them. Not to Sam, Thea, Tanza, Remy, Danzin, Raze—any of the people she'd been with for more than a night.

You don't have to feel this way, Niks thought, wanting to reach out to Rex, shake her free of her own restraints. Furious and concerned, she screamed as loudly as she could: *Tell her how you really feel!*

Shaking her head, Rex paused. I can't.

Wait—did she just hear me?

But before Niks could put any more thought or action to her question, pain surged through her, blanketing her with a darkness that suffocated all light.

Niks shot up, reached out with both arms. "You're not alone—"

Shocked by her own voice and the emptiness of Syra's quarters, Niks shriveled back up, drawing her legs up to her chest. She couldn't be sure what bothered her most: the stark feeling of separation, or the residual loneliness lapping at her mind as she came back into her own body.

"I can't do this anymore," she said, pressing the knuckles of her hand into her eyes. Tears squeezed around them, running down her arm. *I don't want these experiences—these feelings anymore. It's not real.*

"It's not real," she said out loud, trying to convince herself.

Needing her friend—needing someone—Niks reached for her wristband, forgetting she had thrown it across the room.

I shouldn't call Sy, she thought, glancing over at the clock on the nightstand. 0023. At this point, Syra would be clinching her lover or lovers for the night, and/or getting the intel she swore she'd get.

No, she couldn't bother Syra. And James was out of the question.

As Niks sunk back in the bed, bunching up the sheets around her shoulders, she realized she wanted to talk to the only other person that might understand her predicament.

Jin…

Somehow, someway, she'd have to find her, even if it meant risking more than she'd ever dared to before.

For Jin, and for me, she told herself, staring up at the ceiling. Then, as the effects of the sedative took hold again, another thought, terrifying in its implications, drifted to mind: *…and for Rex.*

Chapter 10

Waking up behind Rex's eyes again didn't surprise her this time, but her location did. On the level rooftop of the motel, Rex crouched near the edge, watching the Dominion activity below. Searchlights crisscrossed overhead, drowning out the stars, glinting off the scout ships drifting across the cityscape.

Why is she up here? *Niks thought as Rex drew in a deep breath, the residual smell of smoke and grit making her nose wrinkle. From everything Rex said, the cautious measures she took to see Sam, and the anxieties she felt regarding the Dominion, she should be in hiding.*

"So many of them..." *Rex whispered as soldiers escorted a line of handcuffed people out of a building down the block. Despair and fear soaked into Niks' perceptions, as well as fatigue.*

Not just physical exhaustion, *Niks sensed. The woman felt bone-tired; the soul-weary lassitude after a lifetime hustling the streets, running from the law. Or running from herself.*

The revelation struck her hard, in ways she didn't expect. She had yet to acknowledge Rex as anything but an unwanted dream, chalking it all up to a freak experience and coincidence. But the woman standing over the edge, looking down at the street with a strange sense of longing and futility, felt too human, too real to ignore. The cool composure she had seen and felt in her, the aggression and confidence, dropped away, and the person behind it all, frightened and tired, emerged.

Take me away already, *Rex thought, staring at a soldier on top of a crawler, scanning the street with silver-sealed eyes.*

Why?—no, *Niks said,* don't do this. Go back inside; don't let them take you!

Rex brought her right hand up to her face, looking at the interweaving tattoos starting at her palm and winding around up her arm. Old memories, ties to a distant past, skimmed across her mind: The embrace of a caring mother, the hearty laughter and gentle reassurances from a loving father. Siblings, many of them, running around her in a dizzy whirl of playtime fun and games in a house not big enough for the lot of them. But something dark reached out from within Rex, grabbing hold of what happiness she conjured, and burning it away with loathing and revulsion.

Uglier memories bled through. Niks reared back at the sight of old-fashioned syringes with long needles coming at her, and the bite of their sharp tip as it plunged into her bared stomach. She screamed, fighting the hands that held her down on the cold exam table, begging her mother to make it stop as they injected acid fire into her intestines.

"The Trinane treatments, coupled with electrotherapy, will help suppress your daughters condition," a white-coated man said, reassuring her sobbing mother. "You don't want her to end up like her biologicals."

God, stop, Niks thought, heart crumbling as Rex, no older than six or seven, screamed as the next round of injections began. So young…why are you doing this to her?

Rex shook her head, ridding them both of the torments of her youth. Hands balled into fists, she stared out again at the silver-eyed soldier. "Come and get me, you bastards."

A whimper caught both of their attention. Rex whipped her head around, body tensed to fight or run. When the whimper came again, this time sounding desperate and pained, she relaxed.

Sounds hungry, she thought, walking over to the utilities access unit near the door to the stairwell. A chain bound the double doors, but someone had jammed something into the middle, trying to break the doors apart, succeeding only in creating a small hole. Niks would have already moved on, but Rex did not, peering into the dark space, listening again for the cry. When it came again, she stuck her hand in, feeling around the shelves and control panels until she came upon something soft and fuzzy pressed up against the humming generator.

"Gotcha," Rex said, pulling out a matted black ball of fur. The tiny creature with yellow, saucer-shaped eyes, struggled at first, clawing and biting at her until Niks brought it to her chest. It weighed next to nothing, its ribs prominent and tail limp.

That looks like a kitcoon, Niks thought, remembering that La Raja had a problem with the stray feline hybrids.

Calming herself first, Rex projected her intent through her words, and her gentle touch. "You're alright, little guy." The kitcoon retracted its claws and looked up to her. "You can stay with me for a while."

With a yawn, the kitcoon snuggled into her, purring with satisfaction.

How did she do that?

But Niks stopped herself, no longer able to keep asking the same question. Not now, not after all she'd witnessed.

At a loss for words, she watched as Rex took the kitcoon back down to her motel room, keeping it safe within the wrap of her hoodie until she got inside. When she found Remy in the coffin, eyes closed, naked and jacked into the biofeeds, she breathed a sigh of relief. At least she'd have a few hours to nurse it back to health, maybe longer if she put up enough of a stink.

As she dropped off her wrap and flung her scarf near the door hook, black fur ball still safely in her arms, she paused. On the floor, next to the buzzing coffin and on top of the neat stack of Remy's clothes lay his dog tags. She stared at them a moment, her thoughts drifting away again. Niks felt her pull back when memories of their better times threatened to replay, especially when she shifted her gaze to his naked body.

Still, Niks grafted her preconscious recollections: Remy. Remington, the half-man, half-biotech freakshow. The ratchakker assino ex-captain who had the misfortune of being the lone survivor in a doomed covert ops mission for the United Starways Coalition. Unlike her, he could have returned home, and despite the chak-up, would have been lauded a hero. But no. He stayed with Rex, hustling the streets, building her tech, keeping her secrets—but most importantly, unlike anyone else she'd ever slept with—never asked for more than she could give. In fact, he never asked for anything.

And that's why, after all his sycha, with all her fears of anything long-term, she let him stay.

Rex sifted through a faded camouflaged backpack until she found a few packets of dried food and an instant meal. Remy would be pissed, especially since they were down to less than a day's supply. Still, she'd rather go without food herself than let the little thing starve.

After finding some leftover jerky, she propped herself in the corner of the room, atop a pillow thrown from the mattress days ago, and took a bite.

"Here you are," she said, offering the kitcoon the masticated pulp. The kitcoon sniffed the red mash, and with a bright pink tongue, took a testing lick. Then, a little too eagerly, wolfed down the entire lump.

"Go slow," she said, continuing to offer it more. Her own stomach growled, demanding for her to take some for herself, but she ignored it. "Our secret, though, alright?"

After finishing, the kitcoon stretched out across her lap, it's little belly sticking out over her calf. Tired herself, but not wanting to curl up on the floor again, she grabbed one of the books she'd snuck behind the coffin.

Sam's books, of course, and a few she had coerced from rich clients. Where else would she find such a treasure? Not on a hedonistic hellhole like La Raja. Real books hadn't been manufactured in centuries, and the texture of real paper, the old smell of vanilla and almonds, the heaviness of the book as she held it in her hands—she'd yet to match magic, the purity, of the experience.

Cracking open the book, she tried to make herself as comfortable as possible jammed into the corner, and leafed through to the first chapter. She'd read all five at least thirty times each. Still, tales of adventures, people with supernatural powers, good triumphing over evil—she couldn't get enough of it. And now, as the Dominion forces tightened down on the city, she needed that escape more than ever. After all, where else could she go? The Dominion closed the skyways, patrolled every street, and everyone with half a sense and a getaway vehicle had already fled before they locked down the docks and put two warships in orbit.

The truth sunk in to her bones as she found her favorite chapter. Dominion sirens sang in the distance, calling for reinforcements.

Rex dropped the book and held the kitcoon close as phantom needle-pain stabbed into her stomach. They're coming.

Only one option remained if she wanted to keep her skin. She had to find Boss Akanno.

"Wait, you can't—"

"Can't what?"

Niks snapped opened her eyes, surprised to see Syra half-naked rummaging through the pile of clothing on the ground.

"Sy… I'm sorry," she said, clutching her forehead. A dull ache thudded against her skull, reminiscent of a hangover. "I feel so lost right now."

"Bad dreams?"

Niks hesitated, unsure of the right answer. "Yes."

"Yeah, that drug will do that to ya. I noticed you were pretty restless when I came to bed."

"Wait—when did you come home? What time is it?" Niks asked, rubbing the sleep crusts from her eyes and looking to the clock.

"Around 0100. It's 0430 now."

"Did you sleep?"

"Enough. Come on, us Nagoorians only need about three hours," she said with a wink.

After putting on a scrub top and bottom, Syra came over to her, refurbished bioscanner in hand. "I got a few leads last night. I've got a plan."

Niks scooched up in bed as Syra ran the bioscanner up and down her body. "What happened?"

"Just made friends with one of the cute geeks down in engineering," she said, licking her lips with a smile. "He's going to hook me up with a modified scanner so we can find that missing part to the Med Oculus."

"Sy, no—that's dangerous."

"We can't just leave it down there for the Dominion to find—they are wayyyy too interested in it. Makes me nervous, especially with Jin still gone."

"I'll go," Niks said, swinging her legs over the bed. The headache pounded her back, jabbing ice picks behind her eyes.

"No way, sista. That neuro toxin needs another few hours to flush out of your system."

"What are you doing?" she asked as Syra popped open the bioscanner and fiddled with the internal settings.

"Gonna just swap some numbers, you know, modify things here and there…"

"Sy…" Niks said, pulling her hand away from the screen so she could see what she did. Red arrows highlighted her inflamed intestines. "You gave me diarrhea?!"

"Horrific, crap-your-pants squirts. And gas. Don't forget that."

"Come on, Sy, stop—"

Syra connected the bioscanner to her wristband. "Oops, too late—uploaded it to Dr. Nara. That ol' softie will give you a pass out of work. Now Meow—she'd probably be into you pooping yourself."

Laughing hurt, but Niks couldn't help herself as she laid back down. "Thanks, Sy."

Syra patted her on the stomach. "Always, my gastrointestinally-challenged friend."

"Hey, Sy," Niks said as Syra got up and gathered up her things for work. Thinking of Rex, the impossibility of her dreams, of needing to find something real in all of the illusion, she forced herself to ask: "Have you heard of Trinane treatments?"

Syra raised an eyebrow at her. "Trinane treatments? Why you interested in medieval torture?"

"What do you mean?"

Syra shuddered. "That stuff still freaks me out. Pull it up on your wristband."

Niks revealed her bare wrist.

"You—the rule follower—took off your SOHO wristband?" Syra imitated cat claws with her hands. "Meow's going to have a fit if she can't track you 24/7."

"It's right over there somewhere," Niks said, pointing to one of the mountainous piles of clothing. "I was upset that James wouldn't return any of my messages."

"Fair enough," Syra said, walking over and searching for her missing accessory.

Impatient, and needing to find something to prove herself wrong—that all of her dreams and experiences were just delusions—she persisted. "Tell me."

With a sigh, Syra looked up from her search, to the windows facing the stars. "It was a horrible, unsanctioned method of 'treatment,'" she said, performing air quotes, "that one wacko came up with about twenty years ago to treat young kids with telepathic lineage, under the pretense that it could 'cure' them of telepathy."

"What?" All of the air left the room, and she brought her arms to her chest, terrified and stricken by the weight of her answer. *That means that Rex is...*

The word sang across her mind as she sucked in her breath. *A telepath.*

But how? she thought, fighting with herself. None of the bizarre skills Rex exhibited matched the four recognized species and their powers. The Si infiltrated the weak-minded, the Moro sensed emotions, the Tre stole dreams, and the Prodgy—the most dangerous type—could heal or liquify a person. Giving someone a psionic orgasm didn't exactly appear on the list.

"It involved shocks, hypnosis, caustic medications—that were delivered with antiquated hypos, mind you, into their stomachs and necks. Those poor kids. Some of them had permanent brain damage or physical disfigurements. I think all of them had to come away with some kind of PTSD. Wouldn't you? I mean, could you imagine your parents, the people you trust most as a kid, signing you up to get tortured like that?"

God, Rex—I'm so sorry...

As Niks digested the gravity of the Trinane treatments, a voice whispered up from within: *Maybe that's why she can't attach to people.*

Thea, Sam, Remy—and a half dozen other familiar faces appeared on the fringe of her mind. Niks knew them, had tasted each one of them, touched them in the most intimate ways. And yet, something remained missing, a hole in her chest unfilled by all her conquests, her many wild nights; a void she could not fill, even after each one of them offered her their heart.

"Who would do that to their child?" Niks whispered.

"Mostly parents who adopted kids with a known telepathic bloodline—especially if there was any Prodgy in there. Don't want a Dissembler ripping apart your family at the Sunday dinner table!" Syra said, waving her hands in the air to add further exaggeration. "It was *gorsh-shit*, and it messed up a ton of kids."

"How do you know all this?" Niks said, still holding her hands over her heart.

Syra shrugged, resuming her search for the wristband. "I did my senior thesis on PTSD in pediatric patients, remember?"

"Yeah," Niks said, hearing the subtle waver in Syra's voice. Back in nursing school she noticed her friend taking a particular interest in the subject, but she never put it together until now, years later, as watched Syra find the wristband and walk back to her. Eyes downcast, jaw tightened, her best friend carried her emotion in her face, even as she tried to play it cool.

"Did you choose that subject that because of your parents?"

Syra went rigid, stopping a half meter away from the bed.

"Sy…" Niks reached out to her, coaxing her to sit next to her in the bed. She softened her voice as she took her friend's hand in hers. "I'm here."

"I know. But right now you've got to take care of this nonsense," she said, handing her back the wristband.

As Niks slid it back on her wrist, she swiped the flashing lights. "Twenty-eight missed calls and seventeen text messages?!"

"Ah, Mr. Predictable," Syra said, rolling her eyes.

Niks flipped through the texts, all of which contained the same message: *On the Callieo. Call me ASAP.*

Nothing else, not hint of what the hell was going on.

"I gotta go, Niksy, or Meow will tear me a new one," Sy said, standing up again and heading for the door. "You stay low and feel better, k?"

"Sy—be careful," Niks said as Syra backed out of the door blowing her a kiss.

"Aren't I always?"

"No!" Niks shouted as the doors clamped shut.

He'd better have a good explanation for all this, Niks thought, dialing James up on her wristband.

The blue connection indicator beeped for what seemed like forever. Finally, as she went to disconnect, he popped up on the holographic projectors. Only his face appeared, bags under his eyes, cheeks sunken, as if he hadn't slept in days.

"Where have you been?" she said. "I've been trying to reach you for—"

"Nikkia, listen to me."

Of course he won't let me finish, she said, disappointed with herself for even trying.

"I heard about what happened to you on La Raja with Dr. Naum."

"I didn't sign up with SOHO to be interrogated and tortured by the Dominion, James," she said, hands shaking. "Your military can't treat people like that."

"I didn't have a say in what happened—you know that," he said, taking a paternal tone. "But you need to comply with the military, Nikkia; this is a safety and health issue that can't be dismissed. I've got Rogman breathing down my neck for this."

"Stop calling me that," she said, slamming her fist down on the bed.

"It's your name—"

"Niks. Call me Niks."

"Look, this is serious. I can't make this go away. The terrorist attacks on La Raja, the Med Oculus—this is all being taken out of my hands and sealed by the higher-ups. I've never seen anything like it before. I'm worried about what this means, especially for you if you do not comply."

It took everything she had not to throw the wristband across the room again. "I want to see Jin."

"Jin?"

"Yes. Her 'arrest'—or forced removal—however you're going to spin it—has caused serious tension amongst the SOHO staff. Things are going to get ugly if there isn't some kind of contact with her."

"Like what?" James said, his tone careful and even.

"I don't know," Niks said. She didn't like the stern way he looked at her, or how he straightened out, assuming his most authoritative posture. "The *Mercy* staff signed up for a medical mission—not for experiments and detainment. Someone could contact headquarters, file a complaint—even shoot a message to the United Starways Coalition, give them more ammo for their cause against the Eeclian Dominion."

"That would be unwise," James said curtly.

"Please, James. I need to see Jin."

"I can't promise you anything."

The signal canceled out.

Did he just hang up on me?

Furious, but her stomach twisting in knots, she laid back down on the pillows and stared up at the ceiling.

I don't know what to do.

A lump formed in her throat, her eyes hot and wet. None of her dreams, the impossibility of her connection to Rex, seemed real, but just as she couldn't accept it as true, she couldn't fathom accepting that it wasn't. None of her previous relationships—even her friendship with Syra—matched the intensity of what she felt after being inside Rex's head, sensing her thoughts and emotions. And the sex—

Oh God, the sex…

Niks closed her eyes, remembering the feel of Rex's caress, and how she felt Rex touch others. Before that, she thought she craved James' embrace, and now, having experienced the fires of passion and desire from two different vantage points, she couldn't stand the cold comforts of her lonely, predictable world.

I want more. I need more.

(I need Rex.)

Her eyes shot open again. *But Rex is in trouble.*

In her last dream, the Dominion sounded the alarms for reinforcements—and Rex had made a dangerous decision to seek out Boss Akanno.

I need more information, she decided, pressing the heels of her hands against her forehead, *and if I can't talk to Jin, I'll have to figure this out myself.*

And the only way she knew how was to go back to sleep.

After checking her wristband to confirm Dr. Nara had pardoned her from her shift, she rifled through Syra's nightstand, looking for another yellow packet amongst the sex paraphernalia. Some of the odd-looking toys—silver beads strung together, handcuffs, or the plug-looking thing—she'd have to question Syra about later. For now, the yellow packet she found balled up inside a condom would have to do.

Come on, she thought, staring at the ceiling. Her heartbeat sounded in her ears, rapid and booming. The silence in the room, the confinement of her own body, made her all the more impatient, and she tossed and turned in bed.

Maybe I am crazy. Maybe I should turn myself in, she thought, wondering if Jin had experienced any of this after using the Med Oculus, and the Dominion really was trying to help her.

But her heart wouldn't have it, and any of the doubt left inside her became no more than just a whisper as she thought of Rex, and her sun-fire gaze.

It's me, Niks, she thought, closing her eyes and imaging herself in Rex's embrace. *I'm coming back.*

Chapter 11

Niks crash-landed on the graveled rooftop, pain lancing her knees and ankles. Rolling under a pigeon coop, she waited until the scout ships drifted by overhead, and the searchlights swept over her position, holding her breath the entire time.

Just one more, *Rex thought, adjusting the bag strap across her chest as she eyed the target building up ahead. Despite the broken street lamps and half the buildings without power, she could still make out her pathway with all the light pollution provided by the Dominion occupation.*

Niks tried to get a better bearing of her surroundings as Rex crawled out from underneath her shelter. As she bolted for the next building, Niks caught sight of ornamental tiled façades, blown-out shophouses, decorative columns, and broken neon signs.

The District.

Or at least what establishments remained after the bombings.

Having never been one for heights, she panicked as the gap between her building, and the building ahead, came into view.

We can't make that—

I can make it, *Rex thought, pumping her legs even faster as she sprinted to the edge. She took off with a giant leap, arms stretched out in the night air, dizzying drop beneath her.*

Niks would have closed her eyes if she could, but Rex did not, taking it all in as she soared through the air.

You're coming in too fast—

Misjudging the landing, Rex fell hard onto the tarred surface, knocking the wind from her lungs, tearing the skin on her palms. Niks winced as Rex flailed, gasping and fighting against her spasming diaphragm. Black motes dotted her vision, her head spinning.

Falling into nurse mode, Niks concentrated on Rex, allowing her panic inside her, keeping her voice calm. Slow down, breathe.

Despite the scout ships circling around again, Rex forced herself to relax, her muscles releasing. She took one breath, then two.

Get up, *Niks thought.*

Rex ground her fists into the tarred rooftop and got to her feet. As the scout ships shined their lights, sweeping toward her, she stumbled over to the translucent skylight cracked open for ventilation. A steady, bass thump from overworked subwoofers rattled the muddied yellow glass.

Jamming one of her feet underneath the skylight, she kicked upwards, busting it at the hinge. She shoved the rest of her body through, snagging her hoodie and her jumpsuit, but she didn't care, not with the scout lights coming straight for her, looking for anyone suspicious, especially someone breaking curfew.

The drop down landed her smack in the middle of a table, breaking it in two. Beer bottles, hypos, empty drug bottles, and ashtrays went flying in every direction, showering her with backwash and ash.

Adrenaline rush sprung her to her feet as her back screamed in pain. Despite the thundering bass of the electronic pop blasting from the wall speakers, she couldn't chance that her unconventional arrival hadn't alerted the wrong people, even if she did land in a private booth.

Searching for a way out, she spotted six patrons wearing oblong headgear, heads resting against the curved booth wall, or pitched forward at an awkward angle. Red, yellow, and green lights flashed, indicating how much juice they had left until their sim-stim time ran out. Rex picked the one with the red-lit cranial strip, and pulled him from his sitting position and dropped him in the middle of the broken table. With such low-grade neuro tech, and the suspicious array of drugs she saw scattered around the floor, something like a seizure could have easily caused such damage.

After setting up the scene, she wedged herself behind one of the junkies and secured her hoodie over her face. As expected, two meathead bouncers pushed aside the beaded curtain, red-faced and ready to fight. When they saw the junkie sprawled out on the broken table, they grabbed him by the collar and arms, and dragged him out.

"That's the second one today," one of them shouted above the music.

"Gotta make him disappear or the boss 'ill be pissed."

That's 'cause your tech is poison and junk, Akanno, Rex thought, moving to the curtain. She parted the plastic beads and looked out to the main bar. Subsonics pulsed in her stomach and skull from the gigantic speakers blasting onto on empty dance floor. Not that this kind of bar would attract a dancing crowd, even in better times.

Sticking to the shadows, Rex made her way to the bar. A handful of people hunched over their drinks, some mumbling to themselves, others staring into the cheap, lukewarm booze, foreheads knotted, eyes bloodshot. Rex knew that look, preyed up on it.

Getting drunk means that they didn't have enough cash for a 'real high,' Niks gleaned from Rex's thoughts. *And she wanted that kind of desperation, especially for what she had in mind.*

She waited until the bartender turned her back before approaching the closest patron, a balding middle-aged human man with a pocked face and a pungent odor that rose above all of the other bar smells. Wearing a stained space suit under-layer, he looked like an off-world scavenger, but the track marks up his arms indicated he'd been on La Raja for some time, hooked on Akanno's poison.

"Wouldn't you rather be in the clouds?" Rex asked, sliding into the barstool next to him.

The man didn't look up at her. "Got no cash."

"Don't need any," she said, getting up and walking back into the shadows, away from the speakers.

After a minute, the man shoved away from the bar and walked over to her, a limp in his step. He looked her up and down, lower lip twitching, like a starving dog. "What's the deal?"

Niks didn't like the plan unfolding in Rex's head, or the pitting feeling blackening her stomach. *It was a risk to be in one of Akanno's joints in the first place, and an even bigger one to bribe a strung-out sim-stim junkie.*

"Relay a message to Boss Akanno for me, and I'll put you in the clouds," Rex said, lowering her scarf to reveal her face. "No juice, no hangover—best ride of your life."

The man quirked his head. "Ain't you…?"

"Yes."

Snorting, he glanced back over to the bar, then to her, a grin denting his hideous face. "There's a note on your head bigger than a single ride."

Niks wanted to run, but Rex didn't flinch, not even when the man went to grab at her arm. Instead, she stepped back, offsetting his balance, and hooked his left foot with hers. In one fluid motion, she threw him down, his head splitting against the laminate floor. He grunted, his eyes still open as he lay there, dazed and drooling.

As Niks marveled at her martial skill, Rex hurried back to the private booths, not waiting to see if the incident had been witnessed. But when she went to part the beaded curtain and make her escape, a bandaged hand shot out in front of her.

"I knew you'd be here," a voice shouted above the electro pop. "You've got a death wish."

Rex sighed and stepped back from the curtain. A slender man in his late forties, dressed like a seedy nightclubber, his eyes concealed behind reflective lenses, leaned against the wall. His ears, white against his already pale complexion, looked molded out of wax. "What do you want, Chezzie?"

"Come—have a drink with me," he said, curling a finger at her before disappearing in the adjacent private booth.

She followed, but Niks sensed begrudging feelings, as well as the sour aftertaste of a long-standing contentious relationship. Flashes of back alley deals, swirls of cigarette smoke in dingy bars, arcades booming with electric noise, and black market clinics with hacked restoration coffins swam through her brain.

"You should have known better," Chezzie said, sliding into the curved booth. He offered her a seat across from him, where a sparkling drink fizzed in a tempered glass cup. Raising his beer bottle, he took a swig and then added: "With that price-tag on your head, no junkie would even consider helping you."

After removing her messenger bag and setting it underneath the booth table, she took a seat. Rex pushed the drink in front of her to the side. "Not until they've tried my gear."

The man smiled, chipped teeth popping over his lower lip. "So the rumors say. I've only been on this god-forsaken planet for three months and all anyone can talk about is the Laws of Attraction—the hottest sim-stim, run by the hottest operator."

Rex shrugged. "Sometimes the rumors are right."

"I liked you better when you were my data hustler," he said, sipping his beer and leaning back. "Less ego."

Niks didn't know how she kept so calm, especially as she recalled the details of their relationship surfaced.

"You liked me better as a runaway fourteen-year-old girl naïve enough to work for an assino like you."

Chezzie grinned. Something about it alerted Niks, and Rex, making both of their stomachs squeeze down tight. "You've always had an uncanny ability to read people. I haven't been able to replace you."

"I'm sure you're doing just fine," she said, keeping her tone even. "What are those—series 5,000 ocular implants?"

"7,000," he said, smile waning.

"And I remember you swearing you'd never end up a mule."

What's a mule? Niks thought. *The knowledge splashed over her, like a bucket of water thrown onto a muddy surface. A messenger...*

"It's good money," he said, voice tightening as he took another sip. "Better than hustling."

"As long as you don't mind getting your eyes and ears ripped out."

The man's knuckles turned white around his beer. "You and I both have had worse done to us."

Rex played back a cool smile. "Why are you here, Chezzie?"

"Work. All the bosses in La Raja use mules. But when I heard you were operating around here, I knew we'd end up crossing paths again—and now here I am, with my latest delivery, just for you."

Rex curled her toes in her boots, dug her fingernails into her arms, but didn't change her relaxed facial expression.

"Who?"

"Boss Akanno," he said a little too casually. "The man is a shark; how'd you end up pissing him off so bad?"

Rex eyed the drink Chezzie had bought for her, tempted to screw her gut feeling, as she had been over the last few weeks.

No, Niks *called to her.* Please don't.

"I've got the best neuro tech in the Starways," Rex said. "And your Boss can't handle the competition."

Chezzie set down his beer. "That's just it. I hear your clients don't need drugs, there's no aftereffects—just a good, clean ride, best orgasm you can get off a sim-stim."

"No," Rex said, leaning forward. "Best orgasm you'll ever have."

Chezzie guffawed. "That's a bold claim, even for a talented girl such as yourself."

Wanting to appear bored, she checked her nails and gave him another shrug. But Niks knew the truth, feeling the same butterflies swarming her stomach.

"Who's building your gear?"

"An old friend."

"Gorsh-shit. You don't keep friends," he said, trying to hide an old hurt with another chuckle.

He liked Rex, Niks realized, sensing more of their complicated past. She shuddered as images of him leaving her gifts and sending her salacious texts swam across her mind. ...A little too much.

"And nobody builds tech like that," he added.

"Try a jacked vet with a specialty in cyber-ops and too much time on his hands."

"You don't say," Chezzie said, eyes searching her face.

She's not lying... Niks realized. But she isn't telling the truth either.

Clicking her nails on the table, she sighed. "Just give the message already, Chezzie."

His eyes flicked to her messenger bag. "You carrying?"

"Why?"

"How 'bout a sample?" he said, putting his arms behind his head. "For an old friend."

"Right here? Now?" she said, waving her hand at the flimsy curtain dividing them from the main floor, and the circulating bouncers.

Chezzie nodded. "How much is this message worth to you? It's just as easy for me to call over those bouncers, get you dragged over to the SnakePit across the street..."

"Then you wouldn't get paid," Rex countered.

"You sure about that?"

Sensing her years of street-survival and heightened instinct, Niks expected, at the very least, a cool response, something that would buy Rex time until she formulated her escape. But as the bass throbbed in the pit of Rex's stomach, the subsonic pulses beating away loose ideas of caution or rationality, Niks discerned something ominous lurking beneath the surface.

Jigsaw pieces appeared, fell into place, forming a living picture of sights and sensations. Terror, paranoia crawled up her spine, quickened her breath and hammered at her heart. At thirteen years old, she didn't want to be in her own skin anymore. Looking in the mirror, orange-fire eyes no longer appeared beautiful and unique. Instead, she saw the flames of a monster hiding behind a humanoid mask, a curse that could not be lifted, even after thousands of injections that ravaged her from the inside and sickened her for weeks.

Oh, Rex…

And yet, the same evil her parents could not lift, that she could not resist, promised her survival, liberation from the torture she'd endured, a new life. One amongst the stars, far away from her family, protecting her from anyone who would ever dare grow close and discover her most devastating secret.

No one can live like that, *Niks thought, struck by the loneliness cocooned beneath the conditioned response to run farther, faster, and the even stronger, more dangerous desire that had been brewing inside her for months now.*

No, Rex—that's not the answer—

If she had any material presence, Niks would have pounded her fists against Rex's chest, shaken her by the shoulders, but she could do nothing as Rex succumbed to the insidious poison that had been circulating in her veins and hardening her heart.

"Alright then," she said, reaching into her messenger bag. She removed a wraparound visor that better resembled the Med Oculus rather than the clunky headgear Niks had seen the other sim-stim junkies wear. "You know how my game works?"

"No," Chezzie chuckled, regarding the visor before setting it on his head. Pointing to the compact battery and computational unit on the occipital curve, he asked, "Is this really it?"

"Yes." Reaching across the table, she clicked on the circular power button on the frame of the visor.

"Wait—why do you have one?" he asked as she slid a second visor over her own eyes.

"Other operators jack you with stims, give you some generic simulation, get you off with an artificial push. Mine has a more personal *touch*," she said, emphasizing her words with a seductive hint of a smile.

"Wait a minute—you're getting into my head?" he asked. "What, you some sort of leech?"

"You know me better than that," she said in a practiced tone. "My visor gives me a live datastream, I read your responses, tailor the game to your...needs."

"Ah. So the user's desires bring about the experience?"

"Yes."

"The Laws of Attraction..." Chezzie held the visor up, forehead pinched together. "Now I get the terrible name."

"Afraid to let me see what gets you off, Chez?"

"No," he said, securing the visor in place. "Just never had no operator watching—no, playing—in my sim."

"I'll be gentle," Rex said, touching the back of his hand. "Or maybe that's not your thing."

Chez recoiled at first, but gradually set his hand back down on the table. "For the record, I ain't into you no more."

Rex clicked on the power to her own unit. "We'll see about that."

Chapter 12

Light and sound pulled Niks forward, into another sphere of far beyond herself. Faces rushed past in a blur, an amalgam of sound crashed over her like a surf. Niks tried to come up for air, to find some kind of purchase as the world flipped inside out, and upside down. Instead, she funneled away faster, slaloming through the cacophony, until she hit a dead stop.

Where am I...?

Still reeling, Niks didn't recognize her familiar station behind Rex's eyes until caught a glimpse of the tattooed woman's reflection in the wall mirror. Instead of her hoodie, scarf, and jumpsuit, she wore a v-cut vinyl halter dress and boots that laced up to her mid-thighs. In her right hand, she held a riding crop which she tapped metronomically against her leg.

She looks like... Niks couldn't remember the word that Syra taught her years ago, at least not until she caught another glimpse of the mirror, orange eyes standing out against heavy black liner and shadow. A dominatrix.

Nothing looked familiar, at least not to Niks. The dimly lit private booth had been replaced by mirrored walls on all sides—even the floor and ceiling—and a king-sized bed in the middle of the room, situated underneath a golden chandelier. Chezzie, gagged, stripped naked, and tied down to all four corners of the bed, lay on the red satin sheets.

"What a dirty mind you have, Chezzie," Rex said, boots clacking against the mirrored floor as she circled around him.

Chezzie lifted his head, mouth straining around the red ball logged and secured into his mouth. His words came out in a slobbery garble, but Rex didn't need them. Even Niks heard them loud and clear in her own mind.

Get me out of this, you *baech!*

"Not yet. Not until you get what you asked for," she said, dragging the tip of the riding crop across his shoulder and over his head.

Calmer, she might have taken the time to absorb the knowledge available to her, but Niks couldn't help herself. She didn't want to like the feel of the high-cut vinyl dress, or the reaction she got out of

Chezzie as she climbed on to the bed, her breasts almost spilling out of her top as she kneeled over his legs. But she did. And she delighted even more as he hardened even though he closed his eyes, and fought against the cuffs.

"You're bad, Chezzie," she said, batting his length with the riding crop. He winced, tensing against his restraints, but no longer fighting them. She hit him another time, harder. The erection never softened, even as she hit it again, this time leaving a red mark on the shaft.

"You think you know what you like," she said, devilish grin spreading across her face as she pushed his length against his abdomen with the riding crop. Chezzie's eyes popped open, his cries muffled. Rex glanced over her shoulder at the man and woman she materialized at the foot of the bed. "But I know what you really want."

The woman had red hair that fell to mid back, and eyes the color of raw umber. Curvy and big-breasted, she stood with one leg crossed in front of the other, hand on her hip, the other reaching up for the man.

He looked older; silver streaked his dark hair, and deep grooves ran across his forehead. Still, his symmetrical face, molded from granite, strong and defined, dared anyone to question his virility. Nothing about him was small, especially the engorgement between his legs, intimidating and commanding in its fullness. Niks reacted to him—and her—nerves tingling, warmth spreading throughout her awareness.

Teela…and the man she cheated on Chezzie with? *Niks didn't get it. Why would seeing his ex-girlfriend with another man be a turn on?*

Salvia frothed from Chezzie's mouth, his face turning red as Rex stood up, allowing Teela to crawl on top of him. Through Rex, she sensed that his visible distress did not match the rising heat inside him.

What we want is not always what we can ask for, *Niks gleaned as Rex pushed him even further, squatting by his head and slapping his arms with the riding crop.*

"Do her from behind," Rex said, snapping her fingers at the couple. *The red-headed woman stayed on her hands and knees as the man positioned himself behind her.*

Uncomfortable, but unable to turn away, Niks watched as the man spread Teela open with one hand, and plunged in. Teela moaned, and with each thrust, her breasts bounced against Chezzie's chest. As he gained a steady tempo, she pressed into Chezzie, the friction of their bodies exciting him even further.

And Niks. Despite her conscious revulsion, something inside her continued to react, drawing her into the scene, even as Chezzie struggled against his restraints.

Sensing him nearing a climax, Rex walked back around, wedging her boot in between them and stepping on his shaft. He grimaced and tried to wiggle free, but Rex followed his movements. "Don't you dare."

The man behind Teela grabbed her hair, pulling her neck back. As he rode her even harder, Rex reached behind Teela, dipping her fingers in between her folds. Without taking her foot off Chezzie's shaft, she wiped Teela's scent, her wetness, across Chezzie's lips.

"You can't have any of this, ever again," she whispered, slapping the riding crop down on his forehead. Tears slid from his eyes and he writhed, in agony and pleasure.

I don't understand any of this—

And yet she did. Through Rex, through her eyes, forced open.

(Don't stop—)

Tormented by her own inner conflict, Niks fought against the swelling waves inside her, not wanting to see or feel Chezzie's fetish realized, partake in Rex's delight as she lorded over him, and, least of all, allow herself to find gratification in any of it.

This is all wrong—this isn't—

(James.)

—I can't—

(Why is this wrong?)

She sensed Chezzie's consent, and the careful craft and construction of Rex's virtual world.

(Maybe it isn't.)

Denying him a physical orgasm, throwing him in the face of shame and degradation, didn't put him down as she would have judged. Rather, it fulfilled a deep-seated desire he could not have otherwise put into words, ramping him into an internal frenzy as he succumbed to the denial and pain.

The man grunted as he gave one last thrust, releasing himself into Teela. With a moan, Teela collapsed on top of Chezzie, fluids dripped down her legs and onto his pelvis.

Rex removed her boot and smiled at Chezzie as he lay heaving for breath under the weight of his ex-girlfriend. "How's that for a sample?"

***

"Chak," Chezzie said, ripping off the visor and bracing the lip of the table with both hands.

Rex kept calm, removing her visor and setting it back in her bag. "I take it you enjoyed your ride?"

It took another several seconds before Chezzie caught his breath as sweat dripped down his face. He sounded giddy, his words rushed, mind in overdrive. "How... how did you know?"

Niks knew.

"Told you—best neuro tech in the Starways," Rex replied.

No, Niks thought, *still reeling from the ordeal from the shared hallucination. It's more than that.*

Chezzie didn't buy it either. "No—not possible. E-even I didn't... I didn't know that about myself."

With a shrug, Rex plucked the other visor from the table and placed it in her bag. "You said I had an 'uncanny ability to read people.'"

"But that—what you did to me—"

"Erotic humiliation?"

"—I've never done that before."

Rex twirled her finger in the air. "Is that a thank you?"

Blood rushed to Chezzie's cheeks as he squirmed in his seat. "Chak *you.*"

"Don't stress," Rex said with a casual wave. "I've seen—and operated—much weirder sims."

With trembling fingers, Chezzie ran his hands through his thinning hair, half-laughing as he rode out the rest of his rush. "Why are you here, Rex? With this tech you could own half the Starways by now. Why this small-ops?"

She's not in it for the money, Niks realized, *sliding along Rex's thoughts as the tattooed woman concocted a way to get around a direct answer.*

"La Raja suits me fine. At least before the occupation."

No. *Niks strained forward, listening, feeling her way through Rex's intricate web of self-made truths.* You're afraid of something.

Chezzie stole the drink he bought from her and knocked it back in one gulp. "I can see why Akanno put a note on your head. You're too hot for this world, Rex."

"I'll take that as a compliment." *Rex crossed her arms in front of her chest.* "Now—about my message."

"Alright, jeez," Chezzie said, still shaking as he fiddled with the ocular implants. He paused after popping one of his reflective lenses from the socket. "Hey Rex—I was joking about the death wish."

"Doesn't mean it isn't true," she said motioning for him to hurry.

Rex, *Niks called out to her in a voiceless plea,* why are you doing this?

Chezzie placed one of his reflective lenses on the table, followed by one of his implanted ears as he continued to mess with his augmentations. The sight of the circuit-filled socket, or the shallow, inflamed depression where his fake ear plugged in made Niks' stomach turn. "You always were a heartbreaker."

Rex didn't react to any of it, her voice cold and without regret. "Goodbye, Chezzie."

How can she do something so intimate to him, Niks thought, *and then dismiss him like that?*

"Stay safe, Rex," he said, choking back whatever else he had left to say. With a flick of his head, he sat up straight, spine rigid.

"Hello, Rex."

Rex shuddered, sending shivers through Niks. It wasn't Chezzie, but another familiar voice, this one deeper, smoother, with a heavy Korian borough accent. As he continued to speak, Chezzie's mouth made sloppy, exaggerated movements, like a puppet maneuvered by an unseen hand.

"Still alive, I hear."

Akanno… *Niks grafted, Rex's memory of him overlapping Chezzie's face. Instead of reflective lenses, she saw vat-grown eyes, tweaked bluer than blue, and platinum-blonde hair that belonged on a teenage raver, not on an octogenarian crime boss. Gold-plated teeth sat behind inflated lips, and a plastic-sheened smile.*

"My men failed to kill you—as did the bombings. How disappointing. You, a solo operator, in my city, insults me."

As Rex recalled the event, Niks recognized the alleyway, and the men that assaulted her right before the bombings. Anger and fear laced her thoughts, but Rex kept herself together, focusing on the message.

"But now you can serve a purpose for me, and in doing so, I will forgive this insult."

Go chak yourself, Rex thought, wanting to chuck the glass at the mule's head. But she calmed herself with a few breaths and continued to listen as Chezzie played out Akanno's recording.

"The Dominion's occupation not only poses a threat to the godich leeches, but to my syndicate. They have detained my best operators, seized two of my gear warehouses."

That got Rex's attention. Niks felt her heartbeat increase, her entire body tense, as she thought of Remy, and their defenseless motel room.

"I want Dominion intel."

Rex scoffed. "How the hell am I supposed to do that?"

The recording continued, Chezzie's head bobbing up and down. "Some of the officers patronize the 41st."

A three-dimensional map projected out of Chezzie's lenses and onto the table. "Take this tunnel, and seduce their men."

Rex studied the underground route. This is one of Akanno's drug-runner passages.

Even if she didn't agree to his terms, the information would still be handy to get to the far north side of the city.

"Do it yourself," *Rex said, grabbing her messenger bag and standing up.*

"This is something for the 'Laws of Attraction.'"

Rex lowered the bag and returned to her seat.

Why? *Niks thought, just as confused as Rex.*

"You are my enemy for a reason. Your game is unparalleled; it digs the deepest," *he said, his voice strained, as if he spoke through a clenched a jaw.* "Find out why they are here and I will let you live. Do not deliver, and I will jack you up on Diatox again—"

Niks cringed as Rex flexed her hands against the painful memory of her last kidnapping and beating. Then again, she hadn't been careful, dealing in Akanno's territory, and stealing clients right out of his stalls.

"...and this time, you won't get away."

Why do you have a death wish? *Niks thought, pained by the disregard in Rex's heart.*

Something electronic toned from inside Chezzie's mouth, and his head dropped forward.

Not wanting to wait for him to come to, Rex grabbed her bag and bolted out of the private booth.

Wait, stop—think about this, *Niks wanted to scream as Rex blew past the bouncers on the edge of the dance floor, and headed straight for the alley exit. As she slammed into the back door, practically taking it off its hinges, an alarm sounded.*

Chak everything, *Rex thought, pulling her hoodie over her head and slinking around the drunks in the alley moaning in their sleep,* it's not like any of this matters.

Yes, it does! *Niks cried out.*

The pulsing alarm followed her, as she hurried to the broken fire escape near the edge of the opposing building.

Hurry, *Niks thought as Rex launched off the brick wall to leverage herself up to the half-descended ladder. Her right palm struck the bottom rung, and she grasped on, her left hand slipping off. As Rex hauled herself up with one arm, the bouncers crashed through the back door, alarm wailing into the alley.*

Come on, *Niks panicked as Rex grabbed onto the second rung with her left hand and tried to swing her feet up. The alarm pulsed faster, tone sharpening into a shriek, as the bouncers closed in on the tattooed woman.*

A beefy hand closed down around her right ankle.

"Come here you ratchakker!"

"No!"

Niks bucked forward, careening half off the bed. As she kicked her legs, the feeling of a hand around her ankle dissolved into the taut feel of twisted sheets.

No—not now, she thought, distraught at the sight of the familiar mess of clothing on the floor, and the smell of Syra's perfume.

But the alarm persisted. Or at least that's what she thought as her mind settled back into its normal habitus, and she felt something vibrating around her wrist.

My wristband—

Pushing herself up onto her side, she unearthed her left wrist from the mess and looked at the flashing notification across the face.

Secured transmission

Unknown sender

Niks climbed back on to the bed, sitting at the edge, the alarm continuing to beep.

Rex?—

No, what am I thinking—?

She stared at the blue notification, transfixed.

It's probably James.

(Why did he have to wake me up now?)

Stomach knotted, she accepted the call.

"Niks."

Niks gasped, not expecting the hologram of Jin upper body to pop up on her wristband, and least of all the wide smile struck across her face.

"I heard you were worried about me."

"Jin—God—we're all worried about you," Niks said, bringing her wrist up to her face. The sight of her pulled down on her heart, eliciting an even stronger response than she would have thought. "What happened? Where are you?"

"I'm fine. The Dominion just wants to ensure my full recovery after using the Med Oculus. No one could have anticipated the side-effects of using the device on telepaths."

"No…" Her initial relief melted away as an unsettled feeling crawled inside her belly and weighed down on her gut. Something didn't feel right, even though Jin appeared rested and calm. "I guess they couldn't."

"Just tell everyone I'll be back as soon as I get treated," she said, her smile unabated.

Niks looked again at the call signature.

A secured line. The Dominion could be tapping into this.

Still, she had to know.

Is any of this real, or am I going crazy?

For her, for both of them—

For Rex, she thought, heart racing at the thought of her being caught by the bouncers.

With as much clinical tone as she could muster, she asked: "What kind of symptoms are you having?"

"Maybe later." Jin's smile faltered. "I want you to tell me about Yarri."

"Yarri?" Niks sucked in her breath, unsure of what to say next. Nobody knew about Yarri. At least she hoped not. The revenge she enacted on Syra's violent ex-boyfriend wasn't a story she told anyone, and neither did Syra.

Then how could she...?

As she fought with herself over the uncomfortable possibilities, she caught herself lowering her wrist, and brought it back up to her face. "Yarri... my God, that was years ago. Um, he was an abusive jerk that hurt my best friend."

"After they had an argument, he told her about his STD, right? And then he shoved her away and she fell on that glass table and cut herself?"

"Uh, yeah," Niks said, horrified that she could know so much. *Syra wouldn't share this with her—and I've never told anyone—*

—so how does she know?

Jin blinked rapidly, then asked with greater insistence: "Tell me about that prank you played on him for revenge."

"T-the prank?"

Nobody knows!

The idea sunk into her, hot lead pouring into her gut. *(But she does.)*

Then why is she asking?

(Keep going.)

Niks gave an uncomfortable laugh to fill in the silence between them. "Um, well, Yarri was in the neighboring dorm to us."

Jin said nothing, unusual smile still cutting across her face.

"So, after Yarri put my friend out—"

"Syra."

"Yeah, Sy," she said, jarred by her interjection, "I decided he shouldn't hurt anyone else ever again, especially since the police only gave him a warning."

Niks fiddled with her hands, looking away from Jin. "Syra told me he had a disorder that required he use a halo mod to sleep. I broke into his dorm while he was at practice and messed with the halo."

Jin's eyes widened. "Tell me about that."

"I just set a timer and prolonged the sleep-to-wake cycle so he wouldn't be able to tell if he was sleeping or awake."

"But everything would feel real to him."

"Yes," Niks said, noting the serious inflection in Jin's voice.

"Go on," Jin whispered.

As she recalled the rest, anger tinged her words. "I waited until he hit that prolonged cycle, and then I broke in again. I remember his eyes popping open—that look of terror on his face when he saw me in costume."

"What did you dress as?"

"The devil," Niks said, "the Old Earth kind; head to toe in black, a kid's plastic mask over my face. The cycle paralyzed the rest of his body, so he couldn't do anything, only watch. I used a voice modifier to lower my voice, held a fake butcher knife over his… you know…"

"Wow, Niks."

"Yeah, he was terrified; couldn't tell dream from reality."

"Couldn't escape the nightmare."

Niks felt a twinge of regret as she remembered him wetting himself. "But he deserved every bit of that nightmare. And I threatened to return every night as long as he abused women."

Jin's smile faltered. "I'm surprised, Niks. I didn't know you had it in you."

Shaking her head, she lowered her eyes. "I never want to hurt anyone." She paused and looked back at Jin. "But I'll do anything to protect the people I love."

Jin, no longer chipper, replied in her usual calm fashion. "Don't hide from that story, Niks. It's a good one. It tells you more than you know."

What? Niks thought, confused by the change in her tone and affect. Despite her confusion, she thought to keep her mouth shut, especially seeing Jin's eyes flick off-camera for just a fraction of a second.

"I've got to go. Tell the others not to worry. Goodbye, Niks."

"Jin, I—"

The transmission cut out, leaving her holding up her wrist.

Stunned, she sat on the edge of the bed, trying to process what had just happened. As the conversation replayed in her head, she pulled up the sheets around her shoulders.

Why did she bring up Yarri?

Her mind latched on to Jin's last words, repeating it over and over again in her mind: *"Don't hide from that story... It tells you more than you know."*

Wiping the tears from her eyes, she thought of Jin, James, and Syra. Then, Rex.

"I'm afraid," she whispered, pulling the sheets tight around her shoulders. But as she thought of Yarri, of the violent offender she turned into a whimpering kitcoon, she turned her gaze to the stars, remembering her own words: *"I'll do anything to protect the people I love."*

Lying back down on the bed, she held those words close to her heart, and wished for sleep.

Chapter 13

Several sleepless hours later, Syra returned, looking exhausted and spent, and covered in construction dust.

"*Chak.* I haven't been this tired since I did those brothers from Vetrius in the same night," she said, collapsing face-down on the bed next to Niks. Still wearing her surgical cap and scrubs, she didn't bother to move, even as Niks picked at her dirty top.

"Shouldn't you change?"

"Yes."

Not that she did. With a sigh, she turned her neck in Niks' direction. "Got something for ya."

Niks gasped. "You didn't."

"Oh, but I did," she said, fishing through her pockets and dropping a dirt-encrusted microchip onto the bedsheets. "Even though those Dominion bastards love their *godich* patrols."

Niks brought her legs and arms out of the bedsheets and examined the microchip in her hands. Only a few centimeters wide and coated in a reflective film, it didn't look like any data-storage device or processing chip she'd ever seen. "You think this came from the Med Oculus?"

"It's the only techy thing I found in that alleyway."

"It could be other neuro tech; there are tons of illegal ops in that area," Niks said, thinking of Rex and all the surrounding arcades.

"Well then—there's only one way to find out." Syra pushed up onto her elbows and trudged her way to the medical tote spilling out medical supplies over the sea of clothing. Muttering to herself, she rummaged through the heap of bandages, derm patches, and hemeboosters until she unearthed another bioscanner.

When she returned, Niks noticed accessory parts fused to the bioscanner she'd never seen before.

"What kind of mods are those?" she asked.

Syra took a seat next to her on the bed. "Stuff that helps me scan debris and keeps it unregistered."

"The geeks down in engineering?"

Syra winked. "A little flirting goes a long way."

"Since when is a threesome flirting?"

Bony knuckles popped her in the shoulder. "Do you want to crack this thing or not?" Syra asked as Niks rubbed her arm.

"I don't know," Niks said, staring at the microchip. Icicles formed in her stomach. "Maybe we should just destroy it and forget about it."

"But you want to be sure—and I didn't have time to do more than a cursory scan on Neeis."

"Yeah," Niks said, voice faltering. "…I'm just afraid of what's on it."

Picking up on her hesitancy, Syra scooted closer. "What are you not telling me?"

Niks brought her knees to her chest. "I don't want to get you more involved than you already are, Sy."

"You know me, baby; I go all the way."

Despite herself, a chuckle escaped. "Be serious, Sy; this is really messed up."

"Like the time you traumatized my ex Yarri messed up—or worse?"

"Worse."

Syra put an arm around her. "Then I'm definitely in."

"Alright," Niks said, handing her the microchip. "Let's see what's on there."

After tinkering with the unregistered bioscanner, Syra inserted the microchip into one of the dataports. The bioscanner chirped and buzzed, emitting shrill beeps Niks had never heard before.

"Whoa," Syra said, holding the bioscanner between them as compound data scrolled through the main screen. "The data transfer is incomplete; there must an incompatibility in the software—but it looks like there's an analysis projection."

With a deep breath, Niks whispered, "play it."

Syra hit the processing command, and a green projection field lit up before them. DNA helices, numbers, graphs and charts fanned out in three-dimensions.

"This is the Med Oculus' analysis of the last patient," Syra said, interacting with some of the data. "Wait—I thought you said you tried to help her, but she hit you and ran off? This shows that you performed a treatment…?"

Niks toyed with the bedsheets, trying to swallow the dry lump in her throat. "Yeah. That's right."

Tilting her head to the side, Syra sounded hurt. "Why didn't you tell me?"

"Because… I thought I was going crazy," Niks said, voice wavering. "I had used the Med Oculus on Jin and everything went fine—but not with Rex."

"Rex?"

"Her," Niks said, pointing to the helices.

Syra squinted, interacting with several of the reports. "Rex, huh? Well, your lovely friend is quite the patient. Look at the comparatives."

"What do you mean?"

"These stats make it seem like she's from more than one telepathic bloodline," Syra said, overlapping the blood chemistries and the DNA analysis. "Like this subX5—this says the Prodgies are the only known species to carry that rare gene mutation. And here, it highlights her mitochondria," she said, zooming in on data surrounding the bean-shaped organelle. "This is registering as the same variations as seen in the Moro priests of the Order of Cress—do those guys even breed?"

"I don't know," Niks said, overwhelmed by all the evidence.

"Oh! And a suspicious cluster of genes resembles some of the variations seen in the relatives of the Tre. And who knows what this is," Syra said highlighting an unreadable sequence.

"The bioscanner can't translate all the data," Niks tried to rationalize.

"Maybe. But there's enough evidence here to safely say she's a freak."

The accusation sparked a rush of heat that sharpened her tongue. "She's not a freak."

"Whoa, sorry," Syra said, holding up one of her hands. "But if she is of Prodgy bloodline, she'd have to be a freak to survive the transition."

"Transition?"

"You know all those weird squiggly marks on the old Prodgies?"

"Yes," Niks thought, remembering the trials of some of the Prodgy elders years ago when fears of the death-seeking Dissemblers first came to public light. She remembered their tattoo-like marks weaving around their limbs, and up their necks. Each

Prodgy had a unique pattern, at least according to the reports, and the marks and complexity of the patterns increased as they got older.

"Those marks show up when they come of age, kinda like our puberty. Supposedly it's a horrifically painful process, and no hybrid has ever survived the transition."

Syra's words carved straight through her, cutting down into a memory she didn't realize she had.

Voices came in hazy snatches, clips of harsh language contrasted by breathy whispers. Niks didn't recognize herself, or the searing pain branching through her body like a continuous electric shock as she writhed underneath the protection of a soggy cardboard box. Rain pelted her meager shelter, soaking through and dripping down on her face, the cold fall winds adding insult to her exposed skin. Passersby regarded her with indifference or disgust, but she didn't care, not with the fires burning up her insides, and her frostbitten skin screaming with every shiver.

"She was only fourteen..." Niks said, caught between two worlds. "She ran away from home, was living on the streets. She went through it all alone..."

A man dressed in ratty jeans and an old bomber jacket squatted down next to her as she shivered and shook. Niks recognized him, even without the implants. He had more hair, dark amber eyes, large ears that stuck out on either side of his head.

Chezzie—

"You want a warm bed, hot meal?" he asked, chewing on the end of a coffee straw. He offered her a hand, his fingernails yellowed from nicotine.

"Go to hell," she said through chattering teeth, and curled into a tighter ball in her cardboard shelter.

"Huh?" Syra said, fiddling with the bioscanner. "How do you know that?"

Niks shook her head as other wisps of memory filtered through. *As he walked away, she looked at the skin on her arms. No longer smooth and tan, discolored patches creeped up in odd patterns.*

Disgusting.

She was disgusting. A freak. No wonder her parents wanted to institutionalize her.

"Okay," she said, too quietly at first to get the man's attention. Then, with urgency: "Okay!"

"You know, there were a lot of invasions of Algar, the Prodgy Homeworld, about eighty years ago. Lots of scavengers and mercenaries raiding that world, taking a souvenir or two. Maybe one of your patient's relatives was an abducted Prodgy? It's the only explanation; the Prodgy law is strict—it doesn't allow for hybrids."

"Her grandmother," Niks said absently as familiar touches and smells ghosted her senses. *The smell of lilacs, an elderly, honeyed voice calling out to her across a meadow. A different mother and father, ones who's faces had been corroded by time, held her close as government ships blotted out the midday sun.* "Her parents were special too…"

Soldiers poured out from the mouth of the ships, guns hot. To a young mind, everything happened too fast; colors and sounds dissociated into chaos, mother and father torn apart by the pulse-fires.

"Run," her mother whispered, lifting a bloodied hand and pointing to the forest.

Even then, too young to understand, she did as her mother commanded. She ran as fast as she could, to the protection of the trees, to the shadows that would keep her safe.

"…But they were all separated. When she was found, she was adopted out to missionaries who wanted to give her a 'better life;' one free of telepathic corruption."

"How do you—?"

Niks hid her face, tears streaming down her cheeks. "I have to tell you something, Sy."

"Ok," she whispered, placing her hand on the back of her neck.

"I—I think whatever happened to Jin to make the Dominion want to take her away is happening to me."

"Like what?" Syra said, shutting off the bioscanner and pulling herself in even closer.

"She knew things about me—about the prank against Yarri—that she couldn't possibly know. And I…I know things about Rex, things that are crazy and impossible. And that's not even the start."

Syra held her breath, eyes widened.

Squeezing her hands together, she rushed out the rest before she could stop herself. "Every time I try to sleep, I see her. I'm inside her memories, or behind her eyes; sometimes I'm not sure. She's even come to me, when I wished for something I wasn't getting from James. Ever since…"

"…the Med Oculus," Syra finished, letting out her breath.

"Yes," Niks said, shuddering.

As the silence stretched out between them, worry and doubt pinched at her thoughts. *What if she doesn't believe me? What if I'm just going crazy?*

"I'm sorry, Sy, it's not real—"

"You can't go in that deep without feeling something more."

"Huh?"

Syra looked toward the window to the stars. "Everything always seems so far away, Niks. Even this," she said, touching the skin on Niks' forearm. "Another distance between us. But you felt inside someone; you felt their heartbeat, the blood rushing in their veins, all their hurt. Maybe what happened to Jin, to you, tore down those walls that separate us. It's an incredible gift."

A gift? Niks pressed her palm against her chest, feeling her own heartbeat.

"So," Syra said, glimmer in her eye. "Tell me about Rex. Tell me about these dreams…"

Flopping back down on the bed, Niks draped an arm over her eyes. "Oh my God, Sy."

"What?" Syra giggled. "Please tell me they were nothing but raunchy sex dreams."

Niks sighed.

"Oh hell yeah—tell me every detail," she said, poking her in the ribs until she relented.

"Ow—fine. Me and Rex. Rex and two guys. Rex and other women. Some crazy dominatrix cuckold scene. I can't keep track anymore."

"*Chak,*" Syra said, letting out a low whistle. "I like this chick already."

Niks rolled over, facing Syra as she told her the rest. "She's dominant, sexy, sultry, impossible to reach—or at least that's how she comes off to everyone else. But there's another side to her, one that I don't even think she realizes."

"Like what?" Syra said, lying down next to her.

Pausing, Niks thought back, reaching within herself, and then beyond, to memories on the fringe of her awareness.

"Why won't you ever give me you?"

Thea's words, filled with hurt, as they fought on the rooftop. Niks remembered the feel, the distance Rex thrust between them, even as Thea put forth her interest and affections.

Another memory percolated through, akin to the sentiment. A dingy motel room, no nightstands or dressers, a single flimsy mattress. Amber light streamed through the dusty blinds, onto the half-human, half-machine body lying next to her. Niks recognized his smell first, body odor and aftershave, before he turned his handsome face to her. Blue eyes full of longing and hidden grief, stared back as she sat up and pulled on a t-shirt and pants for a quick departure.

"That's it then?" Remy said, propping himself on one arm. The movement pulled the sheets down, revealing his artificial pelvis and grafted parts. From the looks of it, his sex had been reconstructed several times, but Niks couldn't get past the sheer size of it, and the smoothness of the synthetic skins.

"You were always the best—" Rex started, then stopped herself. Of course he knew that. Women—and the occasional man—paid him for his reliable services. But that's not why he slept with her.

Remy grunted, and pressed down on a mole near his hip. With a quiet whir of internal mechanisms, the erection softened. He didn't look back at her, not even when she got up and threw the rest of her things into her messenger bag.

"Come on, Remy. You're not stupid enough to fall in love."

As she reached for the door knob, he answered back, tenor voice quavering. "What do you know about love?"

Memories shifted, reformed. Niks found herself surrounded by books, most on the ground or scattered across a marbled surface, like a desk. Ink spills dirtied some of the pages. Now that she realized the memory, she remembered the library, and seducing Sam over the poetry of D. Fredrickson in the study area.

Now, post-sex, Sam lay across the desk, naked and heaving for breath, beckoning Rex to come back to her.

Rex did, but only to get one last look, one last feel of her warm skin against hers.

"'Distant stars and human hearts," Sam said, picking up a book and pointing to the passage. "Not so different, are they?' I love that line. It seems like we're all so far apart, but we're really connected, don't you think?"

Bristling at the thought, Rex faded a step back. Sam reached out to her, not understanding her sudden mood shift.

"You shouldn't get attached," she said, pushing Sam's hands away. Spite took form in heated words. "We shouldn't see each other again, Sam."

"She's used to seeing others, all their inner workings, what makes them feel fulfilled... It's how she's survived the streets, made money as a data hustler, and an operator. But she thinks no one sees her," Niks whispered. "Not like she sees them."

"Sounds lonely."

Niks dropped her gaze. "She is."

"Wow, Niks," Syra said, touching her hand. "I've never heard you talk like this."

Niks brought her knees and arms to her chest. "I judged her, wanted to hate her," she said, shifting her eyes away from Syra. Her parents' faces crossed her mind as old prejudices surfaced, then fell away. "She's a leech, a sexual predator—she's everything I've always been afraid of..."

"And yet...?"

Niks looked up at Syra. "She's done something to me... I don't want to wake up anymore."

Eyes misting, Syra reached over to Niks and took her hands in hers. "Oh, Niks..."

"What?"

"That's the realest thing I've ever heard."

With a smile, Niks held back her own tears as she squeezed Syra's hands. "What now?"

"We've got to destroy this thing," Syra said, sitting back up and reaching for the bioscanner.

"How?" Niks said as her friend removed the microchip and turned it over in her hands.

Launching herself off the bed, Syra ran over to the medical tote and dug out a cautery wand. A few zaps later, the stink of melted metals in the air, the microchip turned into an unrecognizable black lump.

"Good enough?" Syra said, presenting her with the smoldering remnants.

Niks smiled. "You're the best, Sy."

"I know," she said, tossing it into the trash compactor.

"Can you help me get back to sleep?" Niks asked as Syra crawled back onto the bed next to her. "I'm worried about Rex. Last time I was in her head, she was running from some bouncers."

"I don't know if you should take any more sleeping pills," Syra said, looking her over. "And even if I gave you more—maybe I should stay up and monitor you, just to make sure this weird connection isn't mucking up that silly brain of yours."

"Thanks, Sy," Niks said, pulling her in for a hug before sliding back under the bedsheets.

"You owe me a *night* of drinking," she said as reached over to the other nightstand and took out another packet of sleeping pills. Stifling a yawn, she flipped open the bioscanner and handed her the packet. "Maybe a few."

"Deal," Niks said, tearing open the packet with her teeth and dry-swallowing the pills.

As she rolled onto her back, anxious for the medication to take hold, Syra chuckled. "Sweet dreams, Niksy."

Blushing, Niks ignored her friend, pushing aside the potential of any invasion of privacy, and closed her eyes.

Niks slowed her breathing, concentrating on her heartbeat, and the one she imagined beating in synchronicity on the planet below. *Please be there,* she thought, anxious to feel her once again.

But as she drifted down into shallows of sleep, a Dominion insignia flashed before her eyes, and a gun barrel pressed into her abdomen. She couldn't move, pinned against a wall, a hand wrapped around her neck.

Niks screamed.

Chapter 14

Despite Niks' fright, Rex felt only amusement as the Dominion officer leaned into the gun barrel she pressed into the tattooed woman's abdomen. Some of the other patrons of the upscale 41st looked up from their drinks, others ignored the scene unfolding near the back wall next to the restrooms. Dominion personnel observed from the bar, but none came to the officer's rescue just yet, trusting that her distinct advantage in the situation would let her negotiate her own terms.

"Back off, scum," the officer said, spitting her words in Rex's face.

It took Niks a moment to orient to her shared environment, and their circumstances in the crowded bar. Dozens of conversations, pitched in loud voices to compete with the instrumental band on the stage opposite Rex, pounded against her eardrums. How did she get here?

In her last experience, Rex was running from the bouncers at another club after dismissing Akanno's offer. Now, pressed against a velvet wall, the loamy aromas of flavored cigars floating over the high-priced liquors and perfumes, she stood with a gun to her gut.

She escaped, *Niks thought, pulling from Rex's immediate memories of the struggle, kicking the bouncer in the face, and fleeing over rooftops, and down into the underground tunnels.* And came here...

But why? Niks didn't understand, especially after Rex's negative reaction to Akanno's demands. Then it came to her in the dark undulations of the tattooed woman's subconscious. A morbid curiosity—

She wants to know why the Dominion is here, too—

—a desire to look death in the face.

(She wants to know her own end.)

Shaken by the realization, Niks forced herself to concentrate back into Rex's immediate awareness. After noticing the bifurcated ears and yellow eyes of the Dominion officer holding the gun, Rex read the nametag affixed above the many medals pinned to her chest: Captain Aramov. She must be Norikan; priggish and ethnocentric.

Rex kept calm, even as Aramov's grasp around her throat tightened. Focusing on their skin-to-skin contact, Rex projected her aura, sending out waves of sexual energy that slipped down her hand and arm, warming Aramov's body.

That's not fair, Niks thought, *feeling the same pulsations coursing throughout her own body. Fright and shock melted away, and curiosity—longing—took its place.*

Grip faltering, the scowl across Aramov's face broke down into a confused knot. "I—I just wasn't expecting you to come up behind me."

"It's alright," Rex said, *freeing herself from the woman's grips, but not moving away from the wall. With a sly grin, she kept Aramov's gaze, each word spoken with cool confidence.* "I'm sure there aren't too many bold enough to approach a woman like yourself."

"What do you mean?" Aramov said, *lowering her gun just a little.*

Niks didn't know how Rex could take her time. Not that she would have ever found herself in such a situation, but she knew she'd have rushed things, probably mumbled some ridiculous response—not delivered each line with such poise and aplomb.

"You're in charge," Rex said, *running the tip of her first finger along the gun barrel to the woman's hand. Aramov twitched, but didn't pull back. Through Rex, Niks felt Aramov's enthrallment, her inability to draw away, even as her logical mind screamed at her to take action against the stranger.* "You're used to control, order, obedience—no surprises."

Aramov's lips trembled. "Yes."

Caught between Rex's mind, and her telepathic gleanings of Aramov, Niks surmised Rex's devious plan, and Aramov's distinct vulnerabilities. The officer, a smaller woman with graying blonde hair wound into a tight bun, hadn't allowed herself more than her military career, denying herself even the slightest of dalliances in the hopes of climbing the ranks to admiralty. But Rex could see past Aramov's callous front, into the swell of unfulfilled urges buried beneath the propriety of her world.

"You can never lose that, can you?" Rex said, *lowering her voice as she moved her other hand off the strap of her messenger bag and up, over the gun. Niks caught sight of her tattoos changing color, from dark blue, to iridescent purple as she touched the captain's jawline. Another wave of light and warmth flowed out of her fingers, and into Aramov's face.* "At least, not here."

Gasping, the captain closed her eyes and leaned into Rex's touch.

"No, I can't," she murmured.

"I can give you what you want," Rex said, leaning forward and whispering the words into Aramov's ear. *Niks shuddered, basking in the pleasure of split perspectives; Rex, thrilling at her position of dominance, seduction, and Aramov's, as she quivered in anticipation, her desires loosened from their hold, wanting only to submit.*

Aramov's voice caught in her chest. "Not here."

"No, not here," Rex said, touching her lips against the side of her cheek.

Slipping out between the wall and Aramov, Rex ducked into the restroom.

What about her? *Niks thought, then stopped herself, taken by Rex's confidence as she entered the last and biggest stall, turned around, and waited.*

Fifteen seconds went by. Thirty.

Good, *Rex thought, rummaging through her messenger bag to find the neuro tech visors.*

Niks gleaned Rex's intention: the other Dominion personnel would see Aramov alone, and voluntarily going into the restroom. No need to follow…

But will she come? She's so uptight and scared, *Niks thought.*

The bathroom door creaked open. Tentative footsteps followed, and the door closed, shutting out all but the metronomic thump of the string bass.

As the footsteps approached, Rex put one foot up against the wall, and leaned back, right hand still inside her messenger back, feeling the smooth rims of the visors.

Niks counted the rapid beat of her own heart as two black boots appeared underneath the stall door. The door swung open. Aramov, eyes trapped wide open, stared back at Rex for only a quick breath before rushing at her.

But Rex turned her head away from her kiss, not allowing Aramov the affections teased out in front of her.

"Not here," she said, cupping Aramov's cheek and holding her back.

"But—"

Rex brought out the visors with her right hand. Before Aramov could protest, she slipped it over the captain's head, and her own.

"I'll take care of you," Rex said, holding her close.

"But I can't—"

"Shhhh." Rex clicked on the power to both visors. "Just feel."

Niks lurched forward as light and sound once again propelled her into a different sphere of consciousness. Random fragments of memory and sound flashed through her, filling her with burning afterimages of drill formations, gunfire, and armored warships blazing through the skies. But unlike before, Rex didn't stop, even as they both gasped for breath amidst the chaos, pushing them down farther and farther, into the deepest layers of the captain's subconscious.

This is too far, Niks thought, her mind stretching over unknown boundaries. *We'll lose ourselves—*

Secret dreams and nightmares rose and fell in great color geysers, giving Rex all she would need to craft Aramov's sexual fantasy. *Then why is she still going?*

Terrified of the blinding separation as her mind and body pulled apart, Niks cried out, but just as Rex pushed them beyond the brink, all came to a stop.

Where are we? Niks thought as her sight adjusted to their new environment.

Thumbtacked posters of indie-electro bands adorned the walls. An action movie played on a mobile holodisk, stacked on the highest point of a messy desk. An antiquated lava lamp projected moody red light. Clothes everywhere—

No, not everywhere. On one side of the room.

This is a dorm room, Niks thought as Rex panned from left to right.

Aramov, rendered much younger, sat at the other desk that mirrored the first, though her side of the room stood organized, undecorated, neat. Hunched over a stack of datafiles, she couldn't help but glance up over and over again at the couple giggling as they fooled around under the sheets in the opposite bed.

Her roommate and her boyfriend... This really happened, *Niks realized, sensing Aramov's familiarity of the surroundings, and the event. But why would Rex take her here? I thought this was all fantasy...*

The answer came to her in a thought pressed close to her mind: Real memories evoke strong emotions, weaken inner defenses.

Niks gasped. Rex?

Aramov's hands shook as she cast her sights away from her roommate. "Why did you bring me here? Nothing happened."

Rex, fully realized as herself, stepped to Aramov, putting her hands on her shoulders. "I know. This isn't about what didn't happen; this is about what you've always wanted."

Walking to the bed, Rex peeked under the sheets at the young man and woman fondling each other. They didn't seem to notice her, even as Rex spoke over them.

"Ava, your roommate, and Jesh, your first crush. She brought him back on this night, and had sex with him while you were studying for your AP astrophysics final."

"Yes," Aramov said, still not looking up, tears in her eyes.

"But you weren't mad at her, even though you forced yourself to be. You and Ava were best friends; maybe more, if you'd have let yourself."

The couple in the bed stopped, looked over at Aramov. With a coquettish giggle, Ava called out to Aramov. "Come on, Clair; join us."

"What are you doing?" Aramov said, looking at Rex first, then back to Ava as she climbed out of bed and walked over to her in only her purple-lace bra and panties. Her lithe figure, and the attractiveness of her dark features, took even Niks aback. Black hair, even blacker eyes, made for an allure that would have challenged anyone's inhibitions.

Rex afforded Aramov only a hint of a smile. "Giving you what you want the most."

Ava kneeled in front of Clair, lights from the action movie dancing across her face, expression intent, but waiting for Aramov's invitation. In the bed, Jesh slid out of the sheets, pushing himself on both elbows, his chest and shoulder muscles flexing, awaiting her decision.

"This isn't real," Aramov whispered.

Rex countered. "Are you sure?"

Through the simulation, but more through Rex, Niks felt Aramov's desires awaken. So close to her now, Aramov smelled the familiar scents of her vanilla body rub, and the floral hint of her hair wash. All the missed touches and unspoken words Aramov had bound in assiduous secrecy from Ava, from the rest of the world—from herself—came boiling through in a heated rush. She reached out to Ava, fingertips grazing her warm skin, breath catching in her chest.

"I've always wanted—"

"I know," Ava said, placing her hands on her legs and pushing herself up to come face-to-face.

That's not Ava, Niks sensed, picking up Rex's confidence, her aggression, funneled through the avatar. Not that Aramov would notice as Ava kissed her lips. Aramov gasped, then grabbed her and pulled her close, relishing in the sweet taste, the soft wetness of her tongue against hers.

As Ava pulled her to the bed, to Jesh, to the attention the two of them would provide, Niks felt Rex's focus split. With Aramov so deeply immersed in the sim-stim, Rex turned to the captain's memories, a place that Niks gleaned Rex could not ordinarily venture. At least not without a sizable distraction, and a reason to risk the extensive reach into another person's mind—and worse yet, detection.

Caught in between the competition between worlds, Niks didn't know where to look. From Aramov's perspective, she felt Jesh's hands travel up her body, under her shirt and traveling over to the tops of her breasts. As he kissed her mouth, he tugged on her nipples, knowing just how much pressure to apply to make her gasp. Ava lent her talents as well, first removing Aramov's pants, then sliding underneath the sheets and between Aramov's legs. A curious tongue parted her, and took a long, savoring taste.

Rex's concern jarred her, pulling her away from Aramov as she moaned with pleasure. Niks didn't know how to interpret the confusion of information coming at her from every direction as Rex dove straight through the captain's memories. Conversations sang out over the sound of gunfire and boots smacking against broken cement. Airlock pressure doors and griddled steel overlapped the dorm room scene, skewing her senses. In one heartbeat, Niks felt

Aramov's surprise as Jesh's cock sprung up in her hands, and in the next, she saw Aramov regarding herself in the mirror with ascetic satisfaction as she twisted her hair up into a tight bun.

I'm not going to find it like this, Rex dismayed, flinging memory after memory aside. Walls came up as she dug deeper, preventing her any farther than the unguarded recollections.

Push her to the limit, Niks thought, feeling the heat between Aramov's legs.

Rex paused, then turned her sights back to Aramov. *Of course.*

(Did she hear me?) Niks thought, excited as Rex focused on Jesh, guiding his moves.

Switching places, Ava came up to Aramov, and pulled her onto her side as she kissed her again, this time holding her by the cheek. Jesh straddled one of Aramov's legs, positioning himself just against her bottom. But Rex wouldn't let him enter her—not yet. He teased her, rubbing his hand along her folds, slipping a finger inside, then teasing the tip of his cock against her opening. Aramov pulled her leg up, holding it with one hand as she held onto Ava with the other, still entangled in her kiss.

Frenzied, she broke from Ava and looked down at him. "Give it to me."

Rex guided the avatar of Jesh inside her. As he pulled back and plunged back in, he gripped her bottom and other leg, yanking her to him. Aramov muffled her groan, but when Ava slipped her hand between her legs, finding the hard bundle and circling around it with her fingers, she cried out.

In some remote sense of herself, Niks felt her own body react, warming to the sensations coursing through Aramov and interpreted through Rex. For a split second she thought of Syra, how her best friend might be looking upon her writhing body, but she didn't care—not then, with craving for release superseding all.

As Aramov grew closer to climax, her body tensing as the great wave within her gathered, Rex injected herself into Aramov's perceptions. Niks didn't know how she did it as she singled out the rising harmonics within Aramov. With practiced skill, Rex held down the chords, kept Aramov's muscles taut, preventing her release.

"Give me all of you," Jesh said, slowing his thrusts.

But it wasn't Jesh, or at least it wasn't the voice Niks heard. Rex spoke the words, lacing in her demands into every part of him, and threading them into Aramov.

"You have it," she said, voice breathless, on edge. She tried to reach for him, but Ava held her down, holding her face into her neck. "Take me. Please, take me!"

Take her! *Niks said, unable to stop herself. She felt it too, the tension of the urge, the part of herself that could not stand for any more delay in gratification. The need for both of them, inside her, a part of her, all bound together in the heat of passion, eclipsed all other desires, any sense of reason or caution.*

Rex's movement pulled Niks over for just a second, just as Aramov reached her threshold, her absolute limit, to the other side of Aramov's mind. No walls, no barriers surfaced as Aramov's entire being channeled into the fervor of her protracted climax. Rex zipped through, absorbing every dark scrap she could that once stood guarded, as she felt Aramov's pleasure turn to agony, threatening the very structure of their simulated reality.

No...

Rex gleaned it before her, but Niks reacted first, recoiling in horror as the truth unfurled within their shared inner dimensions. Secret plans flowered open, detailing the type of toxins to be released in Neeis' atmosphere, as well as the countermeasures.

This is how the Dominion treated the after-effects of the bombs so quickly—

More information bled through in poisonous colors: The flight patterns and refitting specs for two warships, both of which were rerouted weeks ago, in silver and crimson. Bombings that targeted non-telepath establishments and buildings fanning out in ashen grays.

Rex's thoughts echoed across Niks' mind: This was all planned. *The arrest of telepaths, the seizure of Akanno's gear, and the other illegal neuro tech—the entire attack.*

Niks couldn't wrap her head around it. What could the Dominion want with all those telepaths and neuro tech?

It hit her then, as their thoughts and fears merged together: A new angle to the war; something to upset the United Starways Coalition reign over the Starways.

We've got to get out of here, Rex thought, *flinging them both away from Aramov's mind.*

Give her release, Niks cried out, trying to hold Rex back from jacking out too soon. Wrapping herself around Rex's mind, she rooted herself in her own self-assurance and calm, trying to ease the tattooed woman's panic.

She couldn't be sure if she had enough influence to give pause to the operator, but Aramov found her climax, sending ribbons of ecstasy streaming through their shared reality as Jesh gave one last thrust inside her. Niks wanted to stay and bask in the convulsions, the exquisite freefall of fire and pleasure, but Rex hurried them through, disregarding her normal safety practices and jacking them out.

Ripping off the visor, Rex shielded her eyes from the bathroom lights, her eyes sluggish to adjust to the real world. Dull drill bits bore into her temples, but she didn't care about a headache, or the tingling in her limbs.

Got to get out of here—

Niks could do nothing as Rex stuffed her headpiece in the bag, and removed the other visor from Aramov's head. The captain, still reeling from her protracted climax and orgasm, mumbled and moaned as Rex eased her to the ground and propped her against the toilet.

"Wait...come back. Come back!" Aramov shouted, lifting her head from the toilet seat.

Rex rammed through the bathroom door, nearly taking out another patron as she bulldozed through the crowd and made her way to the backdoor.

It'll be ok, Niks thought, trying to get Rex to slow down to no avail. Nausea licked the back of her throat as Rex pushed open the door and spilled into the back alley, nerves still in shock from the abrupt sensory severance.

Rex made it another few meters, taking shelter behind a stack of wood pallets before succumbing to the tide of sickness in her stomach. Sliding down against the wall of the opposing building, she rested her head against the cold bricks, hugging her knees to her chest.

Rex... Niks wanted to do something, anything, as the tattooed woman allowed herself to be swept up into the dark storm of her own mind.

There's no way out of this, Rex thought, *digging her black nails into her legs enough to make Niks wince.*

Old memories seized the opportunity, reforming in both their minds' eye: Tight straps holding her down by the arms and legs, an op-light overhead. Crying out for her parents as needles bore into her exposed stomach, the pain lancing up into her chest and down her limbs. A man hidden behind a surgical mask and goggles standing over her, disregarding her cries as he took his endless notes.

I don't want this, Rex thought. *Disgust and shame potentiated the queasiness of her stomach. Gritting her teeth, she dug her nails in even harder, wanting to pierce through the fibers of her jumpsuit until she could see the red-colored satisfaction she so desired.* They can't have me again.

God, Rex, Niks thought, *sensing down to the roots of her words, to the dark under-layer of all she feared. Thea, Sam, Remy—her adoptive parents, real parents, her grandmother; all hobbled down by the singular fear that overshadowed her entire inner world.* This isn't the end.

Rex lifted her head as a curious kitcoon covered in bits of garbage debris sniffed at her boots. Chancing a bite from the feral animal, she touched its matted fur, needing something warm, something real, against her skin. It stayed, offering her a purr, and an insistent wag of its puffy tail for more than a pet.

But when Rex tried to pick it up, to bring it close, it hissed and scratched at her arm, and took off down the alley.

Disregarding the four beading red scratches on her right arm, Rex looked up to the break between the buildings, to the one star strong enough to shine through the light-polluted sky.

"Distant stars and human hearts...." she whispered. "What a joke."

But Niks saw through her bitterness, past all Rex's life experiences that gave rise to and confirmed her worst fears, to the part of that understood the connections Sam spoke of. After all, she could see the world for all its desires and needs—

But you aren't seen, Niks whispered.

Rex eyed a piece of scrap metal hiding under the last pallet next to her. Dark whispers arose from whatever animus she harbored, promising her the quick and easy solution she thought she wanted. She reached out for the scrap metal.

No, Rex—

Confused, Rex stopped. In that moment, she regarded her hands, but in her anger, saw only the evidence of her spoiled lineage. Cosmetic tattoos and color-changing augmentations covered up the Prodgy marks that emerged during her youth, but not for her. Still a half-breed freak—

No, *Niks cried out as Rex grabbed the metal scrap, sharpened edge gleaming from the hooded light above the 41st's backdoor.*

Rex held her breath, calling out to the emptiness she imagined beyond herself: No one can have me.

No! *Niks screamed as Rex brought the metal scrap above her chest.*

The soft, perfect feel of her grandmother's hugs; rescuing stray kitcoons off the streets. Sam's infectious laugh and Thea's dulcet voice. Watching the sunset outside of La Raja, near the east-side docks, while eating sushi out of takeout boxes. Remy's arms, holding her tight, as they lay in a restoration coffin together, re-patching after a tough run-in with the Takuzi. Reading books until way past midnight, imagining a world far kinder than this one. Family dinners, sharing a bed with her younger adoptive sisters. Memories blinded by pain that Niks brought forth, pressing them against Rex's sights.

I see you.

Rex lowered the scrap, but stopped when she caught her own reflection in the curved piece. Eyebrows pinched together, staring at the mirror image, she whispered: "who are you?"

"It's me," Niks mumbled as hands shook her shoulders. *It's me, Rex—I'm Niks. I'm here. I'm here with you.*

"Niksy, wake up—now!"

Eyes fluttering open, Niks couldn't tell one reality from another as the alley dissolved, and Syra's quarters reappeared. Her best friend kneeled over her on the bed, rubbing her knuckles into her sternum with one hand, empty hypobooster in the other.

"Ow, stop," Niks said, pushing her hands off. "*Chak*—I've got to go back."

"No time," Syra said, jumping off the bed and flinging random pieces of clothing at her. "Get dressed. We gotta go."

"Why?" she said, heart pounding in her ears. "What's wrong?"

The door chimed. Niks looked at Syra's face as her concern fractured into panic.

"Too late."

"Wait, what's—?"

No second chime came, only the whine of a manual override. Still bewildered from the abrupt transition, Niks couldn't tell how many Dominion soldiers poured into Syra's quarters, or what her friend screamed in her native tongue.

"Syra!"

Guns whistled, the air filled with electric charge. Niks cried out as fully-armored commandos grabbed Syra by the arms and bent her forward, then zapped her with a stun gun in the back of the neck. A white-coated figure stepped forward as Niks tumbled out of bed and tried to reach her best friend seizing on the ground.

"Nurse Rison."

Niks looked up. Yellow eyes with vertical-slit pupils stared back at her.

Maio—

Something pinched the back of her neck. Niks tried to paw at the site, but gloved hands blocked her attempts.

As the world around her grew dimmer, farther away, gray lips peeled back to expose a sickle of yellow teeth. "Sweet dreams."

Chapter 15

Niks drifted in and out, faintly aware of the cloudless night sky, or the vast liquid landscape forming and reforming like a restive sea. Voices, in the distance, came and went. Some, discussing her fate, others, ghosts from a different life, too garbled to understand. She didn't care about any of it, not as she floated along, delighted by the shimmering colors swirling by.

"It's you..."

Still floating on her back, Niks turned her head to the speaker. A familiar figure—tall, thin, and muscular, with a partially shaved head, blue and green-dyed hair draped over one side of her face—formed out of the pools of color and light. As she continued to take shape, Niks recognized the orange-fire eyes, the intensity of her gaze.

Rex.

"What's happening?" *Niks whispered, sinking down as the landscape around her slowed, then solidified. A black-mirror surface appeared, extending beyond both of them, into the infinitum of twinkling stars.*

As Niks' bare feet touched down on the glassy surface, she realized more of herself; how she only wore a simple white one-piece, and her body felt weak, cold. Where am I?

"I don't know. You a dream?" *Rex asked, approaching her with cautious steps. She shook her head, forced a laugh.* "Maybe all the sim-stims are finally catching up with me."

"No, I'm real. Is this?"

"As anything else," *Rex said, coming within a few meters of her.*

Niks had only ever seen her once in person, and then the occasional glimpse of Rex's reflection when she sat behind her eyes. Now, face-to-face, she couldn't take her all in, not at once. Angled cheekbones, full lips; the winding twists and intricate designs of her augmented tattoos dashing out of the breaks in her orbital jumpsuit. And her expression—assertive, poised—irresistible—framed by long, dark eyelashes and hint of eyeliner.

"Where are we?"

"Don't know," Rex said, taking another step toward her. "Thought I was asleep."

Niks tried to piece together what happened, access her last memories, but she couldn't hold on to much more than a sting behind her neck, and the sound of Syra's scream.

"Who are you?"

"My name is Niks—"

"You're the nurse that saved me in the alley..."

"Yes," Niks said, fidgeting with her hands. She wanted to do something—hug her, run away—everything, nothing, all at the same time.

"I know you." Rex stopped, then scrutinized her up and down. "I remember some kind of medical tent, a threatening doctor...hurting..."

"Dr. Naum," Niks confirmed. "He tried to get answers out of me."

"But I told you everything would be okay."

"Yes... Why?"

Rex shook her head. "I sensed it. Whatever was happening in that moment, Naum wouldn't find anything on you."

"Rex—"

The tattooed woman held up her hands, taking a step back. "How do you know my name?"

"Something happened back in the alley," Niks said, keeping her distance, "when I used a new medical device on you called the Med Oculus."

Rex assumed a defensive posture. "What's that? Advanced neuro tech?"

"I just wanted to help."

"So now you know my name—what else?"

Niks blushed. "I-I'm not sure how, but your abilities and the Med Oculus—it connected us. Ever since then, I've seen you in my dreams."

"So that's why...?" Rex trailed off, a look of confusion crossing her face. She continued muttering to herself, forehead knotting. "...Must have caused some kind of subconscious trigger..."

Running a hand through her hair, Rex collected herself, a scowl darkening her expression. "This is insane."

"No, Rex, it's not. Something real happened."

"Impossible."

Scoffing, Rex turned and walked away.

"You love sushi, even though you pick off half the rice."

When she didn't stop, Niks dug deeper.

"You hate love stories, but you can't stand tragedy. You find modern day prose too pedantic; you much prefer the aesthetics of the 21st century."

Rex chuckled and waved her off. "What, did Sam tell you that nonsense?"

"You have twelve other adoptive siblings, but no biological ones that you know of. You can't remember your real mother and father's faces anymore. The dark doesn't frighten you, but the smell of disinfectant does."

Shoulders pinching up, Rex stopped dead in her tracks. Slowly, she turned around, orange eyes narrowed. "How are you doing this?"

"You help stray animals before your help yourself. You think hightops are both fashionable and sensible footwear."

Rex stormed back to her, eyes ablaze. "How are you doing this?!"

"You know what people desire, what they need," Niks said, standing her ground even as Rex charged right up in her. "And you love giving it to them; it gives you a sense of control."

"Stop," Rex said, grabbing her by the collar.

"No—you don't want to believe me," Niks said. Terrified, she blurted out the next thing that came to mind: "I know the truth behind the Laws of Attraction."

Rex laughed. "Is that right?"

Closing her eyes, Niks firmed up her voice as best she could. "You charge a high price, but you don't operate that sim-stim for the money."

"Then why?" Rex demanded, yanking her in close.

Niks opened her eyes, staring straight into the orange fire. "It's your only way to feel close to people."

Rex's grip dissolved; she took a step back.

"Your stomach," Niks said, reaching out, only to have Rex pull away even farther. "It still hurts where they injected you all those times. You won't let anyone touch you there, and yet it's all you crave."

After stumbling back a few more steps, Rex stopped, and crouched down to her knees. Niks kneeled down, but didn't advance.

"Rex, please," Niks said. "I know you've seen me, too..."

"This can't be real," she whispered, bracing her head.

"You—the sim-stim operator—really believe that?"

"A connection like this isn't possible. No reputable operator would tell you a reverse feed—or whatever the hell this is—could happen."

"And yet here we are," Niks said, raising up both hands, looking up at the celestial sky. "Dr. Naum, the tent—that was real. You helped me. Please, Rex..."

With tears in her eyes, Rex looked up at her, tentative at first. "You hate it when James calls you Nikkia."

"Loathe it," she whispered.

Clearing her throat, she continued: "You write left-handed, but played football right-footed. Eating anything six hours before a launch makes you nauseated. You once thought about being an artist, but you met your best friend in an intro to medical sciences in undergrad..."

"Yes."

"James has never made you orgasm."

"Well, ok, but—"

Rex's brow furrowed. "You hate telepaths..."

Niks sat back on her heels. "Rex, I—"

"Not just hate... Willing to aid the Dominion in their false incrimination and imprisonment."

"Rex, please, it's not like—"

"No amount of catches will bring your parents back," Rex said, getting up to her feet.

Niks rose, maintaining her gaze. "You know why I did the things I did."

"That doesn't excuse you." Rex sharpened her tone. "You've hurt hundreds of innocent people already—and now, with this way to identify them—"

"I never meant to hurt anyone," Niks said, voice breaking.

"Your parents weren't killed by telepaths." Rex pointed to her head. "You remember the bombs, the rioters, the chaos—but who did you see chanting over their bodies?"

"I don't—"

"A Prodgy."

Niks squeezed her eyes shut as the memory came flooding back to her. The man holding the flag, his Common weighted by a thick accent. So little then, she only noticed the flag he waved, not the fresh marks weaving around his arms and hands.

"He tried to save them, to bring them back. But you didn't see that. You just saw a telepath—a leech. Someone easy to blame."

"I'm sorry, Rex," she said, tears sliding down her cheeks.

Niks expected further berating, expletives; an attack on the ugliness inside her. Instead, Rex lowered her voice and replied: "What do you want?"

Niks didn't know what to say next, how to verbalize the tension building in her chest. Wiping away her tears with her palms, she tried to understand the butterflies in her stomach, the sweat beading across her brow.

As Rex turned to leave again, Niks whispered: "For you not to go away."

Fixing a practiced smile across her face, the tattooed woman replied: "It doesn't matter what you think you know. Three minutes, three days—three hundred years in my head doesn't give you any right to me."

"Rex, please, don't do this."

"You should know better, Niks. I don't do attachment."

Niks' heart sank to her knees, not speaking the words that tore her right open. Too late.

"I'm going now," Rex said, faced away from her. "Don't follow me. And stay out of my head."

Farther ahead of Rex, in the liquid horizon, images of Remy, bloody and beaten, and their ransacked motel room streamed by. She also saw Rex, hiding in a bombed-out arcade, crammed underneath a knock-off sim-stim booth. Blood trickled down her forehead, and her jumpsuit looked ripped across the stomach.

"You're hurt—Remy's hurt—what happened?" Niks said, trying to come after her. But something happened to her feet. When she looked down, she saw them melting into the black mirror, her reflection blurring.

Rex turned her head enough for Niks to hear her, to see the grave expression in her eyes. "There are people coming for me now. Best you get out of my head."

"*Rex—*"

Other voices rained down from above: "I've overriding Commander Hickson's orders."

"But sir, she can't come out of stasis that quickly—"

"*Rex, please,*" *Niks shouted, trying again to run after her. She didn't dare look down, not when she felt herself sinking deeper, past her knees, into the black mirror. A chill ran up her waist, sending a shiver throughout her body.*

A familiar voice, authoritative, harsh, rang in her ears: "Do it, now."

"*Don't go!*" *Niks shouted as the tattooed woman melded into the liquid horizon.*

Looking down, she couldn't keep from screaming. She'd sunk down to her hips, ice scales forming up her chest and into her shoulders.

Rex, *she thought as the world around her folded inward.* I wouldn't ask you to—

Up to her neck, a cold she'd never felt before splintered her bones and cracked open her skin.

—love me back—

Drowning in a world of icy-blackness, Niks held on to one last thought: Just let me stay.

Chapter 16

"Let me stay… Let me stay!" Niks said through numbed lips.

Niks tried to open her eyes, but shut them against the sting of the overhead lights. Movement felt impossible, her limbs sluggish to her commands, immersed in ice water.

Rex? Where are you?

"BP 176/85, Heartrate 150," someone announced. "Injecting 0.5% cryotine."

Niks gasped as her diaphragm contracted and her frostbitten veins spasmed.

"Not so fast—"

"Stop—please," she cried as the muscles in her back, legs and arms cramped. Craning her neck back, she felt the tug of monitors attached to her chest and carotids, felt the sloshing of cryofreeze against her deadened skin.

A husky, familiar voice interjected. "What's happening? Status report."

Niks opened her eyes again, her vision fuzzy, but good enough for her to distinguish the blue shell of her cryotube, her white one-piece freezer suit, and the technicians tending to her overhead.

"She's coming out too quickly. We have to put her back under."

"No." Niks turned her head toward the familiar voice, seeing the muscular outline and cut jawline of the speaker standing over her to the right. "I gave you a direct order. Revive her now."

James?

"Increase cryotine to 1%," the lead technician ordered, hanging another bag of fluid on the IV stand. "Get the cardiac stabilization kit ready."

Don't crack into my chest, she panicked. Once frozen, now her limbs felt too hot, as if filling with molten lead. She couldn't slow her breathing, even as her lungs overinflated and screamed for release. She had to get away from the terrible liquid heat churning through her veins and burning up her insides.

"She's going to arrest," one of the technicians said.

"Tresed," she said through gritted teeth. When the technicians didn't respond, she pounded her fists against the cryo tube. "Tresed. *Tresed*!"

"Uh—try 2mls of Tresed."

Seconds ticked by, monitor alarms shrieking in the background. She felt all of the eyes in the room on her, even as she kept her own shut, trying to will her pounding heart down out of overdrive.

Come one, she thought, praying the benzo/anti-convulsant derivative would work.

Finally, a brisk liquid poured onto the fires in her limbs and core, cooling her back down again. The tension released her chest, and she took a ragged—but satisfying—breath.

"There's my girl." A firm hand patted her on the forehead as she fought to regulate her breathing. "Just relax, babe."

Irritated but relieved, Niks cracked open her eyes again. James leaned in over the cryotube, his baby blues right in her face. "You're going to be okay."

"Sir, we need to titrate her down."

"Leave us," James said, not taking his hand off of Niks' forehead. "Now."

"But sir—"

"*Now,*" he said, sharpening his tone.

The two technicians left, one fiddling with one of the IV pumps before exiting out to the obs and maintenance station.

"God, I was so worried," James said, removing his jacket and then taking hold of her right hand.

Of course—he wouldn't want to get his uniform dirty.

"I came as soon as I heard."

Throat scratchy and dry, she motioned for water, but asked the most pressing question. "What happened? Why am I in a cryotube?"

With one more pat on the forehead, James disappeared from sight, but returned with a paper cup half-filled with water. Niks accepted it, and his help to sit up, as she guzzled it down in one swallow.

"Now may not be the best time for that."

"James," she said, scrunching up the paper cup in her hand. "I need answers."

Glancing over her shoulder at the obs station, James returned to her, voice just above a whisper. "All bioscanners—even refurbished and unregistered ones—have a default trigger to upload any and all information on telepaths to the Dominion server."

Niks bit her lower lip. *Of course.* Chak. *How stupid could we be?*

"The Dominion knows about the patient you treated with the Med Oculus, and about her unusual bloodlines," James said, voice hardening. He paused, blue eyes full of hurt. "Why didn't you tell me?"

"I didn't want you to worry. Or any of this," Niks said, rubbing the tops of her thighs, trying to restore normal feeling again. Her skin tingled, but she could flex and relax her muscles. "Am I captive like Jin Idall now?"

"No, you're still aboard the *Mercy*," James said, jaw muscles tightening. "I stopped your transfer to the *Ventoris*."

"At least your good for something," she muttered.

"What?"

"Where have you been?" she said, voice rising. "Or are you part of this conspiracy?"

"Nikkia, you don't understand—"

"I understand more than you think," she said, ripping off monitors and disengaging IV lines.

"Hey, I'm on your side," James said, trying to get her to slow down as she braced the sides of the cryotube and tested the strength of her legs. "Otherwise I wouldn't have risked waking you—or taking you away."

Niks snapped her head to him. "Why would you take me away?"

Glancing over his shoulder again, James returned to her, a grave expression crossing his face. "Rogman is coming."

All the air left the room. Niks shuddered, her mind spinning in ten different directions. *Rex—oh God—the telepath hunter is coming—*

What will we do—?

What will I do?

How can we escape the Dominion?

"...And he assigned a 'priority one' tag to the arrest and retrieval of your patient, and to your transfer to the *Ventoris* for further investigation by Dr. Naum."

"No," Niks said, shrinking down into the cryotube.

"I'm here for you, Nikkia. I don't believe any of the *gorsh-shit* pseudo-science they're using to detain Jin Idall, or justify arresting and freezing you. I can understand why you didn't think to tell me about treating that patient—but you would have told me if there were side-effects…"

The last part sounded less like the statement, and more like a question. With concerted effort, Niks brought herself up to a sitting position, unable to look James in the face.

"What now?"

"I need to get you out of here as soon as possible," he said, typing in something into his wristband.

"Where's Syra?" Niks asked, throwing a leg over the side of the tube. She noticed another dozen or so cryotubes in a row to her left, all occupied and tagged. Unlike the cryotubes used for the rotating crew shifts, they used higher doses of cryofreeze to keep their occupants in the deepest sleep, and a full lockdown mode to prevent escape upon revival. She also didn't recognize the extra monitors rigged over the head of each tube, recording data waves she'd never seen before.

This is the detention center—

"Wait, babe—not so fast."

As James helped her out of the cryotube, avoiding her question, details of the assault trickled back in: *Soldiers pouring through the door, guns charged, Syra screaming. A burning smell in the air. Her best friend seizing on the ground, something stinging the back of her neck. A white-coated figure, yellow eyes with vertical-slit pupils.*

Maio, Niks thought, holding on tight to the lip of the tube, remembering the charge nurse's terrible smile as she whispered, *"sweet dreams."*

"Where's Syra?" she said, this time grabbing onto James' shoulder.

James took both of her hands in his and held them together. "She's safe. Now, come on."

On shaky legs she followed him over to the storage lockers and retrieved the t-shirt and underwear she had been wearing when attacked in Syra's quarters. James also fished out a pair of fatigues from the next locker over as she shivered and dripped blue cryofreeze all over the tiled floor.

"Just follow behind me," he instructed as she peeled off the one-piece freezer suit and donned her clothing. While slipping his jacket back on, he added: "and don't say anything."

Niks stayed close as he led her out of the cryo unit and through a locked area guarded by Dominion soldiers. Seven months back she'd visited the detention center to bail Azzi out after his verbal spat with Syra in the Cantina, but she didn't remember as many guards, monitoring cams, or mobile analysis terminals linked to the obs station.

How did any of this happen so fast? she thought, avoiding James' hand as he tried to help her onto a lift.

Hugging her arms chest, she tried to keep her balance as the lift whizzed down the corridors and up the vertical transfer shafts.

"I've got you," James said, steadying her from behind as she tipped back.

Niks shrugged him off. "I'm fine."

"What's your plan?" Niks said as the lift dropped them off at his quarters. She followed him inside, not surprised to find an outfit laid out on his bed, including her least favorite bra and panties, and an old pair of combat boots.

"Is that a Dominion uniform?" Niks said, picking up the blue and silver top. "I'm not wearing this."

"It'll be easier getting you out on a Dominion transport," he said, blocking her from the dresser as she tried to pull out her own set of clothing.

Pushing him aside, she dug through the dresser. "*Godich.* Where the hell are all my thongs? *Chak it,*" she said, selecting a pair of scrubs and changing outfits. "I'd rather take my chances in an escape pod."

"Nikkia—"

"Stop calling me that," she said, whipping around. Her fury transmuted into shock when she saw him down on one knee.

"You mean so much to me. These past four years have been perfect. And now, with your contract with SOHO expiring in two months, I would like us to travel the stars together."

"Are you proposing to me?!" she said, backing up into the dresser.

"Yes. I'm in love with you." Reaching into his pocket, he produced a felt box, and cracked it open. A white-gold band with an outsize diamond sparkled at her. "I see our future together."

"Our future. You mean with the Dominion."

"Of course," he said, still holding up the ring. "We'll get this cleared up with the Dominion once I can get you to Central Command and explain the circumstances. Rogman has no right to transfer you to the *Ventoris,* or put you in the hands of that sadist, Naum. You're not a telepath, and you aren't sick."

She shook her head. "James, I can't do this."

"I can help you," he said, removing the ring from the box and reaching for her hand.

"No," she said, jerking her hand away. The expectant look on his face, the way he still reached for her, the garish diamond—

"There were side-effects," she blurted.

James lowered the ring. "What?"

Sliding down the dresser, Niks came to rest in a sitting position just across from him. "I'm sorry."

"What kind of side-effects?"

Letting her head fall back against the dresser, Niks closed her eyes and forced out the truth. "Her name is Rex."

"That patient?"

"Yes. And yes, she's a telepath."

"Nikkia, this is serious—"

"I know," she interjected. "And I can't explain why every time I sleep I wake up inside her head, feel her emotions, hear her thoughts—why I should even think any of it is real…"

"Is that why you've been so distant?" he said. He chuckled, then assumed a more authoritative tone. "Babe, it's a mind trick."

She stopped herself, shocked by the words perched on the tip of her tongue.

I don't want to hurt him…

But seeing his face, the defiance, the insular world he created that would prevent him from hearing the truth, she knew of only one recourse.

"It's more than that."

"What do you mean?"

Niks touched the back of his hand holding the ring, feeling the strength, conjuring the feel of his gigantic palms bracing her hips or holding her cheeks. "I… have feelings for her."

James pulled back the ring, out of her reach. "I don't understand."

"I care about her. Deeply," Niks whispered, relieved and terrified she said the words out loud. Shaken by the truth, she couldn't help but tear up again, helpless against the swell of emotion bursting from her heart.

"Maybe you are sick," he said, rising to his feet. "This is what Jin Idall reported—false visions, feelings—"

"I'm not sick," Niks said, standing back up and grabbing his hand to keep him from walking away. "And neither is Jin. We've experienced something—something incredibly powerful and wonderful—that's changed everything."

"And what is that?"

"Real connection. Seeing a person without walls, experiencing them for all that they are, all their beauty and darkness, unfiltered, raw, genuine."

James eyed the door, as if gearing up to run straight out. Instead, he took back his hand and steeled his blue eyes to hers. "I can't hear this, Niks. Don't force me to turn you over to Rogman."

"I'm not forcing you to do anything, James. But I'm not going to lie to you to spare you what you don't want to face."

"What then? You want me to choose between my career and us—and you're telling me that there might not be 'us' anymore because you're infatuated with some leech you met a days ago? I have a promising career, Nikkia," he said stabbing a finger out at the stars. "Hickson gave me the transfer notice yesterday."

"Transfer notice?"

"Next month I'll be transferred over to the *Callieo*. I'll be Fleet Commander Varkanian's second officer. This is a huge opportunity."

"Well, don't let me stand in your way," Niks said, blowing past him and picking up her slip-on shoes near the front door.

"Nikkia!" he shouted after her as she ran out the door.

"Take care of yourself, James," she said, hopping onto a passing lift.

Without a wristband, Niks inputted the command codes manually to get the lift to change course.

Only one way out of this, she thought, directing the lift to the lowest levels of the *Mercy*.

As the lift passed through to the sub-levels, she inputted one last command into the transport, accessing the ship-wide communications net.

Sy... she thought, writing out a secret message to her best friend. She could still hear her scream, goosebumps popping up across her arms as she recalled the sound of Syra's body convulsing on the ground. She thought of Maio, the evil delight in her voice, the pleasure she must have taken arresting the two of them.

Then it struck her.

Hopefully just arrested.

Pressing her hands over her chest, Niks dared not entertain the terrible possibilities ravaging her heart.

Please be alive.

Chapter 17

"Thank God you're okay!" Niks said, throwing her arms around Syra the second her friend walked into storage room E.

"Ow, careful."

Niks pulled back, but still held on to Syra's shoulders as she looked her over. "Oh, Sy—your face—"

"It's nothing," Syra said, holding Niks' hands away as she plopped down on the end of one of the exam tables crammed up against the wall.

"That's a terrible black eye—and you tagged your chin—"

"Eh," Syra said, shrugging her shoulders, "at least I got some of Meow's beak."

Niks walked over and hugged her friend again. "I was so worried. What happened to you?"

"I got to enjoy some quality time in our lovely detention facilities," she said, squeezing her back.

"How'd you get out?" Niks asked, sitting next to her.

"Dunno. Maio made it sound like after interrogations, I'd be frozen. But they just let me out, I got your message, and came here. No escorts, no nothin'. I even got off an email to SOHO complaining about these bastards and their treatment of us."

Niks frowned. *The Dominion wouldn't just let her go.*

"What about you, Niksy?"

"I got frozen," Niks said, raising a hand to demonstrate the tremulous after-effects of the rapid thaw.

Syra pulled down on Niks' eyelids, turned her head from side-to-side. "You should be in medical."

"I'll be fine," Niks said, lowering Syra's hands. "Sy—I saw Rex in cryo."

"What? You mean they froze her?"

"No—I saw her while I was under. I think she was asleep too. We finally connected face-to-face. Well, sort of."

"What happened? What did you guys do?" Syra asked excitedly.

Niks gripped the ends of the table, trying not to let herself get upset again. Still, her words came out in halting breaths. "She's..."

"I don't do attachment—"

193

"*—Stay out of my head.*"

"…tough. She pushed me away."

Syra put a hand on her shoulder. "From everything you've told me, it sounds like this chick wouldn't be able to handle something like this."

"What do you mean?"

"The connection you guys have. She's used to being in control, Niks."

"But she can see me, too; she should know how I feel."

Syra looked at her, chestnut eyes searching her face. "How do you feel, Niks?"

Tightening her hands around the end of the table, Niks held her breath, uncertain of how to tell her best friend the truth. "Sy, I—"

"Syra! And Gods, Niks!"

Reflexively, Niks grabbed on to Syra as Decks, Dr. Nara, Azzi, Vyers and several other SOHO staff members burst into the already cramped storage room. Decks barreled in for a hug, holding the two of them as she continued to spell out her relief. "I didn't think we'd see you guys again. Not after what happened to Jin."

"MMmfff." Syra pushed Decks' shoulder away from her mouth and tried again. "Did you get my message?"

"Yes—I got everyone I could together," she said, nodding toward the rest of the group. Niks could see a few people around the door and outside.

"What's going on?" Niks asked.

"We're getting out of here," Syra said, typing something on her wristband. "Before the Dominion arrests any more of us."

The others piped in, agreeing with Syra's notion.

"On a transport?"

"No, the Dominion has those locked out," Azzi chimed in. "Gonna have to steal a lifeboat."

Syra nudged her and leaned over to whisper in her ear: "That's the only reason he's here."

"Come on, Sy, you know that ain't it."

"Shove it, Azzi!"

"Don't start you two," Decks said, putting herself between the warring exs.

"Right," Niks murmured back. Although Azzi was the lone SOHO pilot and only person skilled enough to override a lifeboat's automated system to circumvent remote shutdown and navigate them out of the docks, she doubted Syra's sole intent, even as her best friend flipped him off.

"Come on," Syra said, pushing her way through the crowd and out the door. The lift that brought the ten other staff members still hovered in the hallway. After climbing aboard, she motioned for everyone else to join. "Stay close—and let me do the talking."

"You sure that's a good idea?" Niks whispered to her.

"You sayin' I don't have diplomacy skills?" Syra said, hugging up against Niks as the lift went over max capacity.

Niks looked down at Syra chest, to the alterations she made in the neckline of her scrubs so that tops of her breasts popped out. Pressed up against her, the warmth of her body, the smell of her sweet vanilla lotion, she sighed. "Nevermind."

With a click of her tongue, Syra hoisted her breasts up a little higher. "Gotta trust the girls."

The lift got as far as the emergency access corridor before Dominion soldiers flagged them down. Two fully-armored commandos guarded the lifeboat oval access port, while an officer and a cadet reviewed a charter file.

"What are you going to say?" Niks asked as the guards redirected the lift to their position.

"Hell if I know," Syra muttered back.

Outfitted with shoulder-mounted guns, reinforced black-plated armor, and full head gear, one of the commandos addressed the SOHO staff: "Present your wristbands for identification."

"*Chak*," Syra whispered, shuffling Niks behind her as the commando scanned each of their wristbands with a sensor on his glove.

"Who's in charge?" the Dominion officer said, looking up from his datafile.

Niks couldn't see over Dr. Nara's shoulder, but heard her friend speak up. "Me."

"ID?"

"Syra Gaoshin, RN-level 3."

"We don't have any crews going out from this dock, nor at this hour," the officer said.

The second commando circled around them, scanning the rest of the group.

How can we get out of this? Niks thought, rubbing her bare left wrist.

"You. Identification," the commando said, pointing to her as she tried to hide behind Azzi's giant frame

"Lieutenant, we're the relief crew for day shift 1," Syra said, grabbing Niks and pulling her to her side. She leaned over, spreading her chest. "And we're returning this citizen back home."

"In scrubs? All citizens are transported via docking bay 1," the officer said. Pursing his lips, he looked Niks over, red eyes dilating. "Don't I know you?"

Niks had never seen the officer before, and from the looks of all the ribbons on his chest, she guessed he might have come over from the *Ventoris* or the *Callieo* to monitor their crew. *What if he accessed the crew roster?*

No—he couldn't have memorized over 500 faces, she reassured herself. But when he cocked his head to the side, flitting his triangular ears in her direction, she realized his species.

Marmos—

And that he could more than likely hear her rapid heartrate.

"Retinal scan on that one," the officer said, snapping his fingers at the commando.

"Sy," Niks whispered, nudging her friend.

"Faint," Syra said, yanking down on her wrist.

Buckling at the knees, Niks allowed herself to fall, though she didn't get very far. Azzi grabbed her by the armpits and lowered her down as Syra shouted at the others to get into gear.

"She's coding again. Hey—get a medkit!"

Niks tried to relax her body, but the feel of so many hands checking her wrists and neckline made her squeamish, even though they were her friends and co-workers.

"There's nothing wrong with her—get her up," the officer said, slapping his hand against the lift railing

"Is that your expert opinion?" Dr. Nara said. "She's going into cardiogenic shock—we need to get her into a restoration tube, now."

"Then take her back up to medical."

Someone slapped her cheek and rubbed on her sternum. *Ease up!* she thought, fighting the urge to yell at whomever had gotten overly aggressive.

"No time. There's a restoration tube on the lifeboat. Take her now."

A shuffle ensued, but Niks kept her eyes shut, even as the team shouted for the commandos to get out of the way and allow them onboard.

"What's the problem here?"

James.

She heard him, somewhere down the hallway, coming toward them along with the whir of another lift.

"These SOHO personnel want unauthorized access to the lifeboat."

"In case you're forgetting, lieutenant, this is a SOHO starship."

"Under Dominion jurisdiction."

"I authorize it."

James...

A long silence. Hands and arms grabbed her by the armpits and legs, lifting her up.

Niks heard the click of door locks, saw the flickering of lights behind her closed eyelids. *We're aboard.*

"Wait—hold that one," the officer said.

"But I'm part of the team—"

Sy!

Without thinking, Niks opened her eyes and twisted around to see the commandos holding up Syra at the portal entrance to the lifeboat.

"What's the issue, lieutenant?" James said, hopping off the lift.

"Her name is flagged. This report says she was just released from detention, but there's no reason listed—"

Everything happened too fast. Azzi lunging forward, breaking the commando's hold of Syra's arm and pulling her inside the lifeboat, shielding her with his massive body; Dr. Nara screaming as the commando's raised their guns and took aim.

"Sy!" Niks said, wiggling out of the hold of her co-workers and falling to the floor as shots fired.

Everyone else scattered, hiding behind structural pillars or running to the front of the lifeboat. The air filled with smoke and electrical charge. Shouting and more gunfire rang through the portal door, but Niks couldn't see through the haze.

"We've got to get out of here!" Decks shouted.

Hurling herself at the panel lock, Niks pounded her fist against the seal, and the door clamped down.

"Azzi!" Sy screamed.

Niks took one glance at Azzi, then went into action, helping Syra out from underneath him and then returning to his side.

"Oh God, Niks—is he—?"

"He's alive," Niks said, pulling apart his shirt to reveal the smoldering wound that penetrated through his back and out his left upper chest.

Decks came running back, med kit in hand. Outside the lifeboat, sirens alarmed. "Hey, we've got to get out of here, now, before the entire dock shuts down."

"Starting a low-dose zetine drip," Niks said, breaking open the kit and searching for a IV startkit.

"Are you sure? He's tachy," Decks said, applying derm-stabilizers to the surface of the burn.

"Yes; he's compensating. That'll change in less than a minute."

Niks went through the motions, but even as Dr. Nara came over to direct their resuscitation effort, a sinking feeling settled into her gut.

We can't revive him too quickly, not without killing him, she thought as Syra fought through her tears and listed off his crashing vital signs.

Reinforced metal arms pounded on the lifeboat portal door.

"The commandos are trying break through," Vyers said, rushing over to the panel lock and inspecting the readout. "We've got about thirty seconds before they crack the locks."

As Azzi's life-signs dipped again, Niks vocalized her concern: "We have to keep him under or he'll arrest."

"Who else can pilot the ship?" Dr. Nara said as she rescanned his chest and administered another round of medications.

"Niks?" Syra whispered, wide-eyed and trying to keep herself from panic.

She's right. Not knowing any other recourse, Niks closed her eyes and reached out. *Please...help me. Help us.*

Silence.

Despairing, Niks opened her eyes, expecting the same scene—Azzi, supine and blanched, most of the medical team around him in a frenzy trying to resuscitate the pilot before the Dominion crashed through. Instead, she found herself ducking into the cockpit of the lifeboat, and taking a seat at the controls.

"What are you doing?" Decks shouted from across the fuselage.

She'd never piloted a ship in her life, nor did she recognize any of the controls. But somehow her hands knew which buttons to punch and levers to pull, and how to interact with the holograms popping up on her right-hand console.

Rex?

"Override automated pilot?" the ship asked.

Oh God no—

She swiped the red button on the holographic interface.

Vyers took a seat beside her, strapping in and gripping the armrests until his knuckles turned white. "You know what you're doing?"

NO—

But she nodded, keeping her eyes trained on the closed bay doors as the lifeboat lifted from the docking clamps and floated toward the exit.

She punched the request to open the bay doors. Then again, but no response.

They're not going to let us out, Niks thought, eyeing the control station occupied by two Dominion traffic regulators. And jumping within the *Mercy* would destroy the ship, a sacrifice she couldn't fathom.

"Clear!" Dr. Nara shouted from the back. Through the wail of the external sirens, she heard the sound of an electrical discharge.

Come on, she thought, eyeing the control station again, heart thumping against her chest.

Then, she saw him. Appearing disheveled, James came up behind the two traffic regulators and dismissed one from his console. Niks held her breath, watching as he typed something into the control panel.

Stomach tightening, she pressed her hand against the window. *What are you doing, James?*

He glanced up, blue eyes reddened, lips pressed into a tight line.

The bay doors opened.

Why?

"Yes!" Vyers said, clapping his hands together as Niks throttled them through.

As Niks guided them to the safe zone for the first jump, twin vipers appeared off the port bow, closing in on her path.

"Uh, Niks—"

"I know," she said, eyeing the flashing lights on her scanners.

Two signals appeared on the ship's com, one from the *Mercy*, the other from the *Ventoris*. As she reached to answer the hail from the *Mercy*, she stopped herself. *He's already made his decision. And I've made mine.*

Niks withdrew her hand.

"Missiles fired. Evasive maneuvers recommended," the computer announced.

"Niks—!"

Ignoring Vyers, Niks looked down at the jump sites, not knowing what to punch. *Where do we go? We can't go to any of the preregistered coordinates or they'll find us—*

No answer, no invisible pull guiding her touch.

Oh God, Rex, please—not now.

"Just pick somewhere!" Vyers shouted as the internal alarms blared.

Please, Rex, she called out, watching as the Vipers' missiles close in on the lifeboat. *Don't give up on us.*

Exhaling all the breath left in her lungs, Niks let her mind fall back and away, allowing her fingers to fly, inputting calculations she couldn't have known herself. With eyes closed, she hit the punch.

Chapter 18

"How's Azzi doing?" Niks asked, coming up beside Syra and putting her hand on her shoulder. Her best friend didn't move, staring at one of the three slanted restoration tubes in aft compartment of the lifeboat. The rest of the team that had escaped from the *Mercy* gathered in the midship, tending to minor injuries and resting as the engines recycled for the next jump.

"Stabilized. Dr. Nara thinks he'll pull through," Syra said. Muttering to herself, she veered off in her native tongue. "What a dumb *pin'yahto grehia...*"

Niks looked over the graphics readout to the right of the occupied restoration tube. Vital signs, blood chemistries and counts read low, but within sustainable range, as the automated guidance system assisted repair of his wounds.

He's still pale, she thought, looking through the transparent glass. But his pulse remained steady, strong, even under chemical sleep. *The big bear will pull through.*

She wasn't so sure about her friend.

"How you holding up, Sy?" Niks asked, still holding on to Syra's shoulder.

Turning to Niks, her hands in fists, Syra blurted out: "Why'd he do that, huh? Almost got himself killed."

Niks wrapped her arms around her, holding her friends until the tears stopped.

"I can't really say I'm a relationship expert," Niks said as Syra dabbed at her eyes. "But for all the trouble between you two, I'd say he still cares a lot about you."

"Yeah, well, he's still a big oaf who doesn't know what's good for him."

"I'd say he made a good call," she said, poking her friend in the side.

Syra shook her head. "He makes me so mad. When he wakes up, I'm going to tear him a new one for being so stupid."

"Before or after touching his—"

Syra smacked her on the arm.

"Come on, Sy," she chuckled. "I see it."

"What?"

"The fire between you two."

"Oh, there's fire," she said, crossing her arms. "And he'll answer for this."

"What—for saving your life?"

Syra's arms loosened, fell to her side, and she looked down at her feet. "*Chak...*"

"At least you have fire. There are worse things."

"Like what?"

Niks looked over to her left, out of the rectangular window framing the unfamiliar stars twinkling in the distance. "Predictability."

One of Syra's hands wrapped around her arm. "Oh, Niks... I'm sorry."

"Don't be. He thawed me, helped us escape," she said, thinking of James at the traffic control console, opening the bay doors to allow the lifeboat safe passage. "He even asked me to marry him—after, of course, telling me about his career opportunities."

Niks expected Syra to make some joke about 'Mr. Predictable,' or the trappings of relationship comfort and safety. Instead, she looked at Niks, curiosity in her eye. "So, whad'ja say?"

Niks shuddered. "I couldn't say yes. Not with everything that's happened."

"Really?" Syra said.

"The crisis on Neeis, the Dominion occupation, this crazy business with the Med Oculus... I'm not the same person, Sy."

Syra scoffed. "I love you, girl, but swear to God you haven't changed since freshman year."

Something sparked inside her as she gazed at her best friend, seeing the auburn ringlets falling over her shoulder, purple lipstick accentuating the generous curve of her lips. Heat surged beneath Niks' breastbone. She took in the blue tint to her Nagoorian skin, the high crest of her cheekbones; all the familiar features she'd known for years, and would never allow herself to realize.

Syra squinted. "What are you—?"

Stepping forward, Niks slid her arm around Syra's waist, and brought her other hand to her cheek. She slid her thumb across her cheekbone, cupping her jaw, and leaned in for the kiss.

Syra made a surprised noise, but didn't pull away, pressing back into her.

Finally—

The breath ripped from her chest as Niks let go of over ten years' worth of shame and regret, longing and unfulfilled need, and fell into her kiss. She pulled her in, holding her close, the familiarity of her touch, the love she'd known for the best parts of her life, coming through as she savored the intimacy of their exchange.

Niks pulled back. "Well?"

"Holy *chak*," Syra said, trying to catch her breath. A smile broke out across her face, and she gave her another quick kiss. "I am so *goddich* proud!"

"Thanks," Niks said, blushing.

"So all this—because of Rex?"

Niks hesitated. She thought of Rex, of the thousands of patrons she'd served with the Laws of Attraction, pushing past their paralyzing fears and secrets, to embrace true desire. "I don't know, exactly. But before her, I was so afraid to allow myself to feel anything."

Syra beamed. "You haven't changed."

"But I just—"

Grabbing Niks' hands, Syra held them close to her chest. "You're just not afraid to be you."

After a long hug, Niks pulled back again and stood arm and arm with her best friend.

"I'm happy for you, Niks, really. Maybe there's hope for me, too, yeah?"

Niks giggled. "As long as you're not aiming to become a demure, monogamous housewife."

A sharp elbow connected with her ribs.

"Haha, come on, how could I resist?"

Syra looked at her again, her annoyed expression softening into something else. "You know—I've never seen you smile like that before."

"Like what?"

Grinning, Syra pinched Niks' arm. "Just how much has this Rex chick gotten into your head?"

"Okay, come on—"

"No, look at me," Syra said, taking her by the shoulders and squaring herself to Niks. "What has she done to you?"

Chuckling, Niks tried to shrug her off, but Syra stayed firm.

"Tell me."

Niks thought of James, of him getting down on one knee, diamond ring sparkling in his hand, and Rex's warning: *"...get out of my head."*

"I'm scared, Sy."

"I know; this whole situation is *chakked*."

"No, I mean... I've never felt this way before."

Syra quirked an eyebrow. "So, you like her?"

"More than like," Niks whispered back, elated and frightened to hear herself admit it to her best friend. "I feel like a part of me is missing when she's not around."

"Whoa, Niksy. That's a first."

"I loved James—"

"Eh," Syra said, rolling her eyes.

"...but I convinced myself I was in love with him. This is different. With Rex, everything is wild, raw, in-your-face, imperfect, flawed, *hot*..."

She struggled to find the right words to encapsulate the emotions, fumbling with her hands, searching her friend's face for the answer as her cheeks turned red.

"It's real."

"Yeah," Niks said, curling back a loose strand of hair behind her ear. "...and it's terrifying, but I'd rather feel something—take a chance—than stay numb any longer."

"Finally," Syra snorted. Seeing Niks' frown, Syra covered her mouth and pretended to cough.

"But things are messy—she's in trouble, and she pushed me away. I don't know what to do."

Syra looked back at Azzi, and his still form inside the restoration tube. "You know why Azzi's still alive?"

"Good teamwork."

"That, and a good initial call. That zetine drip protected his cardiac cells when we had to deliver shocks."

"Thanks, but I don't see how that—"

"You're a sharp nurse, Niks. You've got good gut instincts. Keep listening to them. And I'll back ya' whatever you decide."

"Thanks, Sy."

Syra kissed her on the cheek. "I cannot *wait* to get you a drink. And don't you owe me?"

"Ha—yes," she said.

They both tipped forward as the ship jumped to the next site.

"Hey, captain Niks—where are you taking us?" Syra asked, steadying herself on the restoration tube.

Niks shook her head. "Apparently Spacey's Port in the Polaris System."

"Isn't that a dog soldier bar?"

"Looks like it from all the flags and warnings that popped up on the search."

"How the hell did you know about that place to begin with?"

Sighing, Niks looked out the windows at the kaleidoscope colors streaking by. "The same way I knew how to pilot this thing."

She didn't like how Syra looked at her, unsure if she was amazed or nervous. "Rex?"

"Must be," she said, grinding the ends of her toes inside her shoes.

"Wow, Niks..."

"I know, the irony, right? Me, the *ratchakker* nurse who hated leeches, the one who figured out a surefire method to screen out telepaths, saved by the very thing I've always feared."

"Well, that, yeah—but I'm just trying to figure out what we're going to say to everyone else. You know those guys are going to ask," Syra said, standing on her tip-toes to look out of the circular window in the door separating the two compartments. Dr. Nara and Decks tended to Choko, the other physician specialist, who had sustained burns to his neck and shoulder from the pulse fire. Everyone else either stood or sat on one of the three rows of benches, some skimming over the yellow survival packs attached to the walls.

"I don't want them to know," Niks said, shuddering.

"Alright, girl," Syra said. "But we better get out there and say something or nosy Ms. Deckers is going to start asking questions."

"Just tell them we were making out."

Syra snorted, and slapped her on the back as they stepped into the midship. "God-dang I like this aggressive side to you."

As they joined the others standing and sitting in the common area, Choko started a round of applause. "To Nikkia—nurse, pilot—what can't you do?" he said in a thick Salvada accent.

Niks blushed, but Syra stepped in before the compliments made her too uncomfortable. "You can thank her when we get to Spacey's."

"Spacey's?" Vyers exclaimed. "Like the pirate port?"

"I think they prefer 'dog soldiers'—pirates are more of a campy Old Earth thing," Decks corrected.

"Um, I don't think that's how Earth history reads."

"Look, whatever— it's mercenary hangout," Syra said. "At least they'll have some crazy booze."

"Nothing regulated," Dr. Nara added. "I would recommend a digestive panel before and after if you plan on libations."

"Goodbye, liver!" one of the techs chuckled.

"Hey, so, what's the plan?" Decks asked, setting down some bandages and looking around at the crew. "Get sloshed at Spacey's, mingle with the dog-soldiers, and hope SOHO gets a signal?"

"We have to alert SOHO to rescue the rest of the crew of the *Mercy*," Dr. Nara insisted.

Choko wagged his finger. "And Jin—those Dominion bastards can't have her. We have to do something about Jin!"

"Gods, Jin," Decks said, pulling her red hair up into a ponytail. "What happened to her? Do you know anything, Niks?"

Resisting the urge to look over to Syra, Niks replied: "I did talk to her over a secured line. She wasn't in distress; she said everything was fine."

"You know it isn't," Vyers interjected.

"No. That's why we're all here. The Dominion is very interested in the Med Oculus, neuro tech, telepaths—and they'll do anything to keep their plans a secret, even if it means taking our own."

"No *chakking* way," Decks said, squeezing a wad of gauze in her hand. "We can't let this happen."

"I got an email off to SOHO headquarters before we left," Syra offered. "I told them everything."

"You're assuming the Dominion filters will allow that to transmit," Dr. Nara said.

Decks stood up. "We have to *do something*."

A low chatter stirred amongst the group, but after a few minutes, all eyes rested upon Niks.

This is all on the fly—I don't know—

But before she passed off the responsibility back to a group discussion, she thought of her last conversation with Jin.

"Don't hide from that story... It tells you more than you know."

Why? she thought, still not understanding her cryptic message.

Then it dawned on her: Yarri, a bigger, more powerful enemy than her, and taking him down with the only advantage she had.

Dreams.

And doing it alone, without endangering anyone else.

Niks exhaled slowly, taking in the faces of her coworkers, her family, and made her choice. "I have a plan."

Chapter 19

"This is a hunk of junk," Syra said, racking her knuckles against the hull of the lugger. "I'm not sure you got your money's worth, Niksy."

Niks looked back at the captain extending his bandaged hand to seal the deal. In a hangar full of chopped and swapped spacecraft, the one he offered her in exchange for the lifeboat had to be the dingiest looking pile of scrap she'd ever seen. Graffiti and naked women adorned the sides of the ship, with other crude paraphernalia dangling from the inside of the cockpit controls.

"She ain't pretty, but that lugger's gotten us through hell. She ain't got no tracers, and can jump up to two systems."

"Any registered ID?" Niks asked, knowing that they wouldn't be able to land on Neeis without some kind of legal identification.

The dog-soldier captain smiled, incisors gleaming. "You gotta 'bout a dozen to choose from, little lady. Depends on what system you're aiming to cruise through."

Niks eyed the captain's first mate, a gigantic, blue-furred alien that hovered over him like a guard dog. *Is that a Talian?* He hadn't done much more than emit a low growl, but she could tell by the way the captain turned his head toward the sound that he got something out of his nonverbal communication. Keeping her voice firm, she added: "I need clothes, IDs, and weapons."

"Now that's getting greedy," the captain said, retracting his hand.

"That's more than fair. My lifeboat is worth at least triple of what you're giving me."

"Ah, but you're desperate," he chuckled, "why else would you arrive in such a vessel, and seek out a ship without tracers? And I'm going to have to strip that lifeboat down and dismantle the emergency beacons before whomever owns that ship comes looking for it."

Niks cheeks got hot, but, thinking of Rex, kept the emotion out of her voice as she eyed his bandaged hands again. "We're a medical crew. Those that are staying behind can provide treatment to you and your crew with what we have left on the lifeboat before you take it."

The dog-soldier captain kept his gaze, but shifted the weight between his feet. She hadn't intended on making him feel uncomfortable, but by the tone of his voice and the way he hid his hands behind his back indicated she'd hit some kind of hidden mark. "We'll take all your meds; maybe I'll have one of you look over the rest of my crew."

"Just leave a lifepack for my crew. Deal then?"

With a wink, the captain threw her the keys to the lugger. "I'll have one of the boys bring by a few sets of clothes, IDs, guns. Can't guarantee cleanliness."

Niks shuddered. "Fine. We're leaving in twenty."

As soon as the captain and the wolfish first mate left for the bar attached to the hangar, Niks returned to Syra's side.

"It smells bad enough on the outside," Syra remarked, lowering the ramp. A waft of air sighed out of the lugger's airlock, making the both cover their noses. Stomach turning, Niks thought of the unkempt party houses from college, especially toward the end of the school year, when the smell of booze, sweaty bodies, and whatever else fermented in the corners had gained dominance. "You sure about this?"

"Unfortunately," Niks said, stepping inside.

The lugger, a secondary transport that served as a shuttle to and from orbit for larger-capacity ships, would normally not serve their needs, but from what little Niks knew of space travel and starships, the dog-soldiers had clearly made modifications and upgrades to allow for other purposes. Any kind of seating comforts had been stripped down or ripped out, allowing for the oversized engine to poke into the main cabin.

Well, at least he wasn't lying about the jump drive, Niks thought, running her hand along one of the cylindrical blue cooling cells.

"How you figurin' on flying this thing?" Syra said, following her into the cockpit.

Pulling off some of the naked female figurines dangling from the overhead control panel, Niks sighed. "I'm still playing this as we go."

"That's not your style, Niks—and we can't do that if you're really planning on charging back to Neeis, sweeping up this Rex chick—and what's his name? Remy? Oh, and somehow rescuing Jin."

Niks brushed off the crumbs and whatever else dusted one of the two pilot's chair and sat down, hoping the answers would come to her as she stared at the ship's controls. "Either way, I can't stay here, Sy; I'm a danger to the crew."

"Come on, that's a little dramatic—"

"No, it's not," Niks said, turning to her. "The Dominion had a big enough priority tag on me to put me on ice."

Syra smacked the back of Niks' chair. "Well then, *chak* 'em, right? You and me have always figured it out together."

"Right," Niks said, fiddling with the controls as Syra took the seat next to her.

"Um, what's that?" Syra said, pressing a yellow flashing light on her control panel.

An alarm sounded from the back of the ship, and lights flashed overhead.

"No, not that—"

"That's the shield generator. Maybe that's the on button?"

"There's no on button for a starship, Sy—"

"You two might be the best nurses in the Starways," a rumbling voice said, approaching from the behind. "But arguably not the best pilots."

"Azzi!" Syra exclaimed, swiveling around in her chair.

"Azzi—you should still be resting," Niks said, standing as the hulking pilot ducked into the cockpit and clicked off a few buttons. The alarms silenced, and the flashing lights turned off.

"I'm a fast healer," he said, opening his jacket. Shirtless, he revealed the mismatched, bright pink skin on his shoulder and back.

"Then lay low with the others, Az."

"Lay low? Do you know Ali Deckers? That crazy red-head has already scared some chump in Spacey's bar into giving her access to his ship's coms. She'll call the USC, get us help."

The thought of not acting spread an ache throughout her chest. "I have to do this, Azzi. You don't have to come."

Azzi eyed Syra as he zipped up his jacket. "I know what I want."

Sensing the tension shift, Niks paused, waiting to see what Syra would say—or do.

"You stupid, big-headed, *assino*..." Syra mumbled through gritted teeth. Her knuckles blanched as she gripped the armrests of her chair.

"Maybe I am," Azzi said. "But I'd take a thousand more blaster hits just so I don't have to miss another day without you, baby."

"Sy—" Niks said, reaching out as Syra lunged at Azzi. For a split second Niks was certain she would hit him for making such a wild statement, especially as she cocked back her fist. But Azzi didn't move, even as Syra grabbed his collar with her other hand.

"Take it back, you big meathead—"

"I love you, Syra Gaoshin."

Syra's jaw dropped to the ground. Tears forming in her eyes, she covered her mouth with her hands, and backed away. "You can't do that."

"But I did."

"You *ratchakker assino*—"

Grabbing him again by the collar, Syra yanked him forward. At first, Niks thought they'd smack heads, but Syra planted her lips on his and locked her arms around his head.

"Mmmpfffff—"

"Shut up and kiss me," Syra said, surfacing for a second, but not letting him go.

Niks smiled, happy for both of them, even as they butted into the back of her chair and smashed her into the console.

"Okay, you two," she said, wiggling out of her chair and dodging Syra's swinging legs as she wrapped them around Azzi's hips. Eventually, she gave up, retreating to the midsection of the ship to let the two lovers have their moment. Rearranging her hair into a ponytail, she shouted to them: "I'll just wait for the rest of the delivery out here."

Not wanting to hear any more of the passionate noises coming from the cockpit, Niks stepped out onto the lugger's ramp. For a few seconds she looked for the dog-soldier captain in the crowd of other mercenaries before her gaze wandered up, past the circling starships and the rippling environmental shield, and out to the stars.

If Azzi and Syra can figure each other out...

She didn't dare think the rest. Not with so much uncertainty. Years of trauma and perioperative nursing taught her how dangerous hope could be.

And yet, as she gazed up to the stars, all of her fears gathering in the cold pit of her stomach, her words escaped in a whisper: "Distant stars and human hearts…"

***

Finding a sliver of space between an access panel and the scratched surface of the interior hull, Niks laid down and pulled one of the dog-soldier jackets over her torso. Under different circumstances, the musky stench, and whatever cologne was used to try and mask it, emanating from the leather would have made her queasy. But for now, it served to compete with whatever else had soaked into the speckled brown carpet, and stained the graffitied walls.

I'll never be able to fall asleep, she thought. Not with only two hours left until they reached Neeis, or with so much on her mind…

Minutes ticked by, but Niks kept her eyes closed, trying to relax her muscles in the tight space.

At first she thought the twinge in her back and the dull ache in her legs was her awkward position, but as Niks tried to reposition herself, her limbs wouldn't respond to her commands.

Why can't I move?

"Stop fidgeting."

Rex—

Light shafts breaking through the rubble illuminated the injured man lying before her on a bloodied tablecloth. Niks found herself crouched over him, back and legs screaming for reprieve, but she couldn't access him from any other position in the bombed-out arcade.

"You're intolerable when you're injured," Rex added, trying to get him to let her change the crude dressing across his stomach.

Remy grunted, but before he could do more than glare at her, his eyes drifted shut.

"No you don't," she said, slapping him on the cheek. "Stay awake, Rem. Come on—"

What happened?

She sensed Rex's pain, from the throbbing headache to the scrapes, cuts, and bruises up and down her body. Even though Remy's injuries looked severe, Rex didn't feel in great shape herself.

Calm down, Niks thought, *forcing herself to relax her mind and extend herself beyond her own boundaries. What happened, Rex?*

Images of Rex running through underground tunnels, alleyways, and across rooftop flashed through her mind, trying to get back to Remy to share the terrible information she found out after seducing Aramov. Hitting her head against a fallen lamppost, tripping and tearing open her jumpsuit only made her run faster. Her heartrate surged as she spotted the smoke chugging out of their motel, and the scout ships circling the area.

Remy—

Sticking to their emergency bailout plan, she found Remy, bloodied and wounded, three blocks away, taking shelter in a dumpster to avoid the biosweeps.

"Got ambushed," he said through cracked, swollen lips.

Rex hiked herself up higher over the lip of the dumpster. "Did you salvage anything?"

Remy flicked his eyes above his head.

Following his gesture, Rex found the camo backpack on the top of all the garbage, and the furry face poking out the top. A pitiful meow followed, and a struggle to escape.

Rex freed the kitcoon, watching it scamper off. "Come on; we can't stay here."

After relocating Remy to the bombed-out arcade, she went to the motel. Not that she didn't believe Remy, she just did had to see things for herself.

I'm so sorry, Rex, Niks thought as Rex *spied their motel room from the top floor of an evacuated apartment complex just across the way. Their motel window and half of the exterior wall had been blown out. From what she could see, everything—all their gear, supplies, her books—had been taken. Even the walls and floors had been stripped, exposing beams and moldy planks.*

Terror-stricken, Niks would have thought Rex *would have sprinted back, collected Remy, and made a desperate attempt to escape. Instead, she stared at the Dominion soldiers scanning the inside of their motel room with odd-looking, hand-held devices. The hopelessness she'd felt in Rex just after she learned the truth from Aramov sank its clutches back into the tattooed woman, and she leaned out of the window into plain sight, inviting the very personal disaster she feared.*

No, Rex—

But the thought of Remy jolted her back. She couldn't leave him, not when he would die alone in the arcade.

Stupid man, *she thought, racing back to him.*

And now, two days later, back in the devastated arcade, she watched Rex try to keep him from losing consciousness amongst the overturned tables and broken sim-stim booths.

Feel his pulse, *Niks called out as Rex opened up Remy's shirt to reassess his injuries. Old scars and fresh shrapnel wounds peppered his entire torso, but Niks was most concerned about his abdomen as Rex peeled back the old rags pressed into the bullet wound. The site oozed blood and a viscous, black liquid redolent of poisoned shock bullets. Rex had already dug out a casing, but some part of the projectile must have remained for the wound to take on the greenish hue.*

When she paused, Niks tried again, this time thinking of herself performing the action. Along his neckline—check there, then by his wrist.

Rex went rigid, her hands turning to fists. I told you to stay away.

Please, *she said,* let me help.

Just help him, *Rex thought, allowing for Niks' instruction as she placed two fingers into the notch along his neck. Niks felt his pulse, though slow and not as strong as she'd like. Same for the one on his wrist. Still, his skin felt feverish, sweaty.*

He hasn't gone into shock yet, *Niks said.* He'll need fluid and antibiotics, but first you've got to get out the rest of that bullet.

I know that, *Rex replied sharply, rolling up her sleeves and hovering a hand over the site.*

Niks thought to give her further instructions, but stopped as she sensed not only Rex's experience guiding her, but her other abilities she dared never use.

Closing her eyes, Rex slipped her fingers into the gunshot wound, feeling around the exposed tissue for the bullet remnants.

Uck, *Rex thought, squicked by the warm wetness of her friend's blood and viscera, and the way his hands twitched and jerked as she sunk deeper.*

You've got this, *Niks encouraged.*

Something shifted within the invisible connection that tethered them from across the stars. Niks fell forward, finding herself less behind Rex's eyes, but beside her.

There, Niks said, sensing Rex's fingertip brush along a round surface.

After pinching the round projectile between her fingers, Rex slowly withdrew, imagining the tissue around the site closing around behind her.

How are you doing that? Niks thought as the bleeding stopped. From what she had always been told, only a full-blooded Prodgy could perform any level of healing.

I'm full of surprises, Rex said, sounding more weary than anything else as she chucked the bullet over her shoulder. *Chak,* I hate blood. What now?

There's a SOHO supply drop not far from here. I can give you the codes to unlock the storage unit and you can get the supplies to treat the poison and give him fluid resuscitation.

Remy moaned, his eyes fluttering open. As his body tensed and he swung his arms at her, trying to guard his abdomen, Rex laid a hand over the site and closed her eyes again. Niks couldn't believe it, even as she sensed Rex soothing his screaming nerves, desensitizing enough of the area until he relaxed again.

That's amazing, Rex—I didn't know you could do that.

A few cheap tricks won't save anybody, Rex said, wiping her bloodied fingers off on the tablecloth under Remy. *Emptying out the camo backpack of what few possessions he managed to save, she slung it over both shoulders.* Show me where to go.

Niks thought to say something of Rex's fatigue, of the need to tend to her own injuries, but sensed the argument would go nowhere, especially with Remy in such bad shape.

Shoving aside one of the single booths, Rex revealed the hole in the side wall of building and crawled through. The air traffic noise, previously muffled by the inside of the arcade, assailed her ears with the thunderous rolls of vipers streaking across the skies and the low drone of scout ships circling lower, across the devastated areas of the city. Rex scanned the back alley, keen eyes looking for any sign of movement amongst the ruined buildings, ears trained to discern any unusual sound. Niks didn't like any of it—the blood-red glare of the sun's afterglow reflecting off broken panes of glass, the bleak emptiness of buildings, the hostility of fractured asphalt and cement. No mewing kitcoons, no insect sibilance—not a single pigeon taking wing across the late afternoon sky.

Everything around her felt abandoned, dead.

Head to Linbarry street, Niks said, trying to keep her nerves out of her voice.

Staying under any cover she could find, Rex cut through blasted walls and skeletal remains of the buildings on the block, high-tops crunching over empty bullet casings and broken glass. The breeze carried dust swirls and the lingering smell of bombs, but Rex kept her attention trained to any sign of the Dominion patrols.

Is that it? Rex said when she spotted the ten-meter storage unit dropped in the middle of an empty street. A few pop-up treatment tents still remained near the unit, but from the few loosed flaps fluttering in the wind, both Niks and Rex deduced the medical teams hadn't been back in at least a day.

Yes. The code is 791997.

Niks heard an echo of Rex's disbelief leak through, and doubt double her already pounding heart.

This is real, Niks said, trying to reassure you. This will save Remy.

Rex took a tentative step out into the street. Then a second. Extending her senses, she didn't detect any biological presence nearby.

Rounding the supply drop, Rex found an access panel and hesitated. A wrong code entry could sound an alarm, take a retinal snapshot—perhaps even deliver a paralyzing shock.

Trust me, Niks thought, opening herself up, her intention, to Rex.

Inhaling sharply, Rex entered the code. The storage door slid open.

Guess this means you really are real, Rex said, scooping up armfuls of supplies before Niks directed her to what she would want.

Are you always this bossy? Rex asked, stuffing her backpack full of antibiotics, dermpatches, boosters, fluid bags and prepkits.

Says the woman who possessed me to fly the lifeboat.

Rex pinched her shoulders up and muttered a string of swear words. But as she formulated a more coherent retort in her mind, a scream pierced the empty street.

Skin prickling, Rex zipped up her pack and slung it around her shoulders, ready to bolt back to the arcade. But when the scream came again, this time punctuated by expletives in Korian accent, she stopped in her tracks.

God, that's so loud— *Niks thought.* Where is it coming from? I know that voice.

Boss Akanno.

She shouldn't care. In fact, she should run as fast as she could. But Rex didn't. If Niks hadn't been injected so deep into her head, she wouldn't have understood her motives.

Akanno would never allow himself to cry out like that, even if tortured, *Rex thought.*

Unless the torture was too great.

Rex followed the sound two blocks east, keeping an eye on the scout ships about a kilometer away to the south.

There's Dominion activity here, *Niks pointed out, trying to get Rex to acknowledge the boot prints in the dust, and tank tracks ground into the street.*

You think that's bad? *Rex said, walking sideways through a narrow passage between buildings to accommodate her broad shoulders. As she emerged, she directed her sights to what was once a city park. Now, flattened out and stripped bare of any vegetation or plant life, drone ships circled the new Dominion encampment.*

Turn back, Rex.

The sheer number of troops, the drones buzzing through the air, the rows of Dominion captives being loaded onto a grounded transport—

This is the worst place we can be right now.

Ignoring her warning, Rex climbed over a slab of canted cement and crawled behind one of the last standing pillars to a brothel. Waiting until a pair of drones zipped past, she peered through a mish-mash of uprooted wire and foundation. About ten meters ahead, under a partially open tent, Akanno sat tied to a chair. Blood dripped from a laceration running across his forehead, and his right eye had swollen shut, but Rex's gaze fixed on the glowing collar wrapped around his neck.

What's that?

Shock collar, *Rex replied.*

Niks spotted a man dressed in a high officer's uniform inside the tent, black-gloved hands clasped behind his back, give a nod to one of the soldiers standing next to Akanno. The soldier holding a remote pressed a button and Akanno shrieked and bucked against his restraints.

He's lost his *sycha,* Rex said, *watching as Akanno slobbered and screamed, eyes dancing in their sockets.*

Niks grafted what she meant by the surge of emotions and memories that overlapped the present: her own torture under Akanno's men—the injection of Diatox, the beatings, pain magnified a thousand-fold, enough to make the strongest person break—

The high officer nodded again, and the soldier standing to the other side of Akanno held up something to his mouth as he screamed. Speakers placed around the entire park, projected toward the rows of prisoners and out to the city, let the entire world hear his suffering.

Brutal, Rex said, *but her thoughts carried a more complex realization. The intricate protocol of the streets, the need to for a boss to be terrifying, commanding, indomitable—meant that a fracture like this would be completely ruinous.*

But Niks saw another side to it: the way the captives didn't resist their restraints, hurrying on to the transports, cowering as one of the most feared crime bosses in La Raja buckled to the tyrannical Dominion.

Rex—I'm coming for you, Niks said, *projecting the image of the lugger as the shocks stopped, and Akanno wept in his chair.* Please, just go back to Remy and stay safe until I can get you.

As Rex took one last look, the high-officer leaned to Akanno, whispering something in his ear. The crime boss's head lolled side to side, drool sliding over his lips and dripping down onto his sweat-stained shirt. As the officer signaled the first soldier, Akanno perked up, sputtering his response.

Close enough now, Rex heard his words *before the second soldier held up the mic for all the world to hear.*

"R-r-r-ex."

The high-officer leaned in again, delivering another message. When he turned around, Niks saw his vicious face, and the thick mustache above his upper lip. No empathy, no compassion reflected in his eyes; only cruelty and domination, all the bleakness of war.

Rogman—

"*Rex—he's c-coming for you.* Chakking *run—run, no, God—*"

Another shock split apart his words, this one longer than the previous. Akanno's screams tore through the city. Rex covered her ears, but she couldn't protect them from the agonized sound, and the truth that blazed through his torments.

Rogman will stop at nothing.

Niks panicked, and even in the remote distance, her arms and legs charged for the run. But Rex didn't budge, even as the screams died off. Instead, she took another look. Akanno had passed out, and the high-officer waved his hand at him in disgust.

Then, a familiar stature stepped out from behind Rogman, passing off a set of datafiles. Niks gasped as Rogman accepted them before departing the tent, allowing them both to see his blonde hair and blue eyes. James.

What is he doing there? *Niks thought, confused as he removed the shock collar and repositioned Akanno's neck and head to prevent respiratory obstruction.*

He doesn't look good, *Rex observed. Dark rings circled his eyes; he looked haggard, sleep-deprived.*

Furious and confused, Niks didn't care to afford him any more consideration. Go, Rex. Please.

No, I can't leave him.

What?!

It's only a matter of time before he leaks everything, *Rex said, calculating the distance between her position and Akanno's, and the instrument carts that could provide shelter once inside the tent.*

But Niks felt something behind Rex's words, beyond her own conscious thought, as she waited for James to leave and the two remaining soldiers guarding Akanno to assume foot patrol around the tent; a strange solidarity, an unspoken bond between two opposing forces on the neuro tech market, bound by secret laws known only to those who never operated by common rule.

Bolting from the safety of her hiding spot, Rex dove sideways under one of the carts in the tent and froze. Boots smacked against the pavement, paused near her position, then continued on.

Sliding out from underneath the cart, Rex stayed low to the ground and crawled up behind Akanno. Niks noticed Rex's tattoos—a solid black—and the cold fear that shored up on both their minds as she struggled to cut the zip-ties binding Akanno's hands behind his back and to the chair.

Hurry, Niks bade.

I know—

Akanno stirred, mumbling as she tore the zip-ties with her teeth and freed his hands.

"Wake up," she said, prodding him in the ribs.

Akanno's eyes shot open, but Rex covered his mouth before he could make any noise.

"You have one chance to get out of here. Run when I say."

He's not in proper shape to—

He's got one chance, Rex said, slinging Akanno's arm over her shoulder and hoisting him up.

As he found his footing, Akanno pawed at his neck, anger igniting his eyes, bring color back to his cheeks.

"I didn't say anything," he said, voice quavering as he looked at Rex through his one good eye.

"I know. Come on," Rex said, peeking out the tent as another drone patrol zipped by overhead. The sound of the two circulating guards grew closer as their bootsteps came toward the front of the tent again.

"Now," Rex said, taking off in a sprint.

In her periphery, Niks saw Akanno break off in a slightly different direction, toward a felled hotel, stumbling and staggering, but finding his footing with every step.

Rex kept her eyes trained on her escape route.

Fifteen meters.

Ten meters.

"You—stop!"

Seven.

Four.

Something bit into her calf. Rex fell hard to the ground, her cheek smacking into the pavement. Dazed, she turned over, seeing the spider-trap latched around her calf, sending electricity up her leg.

Muscles cramping, Rex tried to pry the containment device off as soldiers descended on her position, guns pointed at her head.

Rex—

Niks saw Rogman too, behind the soldiers, mustache twitching as he regarded her from afar. Dark eyes showed no delight, only cold calculation.

Fight, Rex, please—

Gritting her teeth, Rex fended off the first soldier, but the second one tackled her, grinding her face into the ground.

Keeping fighting—

A cold metal device snapped around her neck.

Take care of Remy, *Rex said, closing her eyes as a tingling sensation buzzed up into her skull.*

Rex, I—

White fire exploded up and down her spine. In one gasp, in one flash of afternoon sky, blue and black uniforms, and the taste of copper, Rex was gone.

Chapter 20

"We'll find her," Syra tried to reassure her again, but nothing she did quelled the vice-tension squeezing down around Niks' heart.

Rex is gone Rex is gone Rex is GONE—

Pacing behind Azzi and Syra in the cockpit in what little space she could work out her nerves, Niks looked again at the status board. The *Ventoris*, one of the Dominion warships orbiting above Neeis, had yet to clear them for orbital descent.

"This is the *Lovelug*," Azzi repeated into the com, "requesting clearance for descent to La Raja."

"That is the dumbest name. If we get caught, *assino*..." Syra muttered, unstrapping herself from the co-pilot's chair.

"We're pirates, remember?"

"Dog-soldiers."

"Trust me, baby," Azzi said, throwing Syra a wink as she grabbed Niks and pulled her into the next compartment.

"Hey, you gotta calm down," Syra said, putting a palm to Nik's forehead as if to check for a fever. Niks couldn't help herself, rocking back and forth, unable to keep her focus as her eyes flicked back and forth, in search of something.

"She's gone—"

"I know, hon."

"No, Sy," Niks said, holding onto Syra's shoulders *"Gone.* Like ripped from me. She could be dead—"

"She's not dead," Syra interjected.

Niks held her hands over her heart. "But I can't feel her anymore."

Biting her lip, Niks couldn't tell if Syra withheld a snarky remark, or the stark truth. "Niks—you're not a telepath. Whatever happened between you was a freak thing, alright? And you said she got zapped by a shock collar—"

"So what?!"

"Maybe that severed the connection the Med Oculus made."

Niks' clenched her hands. "No—they can't do that; they can't take her from me."

Blowing past Syra, Niks aimed to smash the com button with her fist and wrestle Azzi for the controls when the *Ventoris* sent their reply.

"We've got clearance," Azzi exclaimed as he set their course. "Hold on to your panties, ladies, the *Lovelug* is diving in!"

With a groan, Syra came up from behind Niks.

"Hey," she said, turning her around again. "I like feisty you—but not this."

"What?"

"This," Syra said, waving a finger between her eyes. "The insane *I'm going to do anything to get my girlfriend back* attitude you've got blazing in the beautiful greens."

"She's not my..." Niks stopped herself, blushing.

"Okay, whatever. But check yourself, all right? Or this lovesickness will tank us."

Lovesickness...

Niks couldn't shake Syra's words as they descended and docked in one of the cleared ports nearest the District. Even as they each disrobed and suited up in the dog-soldier garb—her nose protesting the patterned long-sleeve shirt and the sweat-stained combat chest protector she pulled over her head—the warning looped in her mind.

I'm not lovesick, she told herself, strapping on shin guards and an old bandolier. *I know what I'm doing.*

"Man," Azzi said, face scrunching up as he took a whiff of the only dog-soldier gear that could fit him—a yellowed tank top with the name of some underground band and a playlist scrawled across the chest. "Did these guys ever shower?"

"I think we all know the answer to that," Syra said, fanning the air from her nose. The dog-soldiers had given them some women's clothes, too, none of which seemed to belong to a mercenary, but rather one of their guests.

"At least yours smells like perfume," Niks said, unable to suppress a chuckle at the sight of her friend in a sequins bra and feathered skirt.

"And other things," Syra commented, flipping up the underside of the skirt and frowning.

"Do you have that lifepack?" Niks asked Syra as Azzi grabbed the rest of their gear.

"Yeah," Syra said, tapping the yellow backpack she slung over her shoulder. In the deal with the dog-soldier captain, Niks had bargained for one of the bigger medical kits from the lifeboat, but she worried it wouldn't be enough for treating Remy's deteriorating condition. "How bad is the patient?"

"Bad. We'll need everything in their just to stabilize him."

"Here you go, captain," Azzi laughed, distributing some of the fake ID cards the dog-soldiers traded them.

Niks regarded the bearded man puckering up in the holographic image.

"At least yours is human," Syra said, showing her the chiropteric alien popping up on her hologram.

"Captain….Howdy? What the hell?" Niks said, reading the name on the card.

"I got Cherry Lipz."

"Haha—I get it—Old Earth references," Azzi said. "Horror movie demon, famous porn stars."

"Yeah, real nice there, 'Dick Rammington,'" Syra said, turning over his card.

"Don't worry, you can re-imprint the image, but the name will have to stay," Azzi said, walking them over to one of the secondary terminals and putting the ID into the interface slot one by one to retake the images.

"Pucker up, captain," Syra said, nudging Niks as she stood in front of the imaging scanners.

"Go to hell, Ms. Lipz."

Despite the ridiculousness of their IDs, Niks couldn't believe they go through the docking platforms checks.

"I think it's the smell," Syra whispered in her ear as the Dominion guard, after a cursory check, turned his head away from them and empathically waved them through.

"Come on," Niks said, not wasting time and heading straight for the District.

The Dominion presence thinned near the hardest-hit areas of town already combed through for survivors or whatever else the galactic military deemed important. Niks headed straight for the arcade, relying on what she remembered from Rex's memories to navigate them through the ruins.

"In here," Niks said, wedging herself through the narrow gap between the bombed-out buildings. Finding the hole Rex had left open for her intended return to Remy, Niks paused, waiting for Syra and Azzi to catch up. With his broad shoulders and thick chest, Azzi resorted to crawling on his hands and knees in the wider gap near the ground.

"Sy—hand me the lifepack. You guys wait here," she whispered, wiping some of the soot off her face.

After a grunt and a few awkward twists to slide off the straps in the tight space, Syra handed her over the yellow pack. "Why?"

"He's hurt, but he's still a marine. I can't remember if he's armed..."

Syra grabbed her by the leg, trying to stop her from crawling through the hole.

"I'll be okay," Niks said, prying her fingers off. "Just trust me."

Looking perturbed, Syra let her go, but made a motion with her hand to indicate she only had a minute.

Niks made her way through the hole and assessed the layout of the arcade. Déjà vu struck her with a quick shiver as she looked over the broken tables, booths, and inert gaming modules crushed under the partially collapsed structure or toppled over from the explosions. She'd seen the orange light streaming in through the building cracks and fissures before, just not with her own eyes.

"Remy," she said, keeping her voice confidence. "I'm a friend. Rex sent me."

No movement, no sound. Light-footed, she made her way to the front, where she remembered Rex clearing them a camp site. She spotted a few scraps of cardboard and tablecloths served as bedding, a small pile of personal items, and a solar-powered lamp near a supine body.

"Hey," she said, forgetting herself as soon as she saw him, semi-conscious, reaching for the gun lying next to his side.

"I'm a friend," she reiterated, kneeling next to him and putting her hand over his. Seeing his bright blue eyes turned her stomach into jelly. She'd known Rex's reactions to him—suppressed emotion funneled into an intense loyalty—but not how she'd feel when she saw him for the first time.

I know you, she thought, feeling the weathered skin on the back of his hand. She remembered the tech he'd built with such precision despite his large fingers; the rough feel of his calloused palms against her skin; lonely nights spent curled up beside him, neither one of them speaking, falling asleep to the steady sound of his breathing, knowing he would be there in the morning.

"My name is Niks. I'm a nurse. Rex sent me to help you," she said, lifting her hand to show her trust.

Struggling to his side, Remy managed to look her in the face. Experienced eyes that had sized up countless enemies, deadly threats, assessed her up and down. If she hadn't known him, she would have been terrified, especially with his hand still near the gun, and his face stone cold and unreadable. But she understood his hesitancy, why he waited for her to react in order to gauge her intent.

"I brought a lifepack. I can treat your wounds, give you fluid resuscitation and antibiotics," she added. "There's another nurse with me that can help, and a pilot that will help us transport you back to our ship once we've stabilized you."

"Rex," he said, voice full of gravel.

She didn't understand if meant how she knew her, or where she was. "She's been captured by the Dominion. She told me to where to find you, that you were hurt."

Eyes swimming in their sockets, all he managed in reply came out as a garbled slur.

"Sy—get in here!" Niks shouted over her shoulder.

Sliding in next to her, Syra went into nurse mode as soon as she got a good look at Remy, working in tandem with Niks as she set up the fluids and boosters.

"Can you save him?" Azzi asked, keeping his distance.

Staying focused on the patient, Niks did a quick physical assessment, noting the most serious wound across his abdomen, and selected her medications from the pack.

"Got vascular access," Syra said, placing the transderm unit over his carotid artery.

"We've only got two liters?" Niks pulled out the fluid bag and searched for more.

"It's just a lifepack. Survival essentials only."

The rest of the treatment happened in silence, with only a few patient inquiries by Azzi breaking the quiet. After ten years, they didn't need to talk, not with each of them knowing, and playing into, each others' strength.

"Alright—is that it?" Sy said, sitting back and digging through the lifepack for any more gauze.

After cleaning out the gunshot wound and closing the site with a dermawand, Niks applied the last of the dressing to the site to protect the newly-formed skin. "Yeah."

"Hey—he's coming around," Azzi said, stepping in.

"It's okay," Niks said, spreading her arms between Remy and the other two. "You're safe. We just treated your wounds."

Remy pushed himself up, bracing his abdomen with the other arm, without a grimace or a wince. After regarding himself for a moment, then looking at the three of them, he nodded.

"A real conversationalist," Syra said, removing her gloves and tossing them into the pile of medical trash.

"Can you guys give us another minute?" Niks asked.

"Come on, baby," Azzi said, helping Syra back up and taking her as far as they could go to the other end of the decimated building.

"Look—we're going to get you out of here, but I need your help to find Rex."

Remy tilted his head, sizing her up again.

"Anything is helpful; anything to help me reach her again," Niks tried.

After a long pause, Remy replied in a slow drawl, "What's she to you?"

Niks thought about lying, or about skimming over the truth. But knowing Remy—at least by Rex's understanding—the truth, no matter how unbearable or unbelievable, always worked best.

"I can tell her what you are to her," she said, "better than she ever could. You're her rock; the one person in this world she can trust. The sex was great, but she stopped pursuing it from you when she heard the affection in your voice. She's afraid to be loved, Remy; for her, it's always brought pain."

The veins on Remy's forehead popped out as he ground his teeth together. "She told you that?"

"Not exactly. She's not one to talk about her feelings, is she?"

Remy waited for her to continue, eyes locked in on her face.

"I was one of the SOHO nurses who trialed something called the Med Oculus. I had used it before without incident, so when I saw Rex severely injured after the bombings, I didn't think twice. But when I used the Med Oculus to treat her wounds, something happened... We 'connected.'"

Remy perked up, his eyes narrowing. "Neuro tech?"

"I'm not exactly sure. The Dominion classified most of the information."

After clearing his throat, he asked, "You know what she is?"

"I know she's very special," Niks said. "Rare, mixed bloodlines; Prodgy lineage. She's scared of what she is, but figured out how to use what she's got to survive the streets."

"Better be more convincing than that," Remy said, eyeing the gun again, "for me to even think of helping you."

Niks saw his fingers twitch, already pulling against an invisible trigger. Stomach knotting, she recalled Rex's memories of him finishing off groups of men in bar fights and back alley brawls before they even had a chance to get a hand on their weapons.

Terrified, she blurted the first thing that came to mind: "She never let you touch the scars on her stomach..."

Remy went rigid.

"...never once, even when you showed her your prosthesis, your biomech grafts, everything. You felt she never trusted you, not the way you trusted her with the things you hated most."

"Well I'll be damned..." he said, his voice petering out into a whisper.

Niks hung her head, unsure of herself, or if she had gone too far. "I'm sorry."

Remy grunted. "Huh. That woman gets in everyone's head. Sounds like someone finally got in hers."

"I did," Niks whispered, wiping the tears from her eyes.

"Then you have all you need to find her."

"No—please. You must know something."

Remy stared at her a moment, then replied in the same slow drawl, "you know how the Laws of Attraction works, right?"

"I know you built the tech, and she—" Niks stopped herself as she put more thought into the idea. She concentrated on Rex's sensitivities, her way of knowing a person's deepest ache, their greatest desire, jogging her own subconscious impressions. *Why would she need the tech in the first place?*

Then it hit her: *Sam.* And the orgasm that blasted all three of them through the heavens and into the highest realms of pleasure.

Without tech.

"It's a sham, isn't it?"

Remy continued to look at her, offering her nothing but silence. Not that Niks needed him to confirm or deny what she already knew.

"The Laws of Attraction... Rex is the 'law.'"

"That woman..." Remy said, scooting up against the wall and releasing a great sigh. "...is limitless."

A limitless telepath...

Something the Dominion would most certainly exploit.

"Thank you, Remy," she said before hurrying off to meet up with Syra and Azzi.

"Get him back to the lugger—"

"*Lovelug,*" Azzi corrected.

"—and then get back to Spacey's."

"Wait—what are you doing?" Syra asked as Niks wound her way to the improvised exit.

"Going to get Rex."

"No!" Syra ran over and grabbed her boot as she tried to crawl through the hole.

"You have to let me go," Niks said, twisting around and touching her friend's face.

"I can't—this is suicide; you're lovesick—"

"No—this is the first time in my life I've ever been certain," Niks said, freeing herself from Syra's grasp.

"Of what?" Syra called out after her as she wriggled out to the other side.

With a smile on her face, she ran down the alley and out onto the empty streets. The rhythmic thumping of pulse engines and deep rumblings of tanks got closer as she headed toward the epicenter of Dominion activity in the city park.

So close now, she thought, hearing boots stomping on broken asphalt, and sirens alerting of another transport ready to lift off.

Niks took one last look up above, to the billowy clouds sliding across the infinite golden sky. Fear wormed its way into her stomach as the trappings of gray walls, handcuffs, shock collars unfolded in the back of her mind.

I'm certain, she reminded herself, breaking her gaze and pressing forward.

Winding through the remains of the fallen brothel, she came upon the same vantage point behind a pillar, and spied the interrogation tent Rex had seen not long ago. Drones buzzed through the air as dozens of soldiers bearing military-grade firearms patrolled the trampled grounds. No Rogman—no James—but the same terror tore at her chest at the sight of the vast tyrannical force.

Tears rolling down her cheeks, Niks stepped out from behind the pillar, and raised her arms up to the sky.

Chapter 21

Niks woke up to a distant ringing in her ears and her mouth parched of all moisture. When she tried to wipe off the crusts caked around her eyes, she found her arms tied behind her, and her legs in a similar predicament.

Memories crashed over her in waves as her neck and back screamed at her to shift positions in whatever hard-back chair her captors tied her to: *Stepping out into the sun, into full view of a thousand soldiers. Guns raised, blue and black uniformed men swarmed over her, just as they had Rex.*

The sting of something pushed into her neck.

Sleep.

Then, waking here, half-naked in only her underwear and an athletic bra, in a room that felt more like a metal box baking in the desert.

Wherever here is...

With concerted effort, Niks peeled back her eyelids, blinking until her vision cleared. A single bulb shined down overhead, partially illuminating blank, gray walls. A sliver of light across the room gave hints of a door, and an outside world.

Heart pounding in her chest, she waited.

Any moment they'll come, she told herself. After all, she was awake, and the torture would certainly begin.

Seconds ticked by. Then minutes. Hours. Niks didn't know how much time passed, only that the more aware she became, the greater her panic. Sweat accumulated across her brow and base of her neck, stinging her eyes and sliding down between her pinched shoulder blades.

Something happen—someone check on me—

Nothing. No one came.

Somebody...

Niks bit down on her lower lip, trying to keep herself from crying. She'd felt scared and lonely plenty of times in her life—even in relationships—but never like this. No friends, no allies—no Rex in the back of her mind, whispering relief, answers.

Don't leave me here.

Niks struggled against her restraints, but couldn't budge the cords binding her legs and arms to the chair. The best she could manage was occasionally unsticking her damp skin to the faux wood, only to sink back down in the pool of her own sweat.

After exhausting the last of her energy, she gave in, every once and awhile wiggling her fingers and toes to fight the prickly, tingling sensation of restricted circulation.

Please... No sound to latch on to, not even the purr of a ventilation system, or the sound of footsteps and muffled conversation. Niks closed her eyes, trying to imagine herself somewhere else, surrounded by people. Instead, she thought of James, of all the nights she'd spent trapped and baking in his cuddle, feeling alone when she should have felt gratification, love, with only the light of the stars to give her comfort.

No stars here, she thought.

As tears stung her eyes, her self-pity turned to determination. *Stop it. Think of Rex. Think of how you're going to get out of here.*

(What if she's dead?)

"No," Niks said, twisting against her restraints. "She's not dead."

I'd know, she told herself, trying to dampen the fear quickening her heart.

Footsteps approached. Heavy ones, too numerous to count. Niks straightened up in her chair and tried to wipe her eyes off on her shoulders as the door lock clicked over.

Light poured into the room as the door swung open. Niks turned her head away, her eyes unable to adjust to the brightness. Out of the corner of her eye she watched as the dark figure looming in the doorway stepped through. "Nurse Rison."

That voice—

Something scraped across the floor. Niks chanced a look as the door shut and the man in the room with her took the chair that had been brought in and positioned opposite her.

Rogman!

The telepath hunter. The officer who found war and unrest appeasing. The only man she'd ever known James to fear.

She yanked and fought at her restraints, skin abrading, until blood trickled down her fingers.

"Don't waste your energy. We've haven't even begun," Rogman said, sporting an unusual smile. His face didn't seem well equipped for the expression; the upward slants of his lips made his eyes pop out, exaggerating the insincerity of the gesture.

Crossing his legs, he plucked out a datafile from his jacket pocket and took his time examining it before he started talking again.

"Nikkia Rison, ten years experience as an RN, outstanding reviews and records—and, most recently, credited with the discovery of the new identification process for telepaths with or without genetic markers using a neuro toxin."

Rogman looked up from the report, giving his mustache another twitch. "You have already changed the war for us, Nikkia. We will wipe out entire species—worlds—of leeches."

A tide of sickness rose up through her stomach and into her throat. Swallowing hard, she tried to keep from vomiting.

"But it is not this great feat that interests me in you, Nikkia—it is your experience with the Med Oculus, and this criminal, Rex. Jin Idall's encounters left her with snapshot impressions of patients, unusual emotional attachments—all transient, all easily forgotten with some of our treatment methods."

Niks caught his inflection and cringed. *Treatment methods?*

"According to the results you provided us from your bioscan," Rogman said, glancing again at the datafile, "the encounter with Rex increased the activity levels in your brain, particularly the right hemisphere and hypothalamus, and those areas have remained hyperactive since first contact."

Setting the datafile on his lap, he looked at her with dark-set eyes, his tone ice-cold. "Tell me about your experience."

Niks couldn't believe his gall. "I've got nothing to say to you."

Sporting a wisp of a smile, Rogman got up and crossed to the room to the wall to Niks' left. "I am fully vested in this subject matter," he said, pressing his hand against the gray wall. The wall disappeared, connecting her to a larger room with surgical equipment, overhead lights, and a table. "I am prepared to extract data by whatever means necessary."

A gasp escaped her lips, but she held her breath, too afraid to speak or to release the air in her lungs as Rogman crossed back over to her.

Bending at the waist, he whispered in her ear, "a moment, then, to regard your station."

He walked out, door slamming behind him.

Stars wheeling across her brain, Niks blew out her air and heaved for her next several breaths, unable to satisfy her screaming lungs.

I can't do this—

The temptation to give in to panic, to cry out and beg to be released, grated at her nerves and ate at her stomach. Still, she held herself together by the conviction that got her arrested in the first place: *Rex has to be alive.*

I can't let them take her.

Time ticked by again. One hour bled into another. Thirst raked the back of her throat, dried her tongue. A dull headache broadened into a knuckled fist kneading just behind her eyes.

Rex... be alive, she thought, lifting her head only to look at the empty chair in front of her. *Gods, please...*

Sometime later, long after exhaustion won out and she nodded off, the door to her cell cracked open. Niks stirred, but didn't look up, not wanting to face her tormentor.

Black boots appeared in her field of vision. The hulking figure cast a shadow over her, his breathing sharp, upset.

"I don't know who you are anymore."

Niks craned her head up. "...James?"

He took the seat across from her, but sat at the edge, leaning in as close as possible to Niks. In one hand he gripped a datafile, but he didn't regard it, keeping his eyes pinned to her face.

"I understood you better when you weren't a slave to the telepaths. Maybe you really are sick."

Niks couldn't believe the harshness of his tone. In all their years together, he'd never yelled, or spoken with such venom.

"I didn't understand Chief Rogman's philosophies until now—until I watched my girlfriend manipulated and poisoned by a leech. You wouldn't turn against your co-workers, your friends—me—if it weren't for that leech's influence. The Niks I know wouldn't have turned me down."

"J-James—"

"Don't," he said, raising a hand between them, as if to shield himself from her words. "I don't want to hear your lies, Niks."

As tears formed in her eyes, she caught herself. *Niks. He called me that—twice. That's not like him.*

Daring a longer look at his face, she saw fatigue etched into dark sockets around his ~~eyes, and~~ worry wrinkling his brow. She remembered his expression as he opened the bay doors for them, and the sound of his voice as he told to officer and guards stand down outside the lifeboat dock.

Why did you do those things? she thought. *Why are you doing this now?*

Her gut pulled at her, drawing forth memories from better times—their first date, his first over-enthusiastic kiss; the way he always wanted to hold her close, even when she was too hot, or grumpy, or wanting her space.

She took a chance. "Please… bring her to me," she said under her breath, bowing her head so any hidden cameras could not see the movement of her lips. "Put her in the same room."

James slid back, away from her. All of the expression on his face evaporated, his voice turning to ice. "Comply with Rogman."

"James—" she called after him as he got up and went to the door.

As he took one step out of the interrogation room, he looked back at her, blue eyes rosy with burst capillaries. "You should know where my loyalties lie by now, Niks."

The door slammed shut, leaving her alone again.

"Rex," she whispered, closing her eyes as tears surged anew. "I'm so sorry."

Chapter 22

Niks woke with a start as the prison door slammed shut. Instead of being tied to a chair, she found herself lying on the ground, still half-naked, with the skin around her ankles and wrists rubbed raw.

But as she sat up, relieved at the release from her bonds, she felt something weighted attached to her right forearm.

No—

Niks dug at the octagonal medication dispenser latched onto her forearm like a spider clutching its prey. During longer-term missions, she'd attach similar remote patches to patients to deliver regulated doses of medication, but ones that could be removed with a few interface selections—not one locked out and flashing red.

Someone coughed, stirred. Niks shocked to the sound, rearing back into the wall behind her until she realized the body curled up in the opposite corner of the room.

Is that...?

Dyed hair, dark tattoos. The feminine figure slumped on the opposite side of the room had been stripped down to a tank top and the shredded remains of her ribbed pants.

Rex!

Niks bound over, tripping over herself to get to the unconscious woman.

"Hey," she said, turning Rex over from her side to her back. "Wake up."

After checking her pulse, breathing, and feeling the temperature of her skin, Niks relaxed enough to breathe herself.

"Wake up," she tried again, rubbing the woman's sternum with her knuckles.

Orange-fire eyes peeked open, then fell shut again. Niks did another assessment, checking for any signs of grievous injury.

She's probably broken a few ribs, she thought, feeling the irregularities and swelling along Rex's left chest. A few scattered abrasions and cuts scored her body, but nothing she needed to address right away. *Where's the shock collar?*

Someone had removed it, though a ring of reddened, raised skin remained around her neck.

Niks paused as she rounded again to Rex's face. A sharp jawline, strong cheekbones; tattoos that wound up the right side of her neck and curled just behind her ear; striking features she knew from the inside out as well as she knew her own. And yet the butterflies fluttering in her stomach made her feel as if it was her first time gazing at the woman, at the beauty that rivaled all she had ever known or preconceived.

Niks reached out, touching Rex's skin, tracing the tattoos that wove up and down her one arm. Stolen memories surfaced, seizing her heart with revived vigor.

Feeling ugly; looking in the mirror and seeing only a victim, a disgusting, lank figure with no hope, no future. Shattered glass, a bloody fist. Finding a late-night clinic with no signage, only a reputation. The sting of the needle, the zap of the augmented color adapters burrowing into her skin. On one side, masking the disgraceful marks, but on the other, amplifying and weaving them into more complex designs; changing colors that displayed her innermost fires, letting the whole world see her power.

Niks smiled, understanding the complexity of the memory and the sentiments it carried. "I see you…"

Rex groaned, her head turning toward Niks. Orange-fire eyes cracked open again, this time widening as she realized the person beside her.

"You came for me…"

Niks tried to hold back her excitement. "Of course I did."

Fingers grazed her knees. Niks looked down at the hand that reached out for her and took it in her own.

"I didn't tell them anything," Rex said, trying to sit up.

"I believe you." Niks helped her to a sitting position against the wall, still grasping her hand. "Are you okay?"

Rex squeezed her eyes shut and stifled another groan as she shifted positions. "Yeah. Those *ratchakkers* are just getting warmed up."

"What do you mean?"

"They're going easy on us, getting a feel for our limits. Putting us together is a bad sign," she said, taking back her hand as she stretched out her neck and shoulders. Her eyebrows perked up as she touched her bare neck. "Guess they don't think I'm a real threat."

Niks touched her shoulder. "We'll get out of here."

Cradling her ribs, Rex rested her head against the wall. "I thought I told you to stay away from me."

"I would think you'd know me better than that."

Orange eyes searched her face, lingering on her lips. "I guess I do."

Niks fiddled with her hands, trying to come up with the right words to say. Being in Rex's presence, being aware of her on so many levels, thrilled her, frightened her. She pressed her even closer to the tattooed woman.

"Do you trust me?" Niks whispered, fingers extending, grazing Rex's hand.

Rex's tattoos permuted, solid jet black lines streaked by magenta waves. Fire-born eyes bespoke her answer, even as the loud bang of the prison door stole her words away.

"No!" Niks screamed as two Dominion soldiers burst into the room, guns extended. Rogman followed behind, depressing a remote in his hand.

"Stop—you can't do this—"

Her tongue went numb. Niks looked down at her forearm where the octagonal device flashed green. Coolness traveled up her arm and into her chest, sucking her down and away from herself.

No, I can't let them take her—

Limbs turning to jelly, Niks fell to the ground. Smacking her head didn't hurt, nor did the firm grips of the soldiers as they grabbed her by the arms and dragged her across the room.

"Now, nurse Rison," Rogman said, his image swirling away from her as her eyes drifted shut. "We begin."

Chapter 23

In clement reprieve or wild desperation, Niks hallucinated herself back aboard the *Mercy,* waking in Syra's bed. But the known comforts of soft sheets and a knee or a shoulder in her back disappeared, replaced by bright overhead lights and invisible straps holding her down against a stiff table. As she continued to sober, the smell of perfumes and under-washed sheets faded, and the noisome vapors of disinfectants cleared out her sinuses.

"Welcome back."

Terror awakened with her, eating at her stomach as her wobbly grasp on reality solidified. She realized Rogman standing over her, and her semi-naked body restrained to the same operating table she'd seen earlier when he made the wall to her cell disappear. Whatever force-field held her down allowed her the gross movement of head, hands, and feet, but everything else remained confined against the cold metal.

Turning her head to the left, away from Rogman, revealed an array of instruments and medication vials displayed on two-tiered carts. Some implements she recognized, others she did not. But her mind filled in the gaps as her eyes picked over the pronged, serrated, or bladed edges of the silver tools, or the blood-red or milky-white serums laid out in a neat row in the next cart over.

Squeezing her eyes shut, Niks whipped her head the other direction, unable to stand the nightmare.

"Let her go."

Niks opened her eyes, alerted to the sound of Rex's voice. Craning her neck up and to the right, she spotted her tied down to a chair, eyes blazing.

Rogman leaned down, getting in Niks' face. The sour odor of his breath made her grimace and turn away, but he followed her, putting himself in any direction she went.

"I require information."

"Let her go!" Rex shouted, struggling against her bonds.

"Tell me the details of your relationship, and full account of any and all shared and individual telepathic abilities," he said, typing something into the remote that operated the octagonal medication unit on Niks' forearm.

Tingling warmth flowed over her. At first Niks relished the feeling, like the first wave of an orgasm. But it kept rising, lighting up her senses, flooding her nerve endings.

Oh God—

Niks dug her fingers into the table, pointed her ankles, curled her toes. Everything around her, and within, magnified in intensity. The smell of disinfectants, already pungent, grew so strong she feared her nose had been pricked, and would bleed. Drawing each breath, even a slight one, chafed her vocal cords, assailed fragile alveoli. She didn't want to move, didn't want to breathe, feel the hammering of her heart inside her chest or the cold bite of the table against her skin. Every hair on her body stood at attention, every cell terrified of the hurricane of sensation, the suffocating din of the world.

"What… did you… inject…?" she whispered, ears and tongue aching with each vocalization.

Rogman kept his voice low as he waved in someone from beyond her sight. "Dr. Naum's favorite sensory-enhancing cocktail, Sidious White and my personal favorite, Diatox. Are you familiar?"

Niks shuddered, sending spasms of pain throughout her body.

She had never experienced it—but Rex had. The memories of the tattooed woman's assault and beating right before Niks rescued her in the alleyway came at her with such violence that she split between the memory and the moment, unable to decipher her own experience.

"It's not real, Niks," Rex whispered.

Tears formed in her eyes, stretching her lids with the weight and girth of an ocean. Niks gasped, causing the salty mix to spill over her lids, colliding against her cheeks with bullet-force impact.

It's too much, she thought, wishing Rex could hear her, help her, mitigate the shrieking excess of the world.

"Tell me," Rogman said, fading back as another person entered her view.

Naum—

Masked and gloved, the doctor reached over and grabbed something off one of the carts.

Niks dared a look into the lights, eyes stinging as she forced them to focus on the small object in his hand. A needle, a slight 22-

guage, but several centimeters in length, dangled between his first finger and his thumb.

He didn't give her a chance to collect herself, to swim above the cacophony and drive her tongue to utter any kind of intelligible response. Instead, he lowered the needle, grazing the bevel across the unblemished skin of her abdomen.

Niks screamed, eardrums singing with pain, as a trail of fire erupted across her skin.

"Stop—" Rex said.

Naum depressed the needle near her navel, driving it in no more than a centimeter. Niks couldn't breathe, her nerves exploding with pain. All of her focus, her entire being, centered around the searing pain, the volcanic fire that set her entire body ablaze.

"I'll give you what you want!" Rex pleaded.

"Doctor…" Rogman said.

Naum withdrew the needle and set it down on the cart. Niks gagged and gasped, trying to right her breathing as a droplet of blood beaded atop her stomach.

I can't—oh God—I can't, she thought, watching as he selected a scalpel.

With an expectant look upon his face, Rogman turned to Rex.

"I'll give you the unlock code to Laws of Attraction," she offered.

No, Rex—

"That is of little use now, isn't it?"

Rogman nodded. Naum turned back to Niks, gripping the knife, his hand poised just below her sternum. Dark eyes zeroed in on their mark as the blade descended.

I can't I CAN'T

Nausea swept up her bowels, boiling the liquid contents of her stomach and scorching her throat.

"I—I'll give you the design schematics," Rex sputtered. Voice strained, quavering, she whispered: "Please… leave her alone."

Naum paused, knife-blade glinting in the light.

"But your game's worth is not in its design, is it, Rex?" Rogman said. "That grunt building your gear is no genius, and you're no neuro-wiz."

Naum pressed the very tip of the blade against her skin. Niks restrained her cry this time, fingers twitching, every muscle in her body going taut.

"Stop—it's me, alright?"

"Yes, we're already aware," Rogman said.

Naum lifted the scalpel and changed his grip. Shaking, Niks realized his intent, the way he angled to flay her open from sternum to pubis.

"Tell me how," Rogman said as the doctor's hand hovered in midair.

No, Rex, don't—

"I—I don't know how," she whispered. "I just can. Telepaths, non-telepaths—it doesn't matter. I just react; I know what a person wants, and with the neuro tech, I can create that fantasy for them."

The knife blade inched lower. Niks froze, nerve endings electrified, unable to take her eyes off the sharpened edge.

"How did you create and sustain a connection with Nikkia?"

"I don't know—I was half-dead. That stupid medical device must have caused a subconscious trigger. I don't know—I DON'T KNOW—"

The shock of her voice breaking, of the tears that cascaded down Rex's face, shook Niks from her own pain.

Rogman donned another insincere smile. "You have no idea what you are, do you?"

Rex wouldn't look at him, face blazed red.

"Not to worry. We have ways of eliciting your use. I'll turn you, a despicable half-breed whore operator, into a means to win this war."

With a snap of his fingers and twitch of his mustache, he signaled Naum and another figure waiting outside of Niks' eyesight. When Maio came over, toting a tray full of blood-collection units, she partially-obscured her view of Rex.

Anger set her teeth upon teeth. Niks had never felt such fury, arcing her neck and smacking her heels against the table. Despite the Diatox, pain became a secondary consideration as she watched Maio hold up the collection unit to Rex's neck and siphon off her blood.

"You *ratchakkers*," she said, clawing at the table. "You can't do this."

"Take what samples you need, then prep them both for surgery," Rogman said. He addressed Niks directly, the smile gone from his face. "Telepaths lie, they deceive; it's in their nature. Look at yourself—a once trusted and heralded telepath informant turned sympathizer, accomplice. Trusting you now, even with the slightest of risk, would be unconscionable."

"What are you going to do?" Niks said, watching as Naum and Maio conferred in the corner. Maio glanced at her, vertical-slit pupils dilating with excitement, before they both stepped out into the next room.

Rogman paused, waiting for her full attention, his response just above a whisper. "We will harvest you both for further examination."

All the air left her lungs. Niks stared up at the lights, eyes watering, unable to comprehend the horror he promised as he left the room.

"I'm sorry," Rex said, breaking the silence. "You shouldn't be here. This shouldn't have happened. It's all my fault."

The sound of her voice rattled her awake again. Niks breathed in, noticing the diminished sensations. *The Diatox cocktail is short-acting,* she thought, realizing the fires of her stomach had tempered to smoldering coals.

"Rex, listen to me," she whispered back, twisting her neck to see her. "You're beyond this."

"What?" Rex scoffed.

"You trust me, right? Think of Sam."

"What are you talking about?"

Niks closed her eyes, knowing that her exact thoughts wouldn't transpose, but the sentiment would.

Everything in your life has been about control. Your real parents hiding you, shielding you from the outside world; your adoptive parents trying to treat you, all the experiments to diminish your abilities. Being afraid of what you are, only indulging a fraction of your powers, what you think you can contain.

Let go, Rex.

Niks opened her eyes again, reading the changing expression on Rex's face. By the way the tattooed woman drew in ragged breaths, tightened her fists, Niks sensed her falling back on conditioned beliefs. The torments of the past, from the deaths of her parents, the

Trinane treatments, to her own self-defeating behaviors, wrinkled her brow and unhinged her jaw. And yet, amidst the whispers of her oldest demons, something sparked in her eye as she gazed at Niks.

"I trust you," Niks whispered as the door swung open again. Rogman, Naum, Maio, and two masked technicians walked in. Naum and Rogman stayed by the door, discussing their business as the charge nurse and techs approached them, hover stretcher in tow. "Let go."

Rex looked at her, orange-fires deepening, flames emboldened with something Niks could not name.

"Nurse Rison," Maio said, thrusting her beaked-nose in her face. Niks noticed the chip at the end, where Syra inflicted damage not long ago. "You will not be missed."

As the surgical tech disarmed the force field securing Niks to the table, Niks heard laughter far in the distance, as gleeful as a prisoner released from suffocating confinement.

"Well now," Rex said, a relaxed smile upon her face. "How about we have a little fun first?"

Chapter 24

In the short time Niks had known nurse Maio, she'd never seen anything other than a scowl or cold indifference sour her face. But as the Dominion nurse and the two techs grasped at Niks's arms and legs to pull her over to a hover stretcher, Maio's eyes dilated and her breath halted, giving her a quizzical, almost shocked expression.

Rex—

Niks resisted the urge to look at her, to see what she was doing, how she was affecting not just Maio, but everyone in the room. In the background, Naum and Rogman had ceased their conversation. Even the technicians froze in place, their gloved hands gripping Niks' arms and legs.

Niks squeezed her eyes shut and projected her thought: *Keep going.*

Something prickled up her spine, then skittered down into her bones, branching into tissues, tickling down into her fingers and toes. A presence, a sensation, searching, identifying—

Don't stop—

—finding every nerve fiber, every cell—

Niks opened her eyes to a world suspended between worlds. No longer lying on a table, she stood behind Rex, looking upon scenes she couldn't have imagined in her wildest dreams. Within multiple glowing spheres Rex held their assailants, each engaged in a shared or individual fantasy, against a swirling background of collective memories and desires.

"Since you're a seasoned voyeur…" Rex said before resuming her concentration on the scenes before them.

"My God, Rex; I didn't know you could do all this."

"Neither did I."

Niks watched in both awe and horror as the desires of each of their captors manifested. The two techs, both male, took a female together, taking turns on her, then joining in together. As much as she never wanted to imagine Maio in any sexual context, she didn't surprise at her submitting to Naum, or the doctor thrilling at her obedience. A chill ran up her spine as his appetites delved into sadomasochism, reminding her of her own experience with him, and the pleasure he took in her terror and pain.

"Look away, Niks," Rex said, shielding her from seeing Rogman's fantasy take form. Niks caught sight of a biomechanical creature; something inhuman, an abominable fusion of cadaverous flesh and machine on six spiny legs, as it kneeled down to the Commandant.

"Can we go?" Niks said, shielding her eyes.

"Not just yet. I need your help."

"To do what?" Niks said, regretting another glance at Rogman and the half-dead machine.

"The Diatox; there's still enough left in your blood. I need to connect you to them, just for a moment."

"What?!" Niks said, looking over as Naum spanked Maio's feathered bottom, and she squawked in both pain and pleasure. "I'm not 'connecting' to them."

"It'll overload their nervous systems."

"No!"

"You said you trust me," Rex said, offering her hand. The tattoo wrapping around her palm sparkled hues of blue and green.

"I do—b-but how can some perverted orgy save us?"

A half-smile turned up a corner of her mouth as one of the techs dismounted the woman, and circled around behind his coworker, eager and erect as he pushed him down and spread apart the other man's cheeks. "You were right about my life being about control, and the need to let go. But maybe that's not what this is about. Maybe there's another use for my talents."

What? she thought, confused at the implication. *You know what people want, you can sense their need, give the greatest orgasms—*

Unless...

Niks shuddered at the grinding of metal upon metal, and Rogman's escalating groans.

"I'll be with you," Rex said, gaze unflinching, even as Maio screamed.

Niks took the tattooed woman's outstretched hand. "Ok."

"Ok," Rex said, bringing her in close.

"What do I do?" Niks said, looking up into her orange-fire eyes, hands pressed against her chest.

"Think of the most frustrating sex you've ever had."

An automatic reply leapt from her mouth: "Anything with James."

"*Yikes. Fair enough. Just think of a time where you were at least semi-turned on, but you never came.*"

Too many times to choose from, *she thought. But then she remembered the last time she tried to be aggressive, wanting to give him oral pleasure, but he called it 'weird' and accused her of not acting like herself before pulling away from her.*

As she recalled more details, Rex disappeared, and James' quarters rematerialized around her. She saw him standing naked at the head of his bed, covering his manhood with one hand and tapping on the pillow with the other, expecting her to lie down for him.

Irritated at the sight of him, and knowing what to expect, she hedged.

Rex's voice entered her mind: It's just a memory—but you don't have to if you don't want to.

If it'll get us out of here—

I promise.

Ok.

Niks complied, going through the same motions as she had before as he pulled off her scrub bottoms and then crawled on top of her.

Still okay? *Rex asked.*

Just annoyed, *she said as he kissed her neck and fondled her breasts underneath her scrub top.*

Niks looked away as he aligned himself for his signature move, pushing aside the crotch of his underwear pressing himself up against her opening.

But he didn't enter.

Niks didn't understand what she saw: James looking down, abdominal muscles hardened, ready to thrust, but frozen in place.

What the—?

A feeling sparked within her, not of need for James, but for what satisfaction couldn't be had as she stared at his chiseled features, felt the erection against her, but not in her; the hands and tongue that did not explore her most sensitive areas, the eyes that looked but did not see her spread beneath; all that was lost in the sweat and friction, the disconnect between two people.

The walls of James' quarters fluctuated, became translucent. She saw the others—Rogman, Naum, Maio, and the techs—all betwixt like her, frustration mounting as the pleasure they experienced swept beyond them to some distant, unobtainable horizon.

Almost there, she heard Rex say as Niks' anger rose.

Niks ripped at the bedsheets, the scope of her world narrowing in on the head of his cock pushed up against her, teasing her with all that he couldn't do, never did, and never would: Nights of him bending her over and taking her from behind, hands tied behind her back. Her, riding him on top of him, nails digging into his chest muscles, her hips grinding against his. Strong hands turning her on her side, spreading her, but not entering where he should. Feeling pressure in a different opening; asking him to take things slow—then begging him to go harder, faster. Sucking him as he licked her, wanting more, but not wanting to move, not when his fingers and tongues worked in such divine synchronicity.

No mounting heat, no rising wave; no convulsions of ecstasy. No release.

"*You* assino!" she cried, kicking her leg over and stomping his chest to push herself away.

The world spun out and away, leaving Niks breathless as she awoke once again in the operating suite, supine on the metal table.

"Where—what—?"

Rex slid her arms underneath her torso and lifted her to a sitting position. The world seesawed this way and that, but the tattooed woman held fast to her, not letting her go until she could balance on her own accord.

"Can you walk?"

Niks didn't like the gelatinous feel of her muscles, or the lightness of her head. Still, Rex's urgency, and realizing the Dominion personnel still present made her slide forward off the table. Knees buckling as she hit the floor, she kept upright, but only with Rex holding her up under the armpits.

"What...?" Niks said through a numbed tongue as Rex helped her to the door. Rogman, Naum, Maio and the two techs all stood in contorted positions, heads bent backward, mouths agape, eyes streaming with tears. "What did you do?"

But she knew deep down as they stared up to the ceiling with pinpoint pupils. Connected by Rex, they felt what Niks had, only magnified by whatever cocktail spiked her nervous system—the frenzied, inescapable pull toward the unreachable, the feverish climb that brought them higher and higher, but not to a peak, only into agitation, pure madness.

"Ever heard of 'blue balls?'" Rex said as she punched the door controls.

Niks gave one last look at Maio, her beak-nose quivering, grey hairs on the back of her neck standing on end. "Are they going to be okay?"

Rex dared a glance out of the door, checking the corridor. "Nothing a very long, very cold shower can't fix."

As they took off down the hall, Niks read the signs, seeing designations different interrogation wings and isolation units. "Where are we going?"

"Don't know."

"Do you know where we are?" Niks caught sight of a portal window, and chanced a glimpse out to the stars and blue and red planet below as Rex rushed them ahead. *Neeis.*

"On one of the warships."

Niks' heart skipped. *Jin.* "Wait, Rex, we have to look for—"

Rex clamped her hand over her mouth and pulled her against the wall, behind a support column, as the double-doors at the end of the corridor slid open. Rushed footsteps slapped against the tiled floor; something whirred through the air.

"Hurry—the Commandant requested this fifteen minutes ago," someone said.

Rex put her arm out in front of her as Niks flattened herself against the wall as much as she could, as if somehow she could shield them both from being caught.

A single guard hurried past them first, followed by a group of people in biohazard suits towing two freezer cases behind them.

The sight of it shouldn't have shocked her as much as it did; Rogman told her of his intent. Still, a chill cast over her heart and formed icicles in her stomach. *We have to get out of here.*

"Stop!"

No—

The group turned around, first spotting the speaker, still out of view, and then Niks and Rex.

One of the suited men pointed at Niks. "Isn't that—?"

Alarmed, the guard raised his gun.

Niks shut her eyes, turning away as Rex slid in front of her. Shots fired.

Someone shrieked, drowned out by the pop and fizz of a blasted electrical pod. Rex pulled her down to the ground, still shielding her with her body.

Niks tried to see around Rex's cover. Smoke filled the air from one of the damaged freezer cases, but she spotted a few of the white-suited men fleeing down the hall, and the guard staggering to his knees, clutching his wounded stomach before falling face-down on the tiles.

Panic struck each heartbeat as a few more shots fired, felling the last of the white-suited men.

"Come on, there isn't much time."

That voice—

The tattooed woman reared back to strike the attacker as he stepped out into view.

"James," Niks said, pulling her back and stopping him in his tracks. He whipped around, gun pointed at Rex's head, but dropped his arms when he spotted Niks.

"You're okay!"

"Back off," Rex said, putting herself between them.

"Please—I came to help you escape," he said, waving over whomever stood just beyond their view. "I'm getting everyone out of here."

Niks didn't have the words, especially as Jin emerged, looking waifish and pale.

"Jin!" she said, hugging her tightly at first, then backing off when she felt her wince. "I'm so glad to see you."

"Me too. Please, get me out of here."

Niks looked at her ex, unsure if she wanted to slap or hug him. "This isn't going to help your career, James."

James typed in a series of codes onto his wristband, before picking up the extra gun from the fallen soldier. "All of you—put on a biosuit. Hurry."

After helping Jin, Rex and Niks suited up.

"Can we trust him?" she whispered to Rex as Jin ran down the hall after the lieutenant commander.

Rex watched as he stopped outside one of the unmarked doors and entered in a series of codes.

"I'm sure he's better at escape than sex."

Niks frowned.

"Come on," she said, tugging her along.

James led them down a hallway that connected with a domed security clearance hub. As they entered the access portal, Niks tensed at the sight of all the Dominion personnel, especially the squads of twelve or more soldiers marching down the segmented corridors branching off from the circular checkpoint.

They're going to see us, she thought, lowering the visor in her biosuit's hood to hide her eyes.

James signaled the lift waiting for them near the door.

"Don't say or do anything," he said as they boarded and he inputted another set of commands.

"This isn't going to work," Niks muttered to Rex as the lift zoomed toward the area sectioned off for repairs. Two guards manned the entrance, already fixing on them and their transport.

"I know," she said back.

James overheard them. "Do you want my help or not?"

Rex answered. "The better question, Lieutenant Commander, is do you want my help?"

Removing her glove, she grazed his hand, eliciting a jump, then a twitchy smile.

"Ok. But be quick."

"If that's how you like it."

Rex threw a sly glance back at Niks as the lift slowed to the sectioned-off corridor and the guards approached.

Oh God…what are you planning?

"Identification please," one of them said, overriding the lift with a wave of his hand and bringing it to a halt. Both appeared human-like, with shaved heads and the symmetrical, muscular figures of the born and bred Dominion soldiers.

Niks looked nervously to James. Even with his rank and authoritative air, she didn't know how he could pull off taking a lift down a closed-down section of the starship with three suited individuals and no ID.

The sentiment, ever so slight, touched her thoughts: *Not James. Me.*

Rex leaned down on the rails and removed her head piece, her gaze direct and unfiltered at the guards. "Hello, boys."

The sound of her voice made Niks squirm, feeling something warm swell between her legs. Whatever spark she felt, the soldiers must have experienced in spades as they shuffled-stepped backward, each covering his groin, a drunken smile splattered across their faces.

"Wow…" Jin said, eyes half shut and swaying in place. "What was that?"

"Your move," Rex said, turning to James as he bent over and gripped the rails.

Clearing his throat didn't help. His words sounded constrained, as if he was trying not to gush. "Hold on."

Still bent over and angling his pelvis away from the women, he typed in the commands to the lift, and the transport glided over the barricade and cruised down the hallway.

"Where are we going?" Niks asked, readjusting the crotch of her biosuit so it wouldn't rub against the sensitized tissue.

"This area is being converted to a new training facility," James explained as the lift zig-zagged and dipped up and down over open panels, bundled wiring, and exposed fixtures.

The lift took them through an open area that reminded Niks of a sports arena. Rows of seats surrounded two opposing consoles in the center of the staging area. Niks caught the tag on one of the consoles: *Endgame Player 1.*

"What kind of training facility?" Rex asked.

Niks caught her gaze, noting the size of the smaller seats and low tables in the dining area. *This isn't for adults.*

"The next phase of the war," James said as they passed through another windowless room with more consoles and gaming booths.

James stopped the lift as they entered some kind of control tower overlooking a mock bridge. Most of the interface and operations units had been installed, others, still open and awaiting parts. After trying to adjust himself, James jumped off the lift and awakened one of the consoles.

"Can't you make it, you know," Niks whispered over to Rex, seeing James' tented pants as he booted up the system, "go down?"

Rex smirked. "You encouraged me."

Frowning, Niks made fanning hand motions down. "I don't want to see it."

"Okay, okay," Rex chuckled.

"Enact Gryggs program 1," James said, inputting a series of codes into the computer. Niks sighed, equally relieved as the system allowed him full access to the warship and his erection softened. "Begin countdown."

It took Niks a second to realize what he'd done as the monitor flashed red, and a countdown timer ticked down. Sirens alerted at three second intervals, and an automated voice announced over the com: "Five minutes until critical mass. Evacuate immediately."

"Wait—are you—?"

James jumped back on the lift and sped them down another series of corridors, to one of the access outlets built into every wing of the warship. A row of ten lifepods, equipped to hold up to six people for immediate evacuation, were already lit and fired up by the emergency systems, awaiting occupants.

"No, this one," he said, shuffling them inside a specific pod.

As Niks and Rex helped Jin into one of the six jumpseats, James fiddled with the control panel inside the lifepod. Niks saw specific coordinates on the interface, and a communication receipt pop up on the screen.

"Hold on," James said, strapping himself across from the three women. "This is going to get a little rough."

Niks grabbed the sashes of her five-point harness, ready for the blast that would eject them into space, right into firing range of the other warship and orbiting Dominion vessels.

We can't get out of this—

Gentle fingers settled over hers, surprising her, but her eyes, steady orange flames, calmed the tension in her chest.

"I'm here..." Rex whispered.

Niks didn't hear it in her words, but saw it in the radiating glow of her tattoos, the amber and gold that she'd never seen before, or remembered from her memories. Something new, a color undiscovered, unfelt, and as the lifepod shot them out, straining all four of them against their harnesses.

"I'm here..."

Words unspoken, a silent vow made.

Niks wove her fingers around Rex's and closed her eyes, sure that her smile, though not augmented or luminescent, shined.

Chapter 25

After James landed them outside of La Raja, somewhere in the jungles, Niks expected the worst—Dominion assault teams, guerilla soldiers—not a ratty starship and an equally suspicious dealer waiting for them.

"He had this all planned," Rex said as they watched James exchange something with the dealer, a ghostly-pale man with red eyes and antennae that twitched their direction, and then wave them onto the ship.

Niks agreed in silence, not yet ready to acknowledge the truth about James. Before boarding, she glanced up above, where the fallout from the explosion of the *Ventoris* still rained down in fiery streaks across the skies. Initially, she felt relieved, but then the reality of it—thousands of men, women, and nonbinary beings vanquished in minutes—struck her with such force she could not celebrate her own liberation.

He gave them enough time. Hopefully enough escaped, she reasoned.

Then she thought of Naum. Maio.

—*Rogman.*

She shivered. *Maybe not all.*

Despite a rocky lift-off and a jarring first jump away from Neeis, Niks finally felt some of her anxieties lessen as different constellations and celestial bodies appeared outside the starship window. As Niks unstrapped herself from her seat in the common area, she checked on Rex. The fire-eyed woman had fallen asleep on the threadbare couch, her tattoos grey and inert.

How long has it been since she's really slept?

A great sigh, then rolling onto her shoulder and curling up, answered her question.

Wish I was in there with you, she mused, brushing the hair off of Rex's eyes.

Kicking aside some of the empty food cartons, Niks made her way to the aft compartments. Even though the starship she'd bargained from the dog-soldiers had smelled like a damp armpit, this one came with its own set of mercenary charms, mostly in lewd messages scrawled across the walls or obvious damage and unwashed bloodstains from fighting. As much as she wanted off, she refocused herself on the joy of the moment, and checked on Jin in the captain's den.

"How are you feeling?" Niks said, closing the blast door behind her.

"Tired," Jin said. She sat on the edge of the unmade bed, hands in her lap, staring out the circular window.

"I understand," Niks said, taking a seat beside her. She wanted to reassess her, to check her vitals, do a more thorough exam, but Jin's stiff body language deterred her. Instead, she offered a hug.

"I didn't know how I was going to escape," Jin whispered, hugging Niks back.

Tears dampened her shoulder. Niks held on another second, then withdrew. "I don't know how James did it. But know that we would have found you no matter what. I wasn't going to leave without you."

Jin wiped the tears from her eyes, humoring a smile. "I know."

It took a moment for Niks to realize the inflection.

"Did you… What did you feel with the Med Oculus?"

Jin looked back out the window. "Connection. Deeper than I've ever felt. I never told anyone this, but my mother once told me her grandfather was a Si telepath. I've always had good intuition…but with that device…" Jin turned to Niks, an unsure expression itching at her brows. "Bits and pieces of you. I saw moments of your life, for just a second."

"So that's how you knew about Yarri?"

Jin nodded, eyes widening. "I'm so sorry, Niks—I should have warned. You shouldn't have come for me."

"What?" Niks said, touching her shoulder as she looked away again.

"The attack against La Raja, the Med Oculus, the telepaths and neuro tech—*us*… and that training facility we saw on the warship…" All the color drained from her face. "It's all part of something; something terrible."

"I know. We're going to warn the United Starways Coalition—"

Jin reared to Niks, grabbing her by the shoulders. "Rex—they didn't take any of her blood, did they?"

"Y-yes, they did."

Jin covered her face with her hands. "Gods, no…"

"What? Tell me," she said, taking down her hands. All the moisture left her mouth, her heart thudding in her chest as she waited for Jin to collect herself, to find the words to share her horror.

"They hurt me. Again and again. Until Rogman found what he wanted. His 'key to everything'... Rex."

The breath caught in her chest. Niks didn't want to believe it—not now, when they escaped, when they were on their way back to their friends and the safety of regulated space within the Homeworlds.

Niks squeezed Jin's hand and slowly exhaled. "We're here. We're going to do something about this. We'll do everything we can so no one else gets hurt."

Jin looked down at her hand, her breath halting, whispering her answer as if she wanted to believe: "Okay."

They both lurched forward as the ship jumped again. The cosmos wheeled by out the window, lighting up the room in pinks, yellows, and whites.

"I'd better go check on James," Niks said.

Niks traversed her way back through to the front of the ship, ducking under a broken panel to get to the cockpit. James sat in one of two pilot chairs, hands resting on the controls, but not moving, as the ship executed his orders.

"We'll arrive at Spacey's in two hours," he announced, checking the stats on the monitors. "I got in contact with Syra; everyone's safe and accounted for."

Niks waited for the jump to finish, for the engines to cycle down and the stars to reappear in the background, needing the world around her to be still to find her voice.

"This isn't how I thought..." She stopped herself, feeling stupid. For the first time in four years, she saw him, his uniform jacket missing, his white undershirt torn at one of the sleeves, his chin cut and crusted with blood. His avoided her gaze, but she caught glimpses of the same blue eyes she thought she knew, freighted by doubt, grief, and guilt, and decisions she did not yet understand, and might never. All the illusions she held of him, of the perfection of their life together, of the fairytale she promised herself, dissolved in that moment, even as the same handsomeness that made her heart leap years ago, caught her again.

He was attractive, athletic, protective, intelligent; a great catch.

Just not for her.

"Thank you for saving us," she said.

James tapped at the monitor for a moment before turning to her. "I never meant for you to be in any danger. I did everything I could."

"I know. Thank you."

He assumed a quieter voice, his gaze hardening. "When we get to Spacey's, I'll make sure you and the others get home safely."

"What are you going to do?"

"This is not how I saw my future—our future… but all of this—you—have made me ask some difficult questions. A few weeks ago I would have done anything my commanders asked of me. But seeing you harmed in the name of this war against telepaths made me doubt this fight, myself, my motives. I've decided if I really want to protect the good people of the Starways, I can't do it with the Dominion."

James ripped off one of the Dominion patches affixed to the side of his pants and crumpled it in his hand. "I'm joining the USC."

"Wow, James… but will they take you?"

"A Dominion defector with level-4 classified access? I think I have a good chance."

Niks couldn't believe it. James, the staunch supporter, the one who believed in the Sovereign's war against the telepaths, in the mission of the Eeclian Dominion to protect and preserve the Starways.

"This is huge, James."

He took her hand. She allowed it, even though she knew what was coming next. "I love you, Niks."

"I do too, James, but—"

He called me Niks.

She paused, seeing the tears in his eyes. Heart tightening, she continued: "…but all that's happened to me—I feel like I'm a kid again, just beginning to discover the world. I'm not going to be the person you need at your side."

"I know," he said, withdrawing his hand. "I just hope you'll still be there—or around, somewhere I can find you. I don't want to lose you in my life."

Niks smiled. "Of course. I don't want to lose you either, James."

In an awkward reach over the central control levers between the chairs, he encompassed her with his huge arms, holding her until they both felt whatever had been lost between them resurfaced as something new.

After letting go, he went back to the monitors, typing and interfacing as he shifted in his seat.

Why is he suddenly uncomfortable?

"James…?"

"I, uh, just wanted you to know I think she—Rex—is great. It's just surprising."

"Surprising? Why—because she's a wild female sex operator with tattoos and a dark, mysterious past and I'm a boring human girl who can barely hold her liquor?"

She got a smile out of him, though he quickly wiped it down with one of his hands.

"Okay. But that, um…" he cleared his throat several times, then put his hands on the top of his pants. "I wish I'd known you were a lot more open to things."

"Like what?" Niks guffawed.

Face reddening, James retracted his hand and went back to typing on the monitor.

"James, what?" she said in a soothing tone, touching his shoulder.

His hand returned to his pants and he pulled them down a bit, revealing the line of a black thong. Her black thong.

"I'm not as predictable as you think."

Niks' jaw dropped.

"Forget it," he said, pulling his shirt over his pants.

"No," she said. Crossing her arms, she leaned back in the pilot's chair. "I'm just pissed that you look better in them than me."

James blushed, but let out a laugh.

"We're friends then?" he asked.

"Yes. As long as you stop stealing my underwear."

James smiled, his face even more handsome than she'd ever seen it before. "You got it, Niks."

***

After Jin insisted that Niks take the last couple hours to get some sleep in the captain's den, she finally relented, feeling the tug of exhaustion pulling down her eyelids and weighing against her chest. Rex, still fast asleep, looked comfortable enough on the couch, and as much as she wanted to snuggle with her on the only available bed, she didn't have the heart to wake her.

A smell test didn't yield much more than the faint odor of citrus starch on the sheets. Even if unmade, it hadn't been used by more than Jin.

I hope.

Niks didn't care, at least not enough, as she zipped off the scratchy biohazard suit and chucked it in the corner. Laying on the top of the bed in only her bra and underwear, she closed her eyes for about thirty seconds before the console next to the bed beeped. Groaning, she rolled over and checked the message.

Spacey's port, private link, transferred from the cockpit.

Smiling, she accepted the call.

"Niksy! There you are, my sleeping beauty. So glad to see that gorgeous face of yours."

"Sy, God," she said, popping up on her elbow and turning the flatscreen so she could see the image of her friends. Syra stood in front of Azzi, holding up some kind of transmitter and turning it this way and that so Niks could see the insides of the crowded bar, their escapee crew, and Remy sulking in the background on crutches, trying to get as far away from the social activities as possible. "I'm so glad you're okay. What are you doing?"

"I made a new friend and borrowed his com," she said, panning to a man passed out on a table full of shots.

Niks sighed. "Dear God."

"Never challenge a Nagoorian to a drinking contest."

Azzi chuckled, nuzzling into her neck. "That's my girl."

"Ah, you two getting along still?"

The com jumbled, as if falling from Syra's hands before centering again just around her face. "Shhhh," she said, eyes darting around. "Don't let him think I'm *that* sweet on him."

"Ok, our secret. But wow, Sy—I'm happy for you."

"This is your fault, ok? You inspired me."

"Inspired you?"

Syra grinned. "To be myself."

"Um, right back at you." Still, Niks beamed. "Everyone else ok?"

"Yeah," Syra said, holding up the camera and showing the rest of the crew drinking at a booth. Each of them waved and said hello, Decks being the loudest to declare her appreciation for their adventurous co-worker.

"Everyone toast to Niks, the bad *assino* nurse that will blow up warships to save one of her own!"

They all raised their glasses and cheered.

"You guys are crazy."

"Miss you, honey," Syra said, taking back the com and shuffling away from the rowdy group. She gave the camera a big smooch, smearing her purple lipstick on the lens. "Get here soon."

The message bleeped out.

Niks collapsed back down on the bed, not even caring to move back to a more comfortable position as her head lay half-off the lone pillow, and pulled the sheets up and over her shoulder.

The ship vibrated and rocked, lulling her to sleep as the stars streaked by. At some point, she thought she heard the door creak open, but was too tired to stir, drifting down farther into the arms of sleep.

The sheet inched down from her shoulder. Cold, she tried to reach for it, but it snuck down by her hips.

Niks jolted awake. Rex sat at the edge of the bed, intent look in her eyes, but paused as she pulled down the sheets.

"It isn't a dream this time."

Rex smiled. "Not this time."

Niks grabbed her arm and tried to pull her down on top of her, but Rex resisted.

Confused, Niks rolled onto her side, closer to Rex, but the tattooed woman held up her hand.

"Wait."

Niks did, stomach aflutter as the tattooed woman stood back up. Still wearing the biohazard suit, she zipped it down and stepped out, wearing only a crisscrossing bra and tight-fighting boxers. Niks took her all in, amazed at her figure, as beautiful and sumptuous as she first remembered. She knew every curve by heart, the feel of her muscular shoulders, the roundness of her buttocks—but from stolen impressions and ghosted thoughts. Now, standing less than a meter away, she wanted to feel her, to experience her touch; to make her tattoos burn red with desire and passion.

"What do you want?"

Niks reached for her again, but Rex remained standing, orange eyes lit, unwavering.

"I want to know you," Niks tried, unsure why she would not come close.

"Is that all?"

"No, not all," Niks said, reaching for her again and grabbing hold of her hand. Rex vaulted forward, pushing Niks down on the bed and straddling her chest. As Niks tried to rest her hands on her thighs, Rex held them above her head, coming within centimeters of her face.

"What else?"

Niks tasted her on her breath, a hot sweetness that made her heartbeat quicken. "I want to know your kiss."

Rex bent forward, her lips grazing Niks'. The temptation to raise her head, to take her in, to fight her grips and try for dominance screamed through her muscles, but Niks forced them to relax. *This is a test.*

Rex, the seductress, the heartbreaker, so stunningly prepossessing; the woman no one could have.

I know why. Niks breathed in and out, steeling herself to the twin flames.

"I see you," she whispered.

"Do you?" Rex released one of her hands.

Slowly, cautiously, Niks brought her arm down, fingers first touching Rex's cheek, then sliding down her neck. Even more carefully, she traveled lower, fingertips dancing across the top of her bra, then pausing and she hovered just beneath her ribcage.

Will she let me?

Rex held her breath, lips pursed, pupils dilated.

I have to.

(She has to know.)

Niks reached out. At first, Rex sucked in her belly, but as Niks extended forward, the tattooed woman let out her breath in a huff, and closed her eyes. As her abdomen pressed into her fingers, Niks felt the scars beneath the tattoos and cosmetic treatments scoring both sides. Most people wouldn't see them, not with all the work she'd done to cover them up, and the way the color-changing cells diverted attention. But Niks saw them, not in the millimeter-wide lumps that marked where she'd been injected hundreds of times with the experimental anti-telepathic Trinane, but in the furtive places she'd seen within Rex, within herself, within all patients and people she'd treated and helped.

"Where did you come from, Nikkia Rison?" Rex asked, pressing her hand over and interlacing her fingers with Niks'.

She shrugged her shoulders. "It's the laws of attraction."

"Very funny."

"Very true."

Rex curled a stray hair around Niks' ear, studying her face. "You just want to know my kiss then?"

Before she could respond, Rex bent down and kissed her lips, stealing more than just her breath. The tattooed woman deepened the kiss, pushing her tongue inside, massaging and licking, spreading fire throughout Niks' body.

Our first kiss—

First real kiss, one that shot her into the depths of space, igniting her heart. She brought her freed hand up and held Rex by the back of the neck, not wanting her to stop, to take her in all at once.

"There," Rex said, pulling back enough so that Niks could see the impish expression in her eyes. "You just said my kiss."

"I want more," Niks said, wrestling her back.

Rex resisted, pulling up and away again.

Niks wouldn't let her go. "I'm here," she said, sitting up and holding her by the waist. She traced her hands up woman's back, feeling all the muscles ripple along her spine. When she reached her bra line, she slipped her hands underneath the cloth. Without a clasp, she worked it up and over from behind, Rex helping the final rest of the way.

The sight of her breasts, voluptuous and freed, whet her appetite anew. She didn't know what she wanted first—to feel or to taste them—but her desires cut loose any thoughts. She dove in between them first, hands cupping them from either side and pushing them into her face. Inhaling her scent, her essence, drove her higher yet, and Niks kissed the tops of her breasts, licking her way down to her erect nipples.

The thought touched her mind only a moment; that she'd never done anything like this before, that she'd never been with a woman so intimately. But as she took in Rex's nipple in her mouth, feeling the skin harden beneath her tongue, she realized that none of that mattered.

"*Godich,*" Rex mumbled, arcing her back as Niks sucked on her other nipple, then bit down gently and tugged. Her hands didn't stop either, one caressing the other breast, the second scraping her nails along Rex's spine.

With all her strength, Niks lifted up and laid Rex down on her back, reversing their positions. Rex tried to sit up, but Niks pushed her down and nibbled at her stomach, working her way down.

"I know," Niks said, seeing the struggle in Rex's face, the way she couldn't handle the loss of control. "Trust me."

After sliding the tattooed woman's boxer's off, Niks removed her own bra, then worked her underwear off and tossed it aside. Niks placed her hands on Rex's shut knees, and parted them, wanting to see her, all of her, for the first time.

The sight of her, naked, tattoos transmuting back and forth from amber to green, stole her breath away yet again. Her stomach muscles, cut and defined, expanding and relaxing with every breath; the way her breasts separated as she lie on her back, or the faint stubble around her shaved sex. Everything, all of Rex, tantalizing, mesmerizing, calling to her.

"You're beautiful, Rex."

But she recognized the dismissive expression on that tattooed woman's face. The knowing of her own attractiveness, and the subconscious despising of it; fearing, yet wanting, someone to see past what she outwardly possessed, daring to look into her secret depths, into the places she herself refused to acknowledge.

Niks smiled. She knew what Sam would have done. What Thea, Remy, and all the others tried, what they thought Rex wanted, needed.

"I know," Niks whispered.

Niks traced her finger down Rex's inner thigh, but stopped midway. Separating her legs a little more, she traversed between them, then flipped around, settling her hips over Rex's head.

Lowering herself on one arm outside of Rex's body, Niks kissed her mound, relishing the anticipation and excitement. But as her lips touched her warm skin, tickled by the stubble, she could no longer delay.

She reached with her tongue first, sliding along the slit, scent flooding through her. But just as she marveled at the first taste of her, Rex's own tongue slipped inside her, making her gasp.

Niks couldn't process it all at once. The salty-sweetness of her folds, the way her hips gyrated as she circled her tongue around her tight bundle of nerves; her own body responding to Rex's skilled tongue and fingers. She couldn't tell what she reacted to anymore, overcome by electric need as Rex pumped her fingers, her tongue dancing across her wetness. She worked her own tongue harder, sliding her fingers inside Rex, into the rippled flesh that invited her deeper, harder, with every thrust.

Lost in delirium, she lowered her hips, wanting all of her, just as Rex thrust up, opening herself to Niks.

Niks dared a second finger, then a third. Rex gasped, her breathing faster, her body tensing, tattoos a scarlet red.

"I want you, Rex. All of you," Niks said, half-muffled by her thrusting hips.

"Take me."

Niks swiveled around, keeping her fingers inside of Rex, and pulled her on top of her so that Rex sat on her thighs. With her other hand, she kept her close, drawing her in for a kiss. But didn't expect Rex's reach, even with her long arms, and paused as the tattooed woman entered her again, matching her girth.

Niks looked into her eyes, into the orange flames that had captivated her from the first moment, into all she had once feared and now yearned for.

"You want all of me?" Rex asked, hovering just above her lips.

"Yes."

"Then kiss me."

Heart leaping, Niks craned her neck upward, kissing her, but not expecting the explosion of color and light. She didn't stop, drawn in by the collision of worlds; tongues dancing together in rhythm, fingers thrusting in and out, breath catching, pulse racing. A kaleidoscope of colors fanned out across her awareness, encompassing them both, dissolving all barriers. Niks felt herself and Rex, closer than she had ever felt before, reaching for the same peak, hearts beating as one.

Niks couldn't take it any longer, feeling Rex inside her, being inside Rex, submerged in the warmth of their joined beings. She cried out, surging forth, bringing them both into exquisite release. White light blinded her, sent her skyrocketing to the highest reaches, Rex beside her as she ascended into the ethers.

She held on to Rex, not letting her go until she could catch her breath, felt the blood returning to her limbs, and her sights resolve back to the shoddy den.

"I've never…God, I've never…"

Rex kissed her atop the forehead. "Neither have I."

Niks rolled her on to her side, so that they faced each other. "Thank you."

"For what?"

"Letting me in," she said, kissing her again.

Rex indulged her only a moment before cupping her cheek and pushing her back enough to speak. "I trust you."

"I love you."

Rex held her breath, eyes misting. Words that had been spoken to her a thousand times, but never allowed, never felt. "I love you, too."

A second, third, and then fourth orgasm followed for both of them, until Niks heard the engines cycling down after the final jump.

"We'd better get ready," she giggled, rubbing her legs together, her clit swollen and spent.

"Just give me a moment," Rex said, spooning her from behind, sweat-slicked bodies sticking together.

Niks rolled over so she could look into her eyes, reveling in the moment. "I'm jealous."

"Already?"

"That you can still feel me," she said, pinching her side. "I miss feeling you, hearing you. I wish that hadn't been taken away."

"Me too," Rex said as she ran her fingers up and down Niks' side. "But I'm here."

Niks scrunched up her shoulders. "You mean that?"

"I'll follow you to the farthest stars and back, Niks Rison. You are my forever."

She couldn't help the tears, or the fervor of her kiss, or the fifth orgasm that made her cry out loud enough to cast away any doubt of their activities in the captain's den.

"Just one thing," Niks said as they both pulled on their clothes again.

Rex came back to her, standing with her in front of the window to the stars, tattoos shining like the golden rays of the summer sun.

"Anything."

"Call me Nikkia."

Epilogue

Fiorah. A windswept, hardscrabble world filled with only the hardiest scavengers and the most ruthless survivors, under the merciless gaze of triple suns. Niks hated it—the stifling heat, the lack of any humidity, the constant noise—especially the cramped confinement of the entire city trapped underneath a shielded dome, and the noisome smog that the air filters never seemed to dissipate. She coughed every other step, her lungs burning with each breath. But it was only a quick stop to refuel and get a few supplies before they continued their journey home, back to SOHO, back to the Homeworlds, to warn the USC of the Dominion's criminal activities.

While James and Remy bargained for goods, a few of them explored the city. Deckers, Syra and Azzi, and rest of the bunch *had* to see the main drag, the central attraction to the black-market planet, where any and all desires could be fulfilled. *Any* and *all*.

Niks didn't want to find out exactly what that meant.

"This isn't great for casual sightseeing," Rex said, trying to talk her into going back to the starship for the millionth time. "There's no good part of this city."

"I know," she said, shielding her eyes as she gazed down the block. Rusted hovercars, gutted and stripped along the street, looked like skeletal relics from a forgotten age. Children and stray animals played inside them as street vendors shouted their wares, mostly knock-off jewelry and drug paraphernalia, a few selling expired meal rations or suspicious looking meats. "But maybe we can help someone."

"With what, Niks?"

Niks looked into Lifepack. Half of a gauze pack reminded, and a few topical sanitizers. If she had anything at all, the others would have joined her, helped her give and treat what they could. But there was nothing left.

"I don't know..." she mumbled, gazing down the street.

They walked a little further, keeping close to each other, watching the alleys, and all the shifty dealers waving them in for a look at their flavors.

But as Niks turned around, having had enough of the dark world, Rex grabbed her arm.

"What?"

Rex drew her attention to a man across the street—a Cerran by the look of his tough, yellowed skin—searching his pockets as a vendor screamed at him to pay up or get away from his booth. Three young children, no older than two, crowded around him, shielding themselves from the suns with the tatters of his robe.

Niks didn't understand why Rex stood transfixed, why her hand tightened down around her forearm. Something terrified her, stole the words right from her lips.

"What?" Niks said, taking her hand in hers.

"Rogman…"

"That's not—"

"What if he isn't dead?"

Niks didn't understand the thoughts the tattoo woman threaded together as she stared at the beleaguered man and his children.

"What would stop him…from harming a child?"

A chill seized her heart. Niks understood, even though she didn't have the language to express it in words. Somehow, in that moment of transparency when Rex connected the Dominion personnel to her, when all barriers came down, she saw them. All of them—the techs, Maio, Naum, Rogman—in their full, terrible light. A clarity that she refused to bear a second witness to, burying the memory as far away from herself as she could muster.

Rex rummaged around in her newly acquired motorgear, scrounging up a few trade coins she'd cashed out with the last of her digital credit. Breaking free from Niks, she walked over to the vendor and tossed him the coins.

"Here. That's more than enough."

The vendor, a stout man with a pocked face, muttered a few words in his native tongue before waving them off.

"T-thank you, stranger," the Cerran man said in thickly-accented Common as Niks joined her side.

"Not a problem." Rex's gaze fell to the three young children. Triplets, by what Niks could tell, and not the Cerran's, at least not by the stark difference in their smooth-skinned faces.

Human children—living here? she thought, wiping the sweat drenching her forehead. She coughed again, not understanding how they could draw any breath in the thin, polluted atmosphere. If she could, she would have taken them all right then, given them a full workup, treated them for whatever kept them so thin and frail, helped them get off this unbearable world—

One of the girls peeked out from underneath the tatters. Bright green eyes, as lustrous as colored jewels, defied her tiny frame. She stared at Niks with an intensity she'd never thought possible from a two-year-old child. Curious, she stooped down to talk to her, and as she bent down, a tickle, very faint, like a feather dragging over the top of her skin, started in the back of her mind.

You're not human...are you?

Niks lost herself in the child's eyes, in all of their gazes, as they turned the full wattage of their attention to her. Blood sang in her ears as her heartbeat grew louder and louder, for all the world to hear.

A woman stepped in front of them. Niks shoot up immediately, jolted by her presence.

"We just wanted to help," Rex said, her voice even, steady, as she looked into the woman's face.

"This is my wife, Lohien," the man said, fumbling for her hand. "My dear, this kind stranger just bought our dinner. It's very good. Very good indeed."

The woman said nothing, clutching her basket full of rags. Niks didn't understand the exchange between Rex and the woman, or why the woman kept her sights on the two of them as she continued to put herself between them and her children.

Finally, after a drawn-out silence, she whispered in the most delicate voice, "thank you."

Niks caught one last look at the strange family as they walked away, the girl with the green eyes giving her and Rex a sidelong glance before taking her brother and sister's hands, and disappearing with her parents down an alley.

"What just happened?" Niks said, allowing Rex to pull her under the shade of an awning.

Rex's gaze trained upward, to the dome that sealed in the city. "I'm not sure."

"Those children… were they…?"

Orange eyes burned with the brightest fires. "We have to warn the USC."

"We are," Niks said, squeezing her hand.

Rex's mouth opened and shut, words falling away before spoken. After a vendor shouted at them to buy something or move along, she took Niks' hand and walked them back toward the starship.

"Wait, Rex," she said, stopping her before they crossed over to the docking platforms. The restless crowds skirted around them, Sentients hurrying to whatever delight awaited them around the corner, inside a store, or deep underneath the city streets, in the notorious Underground Block.

Rex turned to her, face pale, worry knotting her forehead.

Niks kissed her cheek. "I'm here."

Grip relaxing little, the familiar, half-smile returned to her face.

"I don't know what's going to happen tomorrow. Or the day after that," Niks said, spotting the rest of the crew boarding the ship. Seeing the two of them from across the way, Syra stopped and stood on her tip-toes to wave. "But let's enjoy everything we have right now."

"Okay."

As Niks waved back to Syra, Rex hugged her, whispering in her ear. "Nothing will ever keep me from you."

Niks closed her eyes, losing herself in her arms, the chaotic world around them melting away. In her heart she felt it; the gravity of the challenges ahead, the tests of friendship, the sacrifices—the loss of life. But she clung to her greatest hope, and the love that would keep them together, forever. "And I from you."

***

The adventure continues in, "Triorion: The Series."

Made in the USA
Columbia, SC
06 November 2017